W9-AZM-671

Praise for the novels of

ANGELA HUNT

"Compelling characterization is the driving force behind this enthralling story of hope...Hunt fuels the completely engrossing story with dual present-tense narration by the two women. Readers are drawn into their lives, sharing their joy and fear as they approach a fulfilling and surprising climax. A touch of suspense adds to the powerful themes of second chances and new beginnings."
—*Publishers Weekly* (starred review) on *The Face*

"Prolific novelist Hunt knows how to hold a reader's interest, and her latest yarn is no exception...Hunt packs the maximum amount of drama into her story, and the pages turn quickly. The present-tense narration lends urgency as the perspective switches among various characters. Readers may decide to take the stairs after finishing this thriller."
—*Publishers Weekly* on *The Elevator*

"Christy Award and Holt Medallion winner Hunt skillfully builds tension and keeps the plot well paced and not overly melodramatic."
—*Library Journal* on *The Elevator*

"Angela Hunt has over three million copies of her award-winning novels in print today, and this poignant tale about breast cancer will only help to make the number rise. Jonah and Jacquelyn are both strong characters, and the medical terminology is well-written without confusing the reader. Both must learn to trust in a God they weren't sure really cared about them anymore, and ultimately find that God's grace will see them through."
—*Romance Junkies* on *A Time to Mend*

Also by

ANGELA HUNT

A Time to Mend
The Elevator
The Face
Dreamers (Legacies of the Ancient River)
Brothers (Legacies of the Ancient River)

LEGACIES OF THE ANCIENT RIVER

ANGELA HUNT
Journey

Refreshed version, newly revised by author

Steeple
Hill®

Published by Steeple Hill Books™

STEEPLE HILL BOOKS

Steeple
Hill®

Recycling programs
for this product may
not exist in your area.

ISBN-13: 978-0-373-78647-3
ISBN-10:   0-373-78647-6

JOURNEY

This is the revised text of the work, which was first published by Bethany House Publishers in 1997.

www.SteepleHill.com

Printed in U.S.A.

CONTENTS

There are two kinds of adventurers:
those who go truly hoping to find adventure
and those who go secretly hoping they won't.
—William Least Heat Moon [William Trogdon],
Blue Highways: A Journey into America

Prologue

She heard the murmuring sounds of water, felt the deck under her feet rise and fall, and thought, *now I am finally dead.*

Borne by an insistent wind, the ship pressed forward, slicing through the silk black water that ran along its side. Jendayi clutched at the railing, then lifted one hand and held it before her widened eyes. She could *see* every line of her palm, scrubbed and cleaned, her fingers tipped with a harpist's neatly trimmed nails.

She shifted her gaze to the glassy surface of the inky river and felt the wings of tragedy brush past her, urging a shiver up her spine. The images of this place did not mesh with the faded visions of her mortal memory. When the gift of sight had been hers, she had looked on a bright and vivid world, but a crimson hue tinged everything in this region, as if the malevolent fiery eyes of Ammit colored everything in his domain.

The boat slid onto a mounded levee, rocking with a soft thump that nearly knocked her from her feet. Jendayi reached for the rail as the bark began to turn. Massive black rocks roared up from the water's edge; no grasses, crocodiles or hippos lived along these shores. This, after all, was a place of gods and ghosts.

She heard the soft sound of sandals shuffling toward the ancient river, then tiny pairs of invisible hands locked onto her arms and propelled her from the boat. She gasped at the first shock of cold on her bare feet as she stepped from the bark into the water. The impish beings pulled her through the water toward the soft sand where a pair of enormous pillars thrust themselves forward from a pale and gleaming stone structure.

Jendayi swallowed, trying to steady her erratic heartbeat. Strange that she should still feel it beating in her chest. Stranger still that she could feel and yet not see the beings that dragged her forward. But she was not afraid of the dark. Being blind had taught her not to fear anything…on earth.

The crimson darkness around her felt threatening, yet she padded after her ghostly escorts and strained to maintain her fragile control. As she neared the twin columns, the dank smell of sun-starved stone filled her nostrils. The hands urged her from the dampness of earth to the paved portico of a temple. The twin pillars, carved to resemble the eternal lotus blossom, loomed before her. Two torches, one thrust into the wall beside each pillar, pushed at the gloom. Some immortal inhabitant of this place had inscribed the columns with passages from the Chapters of Coming Forth by Day, but Jendayi could not read all the hieroglyphs.

Her invisible escorts withdrew. A silence settled about her, an absence of sound that had a physical density. Of course. Each being must take his place in the silent halls of death unaccompanied; no one could reckon with the gods for the soul of another.

A doorway had been carved into the wall between the two pillars, and its edges seemed to glow as she considered the black void beyond the opening. "We will not allow you to enter past us—" the jambs of the door buzzed "—unless you say our name."

Jendayi paused, searching her memory for the myriad lessons she had been forced to learn. "Accurate Plumb-bob," she whispered, her voice fainter than air, "is your name."

A fiendish giggle rent the stillness, sending a little spasm of panic across Jendayi's chest, but she pressed her lips together and waited. They could not trick her.

"I will not allow you to enter past me," said the right lintel of the door, gleaming phosphorescent in the dark, "unless you say my name."

"Pan for Weighing Truth is your name."

More sinister laughter broke out, and Jendayi steeled herself against the sense of inadequacy that swept over her. She had learned the answers to these questions; she was prepared for death.

"I will not allow you to enter past me," said the left lintel of the door, glowing softly, "unless you say my name."

"Offering of Wine is your name."

More laughter, hoarse and bitter.

"I will not allow you to pass over me," murmured the threshold, bright against the dark floor, "unless you say my name."

Jendayi did not hesitate. "Ox of Geb is your name."

The diabolical voices dimmed. The doorway shone with an even brighter brilliance, and Jendayi took a step forward, pausing when the floor beneath her bare feet flashed red. "I will not allow you to tread on me," said the floor, its voice a sleepy purr, "unless—"

"You are the Hall of the Two Truths," Jendayi interrupted.

"Yes," the floor answered, its tone coolly disapproving, "but I do not know the names of the feet with which you will tread on me."

"Flames of Ha," Jendayi answered, "is the name of my right foot. Wnpt of Hathor is the name of my left."

"You know us," the voices of the door recited in unison. "Enter in over us."

She walked, compelled forward by her dislike of the demonic guardians of the hall and by her wish to be done with what lay ahead. As she walked, the floor brightened, spreading outward in a wave of golden tiles that culminated at black walls to her right and left. Shadows canopied the distant ceiling, and a progression of thickset columns appeared in front of her, each inscribed with the name and image of a god, each pillar glimmering with radiance. She knew the columns and images were supposed to intimidate her into confessing her wrongs. Jendayi refused to look up as she passed, but walked with her eyes focused on her hands, forcing her mind to avoid the interview that lay ahead. Her hands were nothing special, merely a composite of bones, connective tissue and flesh, yet they had served as her greatest asset in life...

A sudden bright light flared before her. She threw up her

arms to shelter her face, and then slowly lowered them. A cold
knot formed in her stomach when she recognized the chamber
into which she had wandered. She stood now in the judgment
hall where the immortal ones waited, called from their duties
to hear her confession.

Shadows wreathed the spacious chamber. In the wavering
light cast by a series of rush torches, the images of Egypt's gods
danced on the painted walls. The images did not frighten her,
but every nerve leaped and shuddered when she saw the three
gods. At one side of the room sat Thoth, the scribe of the gods,
a reed stylus in his hand, his fierce eyes glowing as he stared at
her. A man with the head of the ibis, he waited to transcribe the
results of this interview, to record for all eternity whether
Jendayi had passed into eternal life or suffered the second death.
She knew she ought not fear him, for he loved virtue and hated
abomination; he would record the truth.

But behind Thoth sat Ammit, the Eater of the Dead, a
creature with the head of a crocodile, the foreparts of a lion and
the hindquarters of a hippopotamus. If Jendayi failed the gods'
test, Ammit would devour her body so that no part of her might
pass into the Other World.

In the center of the room, behind the golden scales, stood
Anubis. The ears of his black jackal's head twitched as he stared
at Jendayi, and his man's hand gestured to draw her in. In the
motioning hand he held the ankh, the symbol of eternal life; in
the other he gripped a walking stick. As the Opener of Roads
for the Dead, he would send Jendayi on her way to eternal joy
or everlasting damnation.

She stepped forward, her heart thumping, knowing they
wanted her to confess her sins in their presence. Pharaoh's
priests had taught her the words to say when arriving at the Hall
of the Two Truths; she had also been forced to repeatedly recite
the phrases that would purge an individual from all the evil he
or she had committed.

Those words rose to her tongue now, tripped over her fear,
and tumbled out of her mouth. "I have not acted evilly toward
anyone, I have not impoverished associates. I have not done evil
instead of righteousness. I do not know what is not correct. I

have not committed sins. I have not set tasks at the start of each day harder than I had set previously. I have not reviled the god. I have not robbed the orphan, nor have I done what the god detests. I have not slandered a servant to his master. I have not made anyone miserable, nor have I made anyone weep. I have not killed, nor have I ordered anyone to execution. I have not made anyone suffer. I have not diminished the food-offerings in the temples, nor have I damaged the bread-offerings of the gods. I have not failed to observe the days for offering haunches of meat. I have not kept cattle from the property of the god. I have not opposed the god at his procession."

She paused, breathless. She knew some of her statements were not entirely true, for every man and woman sinned at some time, but the gods would overlook her faults if she had recited the formula correctly. And another, more telling test was yet to come.

The ebony eyes of the jackal looked at her, blinked.

"No evil shall befall me in this land in this Hall of the Two Truths," Jendayi stammered, recalling the rest of the ritual, "because I know the names of the gods who exist in it, the followers of the Great God."

When Anubis moved his head, she thought she saw approval in his jet-black eyes. From where he sat, Thoth did not look up, but scratched on his papyrus, the stylus making tiny tsk-tsk sounds in the silence of the hall.

Behind Anubis, Ammit the eater growled, then opened his mouth in a slow, intimidating yawn. Jendayi shivered at the sight of so many jagged crocodile teeth.

She stepped toward the golden scales. In the left pan rested the feather of Ma'at, the symbol of cosmic harmony, justice, order and peace. Into the right pan Jendayi must place her heart.

She lifted her right hand to her left breast and was not surprised when a cold and solid substance slid into her palm. Her heart was no larger than her fist, a stone organ of veined marble, slightly pink in the torchlight of the chamber.

Anubis dipped his head, his round eyes intent on her movements, and Jendayi lowered her heart into the empty pan of the scale. As it clattered there, Thoth and Ammit lifted their heads.

The feather of Ma'at twisted as if blown by a breath of wind, and the horizontal arm of the scale creaked. As Jendayi watched, the beam shuddered and tilted. Then the weight of her heart sent the pan crashing to the marble floor.

Jendayi's blood froze in her veins as a gouging, ripping mayhem filled the Hall of the Two Truths. Anubis lifted his jackal head in a mournful howl; Thoth looked at his papyrus and cawed in dismay. Ammit the eater roared in fiendish glee; even the floor and doorways wailed in horror.

"Your heart is a stone!" A stentorian rumbling filled the hall. Jendayi wanted to cover her ears, to run and hide within the darkness she had known in her mortal life. But though that darkness had always been inside her, she could not hide in it now.

"The principles of Ma'at are not in you," the voice roared, quaking the pillars of the chamber, "for your heart is dead!"

"I can't help it," she whimpered, cowering behind her hands. A rush of cold air brushed the backs of her legs, and beneath the heaviness of her wig her scalp tingled. "The gods have not dealt fairly with me. They took my sight. They took my freedom. How can a heart live within a slave in Pharaoh's house, within a blind harpist?"

"Foolish girl, be silent!"

She covered her eyes, preferring the familiar darkness to this harsh red light, then realized that the gesture might anger the Great God further. Gathering her slippery courage, she peered through her fingers. Thoth, Ammit and Anubis stood silent and still, awaiting orders from the unseen entity that roared from the walls.

"You have loved nothing, you are nothing, you have nothing! I leave you, foolish child, to Ammit! You shall not enter the Other World!"

Paralyzed in the grip of terror, Jendayi breathed in short, painful gasps as the monstrous Eater of the Dead lumbered forward. She struggled to run, but the treacherous floor held her feet. Falling backward, she felt her thin arms hit the tiles, then the floor imprisoned her hands, too, holding her more tightly than the grave cloths of a mummy. She threw her head back, opened her mouth to release a guttural cry of terror…

And felt the tiles beneath her hands soften to the texture of linen.

As the nighttime sounds of the slaves' chamber crept into her consciousness, Jendayi drank in deep breaths, silent but for the pounding of her grateful heart.

EFRAYIM

*And it came to pass after these things, that one told
Yosef, Behold, thy father is sick: and he took with him
his two sons, Menashe and Efrayim.*

Genesis 48:1

Chapter One

The gilded barge traveled as swiftly as an arrow down the ancient river that was the heart and soul of the Black Land. Common folk from the settlements at Herakelopolis paused along the banks to admire the golden vessel; fishermen on their small papyrus skiffs raised their hands in salute as Zaphenath-paneah, the Father to Pharaoh and the Bread of Egypt, passed by.

As Yosef sat beneath the barge's brightly emblazoned canopy, his thoughts whirred above the pounding of the drummer who urged the oarsmen to unity. The message from Re'uven in Goshen had implored Yosef to hurry. Their father, Yaakov, now called Yisrael, lay near death. He waited only for Yosef and his sons to arrive before he would pronounce his final blessing and depart for Paradise.

The barge passed the entrance to a lagoon, black and heavy with the flood's fertile silt. On the mounded bank a pair of young boys waved and shouted as the barge flew by like a giant dragonfly, its oars shining wings in the sun.

Yosef marveled at the ordinariness of life. A bright light was preparing to leave the earth, yet the sun still hovered overhead like a steady, unblinking eye.

The background noise provided by the chanting oarsmen could not penetrate the heavy silence enveloping the barge's passengers. Menashe and Efrayim sat beside Yosef under the canopy, their eyes fixed to the muddy banks sliding by, their thoughts far away. Whatever they were thinking, Yosef knew their thoughts were nothing like his.

He sighed as his gaze returned to the flooded riverbanks. The seasons of desperate drought and famine had passed. For the past twelve years God Shaddai had allowed the Nile to bless the kingdom. The Black Land had blossomed from Goshen to the southern reaches of Nubia and beyond. God had brought Yosef's family to his door for preservation in the time of hunger, and they had remained near him, protected and secluded in Goshen, for the past seventeen years.

His eleven brothers seemed content to remain in the fertile pasturelands of the Delta where they herded flocks of sheep and goats and raised cattle. In his inner heart, Yosef wondered if they remained because they enjoyed living in the area or if guilt compelled them to linger so Yisrael could spend his remaining years in fellowship with the son they had sold into slavery.

But their motivations did not matter. God Shaddai had led the sons of Yisrael to the Black Land, and Yosef, vizier of Egypt, had been their salvation in the time of famine. They owed their lives to him, though Yosef suspected many of them would rather die than admit it. Most of his brothers despised Egypt as devoutly as they had once despised Yosef, for it was a hedonistic kingdom, given to idolatry and wine and the pursuit of happiness.

Happiness had never come easily to the sons of Yisrael, but they had been quick to accept help from Egypt's bountiful fields and generous granaries. And, after begging forgiveness for their harsh treatment of Yosef so long ago, they had accepted their brother and his place in the royal society.

Yosef's mind curled around fond memories of Pharaoh Amenhotep III and the Royal Wife, Queen Tiy. He had been the current Pharaoh's tutor, guardian and counselor for nearly thirty years; he had nurtured Amenhotep through the death of his father, numerous rivalries and crises at court, and the threat of war. He had even advised the young king to marry for love when it became apparent that Amenhotep's heart had fixed itself on Tiy, a commoner.

One of Yosef's many honorary titles was "Father to Pharaoh," but God Shaddai had wrought it in word and deed. Perhaps—Yosef's gaze strayed to the strong profiles of his own sons—he was more a father to Pharaoh than he was to the two young men who rode beside him now.

But God Shaddai had placed him in Pharaoh's life, and had seen fit to keep him in the royal throne room. He had lived fifty-seven years in the shadow of El Shaddai's guiding hand; he had seen the best and worst life could offer. And because he was as certain of his calling as he was of the sunrise to come, Yosef's heart brimmed with peace.

But what feelings stirred in his sons' hearts, he could only imagine.

The sun was not shining over the Delta.

Bilious black clouds, blown from the Great Sea, hung so low over Goshen they seemed to compress the earth. Yaakov's sons and grandsons huddled outside the patriarch's tent, their heads lowered as if they sought to escape the rain to come. As Yosef and his party approached on the trail from the river, Re'uven lifted his hoary head and nodded in a grim greeting.

"He waits for you and your sons," he said, striding toward Yosef in stiff dignity. "He will not rest until he has spoken to you."

Yosef forced a smile and nodded before lifting the flap of his father's tent. Dinah and Tizara stood inside, and their faces broke into relieved smiles as Yosef entered. Dinah moved away toward the brazier, where glowing coals held back death's chill, but Tizara bowed herself to the ground.

"Rise, Tizara," Yosef said, momentarily annoyed by his niece's obeisance. His eyes flitted over the still form on the fur-lined bed. "Are we too late?"

"Of course not, my lord." Tizara lifted her head. "He has tremendous strength, and he waits for you. I will wake him."

Moving as softly as a shadow, she placed a gentle hand on the old man's bare shoulder. Yaakov's cheekbones jutted forth like tent poles under canvas and the fullness of his lips had shrunken to thin lines of gray. Yet an inherent strength remained in his face, and when the heavy eyelids lifted, the faded eyes were still compelling.

"Grandfather Yisrael," Tizara whispered, "your son Yosef has come."

With visible effort, Yisrael sat up and peered in Yosef's direction. "My son?"

"Yes, Father." Leaving the dignity of his own authority behind, Yosef stepped forward, once again a dutiful son waiting to hear his loving father's wishes.

"I am glad you have come." Yisrael's words came slowly, as if drawn from a deep well. "Listen to what I will tell you, for I am old, and will soon join my father and his father."

"I am listening," Yosef answered, his voice thick.

A look of tired sadness passed over Yaakov's features. "God Shaddai was seen by me in Luz, in the land of Canaan. He blessed me and he said to me, 'Here, I will make you bear fruit and will make you many, and will make you into a host of peoples. I will give this land to your seed after you, as a holding for the ages.'"

He paused, gathering strength. "So now, your two sons who were born before I came to you in Egypt, they are mine. Efrayim and Menashe, like Re'uven and Shim'on, let them be called mine! But any sons you beget after them, let them be yours, by their brothers' names let them be called, respecting their inheritance."

Yosef nodded silently. By his words Yaakov had indicated Menashe and Efrayim would share Yaakov's inheritance equally with the other eleven sons—in effect giving Yosef the double blessing due the firstborn, and immediately passing it on to Yosef's children. Re'uven was Yaakov's eldest son, but Yosef was the firstborn of Rahel, whom Yaakov had always considered his true wife. Even though after Rahel's death Yaakov had come to love Lea, his second wife, he never forgot he had intended for Rahel and Yosef to hold the favored legal position of the first wife and firstborn son.

The patriarch squinted past Yosef. "Who is with you?"

"The sons God gave me here, in the land of Mizraim."

The point of the old man's tongue slowly moistened his underlip. "Pray bring them over to me, so I may give them my final blessing."

Immobilized by the shock of grief, Yosef could not turn, but Menashe and Efrayim had heard and were already moving toward their grandfather's bed.

Yisrael lifted trembling arms and searched for the strong shoulders of his grandsons. When his fingers had firmly grasped each young man, he pulled them close, kissed their cheeks and embraced them.

"Oh, my son Yosef—" his voice rang with awe as his arms encircled Yosef's sons "—I never expected to see your face again, but God has let me see your children as well!"

Yosef stumbled forward to kneel at his father's side, and Menashe drew back to make room. In respect for Yisrael's age and position, the young men bowed their heads while Yosef clasped his father's hand and wept. The flash of joy that ignited at their reunion had not dimmed in seventeen years; too soon he would again endure the wretched suffering of parting.

"Now," Yisrael said, his voice fragile and shaking, "bring your sons to me, so I may bless them."

Yosef stood and motioned to his sons. Efrayim had been about to approach Yaakov on the left side of the bed, near Yaakov's right hand, but Yosef made a sharp gesture, indicating that the young men should switch places. Menashe, as the eldest, should receive the greater blessing, traditionally bestowed with the right hand.

Yosef's heart swelled as his handsome sons fell to their knees to receive the blessing. Yisrael closed his eyes, lifted his hands toward heaven and spoke in a voice that rang with command: "The god in whose presence my fathers walked, Avraham and Yitzhak, the god who has tended me from the day I was born until this day, the messenger who has redeemed me from all ill-fortune, may He bless the lads!" Yisrael then crossed his arms. The right hand, which should have fallen on Menashe's head, fell instead on Efrayim's. Apparently unaware of his mistake, the old man continued. "May my name and the name of my fathers, Avraham and Yitzhak, continue to be called through them! May they teem like fish to become many in the midst of the land!"

"Wait, Father," Yosef interrupted. A thin blade of foreboding sliced into his heart as he watched history repeat itself. Yaakov stole Esav's rightful blessing, Lea usurped Rahel's rightful place. Second-born Efrayim should not be favored above Menashe…

"Not so, Father." Yosef took hold of Yaakov's right hand, intending to lift it from Efrayim's head and place it on Menashe's. "Indeed, this one at your right side is the firstborn, place your right hand on his head."

"No, son." Yaakov lifted his pale eyes, the light of intent shining in them. "I know what you are thinking. The firstborn will be a people, he, too, will be great, yet his younger brother will be greater than he, and his seed will become a full-measure of nations." He lowered his gaze to his grandsons. "By you shall the children of Yisrael give blessings to one another, saying, 'May God make you like Efrayim and Menashe!'"

As his spidery hands fell from the boys' heads, Yaakov leaned back in exhaustion, but contentment shone on his face. "I am dying." He looked up at Yosef. "But God will be with you. He will return you to the land of your fathers. And I give you one portion over and above your brothers." He paused, his chest heaving. "Call the others, for I must speak with them before I depart on my final journey."

Stunned by the sound of weakness in his father's voice, Yosef darted to the tent doorway and hoarsely summoned his brothers.

Menashe stood silently in the shadows with the women as his grandfather pronounced his final blessing on his sons: Re'uven, Shim'on, Levi, Yehuda, Zevulun, Yissakhar, Dan, Gad, Asher, Naftali, Yosef and Binyamin. Many of the uncles wore puzzled looks, Menashe noticed, as blessings and warnings poured from Yaakov's tongue; Shim'on and Levi seemed to wilt beneath their father's harsh words. But the blessings Yisrael bestowed had little to do with the men as Menashe knew them, and he wondered if the old man's words were meant to be taken literally. Would God Shaddai bring Yisrael's predictions to pass? And what had Yaakov intended when he gave Efrayim the blessing of the right hand, the blessing that rightfully belonged to the firstborn?

Perhaps he shouldn't allow the gesture to bother him. After all, what was a blessing? A dying man's words, a heartfelt wish for prosperity. Ordinarily the firstborn would receive double the inheritance of any other children, but he and Efrayim would share Yaakov's estate evenly with their eleven uncles. So the blessing wasn't a matter of property or inheritance. Yaakov had said that Efrayim would have more descendants, but in the space of a man's lifetime, what did that matter?

Yet his younger brother will be greater than he. The memory of those words burned in Menashe's brain. He and Efrayim had always engaged in the typical battles and contests of sibling rivalry. Until recently Menashe had been two years smarter, two years stronger, two years taller than his brother. But now that he was twenty-five and Efrayim twenty-three, maturity had evened the ground from which they competed. In time he would be two years slower, two years weaker, two years nearer the tomb…

Why should a blessing bother him? Looking around, Menashe noticed that none of his uncles seemed terribly upset by their father's predictions. Shim'on and Levi, for instance, whom Yaakov had practically cursed for their fierce anger, stood in the back of the room, composed and quietly awaiting their father's passage to Sheol.

From his couch, Yaakov rallied his strength again; the women helped him sit up. "I am about to be gathered to my kinspeople." His breath rattled in his throat and his eyes closed as if he did not have the energy even to look around the room. "Bury me by my fathers, in the cave that is in the field of Makhpela, that faces Mamre in the land of Canaan. There they buried Avraham and Sara his wife, there they buried Yitzhak and Rivka his wife, there I buried Lea."

He murmured a few other comments in a voice too low for Menashe to hear, then Yaakov lay back, curled on the bed and breathed his last.

A pain squeezed Menashe's heart as his weeping father threw himself on the patriarch's body and kissed Yisrael's sunken cheeks.

Jokim, son of Shela, son of Yehuda, sat outside by the fire, joining a circle of weeping men. Though none of them were so foolish to think that a man one hundred forty-seven years old could live forever, Yaakov had always been among them, the one constant in a sea of change and trouble. Yaakov was the one

who decreed that they should always live in tents so they could
move when and wherever God Shaddai commanded; Yaakov
heard the voice of God Almighty in the night. Yosef would be
the patriarch now; he had inherited the blessing of the firstborn,
but Yosef seemed as distant as a mountain on the horizon. He
kept himself in the city of Thebes, and he would forever be
drawn away by his duty to Pharaoh.

Jokim looked over at his father and grandfather. Pain had
carved merciless lines on Yehuda's face and tears streaked his
heavy white beard. Jokim's father, Shela, drew his lips in and
stared at the fire as though the mysteries of Yaakov's life flickered there. Silence, thick as wool, wrapped itself around the
mourners as each man strove to imagine the days to come
without Yaakov's pervading influence.

Uneasy in the somber heaviness, Jokim slipped away from
the old men and wandered among the tents. The women had no
time to mourn; their hands were busy preparing food and
making beds for the guests who would soon descend on them.
The Canaanites traditionally mourned for thirty days: three
days of tears followed by seven days of lamentation, followed
by twenty days of receiving those who came to pay their
respects and offer condolences. Yaakov of Hebron had been
well-known and respected in the land of Canaan. Kings and
princes from the entire civilized world would soon begin to
wend their way to Goshen in order to acknowledge the great
man who had begotten an even greater son.

Jokim stopped at the sight of Menashe and Efrayim near the
animal pens. The two brothers, both of whom were about his age,
were strikingly handsome even though they dressed and painted
themselves in the manner of the Egyptians. They wore fine
Egyptian wigs, neatly trimmed and anointed with oil, and the
white of their kilts dazzled against the somber hues of Yaakov's
tents and the Hebrews' dyed tunics. Menashe, the elder, had a lean
and narrow face. His smooth olive skin stretched over high cheekbones, and his carbon-black eyes seemed to pierce whomever
they studied. A healthy beard had begun to shadow his chin and
upper lip, and Jokim supposed that the Egyptians had not had time
to shave before boarding the barge that brought them to Goshen.

Now Menashe's brow was furrowed, his hands tight on the rail of a pen that confined a group of lambs too young to swim through the encroaching floods.

"Hello, cousins," Jokim said, approaching cautiously. He did not know his Egyptian relatives well, for Yosef and his sons spent very little time in Goshen. Menashe and Efrayim rarely accompanied the vizier on the infrequent occasions when he did visit, and Jokim could not recall speaking to his kinsmen more than once or twice in his lifetime. But here they were, of the same age, and apparently caught up in the same flood of confusing emotions.

Menashe inclined his head in a formal gesture, but Efrayim flashed Jokim a heartfelt smile. "Greetings. Jokim, isn't it? You are Shela's son?"

"Yes." Jokim tried not to let his relief show in his face. Yosef's sons were nearly Egyptian royalty; he had heard they often dined with Pharaoh's children. Yosef's wife, their mother, had been a beautiful Egyptian noblewoman, so Efrayim and Menashe had inherited attractiveness and position from both parents.

Efrayim, Jokim decided, must have received his mother's looks. His face was not as narrow as Menashe's, his eyes not as direct or piercing. At his neck, a dark curl escaped from under the straight tresses of the Egyptian wig, and his smile was wide and quick, immediately putting Jokim at ease.

"Shall we sit?" Efrayim pointed to the rail fence. "We would like to hear what has happened in the past few days. Unfortunately, in Thebes we do not often hear reports from the Delta."

Jokim smiled, realizing that Efrayim was being tactful. Most people in Thebes cared nothing about what happened to the Hebrews at Goshen.

He shrugged and perched on the top rail of the pen. "The weakness came on Yisrael gradually. He grew weaker and more feeble, and last night he told the women to send for Yosef. My grandfather Yehuda saw it coming—for the past week he has said the end was drawing near."

Jokim tilted his head and studied Efrayim's expressive face. "Can you tell me what went on inside Yisrael's tent? My mother said I should not go in."

Efrayim shot a quick glance at his older brother, who muttered something in the Egyptian tongue and walked away.

"Yisrael gave his blessings." Efrayim's left brow rose a fraction. "He included me and Menashe among his sons. We did not expect that, of course, but the most unusual thing—" He paused.

Jokim leaned closer. "What unusual thing happened?"

"It probably won't mean much to you," Efrayim said, moistening his well-formed lips, "but he placed his right hand on *my* head even though I knelt at his *left* side. My father sought to correct Yisrael's mistake, but Grandfather insisted that he meant to do it." A hint of boastfulness crept into his voice. "Yisrael said I will be mightier than my brother."

Jokim leaned backward, astonished by the news and Efrayim's casual delivery of it.

Efrayim lifted both brows as his face split into a wide grin. "Oh, the drubbing I can give Menashe now! He always held it up to me—his being the elder, of course. But he'll never say anything again, because I can answer him with Yisrael's own words. I am to be a mightier man, and from me will come a tremendous nation!"

Jokim stared in amused surprise. The boast would have sounded impertinent coming from anyone else, but Efrayim uttered it with such bold nonchalance that it did not seem untoward or tactless. "What do you think Yisrael meant?"

"I don't know," Efrayim answered, slipping from his perch on the rail. "But I will have a merry time with Grandfather's words while I can. It is not every day that I manage to defeat my elder brother."

Chapter Two

With her fellow musicians in the queen's chamber, Jendayi lowered her head and waited for a cue from Akil. The queen's companions, whomever they were, had fallen silent at the song's conclusion and Jendayi wondered why they did not speak. The uncomfortable silence was an almost palpable reminder that the enslaved musicians were people who needed time to rest strained fingers and breathless lungs.

When Akil snapped his fingers Jendayi pulled her harp close, ready to play again. For years music had been a mindless diversion that helped camouflage the deep despair that colored her days and nights. Ever since she had been abandoned as a small child, she had grown accustomed to pain and loneliness.

The music began, and Jendayi's fingers plucked the strings of her instrument. She faced a lightless future, a life of nightmares and boredom and slavery. Music was her single joy, but it was a bittersweet pleasure, for the love and joy embodied in the melodies only reminded her that she would never experience these emotions herself.

She attacked the harp with nimble fingers and a burning heart, giving voice to the agony of her despair. The women in the queen's company would undoubtedly listen to her music… and think it beautiful.

They would not know anything about the heart from which it sprang.

* * *

Queen Tiy, Mother of Upper and Lower Egypt, Follower of Horus, Guide of the Ruler, and Favorite Lady, shifted in her gilded chair, bored by the music and the gymnastics of her pet dwarf. The ladies of her court, each of whom had dressed and painted herself in an effort to outshine the others, laughed and giggled at the slave's antics, but Tiy smothered a yawn. She allowed herself one hour with her ladies merely to fulfill the role the royal court expected of her; in reality she had no patience with others of her own sex. Only Sitamun, her eldest daughter, held any fascination for her, and Tiy suspected she tolerated Sitamun only through maternal affection.

"Hail to you, my lady!" A courier prostrated himself at the double doors of her throne room, his broad hands slapping the tile. Breathless from running, the man's ribs heaved like the flank of an exhausted stallion. Tiy quirked an eyebrow and signaled the musicians to be silent. Such haste was unusual in Pharaoh's dignified household.

She extended her hand in pardon for his intrusion. "Rise and tell me what news you bring."

Her ladies twittered like birds as the elegant slave approached, and Tiy rolled her eyes, annoyed with their adolescent yearnings. Life in the palace had spoiled them. Her, it had hardened.

The messenger bowed again, about to lower himself to the tile and repeat his salutation.

"Remain on your feet and speak." Tiy laced her fingers and gave the man a gracious smile. "What news brings you into my court?"

"The vizier of Upper and Lower Egypt, the great and noble Zaphenath-paneah, stands outside your door," the messenger said, a blush coloring his cheek.

"Zaphenath-paneah wishes to see me?" Tiy lowered her hands as a curious, tingling shock ran up her spine. The vizier spent every morning with Pharaoh, regularly crossing the river to Amenhotep's new palace at Malkata. He rarely sought her company.

Stricken dumb in her presence, the messenger wagged his head.

Tiy glanced around. She must give the vizier her prompt attention, but she would not receive him before these simpering women, nor would she subject him to the ridiculous antics of the dwarf.

"I will speak to Zaphenath-paneah in my garden," she said, rising from her chair. "Bring him to me at once."

Leaving her retinue to their vapid entertainment, she slipped out a hidden door.

After returning from Goshen with Yisrael's body, Yosef charged Efrayim with the care of Yaakov's remains while he proceeded directly to the king's palace at Thebes. He knew Pharaoh would not be in residence, but the queen would be holding court and she could convey his message.

Yosef did not feel up to the task of wading through the king's harem in order to bare his heart and speak of Yaakov.

Though women abounded in the king's life, no one doubted that his heart and his trust safely resided in the formidable Queen Tiy. Amenhotep had built Tiy an imposing palace at Malkata, but she preferred to spend her time in Thebes, receiving courtiers and overseeing the care of her royal children. As Yosef followed a guard through the gleaming halls of the queen's chambers, he thought it strange that the royal pair seemed bound as much by distrust as by affection.

The messenger stopped at a passageway opening to a roofed and columned portico. Yosef stepped through the opening, where tall columns, painted in stripes of green and gold and mounted by lotus blossom capitals, dwarfed his own substantial height. The ceiling above his head had been painted a deep blue and emblazoned with the white-gold images of stars. Polished alabaster tiles under his feet reflected his image while a landscaped garden and quiet reflecting pool lay beyond the portico. But he did not see the queen.

Yosef locked his hands behind his back and advanced with caution, not wanting to surprise Pharaoh's Great Wife if he had caught her unprepared. The queen tended to be an overwhelming presence, strong and forceful, intense and intelligent. Yosef supposed that some of her sharpness sprang from her awareness of her lowly pedigree. As the daughter of Yuia, a provincial priest of Akhmin, and Tuia, a servant of the Queen Mother, Tiy had been married to Amenhotep when they were both little more than children. Though Tiy probably felt she had to prove her worthiness and ability to reign, Yosef believed the hard edge she brought to an inbred dynasty would improve the royal lineage.

"Zaphenath-paneah." Tiy's piercing voice cut through his musings, and he whirled to face her. Apparently pleased that she had surprised him, she smiled and folded her hands as she stepped out from behind one of the pillars. "To what do I owe this pleasure?"

He lowered himself to the ground, and sighed in relief when she told him to stand.

"I have a most urgent request," he said, his eyes meeting hers. A small woman, barely five feet tall, her face was marked with a pointed chin, deep-set eyes and a firm mouth. He would not have called her beautiful, but her complexion and clothing were immaculate, her headdress regal and imposing. No royal wife in his memory had appeared more conscious of her august status.

"Your request?" A small smile shadowed the corners of her mouth and her voice softened. "You know I would do anything in my power to please you."

He heard something in her voice—an intimation of desire—and he frowned. Over the years, especially since the death of his wife, a host of bored, silly women had offered themselves to him for purposes of matrimony or pleasure, but Yosef had managed to elude them and keep his mind on his responsibilities. Ordinarily he would resort to an artful cat-and-mouse game that dissuaded attention-starved women, but today the matter of his father's burial pressed on his mind.

"If you would please me," he said, bowing as if he'd been honored by her attention, "know that my father, Yisrael, has departed this life and gone to his fathers. I have charged my physicians to embalm him, and we have entered into our days of mourning. But if I have found favor in your eyes, please speak to Pharaoh for me. As he lay dying, my father had me swear that I would bury him in the site that he dug for himself in the land of Canaan. So if you would be kind, beg Pharaoh to let me go to Canaan, bury my father and return."

A tremor touched her smooth, marblelike lips. "Your father has died?"

"Yes, my queen."

"I am so sorry to hear it." Uncertainty crept into her expression. "If you have a difficult journey, you may be gone for some time."

"A small caravan can make the journey in seventeen days. A larger party will be slower, but I do not think we will be gone more than two months."

Tipping her head back, she gazed into his eyes. "What if some harm should befall you? Pharaoh cannot risk losing you, Zaphenath-paneah. You are more than a father to him."

Yosef bowed his head. "Once the days of mourning are passed and my father is buried, I know that God Shaddai will hasten my return. My lifelong duty is to serve Pharaoh—and you, his queen."

Satisfaction pursed her mouth. "Then I will speak to Pharaoh for you. And you may go bury your father, and we will see that your journey is well made. With you shall go all of Pharaoh's chief servants, the elders of his household and the governors of Egypt. The world will see, and know, that one of Egypt's mighty ones has passed into immortality. And thus his name will live forever, as will he."

Yosef bowed from the waist. "I thank you, my queen."

An inexplicable look of withdrawal had crept over her face when he looked up; strong emotion flickered in the wells of her eyes. "I will mourn with you," she whispered, lifting a hand as if she would touch his shoulder. But she did not, and after a moment, she turned, the wind stirring her wig as she abruptly moved away.

Tiy immediately ordered a barge to carry her across the river to the complex at Malkata. The name meant "Place Where Things Are Picked Up," and Tiy was not certain if Pharaoh had meant to refer to the clean look of the place or his habit of acquiring women for his harem.

From the deck of the barge, Tiy could see the pink granite palace rising from its exalted strip of earth. The western mountains that concealed the burial places of ancient kings rose behind Pharaoh's house, the swollen river stood before it. The barge turned into the T-shaped harbor dredged especially for

Malkata, and to her right Tiy caught a glimpse of the lake Amenhotep had ordered his architects to dig in her honor. On festival days, the waters of her lake rocked with barges and boats dedicated to the sun god, Aten.

A narrow canal, camouflaged by thickly growing reeds, broke off from the lake and skirted the entire complex before doubling back to the Nile. Tiy hated the canal, convinced that it served as an ideal nesting place for snakes and rodents, but many of Pharaoh's top officials and couriers used it as a secret entrance and took pride in knowing of its existence.

The late afternoon sun streaked the water crimson, and Tiy fretted at the railing, eager to be off the ship. When at last the gangplank lowered, she hurried past the guards and strode through the pink-tinted columns of the entrance gates. The buildings around her, built of sun-dried bricks and lavishly painted with scenes of life along the Nile, shimmered with the rich colors of life.

Malkata was not merely one palace, but several, a sprawling combination of compounds, each with its own administrative offices, houses for court officials, halls, chambers, chapels and lavish apartments. Homes for the most deserving and skilled artisans had been erected on the site, but the average people of Egypt had been forbidden to settle on this western shore of the Nile.

She hurried along the pathway, ignoring the fawning slaves and officials who fell to the ground like paddle dolls at her approach. The palace built for her son, Crown Prince Nefer-kheprure' Wa'enre', rose at her left hand, but the complex to which she hurried was far larger and more elaborate than the prince's. It was home to the king's vast harem.

Tiy would never forget a dispatch she once found—in it, Amenhotep had instructed his provincial governors to send him "beautiful women, but none with shrill voices. Then the king your lord will say to you, 'That is good.'"

Many kings of Egypt had loved the thrill of battle, but her husband preferred love to war. During his reign he had married additional Egyptian women as well as two princesses from the Mitanni kingdom, two from Syria, two from Babylon and one from the kingdom of Arzawa in Anatolia. One of the Mitanni princesses arrived with 317 ladies-in-waiting, many of whom Amenhotep was terrifically pleased to add to his harem.

Slaves and guards scattered like chaff as she swept into the House of the Women. She found her husband seated in the reception hall, a trio of dancing girls before him, an all-female orchestra behind him, and a pair of concubines at his side. For an instant her temper flared as it had in the early days, then she reeled in her anger and hid it away.

She forced her lips to part in a curved, still smile as his gaze met hers. "Life, prosperity, and health to you, my lord!" she murmured, prostrating herself on the floor.

"Tiy?" Amenhotep's voice cracked in surprise. "I didn't expect to see you today."

She lifted her head and boldly met his eyes. "I have had a visit from your vizier, Zaphenath-paneah. He begs your permission to journey to the land of Canaan to bury the one we knew as Yisrael."

"My vizier's father is dead?" With the back of his hand Amenhotep absently pushed one of the concubines away, then straightened himself in his chair. "The old man? I thought he would never die. None of Egypt's pharaohs ever lived so long."

"Zaphenath-paneah says his god loved the old man," Tiy answered, lowering her gaze. "The god's blessing rested on him."

"As it has rested on Egypt since my vizier's arrival." When Amenhotep's jaw clenched, Tiy knew what he was thinking. As a child, when Zaphenath-paneah had been Pharaoh's tutor, Amenhotep had dutifully given lip service to the vizier's invisible and almighty god. But as he grew older and fell under the influence of the priests of Amon-Re, Pharaoh decided that Zaphenath-paneah's ideas were too restrictive, too conservative. And so he had widened his allegiance to a host of gods, placating both his people and his priests, and Egypt had not seemed to suffer for it. Indeed, after the famine the crops grew back greener than before, and due to the vizier's ingenuity, all the land in Egypt now belonged either to Pharaoh or the priests. Whether this rich blessing had fallen on the Black Land because of her Pharaoh or her vizier, Amenhotep could not say, but he suspected the latter, for his father, Tuthmosis IV, had filled the sacred annals with words of praise for Zaphenath-paneah and the spirit of God that rested on him.

Amenhotep might be vain and hedonistic, but he was not a fool. He would not risk the future.

"What did you tell Zaphenath-paneah?" Pharaoh asked, in a lower, huskier tone.

Tiy stood and clasped her hands. "I knew you would not want him to be unhappy, my king. So I told him to go and bury his father in Canaan. He had sworn to do it."

Pharaoh gripped the arms of his chair. "Tiy, what are you thinking? What if he does not return?"

"He will, my lord." Tiy smiled in the calm strength of knowledge. "I am sending the best of Egypt with him—the elders of your household, the priests, a royal escort, a fleet of chariots and warriors. Such a show of support will bind his heart to yours…and will guarantee his safe return."

Pharaoh sank back in his chair and cast her a glance of pure admiration. "My clever Tiy," he murmured, his eyes appraising her. "Beautiful as well as scheming. The gods were good when they sent you to me." Masculine interest radiated from the dark depths of his eyes as he leaned forward and extended his hand. "Will you eat dinner with me?"

Tiy felt the corner of her mouth lift in a wry half-smile. Ignoring the dancing girls, the musicians and the concubines, she met his hungry eyes and defied them. "My king, I must see to the particulars of our vizier's journey." She lifted one shoulder in an elegant shrug. "If you would retain your vizier, you must allow me to refuse your kind invitation."

"Of course." He dropped his hand. "Go, then, and see to it that our vizier is happy."

"Fret not, my husband." She gave him a confident smile. "On my life, I would not allow him to leave us forever."

Chapter Three

Once the patriarch's body had been washed and loaded onto the barge for transport to Thebes, a heavy, mournful mood settled on the Hebrews around the encampment's central fire. Menashe joined his uncles as they sat and wept for nearly a full day without speaking, some rocking back and forth, some kneeling on their cloaks, staining the fabric with their tears.

Reluctant to confront the confident, superior smirk Efrayim had worn since Yisrael's final blessing, Menashe chose to remain in Goshen until the days of mourning had passed. Feeling like an outsider, he hunched around the fire with the others, his arms drawn close to his chest, his eyes downcast. He had not spent much time with his grandfather, for the demands of Egypt had prevented Yosef and his sons from regularly visiting Goshen, but Menashe held a deep and abiding respect for the man his father had openly adored.

As the sun sank toward a livid, purple cloudbank piled deep on the western horizon, Re'uven stood, wiped his tears and folded his hands. Facing the circle of men, he let out a long, audible breath, then began to recite the story of two babies who jostled each other inside their mother's womb. "God Shaddai told Rebekah that two nations would be divided from her belly," Re'uven said, depth and authority in his voice. "One tribe would be mightier than the other, the elder would be servant to the younger. And when her days were fulfilled for bearing, twins were in her body. The first one came out ruddy, like a hairy mantle all over, so they called his name Esav, Rough One. And then his brother came out, his hand grasping Esav's heel, and so they called him Yaakov, Heel-holder."

Re'uven sat down. In the silence that followed, Yehuda rose. Leaning hard on his staff, he told the story of how Esav sold his birthright to Yaakov for a serving of boiled red stew. "Therefore they called him Edom, Red One," he said, raking wisps of windblown hair from his forehead, "and Yaakov gave Esav bread and boiled lentils, and he ate and drank and arose and went off. Thus did Esav despise the right of the firstborn."

When Yehuda had finished, Dan rose to tell of the time Yitzhak and his sons had moved to dwell in Gerar in obedience to the voice of God Shaddai. "And God said to Yitzhak our grandfather, 'Do not go down to Egypt. Continue to dwell in the land that I tell you of, sojourn in this land, and I will be with you and will give you blessing,'" Dan recited, his eyes sweeping over the men in the circle. "And God said, 'I will make your seed many, like the stars of the heavens, and to your seed I will give all these lands. All the nations of the earth shall enjoy blessing through your seed, in consequence of Avraham's hearkening to my voice and keeping my charge—my commandments, my laws and my instructions.'"

Shim'on stood to tell of how Rebekah and Yaakov had deceived Yitzhak and stolen the firstborn's blessing from Esav. Yaakov had been a wily deceiver in his youth, but Esav had already demonstrated his contempt for his father's blessing. If Esav did not receive the firstborn's birthright, Shim'on's uplifted eyebrow seemed to say, he got what he deserved.

On and on the stories continued, acknowledging Yisrael's vices even as they celebrated his virtues, focusing Yaakov's image in their memories, reviving the old man's youth, his yearnings, his submission to God's commands. Menashe sat like a statue through it all, surprised again and again by his grandfather's unpredictable encounters with El Shaddai.

He had never heard such stories! He had grown up with the tales of Egyptian gods and goddesses, legends of Horus and Isis and Osiris and the primeval waters from which the world was supposedly formed, but he had never felt any personal connection to such outlandish accounts. But now his uncles revealed his own history, unmasking the rivalry between Yaakov and Esav and explaining the trickery which brought Lea, the elder daughter, into Yaakov's tent though he loved Rahel, the youngest.

"In a similar way our father, Yaakov, displeased Yosef before he died," Binyamin told the gathering. "Yisrael crossed his arms so that Efrayim and not Menashe received the blessing of the right hand—"

Menashe colored fiercely when he heard his own name, and Binyamin stopped abruptly, apparently recalling that Menashe had not returned to Thebes with Yosef and Efrayim.

"Go on, uncle, it is all right," Menashe murmured, the misery of the previous day still haunting him. "I'm not sure what Grandfather meant by his gesture."

"He meant nothing." Shim'on leaned forward from across the circle and gave Menashe an almost playful smile. "So what if Efrayim has more children than you? Rejoice! You will have fewer mouths to feed in your lifetime and less worry when you are dead. Count it a blessing, my nephew!"

Shim'on's words brought a measure of comfort, and Menashe managed a tentative smile as he listened to the other stories that poured from the lips of Yisrael's sons. He learned of Yaakov's frantic flight from Hebron after the artifice which cost Esav his father's blessing, of the death of Rahel at Bethlehem, of Yaakov's stunned amazement when his sons told him that Yosef lived as vizier of all Egypt.

Re'uven stood up, his voice rumbling like thunder as he recited yet another oral history. "And El Shaddai said to Abram, 'Go you forth from your land, from your kindred, from your father's house, to the land I will let you see. I will make a great nation of you, and will give you blessing, and will make your name great. I will bless those who bless you. He who curses you, I will curse. And all the families of the earth will find blessing through you.'"

Re'uven paused, his eyes strafing the gathering. "And just as El Shaddai spoke to Abram, later called Avraham, thus did He speak to Yisrael in the night. 'I am the god of Avraham your father and the god of Yitzhak,' He said. 'The land on which you lie I give to you and to your seed. Your seed will be like the dust of the earth. You will burst forth to the sea, to the east, to the north, to the Negev. All the clans of the soil will find blessing through you and through your seed! Know this, I am with you, I will watch over you wherever you go and will bring you back to this soil. Indeed, I will not leave you until I have done what I have spoken to you.'

"After this our father woke from his sleep and said, 'Why, God is in this place and I did not know it! This is none other than a house of God, and that is the gate of heaven!' And so our father, Yaakov, started early in the morning, and he took the stone that he had set at his head and set it up as a standing pillar and poured oil on top of it. And he called the name of the place Bet-El, meaning 'House of God,' but Luz was the name of the city in former times."

"The House of God?" Menashe whispered to Jokim. "Where is Bet-El?"

Jokim shrugged. "I've never been there. I was born in Hebron, and we moved from that region when I was young."

"Don't you want to visit the place?" Menashe nudged his cousin. "And Shekhem, where our uncles slaughtered the city? And the site where Rahel is buried? How can you hear stories of these places and not want to see them for yourself?"

Jokim gave him a sidelong glance of disbelief. "I've heard stories of Sheol, too, and I don't want to go there! Would seeing these places help me be a better shepherd, or make my goats give more milk?"

Menashe spread his hands as he fumbled for words. "That other land is the one God promised to our people! Canaan is where Yaakov wanted to be buried! If one land is like another, why did Yisrael make my father swear to bury him in Canaan?"

For that Jokim had no answer.

Miles away, in Thebes, Efrayim stood in silent respect as the corpse of his grandfather entered through the gates. In order to take full advantage of the best physicians, Yisrael's body had been brought directly to the small temple within the vizier's villa. Pharaoh's own physician-priests had been dispatched to tend to the patriarch of the Hebrews.

While Menashe lingered in Goshen, Efrayim agreed to help Ani, the steward of his father's estate, oversee preparations for the vast funeral procession that would return Yisrael to the land he loved. As busy as a fly with his unexpected responsibilities, Ani assigned Efrayim to the job of overseeing the crucially important embalming process.

Efrayim knew that the people of the Nile had elevated physical preservation to an art form. The Egyptians believed that when a person died, his *ba* and *ka*, elements of the soul, escaped from the body and lived on in the tomb. The *ba* watched over the living family and friends of the deceased, while the *ka* traveled back and forth from the body to the Other World. In order to enjoy true immortality, the *ba* and *ka* had to be able to recognize the body throughout the ages or they could not return to it.

Though Efrayim did not agree with these elements of Egyptian religion, if Yaakov's body were to withstand the long days of mourning and a tedious journey into Canaan, it would have to be embalmed. And so Efrayim followed the corpse, slipping into a dark corner of the small temple to watch the priests of Amon-Re commence their work.

Yisrael's body, which had been enfolded in sheets of linen, was stretched out on a slanted embalming bed within the temple, then reverently unwrapped. After positioning and cleansing the flesh, the priests allowed the water and fluids to drain away through holes in the marble slab. Efrayim watched in fascination as the physicians used a chisel to break through a resistant bone at the back of the nostrils. With an iron probe, they extracted several cupfuls of a semiliquid gray substance. The brain material, considered worthless in this life and the one to come, was thrown away.

Over the course of the next several days, Efrayim rose with the sun, breakfasted with Ani and then joined the physicians in the little temple to observe the continuing process of embalming. After removing the brain, the physicians made a slit in the left side of the body just above the joining of leg to the trunk. Working from this cut, the embalmers removed the liver, lungs, stomach and intestines. After carefully cleansing these organs, the priests rolled them in powdered natron (a grainy, salty chemical gleaned from deposits in the Nile), then placed the organs in separate canopic jars for the journey to the tomb. The heart, seat of the emotions, was removed, sprinkled in natron and replaced inside the chest.

The physicians carefully cleansed the interior and exterior of the body with scented oils, then packed the body cavity with linen and bundles of natron. As they neared the completion of this first phase of the long process, the physicians chanted prayers and stitched across the gaping cut.

As he watched the priests work on Yisrael, Efrayim marveled that the Egyptians displayed such reverence for this father of the Hebrews. A decree from Pharaoh himself urged his people to observe the passing of the vizier's father, and for the past thirty days the citizens of Thebes had mourned Yisrael as thoroughly as had the Hebrews in Goshen. Many nobles of the court sprinkled ashes on their wigs each morning and beat their breasts outside their houses in public acknowledgment of the debt they owed Yisrael, progenitor of their beloved Zaphenathpaneah, the Bread of Life and Father to Pharaoh. Though twelve years had passed since the great famine, most Egyptians remembered that the vizier—under the guidance of his god—brought them through the Years Without the Flooding of Hep-Ur, the ancient river.

Yet why shouldn't the Egyptians and Hebrews work together? He and Menashe, the offspring of a son of Yisrael and a daughter of the Black Land, proved that such a mingling could bring honor to both peoples. The two sons of Yosef had been reared among the glories of Egypt, enjoying the fullness of its splendor and access to its vast treasures of knowledge. They spoke both the Egyptian and the Canaanite languages, and could write the hieroglyphs as easily as the twenty-two consonants of the Hebrew tongue.

And Yisrael blessed us equally with his other sons, Efrayim thought, studying the wizened face in repose on the embalmer's slab. *And he blessed me with his right hand...*

Finished with the suturing of the body, the embalmers

stepped back. Chanting prayers to the gods of the underworld, they lifted painted bowls and ladled powdered natron over the corpse. They continued chanting until the powder lay heaped over the body, enveloping it completely.

Efrayim breathed a sigh of relief. The natron would cover the body for forty days, completely desiccating it. Until the end of the drying time, Efrayim would not need to look at his grandfather's corpse again.

The sun had already begun to melt behind the walls of the villa when Efrayim left the temple. The guards at the gate of the villa stirred in a flurry of activity, and he shaded his eyes to see through the bright glare of the setting sun. A pair of camels stood there, joined by lead ropes to a straggling pack of donkeys. A small group of men, clothed in the linen garments of the desert-dwelling Bedouin, had dismounted to speak to the guards. Efrayim turned away, satisfied that the visitors were traders from the north seeking to curry the vizier's favor before the day's business was done.

"Efrayim!" Efrayim turned when Menashe's voice rang out across the courtyard. He had not heard from his brother since they parted in Goshen, but now Menashe ran toward him, his head turbaned in linen, his slender body disguised by a long tunic. His eyes snapped in greeting. "I have such news!"

Efrayim greeted his brother with a quick slap on the back, then stepped back and rested his hands on his hips. "What can possibly be happening in Goshen?" He flashed his brother a teasing smile. "A new lamb, perhaps? Or has Re'uven found a way to make his cattle grow as fat as Binyamin's?"

Menashe ignored the sarcasm. "Sleepy Goshen will never be the same." He slipped an arm around his brother's shoulder as they walked toward the villa's wide portico. "The entire world comes to mourn Yisrael. Kings from Jericho, Kadesh Barnea and Gaza. I never dreamed our grandfather was so well-known! Though Father often referred to him as a prince, it has been so many years since Yisrael dwelled in Canaan, I did not think the kings of the world would remember him. But within a week of your departure, the horizon filled with caravans, men who had traveled many miles to reach our settlement. They came, they offered words of comfort, they told stories of Yaakov that stirred my blood like nothing I have ever felt before."

"*Our* settlement?" Efrayim lifted a mocking brow. "You speak as if you are one of them." He stepped back and eyed Menashe up and down. "You even *look* like you are one of them."

Menashe flushed with sudden anger. "The Hebrews are our people. If God had not called our father out from among them—"

"They would all be dead," Efrayim interrupted. "And you and I would not exist. But we do. And we are not only Hebrews, we are Egyptians, too. This is the will of God, and Yisrael confirmed it before he died. God Himself married the sons of Yisrael to Egypt, and we are the first-generation offspring."

Menashe's dark eyes narrowed and hardened, but Efrayim did not give him a chance to speak. "Do not let tales of desert barbarians turn your head, for such stories are not your only heritage." He grasped Menashe's elbow. "Your past lies in the glory of the pharaohs, the splendor of Egypt, the strength of the Nile. If God can bless a straggling pack of nomadic shepherds, how much more can He bless those who have the resources of the world's mightiest empire at their disposal?"

Menashe glared at Efrayim in irritated silence. Shrugging, Efrayim dropped his brother's elbow and walked away, a little surprised at his own temerity. Never before had he spoken so forcefully to his older brother, and never before had Menashe let him get away with it.

He tucked his hands into the belt at his kilt and began to whistle. Perhaps he was the mightier man after all.

Menashe shook his head as his brother walked away. Only the sweet grace of understanding had enabled him to hold his tongue, for Efrayim had mourned in the heart of Egypt. He had not spent the past month sitting by the fires of the Hebrews, listening to the stories of Avraham and Yitzhak, Sara and Rebekah.

And what did Efrayim know of his heritage? Nothing! For the first time in his life, Menashe felt as though he fully understood the legacy of his ancestors. The knowledge that he and his people had been chosen to bless the world had left Menashe shaken and awed.

He bounded up the portico steps and wandered through the vestibule. The front hall where his father routinely received guests and supplicants stood empty, but the room had been recently deserted, for the fragrance of incense still hung in the air. Menashe moved through the halls toward his father's private chambers. A pair of guards stood outside a wooden door, confirming his expectations. "Is my father inside?"

One of the guards answered with an impersonal nod.

"May I enter?"

Another stiff nod. Tarik, the captain of the vizier's bodyguard, encouraged his warriors to be stern of demeanor and limited in speech.

Menashe pressed the door open. Like a demi-king in his own personal realm, his father sat in an elevated chair next to a tray loaded with papyrus scrolls. Ani, forever the dutiful steward, hovered near like a watchful guardian.

Ani's beaked face spread into a grin at Menashe's approach. "Master! Look who has returned!"

Menashe lowered himself to his knees and prostrated himself. After a month of the Hebrews' casual, easygoing familiarity, the gesture felt awkward and stiff.

"Rise, my son."

Menashe lifted his head as his father smiled. "It is good to see you." One of the parchments on the tray curled and rolled onto the floor, and Yosef frowned as Ani scurried after it.

"I trust your uncles took good care of you?" Yosef's handsome face, lined now with weariness and the passing of many years, seemed to gentle as he turned back to his elder son. "How are they faring in the north?"

"They mourn," Menashe said, straightening. He shifted and felt his cheeks burn at the honest welcome in his father's eyes. "They mourn, but they are comforted by a stream of visitors from Canaan and beyond. A band of Esav's people arrived just before I left."

"Edomites?" Yosef's brows shot up. "I suppose Esav's sons will forgive the past for an occasion such as this." He glanced again at the parchments on the tray. "So," he said, clearly distracted, "tell me what you have done during your time with your uncles."

"Father, I have learned so much!" Menashe struggled to curb his excitement. "The stories they tell are unbelievable. Jokim assures me that these things are true, yet I find it hard to believe that an angel of God could stop Avraham's hand as he prepared to sacrifice Yitzhak, and Sarah could give birth at ninety years of age."

"El Shaddai has always been a god of miracles," his father answered, reaching for the parchment Ani had retrieved. "From the beginning of the world until this day, He has not taken His hand of blessing from us."

"I know, Father, but—" Menashe paused "—if these tales are so wondrous, why haven't you shared them with us? Jokim could not believe I had not heard the stories of Rahel and Lea, or Yaakov and Esav."

He stopped, afraid to reproach his father further, and saw that Yosef's attention was riveted to the parchment in his hand. He had not even heard the question.

"Peace and prosperity to you." Menashe bowed his head. "I think I'll go wash and change into something—more Egyptian." He gave Ani another smile. "Efrayim thinks I look like a goat herder."

Ani laughed, and Yosef's face wrinkled in an automatic smile. "Yes, go clean up." He dismissed Menashe with a wave. "Perhaps I will find you at breakfast tomorrow."

"Perhaps." Menashe lowered his gaze as he backed out of the chamber. "But I will understand if you do not."

Chapter Four

Forty days passed. The glistening sheets of water left by the inundation thinned but remained on the fields, brilliantly mirroring the cloudless blue sky above. As the vizier's servants went forth to reset the flooded boundaries of his fields, Efrayim met again with the physician-priests. After greeting them in the villa's temple, he stepped aside and allowed the men to begin their work. While lifting rhythmic chants to Amon-Re, the embalmers used palm-frond fans to blow the piles of natron from Yaakov's physical remains. When the last of the white powder had been blown, brushed and swept away, priests sponged the shrunken body and wiped it with oils, ointments and spices.

Efrayim sat on a stool in the corner of the tiny temple, his fingers pressed over his mouth as the priests went about their work. The physicians reopened the body cavity, removed Yaakov's heart, now shriveled from the natron, and placed it inside a special jar. One priest inserted a stone scarab, an amulet in the form of a beetle associated with the rebirth of the sun, in the heart's former position. As the sun climbed across the sky outside, the priests stuffed the body with packets of fresh linen, then plugged the eye sockets and nostrils with beeswax. Crossing the patriarch's arms, they covered his fingernails and toenails with specially designed golden caps. With silken thread the priests sewed the embalming cut together, then covered the wound with a golden plate engraved with the protective Eye of Horus.

After adorning Yisrael with necklaces, rings and bracelets of gold and precious stones, the physicians carefully bound the body with long, narrow linen strips. With infinite patience they individually wrapped fingers, toes, arms and legs. With the care they might have shown Pharaoh himself, the embalmers inserted protective amulets—images of the lotus, the symbol of rebirth, and the ankh, a sign of life—between the layers of binding, then glued every few layers with resin.

The process of wrapping required two weeks and over 445 square yards of fine linen. After twenty layers of binding, Efrayim was relieved to see that the shrunken body had resumed its normal size.

A portrait mask covered the mummy's bound head, a most decidedly un-Egyptian rendering of a bearded man with black, fathomless eyes. The physicians bound the mask in linen, then sealed the entire body with a final coat of resin. When the resin had dried, the embalmers stepped back, folded their hands and looked to Efrayim for approval. Yaakov's mortal remains were ready for their final journey.

Impressed with their reverent care, Efrayim bowed to the physicians and went into the house to report to his father.

Chapter Five

Menashe's mouth tipped in annoyance when he learned that Pharaoh and Queen Tiy had requested the vizier's presence at a banquet before the burial procession could depart Thebes. His annoyance flared to irritation when he heard that he and Efrayim would also be expected to attend the royal dinner. Though he was eager to join his kinsmen on the journey to Canaan, one thought assuaged his impatience as he shaved and dressed for his audience with the king and queen: the banquet would be held at Malkata. If all went well, he might be able to speak with Jendayi, the only girl who had ever made an impression on his heart.

He had first met Jendayi ten years before. He had been a lad of fifteen, still ungainly and uncertain of himself, but his heart had melted when he saw Ani leading a new group of slaves through the vizier's courtyard. This was a special group, Ani explained, escorting the newly acquired servants to the brick building where the slaves slept. They were musicians, and most talented ones. He had spent a hundred deben weight of silver to acquire them, but they were worth every ounce, for the vizier's house should offer the finest music in the land. The slave broker had assured him that no orchestra in the entire world was more talented than the group he now led through the hot sun.

Menashe's eyes had swept over the other women and focused on her. On that day Jendayi had been a petite girl of seven or

eight, with skin as pure as alabaster and hair as dark as kohl.
The desert wind had whipped color into her cheeks, and even
from a proper distance Menashe could see that thick lashes
swept across her cheekbones. A bruised lotus blossom had been
tucked into the fabric of her belt, an incongruous bit of adorn-
ment for a slave.

Even then her gentle and overwhelming beauty sent his
spirits soaring. Though she had to be frightened at her change
of circumstances, she wore an expression of patient endurance
while her posture spoke of strength and determination.

Look at me, he had silently urged her, fascinated by the way
she held the arm of a robust, bald slave whose heavy cheeks fell
in worried folds over the collar at his neck. But she kept her eyes
downcast, even when Ani stopped at the edge of the portico. The
robust man halted, too, but the girl took two more steps, running
headlong into the woman who walked in front of her.

Then Menashe understood why she kept her eyes lowered.
She was blind.

He backed away, stunned by the realization. He had never
seen a blind child. Blind babies were usually tossed to the
crocodiles, for the Egyptians considered anyone with a physical
imperfection accursed. She must have lost her sight at some
point past birth, and she lived still because she possessed some
talent or quality that atoned for her weakness and prevented her
from being a burden.

Over the next few days, Menashe learned the secret of
Jendayi's salvation. Jendayi was a prodigy, as skilled a harpist
as he had ever heard, more inventively musical than even the
harpists of Pharaoh's court. The bald man, Akil, served as the
orchestra's chironomist, a singer who directed the musical
ensemble with gestures. Menashe noticed that Akil gave particular, almost fatherly attention to the girl, urging her to play
beyond her confusion, to give her full attention to the music.

Apparently she heeded his counsel. The first time Menashe
heard her play, he nearly forgot who and where he was. The
occasion was a banquet his father had hosted for a group of
Egyptian nobles. On a lark, Ani suggested that the master's new
musicians be invited to perform during the meal. Zaphenath-

paneah agreed, and the small orchestra tucked themselves into a corner of the room to provide soothing music to spur the flow of the guests' conversation.

As chironomist, Akil presided over the orchestra. He sat before them, his back to the room, his eyes toward his musicians. With one hand on his bent knee, Akil tapped the rhythm, with his other hand he indicated the notes to be played. The inclination of his arm specified the pitch, the position of his fingers told the musicians whether their sounds should be abrupt, smooth, loud or nearly silent. Since she could not see the director, Jendayi stood in the midst of the others, feeling their movements, listening to their breaths, seeming to anticipate the movement of Akil's arm even before the others could respond to him.

Along with Jendayi and her harp, Akil's all-female orchestra consisted of women who played the lute, a double oboe, a lyre and a tambourine. For the most part they performed gentle, unremarkable music that did little but support Zaphenathpaneah's dinner until a lull in conversation gave Akil the opportunity to lower his arms and hoarsely whisper Jendayi's name.

Even through the veil of memory, Menashe could recall the sparkling clarity of the notes she played. The harp broke through the heavy silence of sated banqueters like the shattering of crystal, then trilled in a melodic passage that brought the dinner to a standstill. The nobles seated around Zaphenathpaneah stopped eating; the servants paused in their circuitous routes to the kitchens and stared as the wellspring of sound swept through the hall and over the assembled diners. No one had ever heard such magic from either a harp or a human throat, and the effect astounded every soul at the vizier's dinner.

Sudden tears burned Menashe's eyes as the music spilled through the room. One minute heavy and boisterous, then sweet and light, the poignant sounds touched places in Menashe's heart no human had ever been able to reach. The melody grew bittersweet, brightening the faded memory of Menashe's dead mother, then rushed on to lift his soul to the hope of sunrise and the joy of warbling birdsong. Finally the music softened to echo the sibilant whispers of the spirits of the Nile and the whirring insects in the tall river grasses. Menashe covered his mouth with his hand, afraid lest some inadvertent sound slip out and spoil the effect she'd created, then the girl pressed her hand across the vibrating strings and the sounds ceased.

The silence that followed was like the hush after a whirlwind when the palm branches hang limp and the earth seems to catch her breath. As worn out as if he'd been running, Menashe clung to the edge of his chair and stared at the girl who sat as silent as the Sphinx. A strange and tangible whispering moved through the air, like the trembling breaths of a hundred simultaneous astonishments. "Who is she? Where did she come from? Has a god inhabited her fingers—or her harp?"

Akil, as master of the orchestra, stood and took a bow, then placed one hand across his breast and gestured to Jendayi. Menashe burst out in spontaneous applause, echoed by his father and the other guests. The girl, apparently aware that the attention of every eye in the room had focused on her, stiffened as twin stains of scarlet appeared on her cheeks.

On that day Menashe fell completely in love. He would bide his time, he decided, and wait until she was of a marriageable age, then he would approach his father and ask if she could be his bride. But within three years of her arrival at the vizier's house, news of the child prodigy reached even Pharaoh's ears. As a gesture of loyalty and love, Zaphenath-paneah offered his harpist and chironomist to Pharaoh's service, and shortly thereafter Akil's little orchestra left the vizier's villa for Pharaoh's pink palace.

Though the turn of events left Menashe feeling bereft, God had not been entirely unmerciful. Over the years Menashe had relished his occasional visits to Malkata, not because he rejoiced at Pharaoh's invitation, but because he adored sitting in the same room with Jendayi. A mere ripple of her fingers across the harp had the power to draw tears, and the sight of her diminutive form moving through the halls set his blood to pounding in his temples. He did not know how he would make her his wife, but one day he would. He would never marry unless he married Jendayi.

His determination had only grown stronger through the

years. On the afternoon of Pharaoh's banquet before the departure to Canaan, Menashe dressed with special care before joining his father and brother at the gate of the villa. After they crossed the Nile on a barge, a litter bore the three men to Pharaoh's gleaming palace.

As a pair of Pharaoh's elite Medjay warriors escorted them through the maze of palace passageways, Menashe reflected on the king who now held Jendayi's fate in his hands. Amenhotep was not unreasonable; in fact, many considered him to be Egypt's wisest pharaoh. He neither taxed his people unfairly nor spilled their blood on foreign fields. He had sired a host of royal children and married a woman who proved to be not only fruitful, but capable.

Of course, Pharaoh did have—Menashe grinned, searching for the words his father would use to describe the king—quirks. In addition to his inordinate fondness for women, Amenhotep possessed an enthusiasm for building as strong as his predecessors' passion for war. Along with the palace at Malkata, he had built a large addition to the temple to Amon-Re at Karnak and a larger temple, flanked by an avenue of Sphinxes, to Amon-Re at Opet. Though no one could say which project was the more daring, the most mysterious work had been accomplished at his mortuary complex. Through some magic of design and situation, Pharaoh's builders had erected a pair of colossal stone statues engraved with Amenhotep's image. Precisely at sunrise each morning, the two sixty-five-foot statues produced hauntingly musical sounds.

Pharaoh's chief chamberlain met them outside the gilded doors of the king's throne room and prostrated himself before Zaphenath-paneah. "Pharaoh and the Mother of All Egypt are in the garden," the chamberlain told them after Yosef gave him permission to rise. "You are to join them as they finish their game."

"What game are they playing?" Yosef asked as the chamberlain led them toward the garden.

The chamberlain's broad face cracked into a smile. "Hounds and Jackals."

Menashe cast Efrayim a puzzled glance. Hounds and Jackals

was a trivial entertainment usually employed by wealthy Egyptians as a way to pass long, hot afternoons. He could not imagine the divine pharaoh and the Mother of All Egypt being bored enough to indulge in a board game. He and Efrayim had not played in years.

His father must have guessed at his thoughts. "Pharaoh and Queen Tiy have erected a life-size board in the center of the garden," Yosef explained, casting the words over his shoulder as they walked. "The fifty-eight golden circles on the game board have been represented by fifty-eight golden tiles along the garden pathway. And instead of a splotch of blue paint to represent an oasis on the game board, Pharaoh's men have situated a real pool between the two garden paths."

Players of the game had a simple objective, Menashe recalled. One player managed a team of hounds, the other a team of jackals. To begin, each player rolled the knucklebones, and the first to roll either a one or a six could set out on the trail, moving from tile to tile. The first player to land exactly on the shenu, the royal insignia, won the game.

The challenge of Hounds and Jackals lay in managing the two serpentine trails that connected opposite sections of each pathway. If a player landed one of his tokens at the junction of a tile and one of the serpentine paths, he had to follow the secret trail, either moving ahead by several tiles or falling back by the same distance. To further enliven the game, five special tiles were marked with the ankh, the symbol for eternal life. A player fortunate enough to land on the ankh could roll the knucklebones again and take another turn.

As they neared the garden, Menashe could see that Pharaoh had made a great production of the game. Two winding paths had been cut into the garden on opposite sides of an enormous reflecting pool. A gigantic shenu, a tile engraved with the king's divine name and decorated with gold, red carnelian and lapis lazuli, rested on the ground directly in front of the garden pavilion.

At that moment an official yelled, "Three!" Pharaoh, who watched from the pavilion, pointed at a slave on the path reserved for "hounds." The slave, dressed in a furred headdress and a silver collar, ran forward three tiles. At once a dozen slaves burst from behind a screen of greenery, a replica of the sacred bark of Amon-Re on their shoulders. The boat, a small model of the sacred bark on which the god sailed to his various temples, featured a curved prow and stern carved with the image of the ram-headed god. Long poles supported both the craft and fluttering banners painted with the god's sacred insignia.

The grinning "hound," delighted at Pharaoh's good fortune, climbed into the boat while the bark-bearers carried him over one of the hidden paths to a tile much closer to the shenu and the finish line.

From the security of her elevated chair, Queen Tiy frowned. Stepping up to the rope that separated the playing field from the observers, Menashe noted the position of the players. If his good fortune held, the king would win.

Tiy nodded toward her representative, who tossed the knucklebones into a gleaming bronze pan. "Two!" called the official. With a decided frown, the queen pointed toward one of her men (a jackal, Menashe decided, since he wore a black headdress painted with pointed ears), who promptly stepped forward two tiles. But his move placed him at the exit of one of the secret paths, and as soon as the servant settled on the tile, a pair of priests lifted the lid on a woven basket. As Menashe stared in mystified amazement, a cobra slithered out and "hissed" the queen's player back to the beginning of the course.

"Don't worry," the chamberlain whispered as the reptile wriggled away. "It is an old creature whose fangs have been removed."

Triumphant laughter echoed from the king's chair. "Ah, Tiy, I shall beat you yet!"

"We shall see, my king." The queen laughed, too, but her laughter had a sharp and brittle edge.

Pharaoh rolled the knucklebones again, and the spectators broke out in polite applause as he moved another "hound" forward six tiles.

The queen shot her husband a twisted smile, then gestured to the official. "The bones," she commanded, her spiderlike hand extended. "I will throw them myself."

The official bowed and gave her the knucklebones. Pharaoh leaned back and cupped his hand around his chin. Tiy rolled the bones in her hands as if to get the feel of them, then splayed her fingers. The bones spilled uselessly onto the ground.

"Tiy!" Disappointment dripped from Amenhotep's voice. "You dropped them! You have forfeited the game!"

"Alas, apparently I have." A smile crawled to Tiy's lips and curved itself there like an undulating cobra. "But I would rather surrender to you, mighty Pharaoh, than be beaten by you. Besides, this is not an appropriate time for games. Our guests have arrived, and they are in mourning."

Pharaoh's expressive face stiffened and became almost somber when he caught sight of his vizier. "Zaphenath-paneah," he said, his voice dull and troubled. "I am glad you have come. I wanted to spend this day with you, to strengthen your heart as you once supported mine as I prepared to bury my father."

Now that the royal gaze had fallen on them, Menashe followed his father's example and prostrated himself before the pavilion. "Rise and kiss the royal foot, most excellent vizier, my Zaphenath-paneah." Pharaoh's voice sounded thin and hollow in the open air. Yosef rose to his knees and crept forward to brush his lips across the tops of Amenhotep's red leather sandals. A great honor, this kissing of Pharaoh's feet. Only a select few noblemen were allowed to touch the divine king.

"You and your sons may stand," Pharaoh called, and Menashe rose. Lifting his chin, he assumed all the dignity he could muster, but he always felt like a child in Amenhotep's presence. Though Yosef was the king's most trusted counselor, Menashe and Efrayim had not spent enough time in royal company to feel comfortable in the king's presence. Perhaps no man ever could.

At thirty-one, Amenhotep III stood before the world as a man in the prime of life. Even from this distance, Menashe felt the power that coiled within him, an energy that could not be disguised by the king's air of studied relaxation. Like the other nobles, Pharaoh wore a linen kilt girdled at the waist by an elaborate beadwork belt, but there the resemblance to other noblemen ended. From Pharaoh's belt hung a sporran of beaded strings, each topped by a gold cow's head pendant, a symbol of the goddess Hat-Hor.

Since he could never be seen with his head uncovered, Amenhotep wore the *nemes* headdress, a piece of stiffly folded cloth held in place by a gold band across his forehead. Two striped lappets fell forward over his smooth chest. A model of the serpent goddess Wadjet protruded from the front of the headdress, and under the *nemes,* the king's profile was sharp and confident. His face, bronzed by the wind and sun, was pleasant enough, but his eyes smoldered with the intimidating and fiery pride of Egypt's kings.

"Your sons have grown into fine men." Pharaoh nodded with a taut jerk of his head, then stole a slanted look at his wife. "What do you say, my dear Tiy? I believe the young sons are as pleasing in form as their father."

Menashe felt an unwelcome blush creep onto his neck as the queen rose from her gilded chair. He had avoided glancing in her direction, for Tiy's sharp, restive features and direct gaze had always reminded him of a vulture spying for carrion.

Dragging her pet dwarf on a golden leash, Queen Tiy advanced to Pharaoh's chair. She inclined her head toward her husband in a deep gesture, then swung her gaze over the trio standing before him, her dark eyes lazily seductive. "The sons can never equal the father, for beauty divided could never equal the whole." Her nasal voice cut through the silence like a hot blade. She cast a slight smile in Yosef's direction. "But they are fine sons, my king, and any man would be proud to claim them."

"So I thought." With an abrupt nod, Pharaoh gestured toward his chamberlain, then rose from his chair. "I invited you today for a banquet, Zaphenath-paneah, so let us forgo formalities and retire to my chamber. I want to hear the details of your coming journey without the distractions of the court. Let my wife and my eldest daughter entertain your sons while you and I enjoy private discourse."

Menashe felt his heart constrict a little at the king's words. If the musicians played for Pharaoh, he would not have a chance to see Jendayi.

But Queen Tiy stepped forward and slipped her arm through

his. "Come, young man, and escort me to my chambers where we shall relax and talk of interesting things." Her smile did not reach her eyes. "My daughter waits for us there, along with food and music sweet enough to soothe whatever trouble stirs behind those restless eyes of yours."

Smiling in the hope of better things to come, Menashe inclined his head and led the queen from the royal garden.

His smile broadened in approval when he discovered that the queen had spoken the truth: the banquet she had prepared was simple, quiet and intimate. The four diners—the queen, Menashe, Efrayim and Princess Sitamun, the king's eldest daughter—sat in tall chairs which had been arranged so that each diner faced one of the others. A steady procession of servants brought in bowls of steaming meats, delicious fruits and tender vegetables. These dishes were presented first to Queen Tiy, who sampled them and instructed the slaves to divide the food among her other guests.

Menashe found himself sitting across from the queen, a position that unnerved him until he realized that the musicians, if they came, would sit behind her. He hoped he might be able to appear to give the queen his full attention while he studied Jendayi, but after assessing Tiy's bold, black eyes, he decided she would not be easily fooled. She would know if something other than her royal presence occupied his thoughts.

For an hour they ate and carried on a pleasant and unremarkable conversation. As Efrayim's tongue loosened he began to tease Sitamun, a pampered princess of sixteen. Tall and slender, with a narrow face, the girl possessed such heavy eyelids that she seemed perpetually on the brink of falling asleep. But her eyes gleamed as she bantered with Efrayim, and her wit proved as sharp as her tongue. More than once Menashe shot a smile in her direction when she scored a point against Efrayim in their gentle sparring, and before the first hour ended he realized that the conversation between his brother and the princess had evolved from common talk to the verbal fencing of flirtation.

Apparently Queen Tiy noticed the shift, too, for the faint beginnings of a knowing smile hovered around the edges of her mouth. Menashe was about to distract her by asking about the king's plans for the restoration of the gates of Thebes when a curtain parted and Akil entered the room.

Menashe's stomach dropped like a hanged man. Behind the chironomist came the oboist, the lutist, the woman who played the tambourine, the lyre-player and, finally, Jendayi, led by a handmaid.

Menashe stared at the little harpist in a paralysis of astonishment. He had not seen Jendayi in several months, and then only from a distance. How lovely she had become! No queen, surely no woman in Pharaoh's harem, could rival the girl's beauty. She wore a full wig now, as did all Pharaoh's servants, but the young woman under the wig seemed more delicate and ethereal than ever. The hand wrapped around the wrist of her handmaid was slender, her fingers strong and slim. Her throat looked warm and shapely above the bodice of her dress, the softness of her young body seemed to melt against the linen of her gown. The eyes she lifted toward the windows were as gray and wild as a storm cloud, but Menashe knew that a passionate, intelligent woman lived behind those eyes and that perfect face. One had only to hear her play to know the depths of the soul that lived within her.

He took a deep breath and felt bands of tightness in his chest. How could any man look at her and not want her? How did Akil work with her every day, hear her voice, and not want to partake of her sweet innocence? And Pharaoh! How did he, the connoisseur of beautiful women, resist this lovely flower?

For the briefest instant his eyes met Queen Tiy's. A smile nudged itself into a corner of her mouth and pushed across her lips. "Has anyone ever told you, my young friend—" she lowered her voice to the vaguest of whispers "—that your thoughts shine in your eyes like stars? From the look on your face I know that the king's musicians have entered the room. And—" she leaned toward him "—the light in your eyes tells me you have found some sight for which you yearned. Since most of the women in Pharaoh's orchestra are waspish, unlovely creatures, the gleam in your eyes must be inspired by—dare I say it?—the little harpist."

Menashe stared at her, tongue-tied, but Tiy's smile told him she understood. "The girl *is* lovely, isn't she? A rare treasure, she possesses both beauty and talent. She is, I'm afraid, one of Pharaoh's favorites." She paused, her paint-lengthened eyes studying him, then pressed her hand to her swanlike throat. "Do not be alarmed by what I am telling you. Though our king has a fondness for music, the women in Akil's orchestra have never been invited to join the royal harem."

Menashe felt his heart swell with relief. A thoughtful smile curved the queen's mouth as she regarded him. "I had almost forgotten that such innocence could exist, Menashe, son of Zaphenath-paneah."

He allowed his eyes to drift back to Jendayi. "Surely God never created a more innocent creature."

"I was not speaking of the harpist. I meant you."

Menashe felt his flush deepen.

"Do not be embarrassed, my dear young friend," Tiy purred. "And do not lose heart. Pharaoh is not completely attached to the harpist. With the right encouragement there may come a time when he might be willing to release the girl…to a man he wishes to honor." The queen allowed her words to hang in the silence, then she lowered her gaze into Menashe's. "There may also come a time when you may be of service to your queen, my young friend. Perhaps, in the future, we can help each other."

Though the queen's words hinted at some sort of mystery, Menashe was too thrilled by the prospect of winning Jendayi's release to do more than nod in agreement.

Efrayim dipped his fingers into the tiny water bowl on his dinner tray, then dried his hands on a perfumed square of linen and studied his brother's face. Menashe's unruly eyes had trained on the harpist again, the sentimental fool. Did he not know that Tiy was a jealous queen? She would not take kindly to being ignored. Furthermore, Menashe's mooning over a royal slave was a waste of time. The girl would never be freed from Pharaoh's service, nor would she be allowed to marry. She should consider herself fortunate if she found joy within her music, for most of Pharaoh's slaves knew nothing of happiness outside Pharaoh's will.

"Efrayim." Sitamun tugged on his arm, her hand lingering on his skin.

"How may I serve you, Princess?" He returned his attention to the girl across from him. Sitamun was a demanding companion, never happy unless he was smiling at her, but she was pretty and intelligent, gifted with her mother's genius and her father's persistence. She was also sixteen, ripe for marriage, and a not-altogether distasteful specimen of womanhood. Though he would prefer a creature of lightness and beauty like Menashe's angelic harpist, the blind girl would never bear heirs to a royal throne. Sitamun would. And though the crown prince stood to inherit Amenhotep's kingdom, life was tenuous and the future uncertain…

A smile ruffled his mouth as he listen to Sitamun prattle about the latest court gossip. Why shouldn't he marry a princess? Yaakov's right hand had fallen on his head, and what better way could he lead the sons of Yisrael to greatness than through an alliance with Egypt? His father had begun a mighty work; Efrayim could continue it.

He leaned his head on his hand, studying the pleasant princess before him. "Has anyone ever told you—" he pitched his voice so it would not reach the other two diners "—that your eyes blaze like stars in a midnight sky?"

Though any observer would have believed Akil intent on the music he directed, his thoughts were focused on the circle of banqueters behind him. He knew the sons of Zaphenath-paneah, their natures and their desires, and he distrusted them. The eyes of the elder, Menashe, burned Akil's shoulders as he stared at Jendayi, and the younger, Efrayim, seemed too glib for Akil's comfort. During the three years he had lived in the vizier's villa, he had not been unaware of Menashe's longing looks and Efrayim's bold flirtations with his prodigy.

But he had managed to shelter Jendayi, the most blessed of

the gods, from the boys' attentions. Her blind eyes had never seen the open heart Menashe revealed on his face, and her ears had never heard Efrayim's bold flirtations. Only once could Akil recall having shirked his duty, the afternoon Efrayim had discovered Jendayi in the garden and kissed her in an impetuous moment. Fortunately, Akil had spied the pair before the situation could advance, and had led his stammering ward back to the slave quarters. Efrayim, cheeky as always, had grinned and walked away, probably to find a more willing slave on whom he could foist his attentions.

Akil cast a discreet glance over his shoulder. A soft and loving curve lay on the elder son's lips as he stared at Jendayi, completely unmindful of the queen, but the younger man seemed intent on Princess Sitamun. Good. Let him cast his nets after the slippery princess; those two deserved each other.

At least, may the gods be praised, Jendayi would not see the look of love in the other man's eyes.

Akil turned back to his orchestra and gave his sighted performers an approving smile. The song they played was an unobtrusive, unremarkable tune in which Jendayi did little more than strum an accompaniment to the oboe. He would not draw undue attention to her tonight.

For he had long known that Jendayi held the key to his own prosperity and happiness. As long as the little harpist retained the gift of the gods and remained in Pharaoh's court, Akil would continue to be her musical interpreter. Though Amenhotep had access to the best musicians in the kingdom, he called for Akil's orchestra at every great occasion, both personal and private. As long as Jendayi's harp continued to thrill the king, Akil would remain in the inner circle of Pharaoh's favor…and he would be summoned to play for the queen.

He could imagine no higher honor, no more beautiful or deserving woman. Tiy was the most brilliant star of Pharaoh's world, a paragon of virtue, intelligence and cunning. Akil willingly gave his loyalty and service to Pharaoh, but he reserved his adoration for Tiy, the Mother of Egypt and his own Favorite Lady.

She might never know that he would die for her, but she would never have cause to doubt his loyalty.

* * *

Menashe's soul burned with impatience as the queen's slaves carried their dinner trays away. They still had to endure the ritual chants to thank the gods for their prosperity, then Queen Tiy and Princess Sitamun would take their formal leave and quit the chamber. The musicians might leave before the royals, so he would have precious little time to find Jendayi before the guards would arrive to escort him and Efrayim back to the docks. One did not wander through Pharaoh's palace unescorted...

But he had to speak to Jendayi. He and his family would soon be leaving for Canaan, and it might be weeks before he received another invitation to Malkata. His silent heart had spent years yearning for her, but now she was old enough to hear of his love, to know that he wanted the best for her and would stop at nothing to obtain it.

The servants finished clearing the room; a bald priest entered and chanted a ritual hymn of praise and thanksgiving. When the priest had finished, Queen Tiy rose in a smooth, graceful motion. "We bid you farewell," she said, her voice crisp in the stillness.

Taking her cue from her mother, Sitamun stood as well. A small, suggestive smile touched her lips as she inclined her head toward Efrayim. "A pleasure to speak with you," she murmured, a sweet edge to her voice. The dark hair of her oiled wig glistened like polished wood as she transferred her gaze to Menashe. "You both must come again when you have completed your journey to bury your grandfather."

"We thank you for your invitation, and yearn to accept it," Efrayim answered, not bothering even to look at Menashe. "My brother and I will fly to your side whenever you command our presence."

Menashe locked his hands behind his back. Let Efrayim accept Sitamun's invitation; he would be pleased to accompany his brother if only to catch another glimpse of Jendayi. "Yes." He nodded toward Sitamun. "We would be honored to see you again."

"So be it, then." Sitamun's smile relaxed. "I will implore the gods to grant you a safe and uneventful journey."

Efrayim and Menashe bowed, then Tiy led her daughter

from the room. When both the queen and the princess had gone, Efrayim turned to Menashe in a burst of excitement, but Menashe stalled him with a touch on the shoulder. Leaving Efrayim in the center of the chamber, he hurried toward the corner where the musicians were gathering their instruments. Jendayi had already disappeared through the doorway, but perhaps the chironomist would call her back—

"Master Akil," Menashe called, his voice a great deal shakier than he would have liked.

Akil turned. "May I help you, sir?" The musician wore a frown, and his brows had twisted in a brooding knot.

"I am Menashe, elder son of Zaphenath-paneah." The words rushed together as he hurried to identify himself. "If you would summon Jendayi, I would like to speak to her."

"I know who you are," the chironomist interrupted. "But we are no longer the property of your father the vizier." The man barreled his scrawny chest. "We belong to Pharaoh."

"I know. But if you will call her—"

"Jendayi cannot speak to you. You are a nobleman's son. She is a slave. And you must leave. The guards are even now at the door."

Menashe glanced over his shoulder. The man had spoken the truth; a pair of armed warriors had entered the room and waited to lead him and Efrayim back to the docks.

"But I wish only a word."

"No! Take yourself away or you will make trouble for both of us!"

Menashe stepped back, driven not by fear of Akil, but by the knowledge that any rash action might endanger future invitations to the palace. The chironomist was a stubborn fool, but Menashe had allies in higher places. Queen Tiy herself had intimated that she would help in his quest for the harpist's hand.

"Later, Akil," Menashe called, backing out of the chamber. "I will see you again."

Jendayi followed her handmaid through the palace halls and tried to deny the sour feeling in the pit of her stomach. She was glad Pharaoh would not be summoning her to play again tonight, for nothing but loneliness, longing and pain could pour from her harp now.

She heard Akil's shuffling steps behind her and lowered her head, knowing he would be angry if he read her feelings on her face. "Why do you long for things that can never be?" he constantly chided her. "Be happy where you are. You live in the grandest palace of the most glorious king of the most powerful kingdom in the world. The gods have blessed you, so rejoice and be content."

She tried to be content, but the dream persisted. Her nightmare of death and the Hall of the Two Truths had not lost its power to terrify her. She awoke every morning in a sweat, recalling the fervor with which the god condemned her. *"You have loved nothing, you are nothing, you have nothing!"* Anubis's gaunt jackal face rose before her now, and with a shiver of vivid recollection she pressed closer to her handmaid's side.

Life itself haunted her, for living seemed an exercise she often heard about but would never really experience. She ate, slept, drank and played in the lonely blackness of the blind; every day looked like every night. Each time she rose from her bed she slipped into a tunic that felt like the one she had worn the day before; the sounds that rose and fell around her were the same sounds that had kept her company since the days of her childhood. The people who moved along the fringes of her world raised their voices when speaking as if she were deaf, or they were quick to assume that because she did not make eye contact with them, they could not make any contact with her.

Pharaoh, the queen, the men and women of the royal court lived and laughed in *the world,* but Jendayi and her companions were forever isolated behind the veil of slavery, urged to perform well and scurry away like rats behind a wall. Her experiences had been as uninteresting and bland as warm water, and her stomach knotted at the thought of a lifetime of emptiness, long years of loving nothing, having nothing, being nothing…

She had been given one gift—an ability to hear and create music. Sometimes in the quiet of an afternoon one of the other slaves would tell a story of love or hate or jealousy, and Jendayi would struggle to interpret those emotions through her harp. But even at her best, she knew the tones that flowed from her hands were only shadows of the genuine passion that gripped and motivated the rest of the world. Her fingers strove to speak of love, and succeeded only in imitating the delicate warble of a mother bird that coos to its young hidden in the river grasses. She was an imitator, not an artist. Anubis was right, she was nothing.

"We are here, mistress." Kesi, her handmaid, turned abruptly, pulling Jendayi with her. Jendayi lifted her head and inhaled the sweet lotus blossoms the lutist had arranged in a bowl the day before. They were back in their room, one of many chambers in the slave quarters behind Pharaoh's palace.

"Thank you." Jendayi released Kesi's arm and held out her hand, waiting for the staff she used to guide her steps while in the slave quarters. Within a moment Kesi had slipped the smooth stick into Jendayi's palm and moved away, probably anxious to be rid of her dependent mistress. Tapping her way through the room, Jendayi counted her way past three beds, then sank to the fourth, carefully placing the staff beneath the bed frame. Once she was certain no one would trip over it, she curled on her side and placed her hand under her cheek.

But she could not sleep, for the dream might come again. Would she ever be able to silence Anubis's mournful howl? Could her cold heart find love? Her mother had abandoned her soon after it became apparent that Jendayi's weak eyes had succumbed to the disease that robbed her of sight. She had no real memories of her mother, nor of the slave market where she had been abandoned. In her childhood she had been fed, bathed and tutored in various aspects of servanthood until her gift for music was discovered. But had she ever been loved?

The other women slaves treated her with gentle concern, but no real affection. Akil cared for her, she supposed, but he was more a teacher than a father, more her guardian than a parent. Jendayi suspected that she was the most talented musician in the orchestra, but Akil said she had done nothing to deserve her extraordinary ability. The gods had gifted her, he said, and they could easily rescind their gifts—hadn't they stolen her sight?

Her life seemed as bleak and formless as the darkness, yet occasionally a magic moment disturbed the monotony. Years ago in the vizier's house, one dull afternoon had fired into unexpected vitality when a boy, smelling of sweat and youth, had pressed his lips to hers and pronounced her beautiful. Akil had promptly chased the boy away, scolding him as if he were a naughty puppy, but Jendayi had been profoundly affected by the experience. Human flesh on her lips—the same lips that gave sound to her words and brought her food and drink. Anubis was Lord of the Lips, for lips were the doorway to life, and this boy had placed his on hers! Did he love her? Surely he did, or he would not have kissed her.

From that day forward she had listened for the boy's voice and waited for his scent. She learned that he was Efrayim, the second son of the vizier, a refreshingly candid and openhearted lad. When the orchestra moved to Pharaoh's palace she thought her dreams of him would come to nothing, but tonight she had heard his name again! He had been a guest in the queen's chamber; he had undoubtedly heard her play.

Just knowing that he listened had thrilled her so much her hands trembled over the strings of her beloved harp. Akil must have seen her discomfiture, for he had not asked her to play alone.

Before she left the queen's chamber she had heard the visitors promise to return to Malkata. So Efrayim would hear her play again. And if her music touched his heart, perhaps he would remember his kiss and feel kindness for her. And if she was virtuous and made the proper offerings to the gods, Efrayim might dare to approach Pharaoh and procure her as a slave for his own house. She could be his servant, perhaps even his concubine. Then, if the gods were willing, she would finally experience love, tenderness and honest emotion. Then the gods could not say she had loved nothing; they could not condemn her to eternal death.

The next time Efrayim heard her play, she would be ready. She would compose a song like no other, one that would expose all the hidden feelings in her heart. She would bare her soul before his, and see if he possessed courage enough to hear everything she wanted to say.

MENASHE

And Yosef went up to bury his father: and with him went up all the servants of Pharaoh, the elders of his house, and all the elders of the land of Egypt,

And all the house of Yosef, and his brethren, and his father's house: only their little ones, and their flocks, and their herds, they left in the land of Goshen.

And there went up with him both chariots and horsemen: and it was a very great company.

Genesis 50: 7–9

Chapter Six

During the first month of the Emergence, when the days of mourning for Yisrael had passed, Pharaoh Amenhotep III summoned the governors of all the nomes of Egypt to Thebes. These nomarchs, along with a great host of servants, priests, elders and other important officials, gathered at the royal palace where they were designated as Pharaoh's representatives on the journey to Canaan. Pharaoh himself elected to remain behind at Malkata, citing his persistent toothache and fever as an excuse not to travel.

But even though the king preferred to remain behind, he made certain Zaphenath-paneah would not feel slighted for a lack of royal attention. Tiy urged Amenhotep to bestow great honors on Yisrael for the vizier's sake, and every tribute that could be dreamed of had been awarded. The finest physicians had embalmed Yisrael's mortal remains, the most sacred stone had been used to fashion the canopic jars that held the old man's precious inner organs. Pharaoh himself had approved the design of the carved chest that would house the jars. Inscriptions and relief-work adorned the chest's exterior; rich blue pigment filled the hollows of the carving. Fashioned of purest alabaster, at its four corners the chest featured raised figures of the goddesses Isis, Nephthys, Neith and Selkis, their wings extended to enclose and protect the chest's priceless contents.

Surely even Zaphenath-paneah's invisible and almighty god

must have approved Pharaoh's labor, for the day of Yisrael's departure from Thebes dawned in a spectacular burst of blue. From his private balcony Amenhotep could see the Nile rippling as bright as new silver in the sun, and a cooling zephyr rushed up from the receding river. He hummed quietly to himself. It would be a good day. Zaphenath-paneah would be pleased, Tiy would be content with Amenhotep's efforts, and the soul of the Hebrew patriarch would rest secure in the Other World.

Behind the king, one of the priests who tended him every morning coughed discreetly. Amenhotep turned from the river view, ready to begin his toilette.

Thebes had never seen such a funeral procession. Not even Egypt's pharaohs, who rode in grand style from the valley temples to their vast mortuary complexes on the Nile's western bank, would undertake so long a final journey. Yisrael would leave Thebes in full splendor, travel to Goshen to gather his children, and then depart for Canaan. On the journey the contingent of mourners would travel through often-hostile lands populated by fierce peoples. Though Egypt had formally subjugated the kingdoms from the Mediterranean to the Euphrates as far north as Syria, to guard against any possible aggression Pharaoh had ordered two squadrons of charioteers and an elite corps of shock troops to accompany the vizier.

The members of the procession had been assembling in Thebes since morning, and Amenhotep had expressly commanded that they move slowly past Malkata so he and his family might smile on them with divine favor. A cloud of dust now stirred along the riverbank to the south, and the king settled back in his chair, pleased that his wishes had been carried out. A pair of slaves knelt at his side, ready to do his bidding; a pair of guards lingered in the doorway behind him. His daughters Sitamun, Ast and Hentmerheb, who usually lived in Thebes with their mother, sat at his right hand. Tiy, for some inexplicable reason, had demurred last night when he asked her to remain at Malkata. She would prefer to oversee the procession at Thebes, she told him; she would extend Pharaoh's farewells as Zaphenath-paneah departed from the docks.

He glanced at Sitamun, whose eyes betrayed her feelings. The night before she had dared to suggest that she might join the crown prince on the journey with the Hebrews to Canaan. Amenhotep had stalled his answer, and later Tiy explained their eldest daughter's sudden interest in the journey. "She fancies herself in love with the vizier's handsome younger son," Tiy said, her pointed face creasing into a sudden smile. "At our banquet, he captured her heart. He is quite charming."

"Should I let her go?" Amenhotep asked, searching his own feelings on the matter. His deep fondness for Zaphenath-paneah sprang from nostalgia for his childhood and his mother's high regard for the man, but he had long ago learned the folly of consistently showing more favor to one counselor than the others. Jealousy hissed like a serpent through the royal throne room, and Amenhotep had felt the effects of its sharp bite. The priests of Amon-Re, who held altogether too much power in their hands, had grown more resentful of Zaphenath-paneah's success as the years passed. Amenhotep heard reports—though he was reluctant to investigate should such a shameful thing prove true—that even the history of Egypt had been rewritten. The priests of Thebes, unable to believe that an invisible and unknown god had saved Egypt, recorded that Amon-Re, "Greatest of Heaven, Eldest of Earth," saved the Black Land from famine during the early years of Amenhotep's reign. As the people who lived through the Great Famine passed into the Other World, the truth would gradually disappear like the ruins of the most ancient Egyptians, buried by yet another layer of shifting sand.

Sitamun sighed, interrupting his thoughts, and Amenhotep congratulated himself for having enough insight to listen to his wife. Tiy suggested that Sitamun remain behind, and now he saw the wisdom in her suggestion. If Sitamun journeyed to Canaan with the Hebrews, the priests would see significant and dire omens in the swirling waters of their divining cups; they would read all sorts of dark meanings in Pharaoh's intention. Even now they grumbled about the expense of this great show of favor for the Hebrew patriarch.

The usual assortment of fishing boats and papyrus skiffs on

the waters vanished like grain before the scythe as the royal
chariots approached, two lines in perfect sync on the banks of
the swollen river. The levees had been reinforced for the
chariots' passage, for the muddy soil could not normally withstand the weight of so large a procession. As the gold-plated
vehicles gleamed in the afternoon sun, the charioteers turned
their faces toward the pink-washed palace. Pharaoh sat forward
and studied them intently.

Between the chariots, on the river, floated a host of stately
barges, each flying the standard of the nomarch aboard. The
Egyptian officials preferred traveling by boat than by land,
and Pharaoh lifted his chin in case any of his governors were
sharp-eyed enough to catch a glimpse of his divine presence
on the balcony.

After the nomarchs came the royal barges that carried
members of Pharaoh's own household: the crown prince, nearly
half of Pharaoh's counselors, priests from the leading temples
of Thebes and a company of scribes to record the wonders of
the journey. At one point Amenhotep had considered sending
Queen Tiy with them, then decided against it. A journey through
the wilderness was no pleasure trip. The heat, grumbling camels
and frequent sandstorms combined with the inconveniences of
uncivilized life to make the journey wearisome from inception
to end. Tiy would not find the wilderness to her liking, and
Amenhotep would not be able to forget her displeasure if he
insisted she go.

When other boats moved into view, Amenhotep leaned
forward on his elbows. He recognized a half-dozen barges and
feluccas belonging to the vizier; these were undoubtedly
carrying trusted members of Zaphenath-paneah's household:
his steward, the captain of his guard and other indispensable
servants and counselors. Across from these boats, on the eastern
riverbank, marched a corps of Nubian drummers who marched
in the rhythm of a steady, morose dirge.

"Look, Father, at the dancers," Ast said, pointing. The eager
child scooted forward. "What story are they telling?"

"I don't know, my dear." Amenhotep craned his neck for a
better view. A host of dancers postured and posed on the wide

deck of an oncoming ship, and with a start of surprise Pharaoh realized that Zaphenath-paneah had employed a group of mimes. In order for the illiterate and uninformed common folk who watched from the riverbanks to understand the significance of the procession, the dancers were paid to pantomime the highlights of Yisrael's life. Pharaoh rubbed his chin as a bearded mime, undoubtedly intended to represent Yisrael, beat his breast as another was led away in chains.

Pharaoh pressed his hand to his cheek. "They are telling the story of how Zaphenath-paneah was sold into slavery," he explained. "The man in the long robe is Yisrael, the vizier's father."

His daughter gaped at him. "Who would sell our vizier?"

"No one today, dear one. But long ago, when our vizier was a boy, only his father and his god recognized the seeds of greatness in him. His brothers, you see, were jealous."

Amenhotep regarded the floating drama with somber curiosity. Strange that he, a man without equal, should know how the brothers felt. For though he had always considered Zaphenath-paneah a father, on occasions he had felt the bitter sting of envy when comparing himself to his vizier.

Shortly after Amenhotep's ascension to the throne, the priests had taught him that Amon-Re consulted with the other gods to see who should bear his child. Thoth had suggested Tuya, the wife of Pharaoh. And so Amon-Re assumed the form of Tuthmosis IV and visited Tuya in the night; therefore Amenhotep was conceived as the son of a god.

Why, then, did Zaphenath-paneah possess more godlike qualities than Pharaoh himself? Amenhotep was all too aware of his own shortcomings. His wife was a more able diplomat and manager than he, and Zaphenath-paneah possessed wisdom far above any displayed by the king's counselors, priests or astrologers. And though no counselor, slave or priest would dare to lift a voice against the divine king, Amenhotep had seen countless pairs of eyes glaze over when he offered his opinions. But those same eyes, even Tiy's, blazed with fiery interest when Zaphenath-paneah spoke.

Giving himself a stern mental shake, Pharaoh directed his attention back to the funeral procession. The professional mourners were advancing now. Clothed in the blue-gray color of sorrow, their faces daubed with dust and mud, they beat their breasts and trudged with heavy steps along the riverbanks, their wails reaching even to the king's balcony. Between them, on flower-strewn boats, other servants of the vizier stood guard over baskets of food and supplies for the journey, a rich testimony to Yisrael's worth.

He cast a quick glance at Sitamun. The girl had been pouting all morning, undoubtedly wanting to join her brother on the journey, but this glorious spectacle would lift her out of her black mood. "Look, daughter—the mortuary boat."

The death boat, which Zaphenath-paneah had designed especially for Yisrael, cut through the water as smoothly as a knife, guided only by the pair of slaves who stood at the bow and steered the craft with slender oars. The tall mast of the vessel moved into view, and Amenhotep smiled, impressed with the vizier's efforts. The sides of the boat had been painted in bright reds, yellows and black; images spelled out texts from the Chapters of Coming Forth by Day. In the center of the boat's deck, adjacent to the single mast, a shrine cabin had been adorned with lotus blossoms and palm branches, symbols of the resurrection. Several mourners rode atop the cabin, pulling at their hair while they wailed, and a host of ritual priests stood at the stern of the vessel: the *sem* priest who wore his traditional white linen robe and leopard skin, and the embalmers who had prepared the body for its eternal rest. They had been entrusted with guarding and overseeing the physical remains until the point of safe interment in the tomb.

Through a series of windows in the shrine cabin Amenhotep caught a glimpse of the dull gleam of green stone, and knew he was seeing the granite sarcophagus especially commissioned to guard Yisrael's mummy. The sarcophagus alone had cost Pharaoh's treasury over three hundred deben weight of silver, but such a tribute seemed small in light of the debt Egypt owed Zaphenath-paneah.

Immediately behind the mortuary boat floated the elegant bark carrying the vizier and his sons. Sitamun leaned over the balcony railing, probably trying to catch a glimpse of Efrayim, and Amenhotep felt himself stiffen, half-convinced Zaphenath-paneah would know whether or not he was paying proper attention. The vizier always seemed to know what Amenhotep was thinking, another unnatural ability for which Pharaoh had no explanation and the vizier had no rival.

Sitamun sighed and sank back in her chair. No one moved on the deck of the vizier's boat, and Amenhotep guessed that the vizier and his sons had entered the small cabin to be alone with their feelings. A man ought to be able to mourn in private. Some emotions were not meant for public display. Women, good food and gentle music could do much to relieve the heaviness of a man's wounded heart—

Music. Where were the musicians?

A few other boats followed the vizier's, but none of these flew the royal standard. Undoubtedly they carried slaves and servants who would tend to the officials on the arduous journey.

Amenhotep lowered his gaze to one of the slaves who waited like a statue at his side. "Akil and his orchestra are supposed to be en route with the vizier. Send guards at once, and make sure the musician has departed."

The slave hastened away, as swiftly as a cat.

Satisfied, Amenhotep stood and clasped his hands behind him. As the caravan melted into the northern horizon he gave his vizier a curt nod of farewell. He had done his part to honor Yisrael. Yisrael's god should continue to honor him.

Irritated by the close confines of the cabin, Menashe pressed his lips together. Their father sat with his legs crossed and his back to the wall, not moving. His eyes were closed either in contemplation or weariness, for the planning of this procession had consumed his energies for many days. Efrayim, on the other hand, had done nothing to warrant special treatment, yet he lounged on a small cot, his head propped on his hand, his face spread into a smile as he attacked a bowl of figs. What in the world could he be so happy about?

"Stop smacking." Menashe gave his brother a black look. "You've been gobbling on those things for an hour, and my stomach is beginning to churn. Your manners are deplorable, and what if someone sees you? This is a funeral, not one of your festival parties."

Efrayim lifted a brow in amused contempt. "You think my manners deplorable? You are the one who has fallen in love with goat herders! Besides, no one can see me, for we are quite alone. If I displease you, go outside."

"I will not go out with the slaves. The sun is too hot, and this is as much my place as it is yours. So stop that infernal smacking!"

The smirk left Efrayim's face. "You're not going to order me around. We are not children and I will no longer listen to you."

"Order you around? I'm asking you to exhibit common courtesy."

"You've commanded me since the day of my birth. And now—" Efrayim gave Menashe a look of jaunty superiority "—I'm not going to listen. The fact that you are the elder doesn't mean anything. Not anymore."

Menashe blinked, as surprised as if Efrayim had slapped him. And even though his brother hadn't said the actual words, he knew what Efrayim was thinking: *Yisrael gave me the blessing of the right hand. I am the favored one.*

Menashe took a deep breath and stifled the urge to choke his brother. He was twenty-five, no longer a child, and as brothers they ought to be able to behave as grown men. If only Efrayim were not so infuriatingly juvenile!

He brought his knees to his chest and looked away. He ought to go outside, but the sight of the mortuary boat depressed him, reminding him again of the afternoon when Yisrael had looked at him with the same mild interest Yosef always displayed. Then the old man had *smiled* at Efrayim, those weak old eyes had almost twinkled as they alighted on Efrayim's twisted grin.

The memory edged his teeth. "It is good that Father did not see the way you behaved during our banquet with the queen," he whispered, casting a surreptitious look at Yosef to make certain those lined eyelids remained closed.

Efrayim frowned. "The princess thought I was captivating. And if I did go a little too far, my behavior was no worse than yours."

"I held my tongue, but you talked like running water, and only to the princess. The queen must think you a terrible fool."

"At least Sitamun likes me." Efrayim shrugged, then his heavy brows arched into triangles. "And I have more to be happy about than you, brother. The object of your undying affection does not know you are alive."

"The object of—what?" Menashe was glad of the shadows that hid the flush in his cheeks. "I don't know what you mean."

"Do you think I am as dense as a rock? You gazed at the little harpist the entire afternoon. Sitamun even noticed it. She thought you were terribly funny."

Menashe felt himself flush with humiliation. He had never meant to act like a fool, but he only saw Jendayi on rare occasions. How was he supposed to sit in the same room with her and pretend she didn't exist? Should he glance only occasionally at the one treasure of his heart?

"I don't care what Sitamun thinks." He lowered his voice in case a servant stood with an ear to the papyrus wall. "I think she is vapid, entirely foolish. She lives entirely for pleasure. I never know when to take her seriously. You may find her fascinating, but I—"

"You are no fun at all, Menashe," Efrayim interrupted, grinning. "No wonder Sitamun finds you boring. Well, your loss is my gain. I will marry a princess while you moon over a slave. And which of us will be happier in the future?"

Unable to bear the taunts any longer, Menashe stood. Standing under the hot sun would be far preferable to remaining in the same cabin with his brother.

Several cargo ships joined the convoy a few miles past the palace at Malkata. Flocks of sheep, cattle and goats filled the stalls of these ships, enough to feed the travelers until the journey had been completed. Menashe marveled at the sheer number of animals until he realized that his father's generous estimations had included feeding not only a sizable host of Egyptians, but his ever-growing family in Goshen, too.

Standing at the rail of his father's ship, Menashe's eyes focused on the far-flung shore. The receding waters of the inundation had littered the shore with uprooted tropical plants washed from lands far to the south. Occasionally the reddish-brown water rippled as a crocodile or hippopotamus ducked beneath the surface, eager to be away from human company. To the east and west, the life-giving floods had muddied innumerable small squares of land marked by stone pillars and mud walls. Soon Pharaoh's subjects would come forth to till the refreshed soil. God would again bless Egypt, and another round of bountiful crops would dim men's memories of the seven years when the annual flood had not come, when only the narrow ribbon of land bordering the river brought forth any crops at all. For those years, Yosef had told his sons, God brought him to the Black Land. Because God Shaddai knew the future, His voice could be trusted in all things.

A tiny vessel appeared on the southern horizon, cutting through the winter waters swiftly enough to decorate her bow with a white garland of foam. Squinting toward it, Menashe recognized Pharaoh's standard on the mast. Had Amenhotep decided to travel with them? Surely none of the king's family would travel in a ship so small.

Menashe moved to Ani's side and pointed toward the ship in the distance. "Who comes yonder? In the felucca."

Shading his eyes with his hand, Ani studied the boat, then his lined face cracked into a smile. "By the life of Pharaoh, the king *did* remember." He turned to give Menashe an affectionate smile. "Pharaoh promised to send his best musicians, but I was not sure he would recall his promise. Akil and his instrumentalists are late, but at least they have arrived."

Menashe's heart jumped in his chest. If Pharaoh had sent his best, including Akil, then Jendayi rode on that ship.

Menashe clutched Ani's arm and struggled to keep the eagerness from his voice. "Should they sail so far behind? They are Pharaoh's servants, after all. If they remain back there beyond the cattle, we would not know if they had trouble on the river. Signal them, Ani. Have their rowers increase their speed until they are directly behind us."

Ani eyed Menashe with a lifted brow, then a secretive smile softened his thin lips. "Yes, Master Menashe." He gestured for the slave who handled the signal flags on the mast. "I will see to it at once."

Menashe turned away, his mood buoyant. If Jendayi traveled with them to Canaan, he would certainly have a chance to speak with her. Away from the strictures of Pharaoh's palace, she might feel free enough to open her heart. Anything could happen under a star-filled sky where the wild wind blew away the restraints and conventions that might inhibit love between a slave girl and a nobleman's son.

A trembling thrill raced through him as he turned again to face the water. Soon he would know if love and marriage would be a part of his future. For since seeing the little harpist at the queen's banquet, Menashe had renewed his vow. Unless he could have Jendayi by his side, he would not take any wife at all.

The ancient river broke into seven tributaries as it entered the delta, and the floating funeral procession anchored on the east-ernmost branch, a short distance from the Hebrews' settlement at Goshen. From this point they would journey by camel and donkey and chariot until they reached the burial place near Mamre.

Efrayim strode down the gangplank of his father's boat and frowned at the disorderliness of the Hebrew camp. He had not noticed this confusion when he visited at his grandfather's death; perhaps grief had tempered his vision. But now, fully aware that his Egyptian companions disdained herders of all sorts, Efrayim thought the Hebrew settlement seemed almost slovenly. Stray animals wandered through the tents, gleefully chased by dirt-streaked children, and the smells of dung-fires, cooking food, cows and goats mingled with the scent of dust and dry earth.

Against the gleaming white of the Egyptians' linen kilts, the rough tunics of the Hebrews appeared untidy and dirty. The windblown hair and beards of the men seemed unkempt compared to the cleanly shaven faces of the Egyptians; the Hebrews' heavy tents smelled of animals and age, a distinct and unpleasant contrast to the airy, perfumed villas of the Egyptians. And while the Egyptians moved off the ships in precise, military order, each man knowing his place and responsibility, the Hebrews wandered in careless confusion, like sheep without a shepherd.

Seeing his father's people with new eyes, Efrayim pressed his lips together and folded his arms. No wonder God sent his father to the Black Land! From the ancient and civilized people of the Double Kingdom these Hebrews could learn much. They could rise above these tawdry tents and build fine stone houses; they could use the mud that splashed around their ankles to form bricks that would last for generations. Like the ancient pharaohs who built the pyramids and the Sphinx, the Hebrews could build cities and monuments and settle permanently in this fertile region. For despite their ineffective methods and crude habitations, they had thrived in Goshen. Many babies had been born, and soon the children of Yisrael would be a mighty and populous people.

Efrayim's mind traveled back to the day of Yisrael's death. He would never forget a single detail of the moment when Yaakov focused his pale eyes on him and prophesied that the younger would be the mightier son. Efrayim would never have dared to contemplate such an idea prior to that utterance, but since that day he had been thinking long, deep thoughts.

As the Hebrew son of Egypt's vizier, he could lead both nations to greatness. Some of his uncles might resist Efrayim's ideas, for Yisrael had always insisted that God had promised them the land of Canaan, but wasn't Canaan now part of Egypt? Tuthmosis III had invaded the land as far north as Megiddo; he had conquered Kadesh and tramped over Mount Carmel. Egypt now extended from the Fifth Cataract of the Nile to the Euphrates River, so why couldn't the promised land of God include Egypt, too?

"Good morning, Efrayim. This is quite a company you have brought."

Brought back to reality by the sound of a Hebrew greeting, Efrayim turned toward the voice and saw Jokim, Yehuda's grandson, standing beside him. Managing a polite smile, he lifted his hand to acknowledge the comment. "Yes, but my efforts alone could not have managed such a large group." He shrugged. "Pharaoh has been generous to us. His guards, his warriors, even his cooks are ours to enjoy on the journey."

Jokim's eyes widened. "I knew your father had influence

with the king, but I never dreamed Pharaoh would care so much for Yisrael."

"Perhaps Pharaoh knows the Spirit of God rested on our grandfather as it rests on my father." *As it will also rest on me.* Efrayim gave the younger man a tentative smile. "Are you willing to help me? We will need to divide the people here into companies. The Egyptians will take care of themselves, but the Hebrews are scattered like feathers in the wind. If we are to make this journey in peace and security, we must be better organized."

"I would be honored to help you." Jokim straightened his shoulders. "But where is Menashe? I expected him to be with you."

"My brother," Efrayim said, the corner of his mouth lifting in a one-sided smile, "waits for the musicians to disembark. He has lost his heart to a slave and his good sense to love. Leave him, Jokim, to his own folly." He placed his arm across his cousin's shoulders and turned toward the Hebrew camp. "Never forget," he said, a teasing note in his voice, "who is the most favored brother. I am the leader, not Menashe. If you want results, come to me."

The youth's square face rearranged itself into a grin. "I hear you, cousin."

Akil was not eager to answer Menashe's impatient questions, but he grudgingly admitted that, yes, Pharaoh had commanded that they journey all the way to Canaan and back and, yes, Jendayi the harpist was among the women aboard the felucca. After making certain that the musicians would be comfortable on the ship, Menashe left the river and strode toward the Hebrew camp. His concern for the musicians caused him to arrive later than his father and brother, and that, he sternly told himself, accounted for the fact that no one made a special point of greeting him outside the camp.

Yosef had chosen to pass the night in solitude aboard his ship, so Menashe looked forward to an evening of renewing friendships with his relatives. But Re'uven, Shim'on and Levi, the three uncles with whom Menashe had always enjoyed an easy camaraderie, scarcely glanced up when he entered Re'uven's tent. Shim'on did offer a distracted wave, but Efrayim was seated with the uncles and a handful of younger men around a dinner feast, and he controlled the conversation.

Menashe halted in the doorway, surprised by the nonexistent welcome, and was only half-aware that a slave girl knelt at his feet, tugging on the strings of his sandals. *You are being foolish,* he told himself, shaking his head at the maid. *These are the men who told you the blessing of the right hand meant nothing, that it didn't matter. And it doesn't, for you are still responsible for your actions, as Efrayim is for his, and nothing can change the fact that you are Yosef's elder son.* But the men who had said farewell only a few days before with warm embraces now gestured for him to come near the fire as casually as if he were a servant, not a firstborn son.

On stiff and unwilling legs, Menashe moved toward the circle and crouched in an empty space. Efrayim was regaling the relatives with a step-by-step recounting of Yaakov's mummification. "I oversaw the entire process," he said, an expression of immeasurable satisfaction gleaming in his eyes. "I observed as they removed Yisrael's heart and wrapped it for the ages. For over twenty days I supervised the priests who wrapped our father Yisrael in fine linen."

Re'uven threw a sly grin in Menashe's direction. "And what did our nephew Menashe do while you supervised?"

Menashe wanted to shout that he had been mourning with them in Goshen for much of that time, but the memory seemed to have slipped his uncles' minds.

Efrayim grinned. "Menashe does what he wants to do," he said, his eyes brimming with smug delight. "You, my uncles, have ruined him for Thebes. Ever since he came back from Goshen he has been fascinated by goats and cows. When he is not examining the new goats in their pens, he walks in the fields and studies the cattle. I am afraid I will awaken one morning and find that he has coaxed a bull into our father's reception hall."

As the uncles roared with laughter, Menashe shot Efrayim a glare. Their argument on the boat had apparently escalated into petty warfare, and Menashe had no wish to continue the feud through the upcoming journey.

But this little skirmish was Efrayim's doing, and he should be the one to apologize. Menashe had done nothing wrong.

Chapter Seven

Jendayi lifted her face to the warm fingers of a caressing breeze, relishing the feel of it on her skin. She and her handmaid rode in a conveyance that Kesi had described as "a pair of huge baskets joined at the middle and slung over a camel's hump." After a short while, Jendayi decided that though the swinging motion so high in the air made her a little sick, she liked this form of transportation. Each girl rode in her own private compartment, granting them a rare measure of privacy. A canopy shaded them from the blistering sun, and the fibers of the woven basket remained blessedly cool to the touch. The rhythmic squeaking of the woven reeds and the camel's grumbling soothed Jendayi, helping her to forget that men of considerable importance—all of them her masters—rode in this caravan as well.

Secure in her perch, Jendayi breathed in the sounds and scents of the journey and realized that she had been pampered. Other slaves walked alongside the pack animals and the other musicians rode in cargo wagons, but she and her maid had been given a camel.

She sighed. Undoubtedly her blindness had caused her to merit this distinctive treatment, but being singled out did not make her happy. She wanted to experience *life,* and yet once again she had been tucked away and protected by the watchful eye of a handmaid.

None of the other women of the orchestra had maids, but

Kesi had been tasked with caring for Jendayi ever since the orchestra's arrival at Pharaoh's palace. Free of Jendayi's encumbering arm, Akil had been eager to enjoy his new mobility, and Jendayi had come to depend on Kesi's guiding hand.

But she did not want to need anyone. Sometimes when Kesi was away, Jendayi practiced moving around her chamber with only her walking stick for a guide, and she usually managed quite well. But sometimes another pair of eyes could be useful.

"Tell me, Kesi—" Jendayi strengthened her voice to reach to the other side of the camel's hump "—what is this country like? Where do they say we are?"

"We are in the wilderness," Kesi answered, the basket creaking as she shifted her position. "The sky is blue from rim to rim. There are no clouds and no mountains to mar the horizon. They tell me there is water far to the north, but I cannot see it. The land is the color of a camel, brown and dusty. I see a few tamarind trees and occasionally an oak, but little else. This place is not like Egypt. I have not seen a flower in days."

"No flowers?" Jendayi adored flowers—their scent, their textures and their almost insubstantial weight on her callused fingertips. Kesi kept a continual supply of flowers by Jendayi's bed in the servants' quarters, and Akil occasionally offered Jendayi bouquets when she played exceptionally well. One day, he told her, she would play a song so beautiful that Pharaoh himself would be compelled to lay flowers at her feet. She could not imagine how to play a song more technically perfect than those she routinely performed now, but Akil seemed to think her best music still lay ahead.

She lifted her voice again. "Tell me, Kesi, what you know about the people with whom we are traveling. I know they are Hebrews. I have heard them chattering for miles. I learned the sound of their language when I lived in the vizier's house, but I cannot understand them."

"Nor can I," Kesi admitted. The maid's basket creaked sharply. "From what I can see, most of them are traveling on donkeys. Several women, older children and men with long beards and hair that brushes the tops of their shoulders. They have dark hair like the Egyptians, but the Hebrews do not shave their faces or their bodies. Hair even gleams at the necklines of their tunics."

"The men wear full tunics? Why?"

"I don't know," the maid answered. "Perhaps they do not feel the heat like we do. Most of them wear loosely woven tunics, belted at the waist. Of course, our vizier wears a similar tunic, for his ceremonial robe is long and flowing—"

"What do the vizier's sons wear?" Jendayi interrupted, trying to curb the curiosity in her voice. "Can you see them? Are they both present—the younger as well as the older?"

The basket creaked again. "My sly mistress," Kesi said, a hint of laughter in her voice, "if you wanted to know about the vizier's sons, why didn't you come right out and ask? I am your friend, Jendayi, your secrets are safe with me."

"I don't have any secrets," Jendayi said, her face burning. *And I don't want any friends.* She pressed her hands to her cheeks lest Kesi peer over the camel's hump and see the flush on her skin. "I am merely curious about the young men who used to be my masters."

"Don't be coy, you can tell me the truth," Kesi insisted, her voice closer now. "Which son do you like, the older or the younger? I saw them the other day at the queen's banquet. They are both handsome."

Jendayi paused, tempted to speak her heart. But Kesi might not understand. She would think her mistress possessed of some juvenile notion of romance when all Jendayi wanted was to know that someone loved her. Her heart slept, but if someone cared enough to wake it, Jendayi would be able to stand in the Hall of the Two Truths and place a flesh-and-blood heart into Anubis's scale.

Perhaps Kesi could be of use after all. "I like the younger one," Jendayi whispered, taking pains to keep her voice steady. "When I lived in the vizier's palace, I once went to the garden to practice." She lifted her face sharply toward the younger girl. "Kesi, I will not tell you more unless you promise never to speak of this! If you are loyal at all, you will keep this secret."

"My lips will be silent," Kesi promised. "What happened in the garden?"

Jendayi took a deep breath. "I was very young. But I was sitting in the vizier's pavilion, playing my harp. The sun shone warm on my face, and in those days I could still see a faint glow of its light. I heard only the wind and the warbling of some waterbirds, but then a shadow passed over my eyes and I knew someone stood in front of me."

"Who?"

"He did not tell me his name. But he spoke, and said my song was beautiful, and that I was beautiful, too. And before I could beg his forgiveness for making music without permission, I felt his lips touch mine."

Kesi gasped. "He *kissed* you?"

Jendayi nodded, forgetting that the maid could not see into her basket. It was enough that Kesi understood the story's significance. No kiss between unrelated persons was ever given lightly. No man kissed a woman in public unless he was either drunk or they were betrothed. A drunkard who kissed a woman would undoubtedly suffer the rage of her husband or father, while a man who publicly kissed his betrothed would usually find himself the beneficiary of a quick wedding. Masters rarely even *spoke* directly to their slaves, so for a young lord to *kiss* a slave girl…

"Did he say nothing else?" Kesi asked.

"No." Jendayi sighed and propped her head on her bent knees. "Akil came into the garden and yelled as if *he* were the master and the vizier's son a slave. The boy left me alone and never spoke to me again." She made a face, for in the retelling the old story seemed more fiction than fact. "I don't know what he intended, but I am sure he must have loved me in that moment. Why else would he kiss me?"

"Noblemen do not marry their slaves," Kesi murmured, her voice a doubting drawl. "Never. If a nobleman looks with favor on a slave, he might make her his concubine. Men marry for position, power and politics, but not pleasure. You should thank the gods that Akil came into the garden when he did. If the boy had remained alone with you—"

"Zaphenath-paneah and his sons are virtuous. They would not cruelly use me." Jendayi's heavy eyelids closed in the heat.

"I did not think the vizier's son would harm me. In the following days, I feared only his…indifference."

Her words drifted away, for not even in the privacy of this woven basket did she dare speak all the thoughts that filled her mind. Her mother had shown her indifference; she had cast Jendayi aside as soon as it became apparent that the girl's eyes were weakening. If Jendayi had a father, she did not know him. She had not known the affection of brothers or sisters, cousins, aunts or uncles. Akil fulfilled a father's role in her life, yet he saw her as a responsibility. As long as she played well, Pharaoh called for Akil, and Akil was pleased with Jendayi. But if she did not play up to the level of her master's expectation, or if for some reason Pharaoh did not call for Akil, the chironomist grew surly and uncommunicative. He would cast fierce taunts and threats at Jendayi, his words lacerating her heart. Only another invitation from the king would restore Akil's good humor.

No, Akil did not love her. He guarded her as a possession; he taught and disciplined her only to safeguard his place in the light of Pharaoh's divine approval.

"A secret kiss—what a wonderful story." Kesi clapped her hands. "Indeed, I am nearly crying! The romantic kiss given so long ago still lives in your memory! What if it lives in his, too?"

Jendayi lifted her head. "It will only be a story unless by some miracle the son of Zaphenath-paneah gathers courage enough to speak to me. I have hoped that his feelings have not changed. If I am not too bold before the gods and if he still finds favor in me, I thought he might approach me on this journey. We are away from Pharaoh's house. The gods could not have sent a more propitious opportunity. Unless—" she nearly choked on the word "—he has forgotten all about me."

"Forgotten?" Kesi's voice rang with indignation. "How could he forget you? No, my friend, he will not. No doubt he remembers everything as clearly as you do, and he will know the time is right."

"But he is noble! I am a slave, and nobles do not waste their breath conversing with slaves. He would surely be more willing to speak to a palm tree or the dust beneath his feet than to me."

"Not the vizier's sons," Kesi retorted. "I've heard that all the vizier's servants are treated civilly. Some say Ani the steward is revered like a lord in that house, and even the kitchen slaves are well-treated. If the vizier's son talked to you once, he will talk to you again."

"Then why—" Jendayi forced the words over her insecurity "—hasn't he spoken to me before this? Both of the vizier's sons were at Malkata the other day. And there have been other times when he might have at least greeted me."

"Perhaps he is afraid to approach you."

"I am a slave, how could he be *afraid?*"

"You are a royal slave, and you have an unequalled talent," Kesi answered. "He may be awed to the point of silence. He may think you do not remember that day in the garden. You, mistress, must let him know. You must tell him you want to speak with him."

A thrill of frightened anticipation touched Jendayi's spine. "I cannot speak to him! I had hoped to touch his heart with music. I have been working on a song—"

"Music is a universal language, it touches all who listen in the same way…unless a listener is forewarned." Determination flooded Kesi's voice. "I will speak to the vizier's son for you. Dictate what you would have me say, and I will relay your message in its fullness. Speak whatever is on your heart. If he is not willing to hear your words, he will call me a foolish slave and send me away. But if the words reach his heart, he will come to you. Out here in the desert, what could prevent him?"

Jendayi let her head fall back to the woven wall of the basket. "What message would I give him? I would tell him that I have waited years for him to explain the kiss in the garden. I would tell him that I have listened through the palace walls in hopes of hearing news of him. In Pharaoh's court I have listened to the vizier's voice and imagined it to be the son's instead. At night, when I dream, I can still hear his quickened breath in my ear, his voice and his admission that he thought my song and my paltry form beautiful. And if he loves me, if it is possible that I could serve him instead of Pharaoh, I would like to know."

"I can't possibly remember so much," Kesi answered, a smile in her voice. "Perhaps it would be better for you to speak to him yourself."

A wave of sheer black fright swept through Jendayi. "I couldn't! I am nothing. I could not even approach him!"

Kesi laughed. "The solution is simple. I shall go to the vizier's younger son and tell him that you wish to inquire of his well-being. He will be polite. He will say he is well. If he is as well-mannered as I've heard, he will ask about you. And I will reply that you would like to dedicate a song to him, in honor of the loyal service you once gave to his father the vizier."

Jendayi frowned, but did not interrupt.

"And tonight," Kesi continued, "after I have forewarned him, the men will gather around the fire as is their custom. They will call for music, and Akil will bring out the orchestra. And you will insist on playing an original song, alone."

"What if Akil objects? He has not been allowing me to play by myself."

"You have power, Jendayi, you should learn to use it. Tell Akil you must play alone or you will never play for him again. And when he gives you a moment to play by yourself, open your mouth and sing one of the ancient love songs. If the vizier's son does not remember your time in the garden, he will think you are merely singing one of the old songs. But if the young man does remember, his heart will understand what your heart is saying! On the wings of Nut, goddess of the sky, compassion will rise from his heart and fly into yours!"

Jendayi pressed her hand over her lips, a little stunned by Kesi's bold plan. She could not imagine committing such an audacious act in Pharaoh's palace, but out here in the wilderness such a plan seemed amazingly reasonable. Kesi's idea was as safe as any course of action she might undertake. If the vizier's son was insulted by a slave's approach, Kesi would bear the reprimand. And Jendayi *had* been practicing a song for Efrayim—what better time to sing it than tonight?

"Be it according to what you have said," Jendayi answered. "Tonight, when we have made camp, find the younger son of Zaphenath-paneah. If he will speak with you privately, tell him the next time I am asked to play alone, I will sing and play for him. I do so in appreciation for the kind treatment I received while I lived in the vizier's house."

"Wonderful!"

"Now be silent, I must practice until the fingerings are perfect." Jendayi fumbled for the small practice harp in the basket with her. "I don't know why I listen to you, Kesi. Akil will surely disapprove and scold me. But I must know if the vizier's son remembers. I must know if he might be willing to take me from Pharaoh's house."

As her fingers closed around the neck of her harp, the dark memory of her recurring dream passed over her like a shadow. Her cold and stony heart had clattered into Anubis's scales on too many nights. She had glimpsed love only once in her life, but she would follow where it led her, no matter how perilous the journey.

As the sun began to sink toward the western horizon, the caravan circled and made camp. Kesi held tight to the rim of the basket as the moving mountain of camel flesh dipped and sank onto the ground, then she helped Jendayi out of the other basket so the herdsmen could water the animals.

"Are you still going to do it?" Jendayi whispered, clinging to Kesi's arm as the camel clambered to his feet and shuffled away.

"Later, after we have eaten," Kesi said, moving toward the huddled women who clustered around Akil. "But first I will see that you are sheltered and fed."

Kesi left Jendayi in a hastily erected tent, brought her mistress a hunk of crusty brown bread and some dried goat's meat from a supply wagon, then wrapped a shawl around her head in the manner of the Hebrew women. As the unloading progressed, Kesi saw that the camp had split into two nearly perfect concentric circles: Egyptians in the forefront, Hebrews at the rear. Into which camp had Zaphenath-paneah and his sons settled?

She looked out into the darkness and spied the vizier's white-and-gold tent rising like a phoenix at the confluence of the two groups. She dropped the covering veil and moved forward, relieved that she would not have to search among the Hebrews.

An Egyptian slave dipped her head in greeting as Kesi approached the outer periphery of the vizier's tent. The sides had not been unrolled; the tent remained open for all to see the vizier inside. He sat on a light wooden chair, a delicate, elegant piece of furniture that looked out of place in the midst of the wilderness.

Kesi lingered among a group of slaves, her eyes skimming over the tent's inhabitants. The Egyptian nomarchs had been invited to eat with the vizier; they lounged on cushions and pillows, their postures relaxed, their eyes merry with wine.

The compact captain of the guard stood at the vizier's side, his sharp eyes roaming over the crowd as his hand hovered near the hilt of the dagger in his belt. For an instant his eyes caught Kesi's, and a tiny tremor of fear shook her when he lifted an eyebrow as if to say, *You do not belong here.* She lowered her gaze and turned, hoping to escape into the crowd, but before her guilty feet had carried her four steps, a hand caught her elbow. Another alert warrior escorted her to the muscled captain of the guard, who had moved outside the tent.

"You wear the garb of Pharaoh's slaves." The captain's eyes hardened with speculation. "Why do you take such an interest in the vizier's dinner? Have you no work to do?"

"I have work," Kesi stammered, keeping her eyes downcast. "I am on my mistress's bidding."

"And who is your mistress?" He dipped his head to better see her face. "I don't recognize you."

"My mistress is Jendayi, Pharaoh's harpist."

The guard lifted his chin as if satisfied with her answer, but a slight hesitation remained in his hawklike eyes. "What business does Pharaoh's harpist have in the vizier's tent?"

Kesi clasped her arms across her chest. "My mistress used to live in the vizier's house."

"Go on."

"She asked me to find one of the vizier's sons. They are…friends."

She expected anger, but amusement flickered in the guard's eyes. He shifted his weight and tapped his chin with one finger. "Let's see—who did I hear discussing the little harpist just this morning? One of my young masters, as I recall, praised her beauty to the skies."

"You jest!" Kesi clapped her hand over her lips as soon as the words escaped her.

"I do not make idle jokes." The captain lowered his voice. All signs of severity vanished from his face as he stepped closer and bent to whisper in Kesi's ear. "The vizier's son has often confided in me of his regard for the little harpist. Only providence and propriety have kept him from declaring his feelings. I daresay the lad is bold enough to approach Pharaoh himself to beg for her release."

A thrill shivered through Kesi's senses. Surely the gods had arranged this meeting. "I have a message for the young man," she said, her heart hammering against her ribs. "I should deliver it personally, but I do not want to venture into that tent. No one knows me, and too many people would wonder what business I have there." Her eyes met the guard's. "Just as you did."

"You are wise to be discreet, for one does not speak openly of coveting one of Pharaoh's slaves," the captain answered, grinning. "This is a risky business, so I will give him your message myself. And you may tell your mistress that Tarik, captain of the vizier's guard, owes her a great debt, for years ago the beauty of her music inspired me to propose marriage to my own wife, Halima. We have married, and I am very happy in love."

Kesi smiled in pleased surprise. "Then my mistress bids me tell your master that on account of her fond memories in Zaphenath-paneah's house, that she will play and sing tonight for him alone." Her eyes flitted over the gathering in the firelit tent. "Even though she plays for the vizier's entertainment."

"Then let us not keep love waiting," the guard replied, smiling as he moved away.

Jendayi bit her lip in concentration, forcing her fingers to fly over the strings of her harp. Akil would cut out her tongue if he knew what she planned tonight, for one did not ordinarily sing of love during a funeral procession, no matter how long and protracted the excursion might be. But Kesi had bubbled with jubilation on her return; the message had been delivered.

More shocking than the delivery, however, was the news her

maid had gathered from the captain of the vizier's guard. "Even now, the vizier's son thinks of you!" Kesi crowed, unsuccessfully struggling to keep her voice low. "The captain says the young man is bold enough to beg Pharaoh for you!"

Jendayi's fingers trembled now; they seemed unusually cold and stiff. Why? She couldn't remember the last time she had felt nervous. Playing was as natural to her as eating and sleeping; she thrived on creating intricate improvisations that bewildered or exhausted other harpists. Akil had long stopped trying to direct her solo work. When given the signal to take the lead from the oboist or lutist, Jendayi played the melodies in her head, producing remarkable sensations of sound, rippling passages that drew breathless admiration from all who heard. But tonight her voice would command center stage; the glissandos of the harp would be only a frame around the painting.

"Mistress, Akil waits outside. The vizier calls for music."

Jendayi stood and brushed her damp hands across the linen of her gown, then pulled the harp into the circle of her arms. Tonight, through her music, she would offer her heart…and wait to see if it would be accepted.

While the musicians played a steady stream of dinner music, Menashe struggled to keep his face composed in bland, pleasant lines. Since Tarik had brought him news of Jendayi's intention, his heart had alternately lurched in anticipation and twisted in the agonies of despair. The harpist intended to sing for *him* tonight, Tarik had reported, but what if she sang of the brutality of noblemen or the sufferings of life? What if she offered a sympathetic song to ease the passing of his grandfather, or, even worse, a song to console him for not receiving the firstborn's blessing? Perhaps the palace gossips had filled the girl's ears with news of Menashe's humiliation, and she intended only to soothe him with sweet music.

She did not know how he adored her—how could she imagine a love as deep as the ocean? She was a royal slave who dared not dream of release. Unless Menashe could reach her, she would live and die within the confines of Pharaoh's palace. So it had always been, and so it always would be.

But she did not know how Menashe loved her. And how he understood her. He knew the despair of losing a mother; he knew how it felt to reach for a father and find only a substitute.

But his father had been a slave and was now second only to Pharaoh. So he understood the possibility of change. *So I see you, little Jendayi, not as a slave, but as what you shall be: a great lady, my wife.*

He took another loaf of bread and broke it into pieces. Would Akil never tell the others to be quiet so she could play alone? Menashe was tempted to demand a harp solo, but Jendayi might think him spoiled and foolish if he behaved so impetuously. His father's important guests—the governors, priests and counselors—now slouched in the quiet contentment of satiated men. Their eyes would not remain open another quarter hour. If Jendayi was going to play, she must play soon.

"Most honored Akil."

Menashe flinched as his father's voice rose above the subdued murmurs.

"I wonder if you might allow us to be dismissed tonight with something special. We have passed a long and tiring day in the wilderness where all seemed gray and bleak to my eyes. Surely your harpist has hidden a few emerald grasses and the rush of the river in her instrument?"

Akil bowed his head in a deep gesture of respect, then turned and extended his arm toward his harpist.

One of the other women nudged Jendayi. Menashe leaned forward—did his eyes deceive him or were her fingers trembling? As Akil folded his hands, surrendering the attention of the audience, the girl ran her fingers over the strings. Golden streams of sound splashed into the silence and then, wonder of wonders, she opened her mouth and began to sing.

"How weary is the nobleman," she sang, the sound as light as a flitting bird that wings the air. "Good fate has become true. Verily, bodies have perished since the days of the god. Others taken their place."

Menashe felt the squeeze of disappointment. This funereal song was not what he had hoped for. But still she sang:

"Spend a happy day, son of the nobleman,
Follow your heart for as long as it is yours.
Spend a happy day, ignore all evil and remember happiness
Until the day arrives when you moor in the land that
    loves silence.
Spend a happy day. Do whatever you praise.
Let your heart be very, very happy.
Spend a happy day, son of the nobleman,
Follow your desire so long as you shall live."

By the time Jendayi had finished, Menashe's own heart sang
with delight. How terribly clever of her to mingle her encouragement for him with a sympathetic reminder that life was
fleeting! And since nearly every man in the gathering considered himself the son of a nobleman, the intended recipient and
her message had been hidden in the most obvious of contexts.

The Egyptians applauded, demanding to hear the song again,
but Akil stepped in and directed the oboist in another melody.

Glorying in the moment, Menashe leaned toward his father.
"Wasn't she wonderful?"

"What?" Yosef stirred; Menashe's question was an obvious
distraction.

"The song! Didn't you hear it?"

"Very nice, as always." Yosef smiled and turned to the crown
prince, who sat nearest him. "Akil does a wonderful job with
Pharaoh's musicians. It was most gracious of your father the
king to send them on our journey."

He had not heard; he had no idea of the song's significance.
Menashe listened with dismay as Yosef continued a quiet con-
versation with the crown prince and one of the nomarchs. But
his father's opinions did not matter. Jendayi had sung for
Menashe, sweetly urging him to follow his heart and its desires.
And he desired only one thing, one woman.

Turning away from his father and the prince, Menashe settled
on his cushion and stretched his long legs before him. When
they returned to Thebes, he would don his finest clothes, silver
armbands and cloak, and present himself to Pharaoh. Perhaps
he could persuade his father to write a letter on his behalf. But

through flattery, friendship or finagling, Menashe would convince Pharaoh to return Jendayi to the vizier's house. Tonight he had learned she was willing to be his, and he would not rest until she was free to be his wife.

Menashe lifted his hand and caught Tarik's attention. The captain strolled over, nodding at a few nobles as he walked. He wore a sly smile when he finally reached Menashe's side. "So tell me, young master, has the evening's entertainment been interesting?"

"Yes," Menashe answered, his courage and determination like a rock inside him. "Most interesting, Tarik. The girl is willing! You heard her, now I must go to Pharaoh for her. I will not be happy until she is my wife, and I will tell her so this very night, as soon as my father's guests have dispersed."

The captain held up a warning finger. "You must curb your eagerness, young lion! She is not just any slave. She is Pharaoh's property. And here—" he lowered his voice while glancing right and left "—we are among Egyptians who would not hesitate to tell the king that the vizier's son has taken advantage of the royal favor. You must not speak of your intentions to anyone. You are setting out to climb an impossible mountain, and if you are to succeed, you must carefully plot your course."

"Impossible?"

Tarik shrugged. "Your father would say nothing is impossible for your God Shaddai."

Menashe transferred his gaze to Jendayi's pensive face. She was waiting for his response; she would want to know what he would do. "Tarik, I must speak with her!"

"You must not! Stay away from the girl, do nothing unusual. If anyone later insinuates that you have done so much as touch her, the king will never grant your request. Pharaoh may even deem it necessary to punish you—or he might use her to set an example for other slaves. Tread cautiously, Menashe. Love has quickened your heart, but you must not foolishly pursue it."

Menashe struggled to curb his impulses. Tarik was right; one did not trifle with Pharaoh's slaves, Pharaoh's children or Pharaoh's counselors. He ought to be silent and sly; he would have to put a rein around his eager heart. With one careless word or unthinking action he could destroy both his life and Jendayi's.

He looked up at the guard who had often proved to be a wise and willing counselor. "I will be careful. I will guard my lips so you alone will know of this. But I must let her know that I love her. Find the slave who brought Jendayi's message to you. Tell her I understand. As soon as my grandfather is buried and we have returned to Thebes, I will approach Pharaoh on Jendayi's behalf. Though my own life be forfeit as a penalty for my boldness, I will redeem her from Pharaoh's house."

With a slow, secret smile, Tarik nodded. "I will relay your message."

"He listened?" Jendayi's voice rose in surprise.

"Shah!" Kesi laughed and lifted the thin blanket that covered Jendayi, then snuggled close to her mistress. "I have just spoken to the captain of the vizier's guard, who brought a message directly from the vizier's son. The message is this: As soon as Yisrael is buried and we are returned to Thebes, he will approach Pharaoh and ask that you be returned to the vizier's house. Though the attempt may cost him his life, he says he will not fail."

Jendayi pressed her hands to her mouth, shock wedging words in her throat.

"There is more," Kesi went on, her breath warm in Jendayi's ear. "The guard says you must be discreet with this news. You must speak of this with no one but me, for you are Pharaoh's slave and no man has any right to talk to you, much less desire you as his own. You must not seek out the young man so no one can suspect him of immodest behavior toward you. And you must guard your tongue, lest you slip and reveal this secret."

"I can guard my tongue." Jendayi whispered, still lost in incredulity. The vizier's son was an endless surprise; she had never dreamed he might be truly serious in his concern for her. And he was right; this would have to be a solemn and secret enterprise, for she was not only a slave, but a prized one, certainly worth her weight in silver or gold.

"Can you believe it?" A tremor of excitement filled Kesi's voice as she pressed her hand to Jendayi's arm. "In all my days,

I never imagined such a thing could be possible. You long to be reunited with the vizier's son, and he wishes to bring you back to his house! It is a wish only the gods have power enough to accomplish."

Jendayi smiled, now certain that her heart would learn to live and love. "The gods *will* bring it to pass. I would stake my life on it."

Chapter Eight

Anxious to avoid rogue bands of warlike Philistines, the company journeyed through the desert to the Salt Sea, then skirted that sea's eastern shore and moved north toward the Jordan River. When they came to the threshing floor of Goren ha-Atad, north of the Salt Sea and east of the Jordan, the mixed company of Hebrews and Egyptians set up camp.

Because his duties had kept him in Thebes while his brothers mourned in Goshen, Yosef proclaimed that they would not move farther until he had observed seven days of mourning for Yisrael with his brothers. And they sorrowed there with a great and heavy lamentation.

At the close of the seventh day, the Hebrews and the Egyptians assembled in one circle, around one fire. Ani, who had grown as fluent in the Canaanite tongue as he was in Egyptian, stood in the center of the clearing to interpret for those who had not picked up the other nation's language.

As they had in Goshen, the Hebrews stood and told the story of Yisrael's life. One by one, each of Yaakov's sons recited a tale: Yisrael's birth, his lineage from Avraham, his struggles with his brother Esav, his experience at the gate of heaven, his marriages to Rahel and Lea, the begetting of his twelve sons. Then the Egyptians, beginning with the crown prince, continued the eulogy, praising Yaakov's descent into Egypt, the glory of his son, Zaphenath-paneah, his decision to allow Efrayim and Menashe, sons of Egypt, to be counted among his heirs.

Yosef stood last. "By faith," he said, his dark eyes raking over the silent priests of Amon-Re who watched with undisguised curiosity, "we understand that the word of the invisible god prepared the world. The things we see were not made by visible hands, but invisible."

As Ani's translation rang out over the gathering, the Egyptians and Hebrews alike nodded in assent. The Hebrews knew the invisible god as El Shaddai; the Egyptians knew him as Neter.

"Without faith in the invisible One it is impossible to please God Almighty," Menashe heard his father continue, "for he who comes to God must believe that He is, and that He answers those who seek Him."

The Egyptian priests cast each other knowing smiles. Menashe was certain they had heard rumors about Zaphenath-paneah's strange and invisible god, but thus far they had not heard anything they did not believe themselves.

"With assurance and reverence," Yosef continued, "Noah, being warned by God Almighty about things yet to come, prepared a bark for the salvation of his household. By his obedience he and his family were saved from the great flood, and the world rose from the waters so that men again might fill the earth."

The priests' smiles trembled now. Menashe knew they believed life came from the primeval waters, but the story of Noah was as new to them as it was to him. Too busy with the affairs of Pharaoh's kingdom to personally tutor his sons, like other Egyptian nobles Yosef had left the religious and social education of his sons to Ani and others of his household. But Ani was an Egyptian, and had never spoken of this man called Noah.

Yosef continued: "With trust in God Almighty, Avraham, when he heard God's call, obeyed by going out to the place he was to receive for an inheritance. He went out, not knowing where he was going. By faith he lived as an alien in the land of promise, a foreign country, dwelling in tents in order to advance when the voice of God compelled him to rise and move on. By faith his wife, Sarah, received the ability to conceive even beyond the proper time of life, because she considered God Shaddai faithful and able to keep His promise."

Yosef spoke slowly now, as if carefully measuring each word before pronouncing it. "And so from Avraham came Yitzhak, and from Yitzhak, Yaakov, and from Yaakov, twelve sons. And from the twelve, as God has promised, will come descendants to rival the stars of heaven in number, as innumerable as the sand of the seashore."

Menashe frowned. His father had never uttered these truths before; was it wise to pronounce them before Egyptians who might feel threatened? Menashe glanced toward the crown prince and the priests around him. The boy who would one day be king wore a perplexed expression; lines of concentration had deepened even on the priests' faces. They, too, were at a loss to explain their vizier's comments.

Yet Yosef continue to speak. "By faith Avraham, when he was tested, offered up Yitzhak, a willing sacrifice. Though God had said, 'In Yitzhak your descendants shall be called,' Avraham believed that God is able to raise men, even from the dead."

A ripple of wonder echoed through the Egyptians, punctuated by at least one snort of disbelief. Though they were staunch believers in the afterlife, never had one of their gods restored a man to mortal life.

"By faith Yitzhak blessed Yaakov and Esav, even regarding things to come." Yosef's voice rumbled through the quiet of the night shadows. "By faith my father, Yaakov, as he was dying, blessed each of his sons, and included mine among his own. Like my forefathers, he died in full confidence that God Shaddai would fulfill his promises."

A servant threw a bundle of dry rushes onto the dying fire. The flames leaped up, throwing the darkness back, and Menashe saw his father's form clearly in the tinted darkness. He stood as tall and straight as one of Lebanon's towering cedars, and his eyes gleamed with the same certainty that had lit Yaakov's dying gaze.

"As of this day," Yosef went on, "the Hebrews have no land to call their own. We are a growing clan, but we are still small in number, generations away from rivaling the starry host. But my fathers saw the promises of God Shaddai and welcomed them from a distance, even as I do."

An indefinable feeling of contentment filled Menashe's heart. He slid his gaze to the place where Efrayim sat beside Jokim and tried to catch his brother's eye. Could Efrayim not see how marvelously and uniquely God had blessed their people? God Shaddai, who was far more powerful and infinite than the gods of Egypt, had personally called the Hebrews out from Canaan and would yet return them to the land. This place, this vast, rimless wilderness of Canaan, belonged to *them,* as did the green valleys of the Jordan.

Efrayim's smile was bland, his eyes vacant and fixed on the fire, his thoughts miles away. How could he sit through the testimonies of Yaakov and his forefathers and not feel the stirring of patriotic passion in his blood? The sons of Yisrael had been chosen, destined to bless the world, elected by the holiest Spirit, the creator of the universe…

Yet Efrayim studied his hands as if concerned only about his next manicure.

Yosef moved to the center of the circle and gestured toward the crown prince and his priests. "Depart to your tents tonight in peace, my brothers and friends," he said, bowing deeply. "Take your rest in this place for a few days, for tomorrow the sons of Yisrael will go forth to bury their father. Honored priests, governors and my prince, I ask you to remain here and enjoy the beauty of this fertile riverbank. I will leave my steward with you so all your needs will be met. But I beg you to allow my brothers and I alone to take our father on his final journey."

The Egyptians looked automatically to their prince, and Menashe knew the thoughts skittering through their minds. This was a most unusual request—why would the vizier lead them into the wilderness only to abandon them so close to the grave? The traditional Egyptian burial involved great ceremony at the site of the tomb, many prayers, incantations, rituals, anointings, weeping, wailing…

But Zaphenath-paneah could persuade even a future pharaoh. The prince's alert, handsome face creased into a smile. He nodded, granting Yosef's request, then stood and allowed his guards to escort him to his royal tents. Whether or not they agreed with their prince's decision, one by one the other Egyptians rose and slipped through the shadows.

Menashe stood and wound his way through the tangle of dispersing men. "Efrayim—" he clutched the hardness of his brother's arm "—do you not feel it?" He lifted his gaze to the sky, black and icy with a wash of brilliant stars, then closed his eyes and inhaled deeply. "Don't you sense it?"

A thread of annoyance entered Efrayim's voice. "I feel tired, if that's what you mean. And sorry for the old men. This desert journey will not be easy if we leave the chariots behind."

"I'm not talking about the burial." Menashe struggled for words. "I'm talking about our destiny. Could you not sense a feeling as Father spoke? We are the generation intended to carry the blessing of God Shaddai. It is up to us!" He shifted and rubbed the stubble on his chin, not certain how to explain himself. He had seen everything so clearly while his father spoke; he had *felt* a mantle of responsibility fall onto his shoulders. He and Efrayim were the sons of Yosef, inheritors of the firstborn's blessing. They should naturally rise to lead the next generation—

But Efrayim's dark eyes expressed more challenge than curiosity. "It is not up to *us,* brother," he said, his voice clipped. "If anything, it is up to *me,* for I will be greater than you, remember?"

As Menashe gaped at his brother, Efrayim's dark brows arched in a mischievous look. "I'm only jesting, so wipe that affronted look off your face. You are tired, we all are. Go to sleep."

But his words had cut deep, spreading an infection of doubt. Were Menashe's fervent feelings only the result of grief-induced exhaustion? Were his convictions only the offspring of his fevered imagination? Perhaps the desert had played tricks on him, inflating his hopes for the future with dreams of Jendayi and the false notion that he might prove to be as favored as his younger brother...

Menashe nodded at Efrayim and Jokim and wished them a good night.

As soon as dawn lit the horizon, the sons of Yisrael packed their donkeys and camels and turned them toward the fertile

Jordan River valley. The Egyptians, remaining behind at Yosef's order, would wait for the children of Yisrael to rejoin them after the burial.

Still smarting from their last encounter, Menashe avoided Efrayim's presence, preferring to walk with his uncles. Each of Yaakov's sons seemed as strong and stable as the earth itself. Though stooped with age, Re'uven could control the younger men with a simple flick of his gray brows; Levi displayed a quality of assurance Menashe had never seen in an Egyptian. Shim'on had been gifted with wit, directness and intelligence, while Yehuda possessed an unshakable spiritual force, a presence born of certainty.

Menashe supposed his uncles fascinated him because their lives had been so different from his. Born in a rough wilderness, they had learned to fend for themselves in a cruel environment; he had been born in a polished chamber where slaves brought his food and would have hand-fed him had he commanded it. From childhood the Hebrews' livelihood depended on strength, quickness and courage; he had spent his earliest years learning how to read and write hieroglyphics. Though he had later received military training, Menashe had never feared for his life—indeed, he had ventured into duels knowing he would not be harmed. No one would dare wound the vizier's son. Only Efrayim had ever landed a blow on him.

His uncles were self-confident, sensible and practical; their fierce, protective manner simultaneously amazed and encouraged Menashe. The Egyptians he had known were easygoing and carefree, separated by class differences as cleanly as the Nile separated the cities of the living from the dead. And yet the Hebrews considered a cousin as close as a brother, regardless of his social standing or how far away he lived.

Shim'on, the largest and loudest son of Yaakov, invited Menashe to travel with him and his wife. Menashe accepted the honor, knowing the invitation had been prompted by Shim'on's unique tie to Yosef's family. Years before the brothers knew Zaphenath-paneah was their long-lost Yosef, Shim'on had spent nearly a year as a prisoner in the vizier's house.

Shim'on seemed especially eager to arrive at the burial place.

His long steps left gaping holes in the desert sand, and Menashe grew breathless trying to keep pace with him.

"Once, many years ago, I went to the tomb alone," Shim'on told Menashe as they walked, his hand tightening around the staff in his grip. "Before we descended into Egypt. Before I married Mandisa."

Menashe cast a quick glance at the woman who rode atop the camel. Though protective veils covered her head and much of her face, Menashe could see eyes that shone with a fawnlike beauty. He knew that Mandisa had once been his mother's handmaid, but she left the vizier's house when his mother died. When Menashe searched his memory for his mother, he found only a whisper of sweet lotus fragrance, the ghost of a cool hand on his head, and the melodious tones of a young woman's voice…

"I stood alone at the burial cave—" Shim'on's voice drew Menashe back from the brink of memory "—and there I felt the presence of God. I left the cave a changed man, Menashe. Though I was not yet the man I should have been, my soul burned with the knowledge that a man cannot trifle with God Shaddai."

His dark eyes searched Menashe's face, reaching into his thoughts. "You have been distressed of late," he said, with no expression as he moved with easy grace through the sand. "Would you like to tell me what troubles you?"

Menashe thrust his hands behind his back and tried to organize his thoughts. Would his uncle understand his feelings toward Jendayi? Could he appreciate the love that would compel him to approach Pharaoh when they returned to Egypt? Or perhaps Shim'on had noticed Menashe's longing to know his heritage, his fascination with the history he had just discovered.

"I am not distressed," Menashe said, "but in the past few days I have learned so many things. I had never heard such stories of Avraham, Yitzhak and Yaakov. My father occasionally mentioned the names of my forefathers, but never did he share those stories—unimaginable treasures! I never imagined that God would stoop to make personal promises and covenants with men."

Shim'on grunted in response, but said nothing for a long while. They had left the fertile valley of the Jordan River and now climbed the foothills of a mountain range. Bawling winds scoured the ridges and mountain rims, whistling through skeletal trees and leafless brush as it blew dirt into their eyes and hair.

"I think there is more on your mind," Shim'on finally said, firing the words over his shoulder as he moved ahead to take the reins of his wife's plodding camel. "For I have seen your eyes, and a young man's longing glance is easy to read. Love has taken root in your heart, has it not?"

Menashe lowered his head against the wind. He wanted to cry, *Yes, haven't you seen her?* but Shim'on would think him insane. An iron-core patriarch like his uncle would not understand the throes of love.

But the face Shim'on turned to him displayed an uncanny awareness. "Remember this." Shim'on slowed his step as he lowered his gaze. "If you love, you must be prepared to sacrifice all you have. If you are not willing to surrender even your life, you do not love at all."

In a movement as unexpected as a clap of thunder on a clear day, Shim'on reached up, took his wife's hand and pressed it to his lips. The smile Mandisa gave him in return was as intimate as a kiss.

One day, Menashe thought, the back of his neck burning as he turned his eyes from the tender scene, *Jendayi will smile at me that way.*

Two days later the procession of Hebrews passed Hebron, a prosperous walled city. Two miles outside Hebron, the company halted at the grove where Avraham had resided. While the women set about preparing a meal, the men watered the animals and made camp. "We will pass the night here after our father's burial," Yosef declared. "As soon as camp is established, let us fulfill our vow to Yisrael."

Menashe was helping one of his cousins raise a tent when Shim'on pulled him aside. "Come see this," his uncle said, gesturing toward the grove. He lifted his hand and pointed to a majestic terebinth tree whose massive trunk divided into four colossal branches and spread like wings toward heaven. "Our forefather Avraham sat under that tree," he said, his voice heavy with an almost reverent nostalgia. "He was sitting under yonder tree when the three mysterious visitors from God told him Yitzhak would be born." Shim'on's dark eyes shone with kindness as he smiled at his nephew. "I thought you would like to know."

A stab of feeling caught Menashe off guard. "Yes," he answered in a husky voice he scarcely recognized. "Thank you for telling me."

Leaving his uncle's side, he walked toward the ancient tree and laid his hands on the scabrous, pitted bark. Avraham, the one who bargained with God, had stood here. Perhaps his hands had touched this bark, his flesh had pressed against these rough ridges.

Menashe turned, resting his back against the rugged surface of the tree, then slid down, scarcely feeling the discomfort. What dreams had filled the patriarch's head as he sat here? Avraham had believed God's promise to create a nation from his heirs, but had he known that a ruler of Egypt would rise from his lineage? And from that ruler, two sons? "Would he—" Menashe lifted his gaze to the branches overhead "—have given my brother the blessing of the right hand? Or would he have seen something in me that Grandfather missed?"

He wasn't sure how long he remained there, but the soft sound of the approaching burial sledge distracted him from his reverie. He turned in time to see the ox-drawn sledge, topped by the elaborate sarcophagus and the chest of canopic jars, begin to move out of the camp. Yaakov's sons, six on each side, walked beside the conveyance, their somber faces like stone masks of grief.

Efrayim walked at the end of one line, like a thirteenth son, and Menashe grimaced as he stood and brushed the dirt from his tunic. Yaakov's dying gesture had proclaimed him and Efrayim as sons in name and inheritance, and he realized he ought to be walking with them, across from Efrayim. Quickly he hurried into place, behind Binyamin, and hoped none of the others had noticed his absence.

For twenty minutes they walked in silence, the only sounds the whisper of the sledge and the occasional jingle of the oxen's harness. An unseasonable heat covered the mountain slope like a blanket, drying the perspiration on Menashe's skin before its dampness had a chance to cool his body. He wore a long tunic and cloak in the style of his uncles; now he sent a covetous glance toward Efrayim's elegant kilt. Every bit the Egyptian, Efrayim looked cool even under his heavy wig.

The procession came to a halt outside a large stone outcropping at a brown and barren ridge. A half-dozen rock hyraxes squealed and scurried away as Shim'on's shadow fell across the scree at the base of the cliff. Without comment, Re'uven, Shim'on and Levi advanced and jammed a beam of wood beneath an immense boulder. Wedging a smaller rock beneath the beam for a fulcrum, they pressed downward with all their might. Within a moment the boulder scraped against the wall of stone and moved away.

A fetid breeze broomed the dust, and Menashe peered toward the opening, half-afraid of what he would see. The Hebrews did not ordinarily mummify their dead, and Menashe stirred uneasily at the thought of viewing an unpreserved corpse. Avraham and Sarah were buried here, along with Yitzhak and Rebekah and Lea. Had the arid air of the desert preserved them? Or had their mortal remains submitted to the slow decay of death?

Relief settled over him when he realized he would not discover the answer to his questions. Yosef and Binyamin, the sons of Rahel, pried open the sarcophagus and wooden coffin, then carefully lifted out Yisrael's mummified remains. While the others watched in silence, these two carried the body of their father into the tomb and laid him to rest for the ages. Then Yehuda pried open the canopic chest and removed the jars; these he gave to Dan, Naftali, Asher and Zevulun, who deposited them inside the tomb.

The expensive granite sarcophagus and elaborate canopic chest were left outside the burial place. They were too heavy to lower into the cave, and of little significance to the Hebrews. No Egyptian would think of entering the Other World without adequate protection for his remains and enough worldly goods to sustain life in the spiritual realm, but Menashe knew his father placed no faith in the Egyptian beliefs. He had allowed the priests to perform a ceremonial mummification in order to preserve the body, but Yaakov would be buried according to Hebrew tradition.

When Yosef and Binyamin finally trudged out of the cave, their faces drawn with grief and weariness, Levi, Re'uven and Shim'on maneuvered the guardian stone back into place. When it had settled back into its customary position, the brothers looked to Yosef, expectation on their faces.

He drew a ragged breath. "I love you, O God, my strength," he said, lifting his hands to heaven. His words echoed among the rocks. "God Shaddai is my rock, my fortress, my deliverer. He is my god in whom I take refuge, my shield and the horn of my salvation, my stronghold. I call on El Shaddai, who is worthy to be praised, and I am saved from my enemies. Though the cords of death encompass me and the torrents of ungodliness terrify me, though the cords of Sheol surround me and the snares of death confront me, in my distress I will call on God Shaddai. He will hear my voice and my cry before I even speak it."

The uncles' somber faces seemed to relax at Yosef's reassuring words. They breathed more easily, for their responsibilities had been fulfilled and their father laid to rest. The day of Yaakov had passed; they were the fathers now.

"God Shaddai sent help from on high," Yosef went on. "He drew me out of the pit. He delivered me from my strong enemy and from those who hated me. They confronted me in the day of my calamity, but God Shaddai was my stay. He rescued me because He delighted in me."

Menashe's emotions bobbed and spun as he stared past his father into his own thoughts.

God Shaddai ordained a covenant with one man, Avraham, in order to bless the nations of the world.

God Shaddai reached down to rescue his father from the prison pit in order to preserve Avraham's seed.

God Shaddai not only ruled the overreaching affairs of nations, He reached down to offer help and solace to individual needy souls. The god of many was also the god of one.

"You have delivered me from the contentions of the people. You have placed me as head of the nations." Menashe heard his father's voice as if it came from far away. "A people whom I have not known serve me. As soon as they hear, they obey me. Foreigners submit to me."

A hush settled over the men congregated at the tomb; Menashe heard nothing but the distant drone of his father's voice and the pounding of his own heart. He looked toward the sky, almost expecting to see the heavens open before his eyes.

New insights filled his head, the stories of his forefathers now fitted into a pattern he had been too close to see. The old ones buried in this place had heard the voice of El Shaddai and obeyed it. Forsaking all, ignoring those around them who worshipped the powers of nature, they sought and followed the Originator, the creator of the world.

"God Shaddai lives," his father continued. "Blessed be my rock, and exalted be the god of my salvation, the god who subdues peoples under me and delivers me from my enemies. Therefore I will give thanks to You among the nations, God Shaddai, and I will offer praises to Your name."

In a breathless instant, Menashe understood the connection between the oft-repeated story of his father's miraculous rise to power and the god his grandfather had worshipped. The god who had blessed Yosef in the Black Land also sent him away from Canaan. God Shaddai's divine will guided the jealous brothers who drove Yosef away from Yaakov's camp. God Shaddai was infinitely more complicated than the single-minded Egyptian gods, for He held things together, He connected past and present, He fulfilled the longings of desperate human hearts and worked His will in the direst of circumstances.

For generations El Shaddai sought men who were willing to follow him, and only a few had answered that divine call to total, obedient surrender. Avraham. Yitzhak. Yaakov and Yosef. Shim'on, certainly, judging by the look of reverent awe on his face, and Yehuda. But many of the others had not, and Efrayim had not. And until that moment, Menashe realized, he had not completely understood what God Shaddai expected of a man.

Obedience. Total, sacrificial, blind-and-yet-seeing obedience. His father had used another word for it at Goren ha-Atad: *faith.*

Leaving the funeral sledge at the tomb, the brothers unhooked the oxen, then returned to the camp they had erected near the grove. Efrayim frowned as he walked; the entire burial had been a frustrating and troubling experience. He was glad the Egyptians had not accompanied them to Mamre, for they would have severely criticized the sons of Yisrael. No treasures, no supplies had accompanied the body into the grave. The uncles had not even carried the majestic canopic chest, Pharaoh's gift, inside the humble cave. No wonder his father had asked Pharaoh's representatives to remain behind!

He seethed with quiet anger and humiliation. The uncles might as well have dug a hole and tossed Yaakov into it. The meanest nobles of Thebes were buried with professional mourners, weeping women and marvelous ceremony. But what did they do to honor Yaakov, the father of twelve sons? They laid him in another man's tomb, with nothing but grave cloths to protect his body. Canaanite grave robbers would roll away the stone once they had gone, and they would mock what little was provided for the father of Egypt's noble vizier.

The mood of his uncles had lightened considerably since the burial. The sons of Yisrael now walked in companionable groups of three and four, but Efrayim found himself walking alone behind his father. The Egyptians of Thebes, including Pharaoh, would be hurt and angered if they knew the boatloads of supplies had not followed Yaakov into the tomb, but had been used to provision the funeral procession. Though his father did not believe material comforts were necessary to provide for an immortal soul, those burial customs had strengthened Egyptian society for generations. The people of the Black Land were so much more advanced than the Hebrews who lived and died with only the barest necessities, still clinging to their smelly, dusty tents…

A wild ass, startled by the company's approach, looked up from his grazing. He stared at Efrayim for an instant, a shred of tough desert grass hanging from his mouth, before turning and trotting away.

Go, Efrayim silently urged him. *You are a creature of the desert, but my people are not.*

He must convince the others to change their ways. Only a lingering respect for Yaakov had stilled Efrayim's tongue thus far, but now Yisrael rested with his ancestors. Efrayim would rise to leadership among the sons of Yisrael, and they would listen to him, for he was the favored son of the favored son. Though his father held the reins of authority, Yosef's duties to Pharaoh would leave him little time for the Hebrews in Goshen. So Efrayim would move to influence them. He would teach them about the glories of Egypt, about strength and power and how to maintain influence in Egyptian society...

He licked his lower lip, managing to quell his unrest by anticipating the victory to come.

Chapter Nine

The sons of Yisrael camped at the grove near Mamre. Insistent breezes blew down from the hills, pushing the suffocating heat toward the arid region to the west. Menashe unrolled his cloak on the ground at the base of the ancient terebinth tree, preferring to sleep under a canopy of branches and the endless plain of stars than in one of the dusty tents.

But sleep would not come. He lay for some time in silence, his fingers linked on his chest, his head spinning with the events of the day. Above him, the moon bathed the area with dazzling light. His exhausted uncles and kinsmen slept around him; many snored irregularly through the silence of the night.

Leaning back on his elbows, Menashe sat up and studied the nearby Hebrews. Efrayim slept not far away, quiet and still, and Jokim lay near the firepit, his face reddish-gold in the gleaming embers' light. Menashe yearned to talk, to compare his experience at the tomb with someone else's, but all the others seemed to sleep as soundly as Yaakov in his grave.

He glanced over at his father's tent. Tarik might understand if Menashe chose to wake him, but Yosef would not appreciate being aroused in the dead of night. He was undoubtedly tired; for as long as Menashe could remember his father had smiled at him with exhausted eyes. Tonight, as Yosef slipped into his tent, Menashe caught a glimpse of his father's haggard face.

Fatigue had settled in deep pockets under Yosef's eyes, and he bid his brothers goodnight in a pose of weary dignity.

No, his father would not want to hear Menashe ramble on about the mysteries and intentions of God Shaddai. Not tonight.

He slouched out on his mantle, bleary-eyed and restless, until his mind drifted into the fuzzy haze of sleep. After an immeasurable interval—it might have been a few moments or a few hours—he dreamed that he walked along the Nile with Jendayi by his side. The sky was a faultless curve of blue above him and the river, bright with the verdigris of summer, ran without a ripple in the windless calm. A choir of songbirds sang from a stand of trees on the shore, and Jendayi's deep gray eyes moved into his and shone with love.

He linked her hand through the crook of his arm and felt his heart turn over. In all his life he could never remember such a feeling of contentment, of bottomless peace and satisfaction. This was how life should be, how his life *would* be if God Shaddai answered prayer...

His thoughts must have summoned the Almighty, for the sun brightened and descended with a terrific downward swoop. Menashe threw up his hands to shield himself from the blinding light; sweat poured in rivulets down his back and arms.

The dreamy silence shattered, and over the roaring of blood in his ears he knew he was hearing the voice of his father's god. "Cursed is the man who trusts in mankind and makes flesh his strength," the voice insisted, a surprisingly gentle softness in its tone, "and whose heart turns away from the Lord. For he will be like a bush in the desert. He will not see when prosperity comes, but will live in stony wastes in the wilderness, a land of salt without inhabitant."

Menashe froze as if rooted to the riverbank. Would the Almighty God really speak to *him?* Or had this dream been conjured up by the day's momentous events?

"Blessed is the man whose trust is in God Shaddai," the voice continued. "For he will be like a tree planted by the water, that extends its roots by a stream. He will not fear when the heat comes. But his leaves will be green. He will not be anxious in a year of drought, nor will he cease to yield fruit."

Above the blazing orb the blue sky darkened; the preternatural voice echoed with entreaty. "Speak, son of Yosef, to the sons of Yisrael. Say to them, 'When you cross over the Jordan into the land of Canaan, then you shall drive out all the inhabitants of the land from before you. You shall destroy all their figured stones and molten images and demolish all their high places. And you shall take possession of the land and live in it, for I have given the land to you.'"

"Canaan?" Menashe asked in a suffocated whisper. "We are to possess Canaan...now?"

He squinted to look at the hand before his eyes—it was solid, of substance, so this was no vision. When he lifted his gaze, the dream world went black around him. The blazing fireball and the river had disappeared, so had Jendayi. He lay on the packed earth of the grove; above him loomed Avraham's ancient tree, backlit by the starry plain of evening.

And yet the voice lingered. "I am YHWH who brought Avraham out of Ur of the Chaldeans to give you this land, to inherit it."

Menashe breathed in shallow, quick gasps, silently waiting for his heart to settle into an even beat. If he had been asleep, he was definitely awake now. And he had heard the voice in the darkness of the grove as clearly as in his dream of Jendayi.

When he was reasonably certain his voice would not crack in terror, he sat up and crawled to Efrayim's side.

"Brother." He shook Efrayim's shoulder. "Did you hear something?"

Efrayim wiped his hand across his eyes and blinked. He tensed when he read the expression on Menashe's face. "Is there danger?"

"No." A great exultation filled Menashe's chest. He squatted on the ground and looked up at the sky. The silence of the night was broken only by the light applause of fluttering leaves from the tamarind and terebinth trees. "I had a dream. But when I woke, I could still hear the voice from my dream." He took a deep breath, forcing himself to calm down. "Did you hear anything?"

Efrayim frowned. "You woke me up on account of a *dream?*"

"It was not just a dream. I think it may have been like the vision in which Yaakov saw the ladder to heaven."

"You are insane, Menashe. You have lost your mind."

Menashe glanced over his shoulder. Fortunately, the others did not stir.

Efrayim's expression darkened with unreadable emotions. "You will go back to sleep and forget about this...*vision*." A thread of warning laced his voice. "The uncles' tales have filled your mind with all sorts of fanciful stories. If you say anything to the others, they will laugh at you."

"But El Shaddai spoke! I heard Him."

"Why would God speak to you?"

Menashe crossed his arms and looked away from Efrayim's accusing glare. Why wouldn't his brother believe him? For though God Shaddai could have chosen Yosef, Yehuda, Re'uven, Shim'on or any of the others, He had spoken to Menashe.

Waking Efrayim had been unwise.

"I don't know why He would speak to me," Menashe finally murmured, dismayed to hear a quaver in his voice. "But I know I heard Him."

Efrayim shook his head as he lowered himself to his cloak. "Now you have a story to tell when the sons of Yisrael next gather around their campfire. That is all you wanted."

Menashe opened his mouth to protest, but Efrayim closed his eyes, a clear signal that he would not listen to anything else.

The next morning, as the sons of Yisrael gathered their belongings and prepared to rejoin the Egyptians at Goren ha-Atad, Menashe walked into the center of the company and lifted his hands. "Sons of Yisrael, uncles and cousins," he called with quiet but desperate firmness. "Last night the voice of El Shaddai spoke to me in a dream."

The noise of the camp ceased. Waves of silence began from those nearest him and spread outward to the servants who were loading the donkeys.

But no one interrupted, not even his father. Emboldened, Menashe thrust back his shoulders. "El Shaddai spoke to me and said—"

"God Almighty spoke to *you?*" Re'uven stepped from the cluster of his sons and took two steps toward Menashe, an expression of pleasant curiosity on his face. "Why would El Shaddai speak to you?"

Re'uven's implication was clear. If God had a message for them, why wouldn't He address one of the elders?

"I don't know why He chose me." Menashe lifted his jaw. "But I am certain He did."

"What is Yosef's son saying?" Dan, who had grown deaf over the years, called through the silence. "What is the boy telling us?"

A cacophony of voices rose in response.

"What sort of madness is this?" Gad demanded.

"Yosef, what has happened to your son?" The question came from Yissakhar.

Efrayim stepped forward, his arms folded tight as a gate. "I warned you not to speak of this!"

Menashe's breath quickened and his face grew warm. Crimson with confusion and humiliation, he crossed his arms.

The noise ceased when his father stepped through the crowd, resplendent in his gleaming vizier's robe and the Gold of Pharaoh's Praise about his neck. Yosef's steps slowed as he lifted his gaze to Menashe's face in a keen, swift look. "Tell me, son." Yosef's eyes flickered with interest. "What did El Shaddai say to you?"

Yosef's question silenced the doubters.

Surprised as much by his father's apparent support as by the stillness, Menashe hesitated. "God Shaddai—" his breath caught in his lungs "—said we should enter the land of Canaan and possess it."

A new and unexpected warmth surged through Menashe as he proclaimed the message. He lifted his chin, amazed at the thrill racing through his soul.

The sons of Yisrael broke into laughter.

"Possess Canaan?" Shim'on looked at Menashe in amused wonder. "With what? We have no army."

"We have two squadrons of Egyptian chariots and a company of warriors waiting at Goren ha-Atad," Menashe said, taking an abrupt step toward Shim'on. "The Canaanites are afraid of us. All we would have to do is make a stand. They would not resist us."

"What of our flocks and little ones in Egypt?" Shela grimaced in good humor. "Would you have us leave them behind? I would not mind leaving my mother-in-law, but it would pain me to leave my wife and six children who wait in Goshen."

"Not to mention your cattle," Dan quipped. "Which would it pain you most to lose, Yehuda—your wife or your cows?"

"We could send the Egyptians troops to Goshen. They will return, escorting those we have left behind." Menashe opened his hands. "The crown prince could act as our ambassador and explain our situation to Pharaoh. The king would understand if we tell him our god has spoken."

Yosef regarded Menashe with open amusement. "You do not know Pharaoh like I do, son. One does not simply send a message to the king and expect him to understand."

Efrayim swaggered forward, a bold grin on his face. "You surprise me." He lowered his voice so only Menashe could hear. "What of the little harpist you love so dearly? If you think you can keep her in Canaan, you are sorely mistaken. She is Pharaoh's property." He shook his head. "You will not live long if you persist in this foolish notion."

Menashe frowned and fell silent. He had not considered Jendayi's situation. Because she had been in his dream he imagined she would remain with him always, but how could he win her freedom if he remained in Canaan? Did God expect him to send her back to Egypt? Surely a loving god would not demand his heart's desire!

His mind spun with bewilderment. Perhaps he had imagined the dream and the voice. Yesterday had been a long and trying day. His heart had been rent by grief, his body wracked with weariness. His longing for Jendayi might have been transmuted into a longing for El Shaddai, his desire to return to the roots of his forefathers into a desire to return to the land of promise.

Undiluted laughter floated from his relatives as the men returned to their packing. "Even so, He did say to possess the land," Menashe murmured. He turned and saw his father watching him. The vizier's brow was creased with worry, his mouth set in a careful smile.

"It's all right, Father." Efrayim stepped forward to deflect

Yosef's attention and cast their father a disarming grin. "Our Menashe has often been troubled by nightmares. You can ask Ani or Tarik. On many a night he has awakened them with his screaming."

Menashe glared at his brother. "I haven't suffered from nightmares since I was a child."

Efrayim ignored him. "Last night he woke me—" he waved his hand in a gesture of reassurance "—but he will be himself soon. No need to worry."

Yosef studied Menashe for another moment, then he nodded at Efrayim. "Grief weighs on all our hearts," he said, swiveling his gaze to Menashe. "But soon we will be home, and back to life as we have always known it."

"We look forward to it, Father." Efrayim looked briefly over his shoulder at Menashe. "We will all be better when we are home again."

Yosef smiled and turned toward his chariot. Efrayim waited until Yosef moved away, then he tugged irritably at his wig and glared at his brother. "Do not speak of this again. They will not listen, they will only mock you and laugh at our father. Soon all of Egypt will be laughing. Do you want to bring shame to Zaphenath-paneah's household?"

Menashe's soul roiled, but he dropped his eyes before his brother's steady gaze. "No."

"Then remain silent," Efrayim muttered. "Say nothing of this to anyone else. Forget what you think you heard, for you heard nothing."

Jokim ran his hand over the back of his neck and winced when his nails scraped his sunburned skin. Yesterday he had followed the burial sledge with his long hair tied back with a strip of leather, and now the flesh was tender. He jerked the leather out of his hair, reasoning that it was better to have heavy hair on the nape of his neck than to wince every time his rough tunic scraped irritated flesh.

They had been traveling for half the day, and Jokim had purposely kept to himself. He had journeyed to Mamre with Efrayim, but Yosef's younger son now walked behind the vizier's chariot, a measured distance away from his brother. A pall of humiliation seemed to hang over both young men. Apparently Menashe had not recovered from the storm of protest that met his bizarre pronouncement, and Efrayim seemed embarrassed for his brother. Not knowing them well enough to intervene in an uncomfortable situation, Jokim left them alone.

He quickened his pace until he walked alongside his father and grandfather. "Perhaps Menashe's idea is valid," Shela was saying. He shrugged. "Perhaps we should consider moving back to Canaan. After all, we came into the Black Land on account of the famine, and that time of starvation has long past."

Grandfather Yehuda frowned. "But Yosef remains in Egypt. And after the wrong we committed against him—"

"That is another matter for concern," Shela interrupted, his voice rough. "While Yisrael lived, Yosef would not dare to lift a hand in vengeance. But his beloved father is dead. What if he turns against you now? The grief in his heart could easily blaze into anger."

"At the tomb," Yehuda murmured, stroking his beard, "he did say something about God delivering him from those who hated him."

"He meant you and the others." Shela ground the words between his teeth. "You were the ones who drove him to a day of calamity and he has not forgotten. Even at his father's grave he spoke of his time of trouble." He lowered his voice. "How do you know, Father, that he does not despise all of you? If we return to Egypt where he wields the full authority of Pharaoh, he may use his power against us. He brought you into the Black Land for Yisrael's sake, but now he may destroy you to satisfy his own thirst for vengeance."

Yehuda's brow furrowed. "So you think we should run back to Canaan? We have no place there and our father is dead."

"I'm only saying that we should consider the idea of return-ing," Shela answered, wearing an expression of pained toler-ance. "Don't allow a few of your brothers to make a decision for all of us. Now the sons of Yisrael are more than twelve, we are more than three hundred. Your sons and grandsons should also be consulted, lest they and their little ones suffer for the evil you and the others committed long ago."

"We will see," Yehuda murmured, staring forward at the caravan. "We will talk to the others."

"How can you sit there and play that same tune over and over? I am going crazy. I am bored, bored, bored!"

Back at the Egyptian camp, Jendayi stopped playing and turned toward the sound of Kesi's agitated voice. The maid had been pacing in the tent all morning, and only through concentrating on her music had Jendayi been able to block the sounds of the girl's annoying shuffling.

Jendayi stilled the strings of her harp. "You might find something to do."

"There is nothing. My only job is to serve you."

Jendayi bit the inside of her cheek, momentarily wishing that she did not require a maid. Sometimes Kesi rendered more aggravation than help, especially when the maid was restless. But Jendayi had already passed through the rebellious stage of denying her blindness and trying to pretend she was no different from anyone else. She *was* blind, she needed help, and nothing would ever change that truth.

She cast a suggestion over her shoulder. "You might help one of the other servants."

"Bah! I am not a kitchen slave."

"One of the other musicians, then. Surely Akil could find something for you to do."

"There is nothing to do but wait, Jendayi, and the Hebrews are taking forever to bury the old man." A teasing note slipped into Kesi's voice. "I had thought to wander among the Hebrew women and see if I could discover anything interesting about your friend, the vizier's son."

Fear shot through Jendayi. "You didn't say anything to anyone, did you? They must not know."

"I said nothing," Kesi interrupted. "Do not worry. I understand. I intended only to ask about the vizier's younger son while saying nothing about you, but the Hebrew women are all gone on the journey. Only a few of their slaves remain."

Jendayi took a deep breath as her heart slowed to its normal pace. She was as nervous and pent-up as Kesi, so perhaps a walk would do them good. She put her harp aside and stood, carefully brushing wrinkles from the stiff linen of her dress. "Let us go outside. The air by the river will refresh us both."

"Wonderful!" Kesi's hand closed around Jendayi's upper arm. "Several handsome soldiers have been posted along the riverbank. I was hoping for a chance to see them at a closer range."

Jendayi lifted the sheer veil on her shoulders to cover her head. If Kesi insisted on dragging her out in the hot sun, she would at least protect herself from it.

"Lead on," she called.

Eager to be on her way, Kesi led Jendayi from the tent and filled the silence with complaints about the boredom of the journey, the dreary landscape and the rude behavior of the warriors who would not pay her proper attention.

Jendayi ignored the girl's whining by concentrating on the scents and sounds around her. The sun was warm on her face through the gossamer veil she wore, the atmosphere surprisingly mild and pleasant. It was the season of Proyet, the Emergence, and soon the heat of summer would be on them in earnest. But she might belong to a different master by the time summer came. If all went well, she would be a slave in Efrayim's household. If he truly loved her, she might be his concubine.

Since the night she had learned that Zaphenath-paneah's son intended to ask Pharaoh for her, a thousand questions had pestered her brain. What sort of man was Efrayim? She had heard he was handsome, but what did handsome look like? How had he matured? She was not certain she would know his voice if she heard it, for though she had heard him in a group, he had not spoken directly to her since his adolescence. Was he still as bold as he had been that day in the garden? She hoped so, for it would take a bold man to approach Pharaoh and ask for one of the royal slaves. She felt a blush heat her cheeks. Did he still think her beautiful?

Light, liquid laughter filled Kesi's voice. "You are thinking of him! I see it in your face."

Jendayi opened her mouth to protest, then decided it was

useless to lie. Kesi knew her too well. "Of course." She shrugged. "You are always talking about one man or another. Why shouldn't I think about the one who has promised to ask Pharaoh for me?"

"I hope he is as wise as he is courageous." Kesi's steps slowed. "I don't know how he can expect Pharaoh to grant his request. You were a gift to Pharaoh from the vizier. Only a fool would ask to have a gift restored after it has been given to the king."

"Pharaoh and the vizier have a close relationship," Jendayi answered, hoping her words were true. "Efrayim would not promise to ask for me if he did not believe he would be successful. Perhaps he plans to find another harpist for Pharaoh. His father might wield his influence. But if Efrayim has made me a promise, it will be done."

"There has been no news of the Hebrews since they left," the handmaid said after a moment. "I knew you wouldn't ask, so I've been inquiring every day. The warriors at the river are to sound the trumpet when they see the sons of Yisrael approaching. The vizier's servants are to prepare a great feast in honor of his return, so they will need every moment of warning to make ready."

"The vizier's servants?" Jendayi's thoughts came to an abrupt halt. "The vizier's servants remained here, at the river?"

"Of course." Kesi halted. "They are not Hebrews, so the vizier asked them to remain behind."

"Then someone here might know something of him." Jendayi's hand went to her throat as her heart fluttered in unexpected anticipation. "I have not dared ask of him, but if we are discreet, the vizier's servants might put my mind at ease."

Kesi laughed. "I was beginning to wonder if you were made of stone. A young man promises to ask for you, and yet you say nothing, you ask no questions, you accept his promise as calmly as if I had just announced that dinner was being served—"

"Stop talking—" Jendayi clutched her maid's hand "—and lead me to the vizier's tent!"

"With pleasure," Kesi answered, pulling Jendayi by her side.

They walked for a short distance, and Jendayi followed Kesi's cue, nodding in the direction of voices that called out greetings. She smiled until her cheeks felt stiff and lifted her sandals through the sand in dainty, mincing steps, all she could manage in her fitted gown.

"Here is the vizier's compound." Kesi turned so abruptly that Jendayi stumbled and filled her sandals with sand. "Nearly all his servants remained behind while the sons of Yisrael went to the tomb. Perhaps one of the slaves here will answer your questions. There are no men in the area, only a handful of serving women. Shall we go inside and speak to them?"

"Do they look trustworthy?" Jendayi whispered. "I don't want them running to their master with gossip."

"One of the women inside is old, but seems to be of a pleasant disposition. She is probably able to hold her tongue. But to put your mind at ease, we will say nothing of Efrayim's promise to you."

Still uncertain, Jendayi resisted, but Kesi dragged her forward. The musical murmur of servants' voices stilled as the pair moved into the cool shade of a tent, and Jendayi felt herself being drawn through a silence that was the holding of curious breaths. If only immortality were not so important! She had managed without love in this life, she could do without the life to come if only she would not be eaten by Ammit…

Feeling self-conscious, Jendayi stepped forward.

"Long life and peace to you," Kesi said, greeting someone. Who, the old woman?

Jendayi blinked in surprise when the servant returned the greeting in smooth, well-modulated tones. She had been expecting the withered voice of a hag.

Kesi wasted no time. "My mistress, Pharaoh's harpist, used to belong to Zaphenath-paneah. Though she was only a child, she once had occasion to speak with the vizier's son—"

"Which son?" the servant interrupted, a spark of curiosity in her voice. "The master has two fine sons, both of whom are with their father on the burial journey."

Jendayi summoned her courage. "The younger one."

"Efrayim." The woman answered in a mild tone, but there was no mistaking the approving smile in her voice. "Efrayim is quite the charmer. A more smooth-talking persuader I have never seen."

"You speak as though you know him well," Jendayi offered.

"I do," the servant answered. "I have known Efrayim and Menashe since they were children. I served as a kitchen slave in the vizier's house until Zaphenath-paneah allowed me to marry the captain of his guard." A faint bite slipped into the woman's dulcet voice. "Why would one of Pharaoh's slaves be interested in the vizier's younger son?"

Jendayi felt a sudden chill. How could she explain her interest without revealing her secret?

Kesi came to the rescue. "I wanted to know about him," the maid said in a confident and breezy tone. "I have lived in Pharaoh's house all my life, and could not believe a nobleman's son would actually speak to a slave. Yet Jendayi tells me the situation is different in Zaphenath-paneah's house. She says masters and slaves often converse together."

"Yes." Jendayi could hear no trace of suspicion in the woman's voice now. "Things *are* different in the vizier's house."

"And this Efrayim, the one who spoke to Jendayi, is a man of his word?"

Kesi was being far too forward. Jendayi would have scolded her if she hadn't been so interested in the woman's response.

"Efrayim is honorable, and much like his father," the servant answered. "He is a natural leader, and more at ease with people than his older brother. He possesses great zeal, and attracts followers like honey draws bees. His name means 'doubly fruitful.' At times I wonder if he has not been blessed even more than Menashe."

The woman lowered her voice. "They say Yisrael gave the blessing of his right hand to Efrayim, the second-born, instead of Menashe. Many in the vizier's household see this as a sign from the gods, but Efrayim seems to think little of it. And what Menashe thinks, who can know?" Jendayi heard the gentle rustle of the woman's gown as she shrugged. "He is a man of few words."

"Doubly fruitful," Jendayi echoed, running the phrase through her mind. It was a good meaning and a good name. She reached out and smiled when the woman's hand slipped into hers. "Thank you for your help. May the gods of heaven and earth bless you!"

"I have already been blessed," the woman answered. "By the vizier's God Shaddai."

Chapter Ten

Yosef clung to the soft darkness of sleep as hard as he could, refusing to open his eyes, but an insistent hand rocked his shoulder. "Master, you must wake." The voice, tremulous with age, belonged to Ani, Yosef's steward. "Your brothers have assembled outside your tent, and they have commanded me to bring a message to you."

Yosef reluctantly quit his sleep and opened his heavy eyes. He and his brothers had rejoined the Egyptians on the previous night. Exhausted beyond words after the ordeal of Yaakov's burial, Yosef had immediately retreated to his tent.

"They are outside now?" he said, his voice clotted with sleep. "What is so important it cannot wait?"

"They did not sleep last night," Ani murmured, fetching Yosef's robe and sandals. "I heard them talking through the darkest hours. Sometimes they argued. Once or twice I heard men weeping. And this morning they came to me before sunrise and begged me to wake you at once."

"All right." Yosef slung his legs off the low bed and slipped his feet into soft leather sandals. Covering his face with his hands, he let out a long exhalation of breath, then lowered his hands to his knees. "I hope you know what they want."

Ani bobbed and twisted his hands. "Yes, my lord, I did hear a word or two of their concerns. They are afraid. They have realized that their father acted as their protector. Now that he is dead, they fear you will take vengeance on them for the shameful way they treated you years ago."

The room around Yosef sharpened into focus. "They fear me? They talk of vengeance?"

"Yes, master." Ani lifted his hands in a primitive gesture of reassurance. "I know they are being unreasonable, and I tried to tell them not to wake you, but they have come with an offer."

Listening in bewilderment, Yosef shook his head. What did they think of him, these sons of Yisrael, his own flesh and blood? For the past seventeen years he had tried to live with them as brothers. Even though the distance between Thebes and Goshen separated them physically and the gulf between royalty and common folk separated them socially, he had strived to provide for them, lead them, do everything an elder brother should. And now they quaked like mice before a cat, believing only Yaakov's wrath had prevented Yosef from taking his revenge.

He swallowed hard and tried not to reveal his anger and hurt. "Summon them." He pointed toward the opening of his tent. "Assemble all the people of Yisrael, Yaakov's sons and grandsons, their wives and servants. I will speak to them as soon as I have dressed."

"Don't you want to hear their offer?" Ani asked.

"I will dictate the terms of our relationship from this day forward." Yosef closed his eyes against hot tears of disappointment. "Tell them to assemble, then come back in and help me dress. If they have not slept, they are tired. And I will not keep them waiting."

When he stepped out of his tent an hour later, Yosef approached his brothers as a representative of Egyptian splendor. Ani had lined his eyes and painted his lids in the stern, formal manner of an Egyptian nobleman, and the most elaborate wig in his possession now covered his head. The heavy Gold of Praise, representing Pharaoh's favor, hung about his neck. He wore his vizier's robe, as white as faultless ivory, and fine leather sandals graced his feet. A company of armed warriors spread out at his approach, and a pair of fan-bearers took their places by his side as Yosef stepped up onto the dais and turned to face his brothers.

He intended for them to be impressed. If his brothers insisted on fearing him even in light of his mercy and forgiveness, he would let them be afraid. When faced with the enormity of the punishment Yosef *could* choose to inflict, perhaps his grace would be appreciated.

Re'uven, the spokesman for the group, stepped forward and prostrated himself on the ground. Yosef stared, amazed that the brother who had embraced and wept with him at Yaakov's tomb could now grovel before him like a slave.

Perspiration streaked Re'uven's furrowed face when he lifted his head. "My lord." His dark, deeply wrinkled eyes squinted toward Yosef. "Your father, Yaakov, charged me before he died, saying, 'Thus you shall say to Yosef, "Please forgive, I beg you, the transgression of your brothers and their sin, for they did you wrong."'"

Yosef took care that the lines of his face remained set. For an instant he experienced the unsettling sensation of déjà vu— on another day, much like this one, he had sat in judgment of his brothers and pretended to feel one emotion while his heart twisted in the throes of another.

"How odd," he said finally, gazing at Re'uven. "I was with our father when he died. I heard all the blessings, I heard him charge me to bury him with Lea in Canaan. I closed his eyes after his last breath. But I do not recall him charging *you* with anything."

"He did so before you arrived from Thebes." Yehuda stepped forward to intervene. Like Re'uven, he fell to the ground and pressed his hands to the dusty earth. "And now, please forgive the transgression of the servants of the god of your father."

As one, the other brothers knelt, prostrating themselves in abject humility. "Accept us as your slaves, only do not look with anger on us," they pleaded, just as they had when they first came to Thebes and did not recognize the brother they had sold into captivity.

The old feelings of abandonment surfaced in Yosef's consciousness and pulled at his heart, dragging him down into the deep well of memory and loss. Even after years of enjoying his protection and provision, did his brothers not know and trust his heart? Did they doubt the tears of joy he shed at their reunion? Were they blind to his tender care of them?

He could no longer pretend to be angry; he loved them too much. With a choking cry he tore his gaze away from the sight of their humility and pressed his hands over his face.

"Do not be afraid," he murmured, struggling to compose himself. Their desperate pleas ceased; he could feel their eyes on him, waiting.

Slowly he lowered his hands and looked out at them, his gaze clouded with tears. "Am I in God's place, that I should judge you? You planned evil against me, but God planned it for good so this day might come to pass. You are alive, you and your little ones, by the hand of God Shaddai. So do not be afraid. I myself will sustain you and your children. You need not fear anything as long as you are in Egypt, for I will care for you."

An almost palpable sigh of relief swept through his brothers and their sons. A half-smile crossed Re'uven's face, the countenances of Shim'on and Levi brightened. One by one, the brothers rose and turned with open arms toward their families, where they were met with newly confident smiles of rejoicing. They had not slept last night, Ani said. They must have been worrying for days, each man confiding his fears to his wife, his sons, even his servants. Now they rejoiced at Yosef's reassurance of love and loyalty, and they would fly back to Egypt on wings of contentment and release.

And as Yosef watched them go, each man to his own family's tent, he had never felt more alone.

"Are you saying I was wrong?"

Menashe turned from Yosef, frustrated by his father's logic and unflappability. "No, you weren't wrong to forgive your brothers, but why did you promise them protection in Egypt?" Menashe struggled to resist the vitality his father radiated like the sun. "*This* is the land God promised. Why didn't you encourage them to remain here in Canaan?"

"I belong to Egypt," Yosef said, looking at his hands. "By the will of God Shaddai they sold me to Egypt, and now I cannot leave. Pharaoh relies on me. The king was gracious to allow me to journey to Mamre."

"You speak as if Pharaoh truly controls you." Irked by his father's cool, aloof manner, the corner of Menashe's mouth twisted. "He does not. Amenhotep listens to you, but you could do anything, you could suggest any idea, and somehow make Pharaoh agree with you." *You could even ask for a royal slave to be your son's bride...*

Yosef stiffened as if Menashe had struck him. "You ought to be glad no one else heard that," he snapped, his voice like steel. "Those are the words of a traitor."

"I meant no treason."

Yosef sighed and locked his hands at his waist. "There was a time when Pharaoh listened to me, but those days have passed." A brooding quality echoed in his voice as he stared at the floor. "Now I am like the father of a grown child. Pharaoh needs me, but he will not admit it. Neither will my brothers. They have the forgiveness they sought. They will go back to Goshen and be happy. And they will forget about me."

"They are not *you,* Father." To his dismay, Menashe heard a note of sarcasm in his voice. "*They* do not have to go back to Egypt, for they do not belong to Pharaoh. They are the sons of Avraham, and Canaan is their promised land."

Yosef's lips thinned as he looked up. "I know who they are, Menashe. And I know them far better than you do. In a way they are like children. They quarrel and bicker and would harm one another if left to themselves. If I allow them to remain in Canaan, within a year their sons will marry Canaanite women, within two years they will be worshipping the idols we passed on our journey." He glared at the floor, frowning. "But I can watch over them in Egypt."

"If they are like children—" Menashe stepped toward his father "—then they must grow up. Can't you see the time has come to push them out of the nest? We are in Canaan now, and possession is half the battle. You are here with two squadrons of chariots and a hundred warriors ready to do your bidding. You could move to Hebron under cover of darkness and seize the city. Build a fortification, leave a hundred men to guard it, and return to Egypt if you must. You have the authority to arrange an escort for the women and children who remain at Goshen."

Caught up in his eagerness, he knelt on one knee at his father's feet. "I know you don't believe me," he said, his voice hoarse with frustration, "but God Shaddai spoke to me the other night. He told me the land is ours. We are to take it, possess it, live in it."

For a moment Yosef studied him with a curious intensity, then his eyes clouded and he waved his hand in a gesture of dismissal. "You do not know our people," he said, his voice heavy and final. "While I admire your spirit and your sincerity, you speak with the naiveté of youth. They are my people, and my responsibility. Until I die, I will keep them in Goshen. They want protection—didn't you hear them this morning? So I will be their protector. I have promised to take care of them, and I will keep my word."

"But God said Canaan is ours!"

"And it will be. But not yet."

Like an old wound that ached on a rainy day, Menashe again felt the distance between himself and his father. Yosef was the vizier, the Bread of Life and Sustainer of Egypt. Menashe was an ill-favored son, an unfortunate dreamer. Nothing more.

When Menashe had gone, Yosef leaned his head on his hand and closed his eyes as jagged and painful thoughts whirled inside his head. He had rejected Menashe's idea as absurd, but doubt reared its ugly head in the silence of his empty tent. How could he have spoken with such perfect confidence? He did not speak for God. He had dreamed no dreams of late; he had not heard the quiet inner voice he had come to recognize over the years. Either God Shaddai had fallen silent…or He was now speaking to someone else.

But would He speak to Menashe? Yosef doubted it. Menashe had fine qualities; in fact Yosef had always favored toward the boy, for Menashe reminded him of a younger version of himself. But while Menashe was bright and intuitive, Efrayim was more suited for leadership. Even Yaakov had recognized the difference in Yosef's sons. Yisrael had revealed a unique depth of understanding when he crossed his hands during the blessing…

Perhaps…I am no longer fit for God's service. The thought

made his right temple pound, and Yosef rubbed the throbbing area as his eye watered. Another headache, and this would be a severe one. Soon he'd be in bed, overcome by nausea and weakness, ashamed to allow anyone but Tarik or Ani into his presence.

The headaches had first begun to afflict him during the years of famine. Once his own family was safely ensconced in Goshen, Yosef had turned his attentions to consolidating Pharaoh's power. In those days Amenhotep had been young and unsure of himself, and Yosef secured the king's position by trading stored grain for silver, then cattle, then the land itself. When the people had nothing else to give, they surrendered themselves in total allegiance, swearing to align themselves with Pharaoh's purposes. Yosef wisely distributed Egypt's citizenry from one border to the other, uprooting age-old loyalties to cities and regions, until the land and its people were united in service to Pharaoh alone. Only the priests had remained outside Yosef's sweeping reforms, and he had been keenly aware that they despised him. He did not worship their gods. He might have even persuaded the king to worship El Shaddai, but the priests held one undeniable advantage: Pharaoh ruled as the divine son of Amon-Re. If he denied that god, he denied his own divinity and his right to rule.

Amenhotep was inexperienced, but he was no fool.

The pain pounded like a tom-tom behind Yosef's eyeball, and he clenched his fists, trying to will it away. His physicians had tried every sort of ointment, chant and massage, but nothing soothed his agony but darkness and quiet.

His thoughts whirred and lagged as he massaged his temple. Had he been wrong to work so diligently for Pharaoh? Had he been too acquisitive? No. He did not confiscate the silver and cattle for his own benefit, but for Amenhotep's. And the vizier's estate surrendered a fifth of its produce to Pharaoh like every other nobleman's manor.

Opening his eyes, Yosef came back to reality. His estate, his work, waited in Thebes, and he longed to return to it. And just because God was silent did not mean He would not speak. Yosef had known times of silence before, long years of unjust imprisonment, other years of slavery. But even during those times of testing, Yosef had known God had His hand on him. He had only to wait until God revealed His will.

And he would wait now. Until God spoke and indicated otherwise, Yosef would keep his people in Egypt, under his protection. And when the time came for them to leave, Yosef would know it.

A light, relaxed mood filled the entire camp as the Hebrews and Egyptians finalized details for the journey home. Yaakov had been mourned and buried; Yosef's forgiveness had been asked and received. As Menashe glanced around at the cookfires and festive gatherings, he wondered why none of the others had considered that this might be the ideal time to discuss the possibility of remaining in Canaan.

A large ceremonial fire burned in the clearing before his father's tent, and around its welcoming flames a host of Egyptians and Hebrews had gathered to share stories. With Jokim on his left hand and the crown prince on his right, Efrayim served as the center of attention and interpreter for the convivial group. Yosef, Menashe noted, had not come out to join in the revelry.

Glumly, Menashe found a place in the company and pressed his sandals into the dirt, only half listening to the lively conversations around him. He did not want to talk. His own feelings were too raw to discuss, his recent defeat beneath the opinions of his father too fresh in his mind.

A servant threw a shovelful of dung onto the fire, and its impact sent a volcano of sparks into the night sky. As Menashe stared at the glowing, maniac cinders, soft shuffling sounds broke his concentration. His heart leaped when he saw Akil enter the circle with the musicians.

"If it please you," the chironomist said, bowing to the crown prince, "I thought a little music might strengthen your heart for the journey home."

The prince applauded, his young face wreathed in a smile. "Yes, please."

"Excellent idea, Akil." Efrayim lifted his hand in salute. "Please, play a happy song, a song of praise."

The men in the circle parted to make way for the musicians. The women came shyly forward and took their places in the sand before their director. Menashe felt his weary heart expand as Jendayi moved into the glow of firelight, her harp in her hands.

He lifted one knee and rested his arm on it, contemplating her lovely face. Regardless of whatever happened between the Egyptians and the Hebrews, he would soon go to Pharaoh to ask for her. If by that time he had managed to convince his uncles to return to Canaan, perhaps he and Jendayi would make their home in Hebron. If not, they might live in Thebes—

He frowned, finding that idea distasteful. Jendayi needed to be free from Pharaoh and the people who had enslaved her. If he could not take her to Canaan, he would make a home for them in Goshen where she could live and create her music at her own whims, not those of a master.

Would she care, he wondered, that he had just fought—and lost—one of the most personal battles of his life? He wished she could have been by his side as he confronted his father. Though she might not understand the significance of God's promise to Avraham, as a slave she certainly would understand his desire to be free from Egypt. Oh, what he would give in exchange for the right to freely talk to her! He yearned to discover the secret joys and sorrows that ruled her lovely frame. But until she was his, he had no right even to approach her.

Akil beat a soft rhythm on his knee and the women began to play. The sharp, nasal tone of the oboe whined against the darkness; the soft strum of Jendayi's harp blended with the fire shadows dancing on the faces of the jovial men. Ignoring the others and their feeble attempts to enjoin him in conversation, Menashe studied Jendayi, impressing her enchanting image on his wounded heart as if it were a salve that could heal the wound he had received.

In time, he would find a way to lead his people to God's promised land. Jendayi had certainly known loneliness, pain and sorrow, but she had persevered with her gift, finding fulfillment and joy in it even as a slave.

And he would rejoice in his holy calling. His father might deny him; Efrayim might mock him. The others might not believe. But if God Shaddai had truly called him, God would equip him for whatever lay ahead.

As the music stopped, the men around Menashe lifted their hands and voices in appreciation. Akil stood, bowed from the waist and managed a tentative smile. "I know what I am about to propose is unconventional." His eyes wandered over the men assembled by the fireside. "But Pharaoh's slave, the Harpist-Most-Blessed-by-the-gods, has asked permission to offer a song tonight."

"Bravo!" Efrayim called, the whiteness of his smile dazzling against the darkness. "Bring her forward, Akil!"

Others took up the chorus, urging Akil to allow the girl to sing, until the man finally lifted both hands in mock surrender and gestured toward her. "Listen, then, to the Harpist-Most-Blessed."

Menashe stirred in his place, searching for a plausible explanation. Did this unexpected gesture have anything to do with him? He did not dare hope that it did, but Jendayi now knew he cared for her. Perhaps this song, like the one she had offered in his father's tent, would contain a subtle message of encouragement.

A confusing rush of anticipation and dread whirled inside him as he leaned forward. He longed to announce his love and his intentions to the world, but only a fool would boast of loving one of Pharaoh's slaves. Men had been executed for comments far less brash. But Jendayi must be careful as well. Any message to Menashe would have to be merely insinuated.

The semicircle of musicians parted; every eye focused on the harpist's slim young figure as she stepped forward and sank to the sand. Her wig, intricately braided with golden strings and tiny beads, fell past her shoulders in a soft, dark tide. Her smile lighted her face from the inside, like a candle in translucent alabaster. She steadied the harp against her shoulder, then her long, sensitive fingers caressed the strings and released the delicate, trickling sounds of running water.

"My beloved master," she sang, and at her words several of the men smiled in anticipation. Menashe shivered, half in fear, half in hope that she would sing of him. But she was discreet, her "beloved master" could be Pharaoh, beloved to all his people, or Menashe, the husband she hoped to have.

Her voice carried the melody while her hands provided soothing sounds of accompaniment.

Of whom shall I sing today?
Of my beloved master, who is a leader among men.
My beloved master, who persuades others to do his bidding.

Menashe felt heat steal into his face. If she intended the
song for him, she had obviously not heard how he had failed to
convince his Hebrew relatives to follow him.

Of whom shall I sing today?
Of my beloved master, born to the Great Provider,
My beloved master, the favored one.
Like a vineyard, he is generous to his people,
Like fine wine, his kiss is sweet on my lips.

Despite his embarrassment, Menashe felt a warm glow flow
through him. *He* was the son of the Great Provider, Zaphenath-
paneah. One day the men who had mocked him would remember
this night and realize that Jendayi had sung of him, not Pharaoh.
Then their cowardly hearts would shrivel with jealousy!

Of whom shall I sing today?
Of my beloved master, who will lead his people to great-
    ness,
My beloved master, the blessing of double fruit.

Menashe blinked in stunned silence as the circle of men
erupted into exclamations of raucous delight and surged toward
Efrayim, eager to clap him on the back. Jendayi had apparently
forgotten that many in the gathering spoke Hebrew; her meaning had been plain enough for half the company to understand.
The Hebrew word for "double fruit" was *Efrayim.*

She had sung of a kiss Menashe had never given her...and
of *the favored one.*

One cold and lucid thought sliced through the misty dreams
that swirled in Menashe's head. Efrayim was the favored one.
Yaakov had decreed it. Jendayi had sung of Efrayim, not
Menashe, from the first word of the song.

A suffocating sensation tightened Menashe's throat. He had

been foolish enough to misunderstand everything. She sang that her love had kissed her, and Menashe had never dared to take such a liberty; he would not even dream of doing so until he had spoken to Pharaoh.

Had Efrayim? He lowered his head, cringing with anger and humiliation. Of course! His bold and impudent brother had probably kissed a hundred women; he wouldn't care whether they were slave girls or princesses.

Menashe rose from his place, unwilling to look on his brother's smirking smile. This time Efrayim had gone too far. Menashe knew his brother longed to marry Princess Sitamun, but Sitamun had remained in Thebes, while Jendayi was here, vulnerable and within reach.

Numb with confusion and shock, Menashe whirled away from the fire and retreated into the darkness, desperate to be alone.

An oddly primitive warning sounded in Jendayi's brain at the sound of the riotous clamor around Efrayim. She had been certain he would grasp her hidden message, but she had never dreamed anyone else would guess that she sang of any master other than Pharaoh.

"By all the gods, Kesi, what are they doing?" she whispered, reaching out through the darkness. "Why are they calling Efrayim's name?"

"Do not fear, Jendayi." Kesi crept closer. "Efrayim smiles and laughs as the others tease him. Even the crown prince seems to be impressed at your wit. No one is angry, except perhaps—"

"What are you doing?" Akil's curt voice broke into the girls' conversation, and Jendayi flinched at its harsh tone. "You foolish, insolent girl! Sing again, and sing of Pharaoh or you will find yourself working in some temple kitchen! You are as stupid as stone, as ugly as a baboon. If you value your life, you will play again!"

"I only meant—" Jendayi faltered, fumbling for her harp.

Kesi thrust the instrument into Jendayi's arms. "Play quickly. Akil is right. Oh, mistress, this was a rash act!"

Why? Jendayi wanted to shout. She had spoken in the only way she could, for a slave could not approach a nobleman, especially the son of a ruler like the vizier. And apparently her song had its desired effect, for Efrayim had smiled…

"Play!" Akil's voice hardened. "Obey me, or I shall sell you to the temple priests myself! Sing about Pharaoh!"

Her fingers trembling, Jendayi began the song again.

Chapter Eleven

Menashe did not sleep, but paced for hours in the desert, not caring if a lion or bear or darting snake should catch him unaware. He thought about walking west toward the Great Sea. Part of him wanted to walk into the water and feel it rise over his arms, his shoulders, his head and his life. He had spent his youth preparing to undertake a role as significant as his father's, and within the past month his heart had been moved to adopt two destinies: Canaan and Jendayi. But within the space of twenty-four hours, both dreams had been denied. For what, then, had he spent his life preparing?

His feelings were a mass of confusion, one powerful yearning melded with another. He had dared to think God Shaddai might speak to him, but his father had defeated that dream with a few well-chosen words. He had dared to hope Jendayi might love him, and the girl herself had dispelled that notion with a simple song. Her heart yearned for the favored one, Efrayim, who collected the attentions of women as easily as other men collected weapons or horses.

When he arrived back in the camp, no one seemed to notice either his bloodshot eyes or his disheveled appearance. Slaves and servants scurried about, rolling canvas, coiling ropes and loading pack animals. The camp would disappear far more rapidly than it had risen. They would leave Canaan within the hour, and each step would take them farther away from where God eventually wanted them to be.

Soon Menashe would begin his work to bring them back. But first he must take care of another matter.

Shouldering his way through the milling crowd, Menashe ignored the servants and guards working around his father's tent until he spied his brother. He clapped Efrayim on the shoulder and spun him around.

"Menashe! Where have you been?" As always, mischief gleamed in Efrayim's eyes. "You look terrible. Did nightmares keep you awake again last night?"

Several of the nearby servants snickered, but they fell silent when Menashe rebuked them with a stern glance. "Last night—" Menashe's eyes narrowed as his gaze returned to Efrayim "—Jendayi sang of you...and a kiss. What have *you* been doing?"

The question seemed to amuse Efrayim. "Surely you don't think I have been toying with Pharaoh's harpist?" He broadened his smile and winked at one of the guards. "I haven't time for such pleasantries." His dark eyes moved into Menashe's and his smile faded. "Nor the inclination."

"She wouldn't lie. You have kissed her."

Efrayim's mouth twitched with amusement. "Maybe I did once, years ago. I can't remember."

"You will remember!" Menashe crossed the space between them and pressed his hands to Efrayim's shoulders. He had wanted to confront his brother, to rebuke him for his distasteful behavior, and yet his fingers, as if possessed with a jealous fury all their own, yearned to slide upward to his brother's neck and choke the air of life from his throat.

A steel will kept Menashe on the edge, one step away from irrational fury...

In a blur of movement, Efrayim brought his hands up before his face, then spread his arms wide, effectively knocking Menashe's arms away. The defensive maneuver was simple and familiar, for Tarik had taught it to both brothers, but the Hebrews had never seen anything like it. Jokim, who stood behind Efrayim, gasped in admiration.

Menashe stepped back, unwilling to remain on the knife-edge of fury. Jealousy had fueled an anger unlike any he had ever felt, but he would not hurt his brother.

Barreling his chest, Efrayim stepped forward, close enough that Menashe could smell the scented oil on his skin. "I did kiss her once," Efrayim whispered, the glitter in his half-closed eyes both possessive and defiant. "And apparently I made quite an impression. But it was long ago, Menashe. I have not touched her. I have not even spoken to her during this entire journey. So calm yourself and sheathe your anger. There is no reason for you to make us look foolish before the Hebrews and the Egyptians."

"If you do touch her—" Menashe met Efrayim's gaze straight on "—you will be more than foolish."

Efrayim took a half-step back and strengthened his voice so the others could hear. "Pharaoh's slave is a pretty thing," he said, eyeing Menashe with cold triumph. "And apparently she approves of me. Perhaps after Pharaoh allows me to wed Sitamun, he will present us with the little harpist as a wedding gift. She would make a sweet concubine."

The biting words unleashed something within Menashe and he lunged, his treacherous hands again intent on Efrayim's throat. Instantly the crowd around them boiled to life; men who had been busy packing donkeys dropped everything to rush forward and separate the brothers. Menashe felt hands scraping his arms, his legs, even his chest, but he could only think of causing Efrayim pain equal to the hurt he had just inflicted.

Strong arms held Menashe and pulled him from the place where Efrayim lay on his back, his face marred by a wise-cracking grin. "See, friends, what a fighting spirit my brother has," Efrayim joked, accepting the hands that offered to lift him up. "No wonder he wants us to remain in Canaan. No doubt he intends to single-handedly defeat the Canaanites."

The men around Efrayim laughed, then helped him brush sand from his cloak and kilt. Though he seethed in silent resentment, Menashe jerked his head in a tense nod and shook the restraining arms away, wordlessly agreeing that he would not attack his brother again.

He turned and lowered his gaze, unable to look his relatives in the face. He was an angry, jealous and resentful youth, unable to lead or command the others. He couldn't even command his own emotions! His spirit was willing to lead and obey God, but his heart was given to treachery, despair and confusion…

When the intervening Hebrews and Egyptians had finally gone back to the business of packing, Efrayim turned to face Menashe.

"A pity Grandfather Yisrael did not see this stouthearted side of you," Efrayim said, lifting a brow as he folded his hands. "Perhaps he would have been more inclined not to cross his arms."

Resentment bubbled again in Menashe's soul, but before he could react, Efrayim grinned and darted away, hurrying toward Tarik's chariot.

Far in the back of the caravan, Jendayi sat in her woven basket and rested her forehead on her knees. Her song had been a dismal failure, for though the men had applauded and howled their appreciation, Efrayim had not responded. Had he approved of it? Or had she embarrassed him beyond recourse? If he cared for her as he vowed he did, shouldn't he have had some response, and shouldn't she have heard of it by now?

Had he flushed, preened or wept as the words poured from her heart? Clenching her fist, she silently cursed her blindness. If she had sight, she would have been able to look around the circle and judge the effect of her song on its hearer. She might have caught a warning glance and stilled her voice before going too far.

Afterward, of course, she heard Akil's dreadful outburst and sought to repair the political damage by offering a song of praise to Pharaoh, her true master. But perhaps she had unwittingly caused Efrayim irreparable harm.

If only she could freely approach him! But even if she were free from Pharaoh's ownership she would have no right to speak to him. She did not know him, and he had not spoken to her since that long-ago afternoon in the garden. Her memory could not recall his scent, and she had never taken the liberty of touching him. She knew only the sensation of his lips on hers, but that caress had been enough to convince her that he cared.

She pressed her fingertips to her lips, remembering. If he still cared, he would find her. She was a powerless slave, so she could do nothing but offer prayers to the gods of Egypt…and wait.

Menashe walked alone over the dun-colored sand at the side of the caravan, consciously setting himself apart from both the Hebrews and the Egyptians. Movement atop a nearby hillside caught his eye, and when he looked up he saw a band of armed Canaanites scurrying away from the ridge. He had felt the pressure of spying eyes all morning; the residents of this area must now be preparing to offer sacrifices of gratitude to their gods. All over Canaan tonight, men and women would sigh in relief that they would not be called to defend the land that had been promised to another nation. All because the sons of Yisrael, led by Zaphenath-paneah, the Hebrew with an Egyptian heart, did not have courage enough to claim what God had willed for them to possess.

And as Canaanites danced around their heathen idols and offered sacrifices to gods of wood and stone, the Hebrews would continue into the Black Land, choosing comfort and provision over a season of faith.

Somewhere, Menashe thought, looking over the rutted road ahead, Yaakov, Yitzhak and Avraham were sorrowing.

JENDAYI

And Yosef dwelt in Egypt, he, and his father's house...
                                    Genesis 50:22a

Chapter Twelve

"Again! By the life of Pharaoh, I *am* as dumb as a post. Why can't I play this?"

In a flurry of frustration, Jendayi slapped her palms to the vibrating harp strings. She had been diligently attempting a melodic run that had rippled in her head all morning, but her fingers balked at the maneuvers required of them. It was as if her hands expected to play for Efrayim, not Pharaoh, and refused to cooperate until they had been returned to the vizier's house.

But Jendayi had heard nothing from the vizier's son. They had been back at Malkata for ten days, and there had been no news from the young man who had promised to risk Pharaoh's disapproval for Jendayi's sake. Had he been teasing her? Or had Kesi invented those messages in an effort to bring hope to a life that had none, that would never have anything.

A hot tear rolled down her cheek and Jendayi angrily dashed it away, then returned her hands to the harp. "As Merit lives, you *can* do this," she told herself, concentrating. She took a deep breath and began the passage again.

A soft footfall sounded on the tile behind her, but Jendayi smelled the particular oil of lilies that Kesi used and did not turn around. It would be better for everyone if the maids bathed more often and used fewer unguents...

"Mistress, Akil bids me tell you that Pharaoh plans a banquet tomorrow."

"So?" Jendayi heard a note of impatience in her response. She kept her fingers moving; such news need not interrupt her practice. "Pharaoh has a banquet nearly every day."

"But this one is special. He will most certainly request a new song from you. Akil suggests that you compose a proper hymn of praise."

Jendayi clenched her mouth tighter. "I will give him a song he likes." Her fingers moved over the strings as her head counted the demanding rhythm: *one-Or-sir-is, two-Or-sir-is, three-Or-sir-is…*

"There will be guests."

"There always are." *Four-Or-sir-is, no, no!* The rhythm was wrong; this was not what she had imagined.

Kesi continued, a coaxing note in her voice. "This banquet, mistress, is to honor the vizier. Pharaoh wants to hear the details of the burial journey. And since his sons will be present, I thought you might want to be forewarned."

Jendayi slapped the strings in frustration. "What do I care about his sons?" She lifted a brow and turned in Kesi's direction. "I was wrong to be hopeful, Kesi, so do not think my heart is broken. I am a slave. I will always be a slave. Apparently my last song was not to Efrayim's liking and he has decided to find a more talented harpist. So I am content with my lot. Humiliated—" she felt herself flush "—but content."

"You are not humiliated." Kesi's hand fell on Jendayi's shoulder. "No one knew anything about your hopes. You followed the song about Efrayim with a tribute to the crown prince. The Hebrews probably think you merely meant merely to sing a song to praise those noble sons. Such things are often done."

"No." Jendayi's anger faded to fear. "My song did not win his heart. Somehow it turned him against me. And last night I had the dream again."

Kesi moved closer and lowered herself to the floor. Her warm hands clasped one of Jendayi's. "Not the old nightmare."

Jendayi blinked, annoyed that tears had risen in the sightless wells of her eyes. "Anubis again asked for my heart. I brought it forth, and nothing filled my hand but a stone! And the stone was not even smooth and beautiful, but hard, pitted and ugly. I could not place it in the scale, knowing I would surely fail the test, so I clutched it and screamed and woke—"

"Hush now." Kesi's arm slipped around Jendayi's neck. "Do not let these dreams trouble you. I know you haven't been eating, and there are dark circles around your eyes. Forget the dreams, Jendayi. Concentrate on pleasing Pharaoh."

"Anubis says my heart is dead," Jendayi insisted, fear and anger knotting inside her. "But how can my heart live if it is not loved?"

"I love you," Kesi said, her voice artificially bright.

Jendayi gave the girl a weary smile. "You are my handmaid." She pulled out of the girl's embrace and leaned her forehead on the stem of her harp. "If Pharaoh gave you to one of his wives or his daughters tomorrow, you'd be happy to leave me."

Kesi remained silent, and Jendayi knew the girl would not dispute her. Friendships among slaves were shallow and brief, for a slave's ultimate bond was to her master. Any other attachments ran the risk of being broken.

"Sometimes you are as silly as a tipsy widow." Kesi tried a more playful approach. "Of course you are loved! Akil is devoted to you."

Jendayi snorted softly. "If I refused to play the harp, Akil's devotion would disappear like a leaf in a windstorm."

"Even so, you are loved. I am certain that people of your past adored you—your own mother, for instance. Every girl is loved by her mother."

Jendayi stared into the deep well of her memory, back to the days when her diseased eyes had been able to discern fuzzy images and outlines. Perhaps there had been a woman who tended her, but any sense of protective and tender care had faded with Jendayi's sight. Over the years several women had moved through her life, many who played instruments of music and sacrificed to Merit, the goddess of song. These women, who combined in Jendayi's memory as a whirlwind of soft voices, sweet scents and twirling music, had often admired, petted and disciplined her. But had they *loved* her? She didn't think so.

She could not recall a gentle hand combing her hair, a tender kiss at bedtime, or anyone gathering her into a sincere and warm embrace. She had no idea when she had been born, or where. She had no knowledge of father or mother, grandparents, aunts, uncles, brothers, sisters, cousins…

Sometimes she felt that she had dropped into the world like a raindrop, utterly without significance or meaning.

"Jendayi, you are ungrateful!" Kesi's outburst was sudden and raw. "Merit herself loves you, and she has given you a talent far beyond any other woman's. Your fingers fly faster than anyone's. Sometimes I wish you could see Akil's eyes widen when you play one of your songs. I have seen Pharaoh drop his cup in order to lean forward and watch you play! Even the queen approves of you."

"If Merit loves me—" Jendayi lifted her head as her fingers moved back to the strings of her instrument "—then she will save me from the fate I must suffer in the Other World." Her mind replayed the troublesome passage she wished to master. *One-Or-sir-is, two-Or-sir-is, three-Or-sir-is, four—*

Another thought whipped into her consciousness. *I pray Merit's love is more steadfast than that of the vizier's son.*

Efrayim gaped when he entered the king's banquet hall with his father and brother. Amenhotep had charged his chamberlain and steward with preparing a magnificent feast to honor the vizier's father, and those officials had spared no extravagance. As he stared around the sumptuous hall, Efrayim could think of only one or two previous state occasions that would rival this one in splendor.

A company of the famed Medjay warriors, the king's elect Nubian guards, had greeted their boat at the small harbor outside Malkata and escorted them to the glorious banquet hall. Other warriors in resplendent white kilts, shining leather sword belts and leopard-skin sashes stood like posts around the walls of the chamber, their arms hanging rigid, awaiting Pharaoh's command. Several nobles had already been seated in gilded chairs scattered throughout the chamber, and a pygmy with jingles tied around his ankles danced his way through the assembled guests.

In the center of the vast hall an Egyptian drummer held his instrument at a jaunty angle and thumped out a steady beat. A line of trumpeters blew their instruments; one man lifted his horn toward the painted ceiling in a vain attempt to make his instrument heard above the others. A group of Libyans, recognizable by their ornate feathered headdresses, beat their clappers in a staccato rhythm, while in another corner a band of priestesses played their sacred sistra, the delicate thumping sounds echoing through the room. The chamber seemed alive with noise, the sound rising from the musicians and dancers and then spiraling down again from the tall ceiling.

The king's chamberlain led Zaphenath-paneah and his sons to seats of honor near the raised dais where Amenhotep and Tiy would sit. Efrayim sank back in his chair and sat on his hands as he looked around the room. Menashe, who had said little since they landed on the western riverbank, sat next to him, his drooping eyes fixed on a bas-relief painting of Pharaoh on the opposite wall.

Efrayim leaned forward to whisper in his brother's ear. "Do not fret, Menashe. Pharaoh would not give a feast without the little harpist. He will save the best for last."

Menashe's lips thinned with anger, but a sudden blaring of trumpets cut off his retort. A group of ladies, adorned in identical wigs with tall unguent cones of fat on their heads, danced into the room. They waved acacia branches as they came, and the diaphanous material of their sheer gowns reinforced Efrayim's opinion that the king had an expert eye for feminine beauty.

After the women came a group of men, shaven and oiled, walking with dignified and erect postures as they carried gigantic vertical bouquets. Hundreds of fragrant lotus blossoms, poppies and cornflowers had been tied to long river rushes and palm branches in tiers, the smaller flowers filling the space between the larger ones, so the slaves carried a profusion of blossoms on a single stalk. Efrayim could smell the flowers even from a distance, then the men spread throughout the chamber, infusing sweet fragrance to every corner.

After another blare of the trumpets the royal children entered. Efrayim smiled as he counted heads, realizing that Amenhotep intended for this to be a truly significant occasion if he had invited Tiy's children—even Yosef had once remarked that Tiy's offspring were as wild and unruly as unbroken horses. Yet here they came, on their best behavior, eyes downcast and their hands clasped in front of them: the princesses Ast, Hentmerheb, Hentaneb, Baketamun and Sitamun. Behind the royal daughters, in a circle of glory all his own, strutted Neferkheprure' Wa'enre', the crown prince and future king.

Efrayim gave a polite nod of recognition and acknowledgment to the prince, then ran his hand over his chin and sought Sitamun's eye. She had been seated on the opposite side of the chamber, but with any luck, she'd soon be sitting beside him and blocking his view of dour Menashe. Pharaoh's formal banquets tended to be drawn-out affairs, and diners frequently moved about during the meal.

When Sitamun finally looked up, Efrayim's eyes caught and held hers. Her gaze swept over his face approvingly and he grinned, making no attempt to hide the fact that he had been watching her.

Another trumpet blast, this one deafening, pulled him to his feet. Every man and woman in the chamber, including the royal offspring, prostrated themselves on the floor. Efrayim blinked at the painted tile beneath his nose, knowing it would take some time for the king and queen to walk to the dais where their chairs waited. Finally the chamberlain's voice broke the silence. "Rise, all of you, and be blessed by the presence of your god and king, the Son of the Sun, Son of Amon-Re, God of gods, Lord of lords, King of kings, King of the gods!"

The diners rose and stood by their chairs. Pharaoh walked before them, his arms crossed over his chest, the ceremonial crook and flail in his hands. Though he stood only five feet tall, far shorter than any of the Hebrews, his narrow face suited his small frame and gave the impression of compact musculature. His almond-shaped eyes, topped by heavy lids, seemed almost elliptical under the heavy black lines that flew outward from his lids. Both the king and queen wore elaborate collars of blue glass beads and fresh lotus blossoms, the floral symbol of rebirth.

The royal couple stood with somber eyes, mournful faces and slightly sagging shoulders—the appropriate body language of sorrow. All to honor Yisrael.

"You must tell me, Zaphenath-paneah—" the king's gaze moved toward his vizier "—of the burial of my friend, Yisrael, son of Yitzhak. Did you have a good journey? Does he now rest with his ancestors according to his wish?"

"Yes, my king." Yosef stepped forward. He pressed his hands to his breast in a humble gesture and bowed before Pharaoh. "And we offer our thanks to you. You generously supplied us with so much, including the presence of your beloved son. My family will be eternally grateful to you. The sons of Yisrael will forever speak of your kindness."

"And so I will be as immortal as Yisrael." A soft smile crinkled Amenhotep's lips. He took a quick breath as if he would say something more, but apparently changed his mind. He smiled at his wife, and together the royal couple took their seats. Cautiously, the guests slid into their chairs while Pharaoh inclined his head toward his steward. The slave clapped his hands, and within a moment the room flooded with servants bearing trays.

The delicacies were presented to the dancing beat of drums. First in the rich procession came a multitude of breads and sweet cakes, some baked in loaves as large as a man's head and others so small that five could fit on a man's palm. After the breads, slaves brought in baskets of roasted onions, followed by nine kinds of meat, including beef kidneys, goose, duck, teal, roast beef, dried and salted fish and roasted pigeons. Two different kinds of cheese filled a carved wooden bowl so big that two slave girls struggled beneath the weight of it. As was customary, the foods were presented first to Pharaoh, who waved the parade on with a subtle flick of his royal wrist. Only after a dish had been offered to the divine pharaoh could it be whisked away to fill the dinner trays of mere mortals.

Efrayim plucked a dainty shat cake from a passing platter, then raised his eyes to find Sitamun watching him from across the chamber. Her teeth, even and white, contrasted pleasingly with her olive skin and dark wig. Her smile shimmered toward him like sunbeams on the surface of the Nile, then she looked away and murmured a comment to her sister. Fully aware of Efrayim's watchful gaze, she leaned forward and carefully brought a slice of the juicy melon called *sekhept* to her rosy lips.

A wave of warmth trilled along Efrayim's pulses. In his twenty-three years he had never given serious consideration to the sort of woman he might take for a wife, but sparks of unwanted excitement shot through him as he watched her. She favored him, the eager affection radiating from her was as evident as the sun at noon. And she was a princess. Since he had grown up in the second most influential household in the world's most powerful kingdom, it was only natural that his heart should yearn toward Pharaoh's household. If he took a royal wife, he might become a man even more powerful than his father. If Sitamun would not have him, he could marry Hentaneb, Baketamun, Ast or Hentmerheb. Pharaoh was rich with daughters.

He was about to ask Menashe which princess he considered most beautiful, but at that moment Akil appeared between two painted pillars. Efrayim stuffed a piece of bread in his mouth, knowing Menashe would be unfit for conversation for some time. Behind Akil, with one hand on her maid's arm and the other around her instrument, walked the little harpist.

"Grace and prosperity to you."

The throaty voice in his ear was familiar, and Efrayim turned, surprised that Sitamun had been able to sneak up without his notice. "Grace and peace to you," he answered, releasing a short laugh touched with embarrassment. "Forgive my manners, but I didn't hear you."

"I didn't want you to hear me." She sank onto a low cushion by the side of his chair and casually tucked her legs under her. "Our fathers will talk of the burial for an hour to come, and— forgive me, please—I am not interested in a man who has passed into eternity." Her eyes danced as her mouth tipped in a faint smile. "I prefer a man who is alive and well."

Flattered, Efrayim leaned forward and lowered his voice. "I am glad you came to join me. I had considered venturing to your side of the hall, but did not think my father would approve. He already thinks me too forward."

"Your father is a powerful man—" her eyes boldly raked over him "—but my father is Pharaoh, and he will not care if I kneel at your feet. I was nearly able to persuade him to allow me to accompany you into the desert." She lifted one small, bare shoulder in a shrug of disappointment. "But my mother convinced him I should remain in Thebes."

Efrayim laughed and she smiled, and for a moment they simply stared at one another. From across the room he could hear his father telling Pharaoh about El Shaddai and the jealousy of the Almighty God, but his mind was rapidly filling with jealousy of a different sort.

By all the gods, was this love? His thoughts seemed to be drifting on a cloud; a strange tingling in the pit of his stomach had overpowered his appetite. His gaze traveled over Sitamun's young body, then moved over her face, searching her eyes. Yes, if she were his wife, he could freely give himself and all he possessed to her. Even from across the room she drew him, the smoldering flame in her eyes intriguing him. And if they could be married, Pharaoh would be honor-bound to place his daughter's husband in a position of authority. He might even name Efrayim vizier of all Egypt, because Yosef was growing older…

Without taking her eyes from his, Sitamun inclined her dark head toward the dais where Pharaoh and his vizier debated. "Your father is speaking of his god again." Her mercurial black eyes sharpened. "What think you of this Almighty God? Your father says he has never worshipped any other god, and yet he is sworn to serve my father, the son of Amon-Re."

"El Shaddai is the god of the Hebrews." Half of Efrayim's brain struggled to weigh his words while the other half hummed with perilous, erratic energy. "But He welcomes anyone who comes to Him. I've heard that Queen Tuya worships God Shaddai. And Tuthmosis, your grandfather, sought knowledge from my father's god."

"The Queen Mother is an old woman." A rush of pink stained Sitamun's cheek for no apparent reason. "And Tuthmosis has been dead many years."

"Tuya is no older than my father." Efrayim tore his gaze from Sitamun's delicate oval face and glanced over at his father. Yosef was moving his hands in tight, intense gestures, pouring out his heart to Amenhotep and Tiy. The queen looked bored while Pharaoh stared straight ahead, a patronizing quirk at the corner of his mouth.

Efrayim suspected that this king would never worship God Shaddai. Tragedy had driven Tuya and Tuthmosis to seek the Almighty God who could deliver them, but Amenhotep had known nothing but blessing in his life. Though from his childhood he had been presented with the Truth, he had let it slip from his grasp, choosing instead to placate the priests of Egypt and his enormous appetite for pleasure.

That thought had barely crossed Efrayim's mind before another followed. If Yosef would never persuade Pharaoh to accept God Shaddai, Zaphenath-paneah would not be the man God would use to implement a Hebrew-Egyptian alliance to bless the entire world. God would have to use someone else.

"Efrayim." Sitamun placed her hand on his, and his flesh prickled at her touch. She smiled with satisfaction when he turned back to her. "Tell me what you are thinking. Sometimes I think you like to take your thoughts from me."

"Never," he assured her, rewarding her with a larger smile of his own. "My thoughts would love to remain with you all day long. They would play with you in your garden, and sit with you at your dressing table as the maids apply malachite to your lovely eyes…"

One corner of her mouth dipped low. "Stop, my friend, or your thoughts will be following me into chambers where they had best not go. Tell me instead what you were thinking when you looked at my father. Your countenance closed as if you are guarding a secret."

"I was thinking—" Efrayim paused. "They are unusual thoughts. You may not appreciate them."

"Go on," she urged, and for an instant wistfulness stole into her expression. "I want to know you better."

"If the truth can be told, and your heart can be trusted—" he took her hand in his "—I was thinking that your father will never be the man my father would like him to be. Your father is a man of many gods, while my father worships only one."

Her face fell in disappointment. "That is no great revelation."

"But it is." He squeezed her hand. "For it demonstrates that

God Shaddai will not conclude His work in this generation. Don't you see? God promised my forefather Avraham that He would bless the entire world through Avraham's descendants. He also promised to give us the land of Canaan as an eternal dwelling place."

Sitamun stared at him with a look of mingled ignorance and annoyance.

He would have to try another approach. "Consider this, pretty one." He bent closer to her. "Which is the greatest kingdom in the world?"

She lifted her chin. "Egypt, of course."

Efrayim nodded. "And through Egypt's bounty the entire world has already been blessed. Now, which kingdom has the greatest military power in the world?"

"Egypt," she answered again, her lips pursing.

"You are bright as well as beautiful." He broke into a wide, open smile. "Now, which kingdom's past king conquered much of Canaan? And which kingdom could easily conquer the whole of Canaan if it desired?"

Her narrow brows rose in obvious pleasure. "Egypt again."

Efrayim paused to let the full import of his words sink into her brain. "God Shaddai has promised to bless the world through the Hebrews, and what could be a better channel for blessing than the power and glory of Egypt? God promised to give the sons of Yisrael a permanent home in Canaan, and what better way to attain it than through the military might of Pharaoh's forces?"

He leaned to whisper in her ear. "But these things will not come to pass in my father's lifetime, for he is content with the way things are. And so I suspect our destiny—yours and mine, Sitamun—must wait. When my father is no longer the vizier, perhaps your father may be persuaded to act."

When the sound of clanging brass broke the stillness behind him, Efrayim jerked around. The crown prince stood behind Efrayim's chair, his heavy eyelids wide-open, a startled expression on his face. A slave scurried to pick up the goblet the prince had dropped, and for an instant fear twisted around Efrayim's heart—had he said anything that could be considered subversive? But the prince's startled look melted into a look of mad happiness as he smiled at Efrayim.

"The gods have blessed you with wondrous thoughts," Neferkheprure' Wa'enre' whispered, bending close so only Efrayim and Sitamun could hear. "But say nothing of this to anyone else. A man's destiny will come in its own time."

Across the room, Jendayi strummed her instrument and tried not to think about the pain in her heart. The soft sounds of laughter and conversation filled the empty spaces between the orchestra's songs; the gentle clap of Akil's hand on his knee rooted her to reality. Though her heart was breaking, no one could see. The revelers in the banquet hall had scarcely noticed the musicians; there had been no requests for special songs, no offerings of praise to the gods.

After an hour of eating and drinking, the funereal atmosphere lifted. Pharaoh seemed in rare spirits, his rhythmic laughter often broke from the sounds of the others, and the shrill timbre of the queen's voice drifted around the room like the sharp clang of a bell.

Yet through the dissonance of muted conversations, the whispers of slaves and the percussive clatter of serving bowls, Jendayi recognized the vizier's resonant voice and knew his sons must be in the room. The elder son was a cipher with no place in her memory. The younger one, she sternly told herself, was a charming joker whose foolish flirtations had raked her heart. She had spent hours pondering the myriad ways through which Efrayim might have been prevented from keeping a sincere promise to obtain her, but time after time she arrived at one truth: he was a free man and an influential one. If neither Kesi nor the vizier's captain had lied—and Jendayi was certain they had not—then by this time Efrayim should have spoken to Pharaoh about her. But he had not, so he did not hold her in any regard; he had merely toyed with her as a diverting amusement. He had listened to her music, the offerings of her innermost soul, and had considered them nothing but idle entertainment.

Plucking the notes of the root chord, Jendayi heard the other instruments blend into the cadence of completion. A smattering of light applause sounded across the banquet hall, but the constant thrum of conversation did not cease. Jendayi shifted on her feet, wishing Akil had allowed her to bring the small harp she could play while sitting down. Even though she could not see the diners in the chamber beyond, standing before them left her feeling exposed and vulnerable.

Was Efrayim looking at her now? Laughing behind his hand? Sharing a joke with his elder brother?

Leather sandals slapped the nearby tiles, then a slave buzzed in Akil's ear. Jendayi lowered her eyes and hoped the slave had requested a dancing song. The princesses were fond of dancing; perhaps they wished to impress the king with some new artistry—

"Jendayi." Akil's voice cut through her thoughts like the flick of a whip. "Pharaoh wishes you to sing an anthem of praise."

She felt as if a hand had closed around her throat. She couldn't sing, not while Efrayim watched. *Twice* she had sung for him alone, twice he had ignored her. Not even for Pharaoh could she repeat that humiliation. She would die first.

"I can't." She refused in a hoarse whisper.

A soft gasp escaped the chironomist. "What?"

She clung to the neck of her harp as though the instrument would protect her. "I can't."

"You must, girl!" She stiffened before the jagged and sharp threat in his voice. "Only a stupid slave would dare refuse Pharaoh! If you would live to see Re sail across the sky tomorrow, you must do as the king commands."

She lowered her head, wishing the floor would open and swallow her, and something in her posture must have given Akil pause. When he spoke again, his voice had gentled somewhat. "Listen, girl, and perhaps you will find your courage. We will perform the story of music. It is one of Pharaoh's favorites. I will begin for you. I will tell the story while you play the accompaniment, then you will sing."

Soft currents of air brushed past Jendayi as the other women silently picked up their instruments and moved away, leaving her alone with the chironomist. Torn between rebellion and obedience, she straightened and heard Akil clap his hands for attention.

In an instant of black silence she felt the touch of a hundred pairs of eyes. Her fingers trembled as she pressed them to the strings.

"Oh, divine king, live forever," Akil began, confidence in his voice. "Long ago, Thoth observed the orderly arrangement of the stars and the harmony of the musical sounds and their nature."

A river of apprehension coursed through Jendayi, but her hands remained on the harp, creating a gentle stream of sound beneath Akil's recitation.

"Thoth made a lyre and gave it three strings, imitating the seasons of the year—the Flood, the Emergence, the Drought. Then he adopted three tones, a high, a medium and a low, and gave high to the summer, medium to the spring and low to the winter."

Jendayi tried to keep her heart cold and still, but her pulse began to beat erratically. Efrayim was watching her, *now.*

"The genius of Thoth led him to build a bigger harp," Akil went on, "and to fashion mortals who had the gift of music. Then he created Merit, the personification of harmonic melody, and taught her to sing through the lips of mortal men and women. Merit has gifted this girl before you, divine Pharaoh, like no other woman before or since. Listen to her now, as she seeks to please your divine heart…"

The pounding in Jendayi's ears drowned out Akil's voice. She tried to play, but her mutinous hands deserted the harp and fell to her side. The floor seemed to shift beneath her feet. Her head swam. The harp, no longer supported, crashed to the floor in a sickening clash of sounds.

The familiar darkness thickened, muffling all sounds and sensations. She struggled to lift her leaden arms, then blackness swarmed like a cluster of bees and carried her away.

Chapter Thirteen

"Look at that." Efrayim leaned forward in sudden interest. "The little harpist has fainted—and my brother has forgotten himself." Menashe had leaped from his chair in the first moment the girl appeared to sway; now he knelt at Jendayi's side while the alarmed chironomist stood wringing his hands.

"Let the servants take care of the slave." Sitamun's hand gripped Efrayim's arm. "And pray my father shows mercy to your brother."

Efrayim sat back, speechless with surprise. Menashe's lunge toward the slave flaunted all protocol, tradition and common sense. His mindless dash to aid the girl had carried him directly in front of Pharaoh's chair; therefore he had risked death to tend a fallen slave. According to Egyptian religion and tradition, the cobra affixed in Pharaoh's headdress, a model of the serpent goddess Wadjet, had the power to deal out instant death by spitting flames at any enemy who approached the king. Either Wadjet had failed in her duty as Menashe ran willy-nilly across Pharaoh's dais, or the goddess had known he was not an enemy. Amenhotep would decide the truth of the matter.

Efrayim thought his father went a little pale as Pharaoh stiffened in his chair. The king blinked, as if he was not quite certain he had actually seen someone invade his private space, then he fastened his gaze to the spectacle of the fallen slave and the hovering vizier's son.

"It would seem, my king," Yosef said, his voice tremulous and weak, "that my son has forgotten his manners in his hurry to aid your harpist."

Pharaoh's dark brows slanted in a frown. "I must agree, Zaphenath-paneah." He gazed at Menashe with chilling intentness and Efrayim held his breath, certain the royal anger was about to explode in reckless fury. Menashe had not only intruded on the king, but now knelt next to the slave as if he, not Amenhotep, owned the girl. If Menashe was not careful, in another moment Pharaoh would see the light of love in his eyes.

Menashe might be a romantic fool, but Efrayim still possessed his wits. Without pausing to glance at Sitamun, he sprang to his feet. "Live forever, most glorious Pharaoh," he called, prostrating himself on the floor opposite the area where Menashe fretted over the fallen girl.

Distracted, Pharaoh turned toward him. "Who speaks now?"

Efrayim lifted his head and broke into an open, friendly smile. "I am Efrayim, the younger son of Zaphenath-paneah. I would beg you, divine king, for news of your new temple at Southern Opet. Since we have been away, I have not had an opportunity to visit the site."

Pharaoh tilted his head and smiled, warming to the subject of his beloved temple, and Efrayim knew the episode with Menashe would soon be forgotten. Next to beautiful women, Amenhotep loved building. The temple he had dedicated to Amon-Re was one of his favorite projects.

Pharaoh cast an approving glance at his vizier. "You have a most astute son." His dark eyes sparkled when he turned again to Efrayim. "I have recently commissioned artists to adorn the walls with reliefs depicting my birth and my royal parents," the king explained, shifting his weight in his chair and folding his arms. "Six statues, more colossal than any before built, will adorn the area leading to the second pylon…"

The king continued, unmindful of his guests' drooping eyelids, and Efrayim remained on his knees, ignoring the pain of his bones grinding against the hard tile floor. But though he kept his gaze fastened to the king's face, with his peripheral vision he could see Menashe lifting the harpist into his arms. Guided by the chironomist, he carried her away, safely out of sight.

Efrayim smothered a smile and lifted a brow as if vitally interested in the king's architectural plans. He had been hard on Menashe that last night in Canaan. Perhaps his jests had been too brutal. But he had imagined his brother the victim of a foolish infatuation, not sacrificial love.

Perhaps he'd been wrong. And if his penance was enduring a pair of bruised knees, he would suffer this small agony in silence.

A flurry of wild, improbable dreams assailed Jendayi, then awareness hit like a punch in the stomach. She thrashed, feeling unfamiliar hands on her arms, but a male voice thundered through her fear. "I won't hurt you," he said, and the pressure of his hands lifted.

Jendayi froze. Where—and with whom—was she? Panic like she'd never known before welled in her throat.

"You fainted." The man's voice was soft and eminently reasonable. "Akil has left me to take care of you." Jendayi shivered, slightly reassured. Akil would not leave her with a monster. This man had to be one of the servants, or perhaps one of Pharaoh's bodyguards.

Her memory returned with a rush and she cringed, imagining the scene she had just caused. She pressed her hand to her forehead. "Is Pharaoh very angry?"

"Pharaoh is—" she heard a smile in the slightly familiar voice *"—busy.* Efrayim has asked him about the work at the temple of Opet. By now Pharaoh has forgotten all about your unfortunate tumble."

Efrayim had come to her aid! She slid her hand down over her eyes, afraid that a sentimental tear might slip out and wend its way down her cheek. And she had imagined Efrayim cruel and flirtatious! He *did* care, or he would have simply gawked at her like the others. Instead he had risen to divert Pharaoh's mind from her folly; out of concern for her he had risked attracting Pharaoh's displeasure.

"Are you all right?" Her guardian's voice now seemed husky and golden and warm as the sun. He spoke with the clear accent of an educated nobleman, so he must have been raised in an important household.

"I am fine." She pressed her hands to the floor to push herself up. "It's just—" She paused, her head swimming with dizziness, and felt the warmth of his touch on her shoulders.

"Should I call the physicians?"

Despite her pain, she couldn't control a burst of laughter. What a joker this one was! As if the royal physicians would attend to a slave!

"Though I have heard your voice before, I don't believe I know you," she said, allowing him to help her upright. "But you are very kind to sit with me. I'm surprised Akil did not have me carted to the slaves' quarters and dumped on a mattress." She turned her face in his direction. "Do you work in Pharaoh's apartments? Queen Tiy's, perhaps?"

The stranger's gentle laugh rippled through the air. "I do not serve Pharaoh." His tone was slightly apologetic.

She paused. "The vizier, then. Are you of his household?"

"Yes." His words were clipped, exact. "I serve the vizier."

She caught her breath and forced her heart to remain calm. This man lived and worked in Zaphenath-paneah's household, so he might know the reasons behind Efrayim's reluctance to speak to Pharaoh. He might even be willing to carry a message for her.

"Will you tell me your name?" She tilted her head as if her sightless eyes could study his face. "I could use a friend at the vizier's house."

"You want me to be your friend?" Something caught in his voice.

"You seem to be the only one around." She gave him a dry smile. "Look about, do you see others here to help me? Even my maid has fled away, for they all think Pharaoh's wrath will descend any moment. As it would, if not for Efrayim—"

The words caught in her throat, and she pressed her fingers to her chin in a vain effort to stop it from trembling. The gods had spoken tonight. They had shown her that Efrayim did care. He was doubtless biding his time, weighing his options, trying to design a faultless plan with which he could bring her back to Zaphenath-paneah's house. Men had been killed for far less temerity than asking for one of Pharaoh's possessions. Efrayim had not yet acted because Zaphenath-paneah had warned him against such foolhardiness, or he was trying to discover another way to earn her freedom.

"I would be happy to be your friend, Jendayi." The stranger's voice was like a warm embrace in the vestibule's chilly air. "You seem to need one."

She turned toward him; something in his voice assured her he could be trusted. "Then, friend, since you know my name—" she smiled through the tears that stung her eyes "—tell me yours."

A long, careful silence followed. "The vizier's people know me by a Hebrew name, but you may call me Chenzira." She stiffened in surprise when his strong hand lifted hers and held it gently. "It's an Egyptian name meaning 'born on a journey.' But you probably knew that."

"I didn't." She closed her eyes and wished that the warmth against her palm had been provided by Efrayim's hand. "Were you born on a journey?"

"Yes," he answered, his voice as soft as a caress. "I think I was."

"Then, Chenzira, if you are my true friend, take this secret with you to the house of Zaphenath-paneah. If you have an opportunity, speak to Efrayim, the vizier's younger son, and offer him my life. Tell him I will serve him in any way I can, but I am waiting for him to take me from Pharaoh's house."

"Is life so hard in the palace?" His voice rang with doubt and something else—jealousy?

"Chenzira," she chided. "Pharaoh is no better or worse than any other master. But in the vizier's house I hope to find love."

His hand fell away from hers, and for a long moment she heard nothing, not even the sound of his breathing. Had she asked too much? Did he fear to carry such a personal message? A whisper of terror ran through her. Was she still dreaming? Would she awaken in a moment and discover that she had just confessed her innermost secrets to a spirit?

Abruptly thrusting out her hand, she felt the smooth bare skin of a man's chest beneath her fingertips. "I am still here." He spoke in a strained, yet gentle tone. "And you ask a lot of a man."

"I know." She lowered her eyes. "I know a slave should not

be so forward with his master. But if you will speak to Efrayim for me, I am certain he will not be displeased. He and I are…old friends." The memory of Ammit's gleaming eyes compelled her to explain. "I must keep his friendship or die forever."

Chenzira's hand squeezed hers. "I will do anything I can to help you, Jendayi."

Restless and irritable the next morning, Menashe paced in his small chamber and considered his options. Last night had been a dream and a nightmare, agony and ecstasy. He had never felt anything like the dizzying current that raced through him when he lifted Jendayi into his arms, nor had he ever been as stunned and sickened as in the moment when she confessed that she would give her life to serve Efrayim.

Once again, without even trying, Efrayim had wrested away something that rightfully belonged to Menashe.

Assailed by a bitter sense of injustice, Menashe sank onto his low bed and knocked a fist against his forehead. Had some evil priest put a curse on him? He could not think of anyone who hated him enough to invoke the forces of evil against him, but there had to be some reason for the incredible events of the past few months. Throughout his entire life he had been well liked, even spoiled, by his father's servants and Pharaoh's household. He was quick and capable, a little too sure, perhaps, of his position as the vizier's elder son, but he had never done anything to warrant the torment ripping at his heart.

He lifted his eyes to the high, narrow window that directed a sliver of sunlight into his small chamber. Even God Shaddai had worked against him. The god of Yisrael had spoken to him in a dream and then hardened the hearts of Yaakov's people.

Menashe ran his hands through his hair, weary of his dilemma. Why should he concern himself with thoughts of Canaan and God Shaddai? He had obviously been mistaken. He had experienced a strange dream invoked, no doubt, by the spirited stories of his uncles. What he took for inspiration was nothing more than the product of a vivid imagination. If God had wanted to give a message to the sons of Yisrael, He would have spoken to Yosef or one of the uncles, not to a dishonored elder son who knew less than any of the others about Avraham's Almighty God.

And Jendayi—Menashe covered his face with his hands. God's cruelest joke was that a slave girl who knew neither of Zaphenath-paneah's sons well had chosen to love the one least likely to return her devotion. Though last night she had been too shy and discreet to say the word *love,* now he knew her attachment to Efrayim went deeper than mere infatuation. She was obviously unhappy at the palace and desperate to return to the vizier's villa.

And he had promised to help her. Menashe supposed he could attempt to speak to his father to see if Pharaoh might trade another harpist for Jendayi, but wouldn't she be more deeply hurt by Efrayim's indifference if she had to encounter it every day? If she returned to the vizier's house and learned that Efrayim had never loved her, she would bear the same grief Menashe had come to know.

He laughed bitterly. Perhaps he would comfort her as the slave Chenzira. And if God was good—

What was he thinking? God was not good. God was a cruel trickster, a force beyond the strength of mortal men. Who would hope to win the struggle against Him?

"If you had only moved one of them to support me," he whispered, resting his heavy head in his hands. "Efrayim. Or my father. Anyone. But you have left me alone, and I cannot do what you asked of me."

The sun stood like a bright, baleful eye over the courtyard as Efrayim wiped a trickle of perspiration from his temple. Under Tarik's watchful eye, he lowered a shining blue-gray sword to the level of Menashe's chest and squinted down its length. "It is a good blade," he said, taking a practice thrust as Menashe leaped away. "But this iron is heavy. It will weary a man's arm faster than a copper sword."

"Heavier, yes, but the metal is strong enough to break a copper blade." Tarik thrust his own blade between the restless points of the brothers' weapons. "And iron is more valuable than silver. It is a precious rarity. I've heard that Pharaoh keeps an iron dagger by his bedside."

With graceful determination, Efrayim parried Tarik's blade and feinted to the right, then lunged to Menashe's left, lightly kissing the skin of his brother's rib cage with the sharpened point of the blade. Glancing down, Menashe let out an oath.

Efrayim grinned. "Do not drop your guard, brother, when I am armed." He tossed the sword to a servant who waited nearby. Sweat and blood from an earlier mishap soaked the hair of his own chest, and another slave handed him a square of linen to clean himself. "Tell me, Tarik—" he glanced at the captain as he toweled off "—which of us is the best swordsman?"

The guard pasted on a diplomatic smile. "You are equally good and equally headstrong." He took the sword from Menashe's hand. "But you have not been truly tried. What a man does in the practice ring, Efrayim, is not always what he will do on the field of battle."

The captain's wry remarks weren't enough to dispel Efrayim's good humor. He was about to taunt his disgruntled brother again when a slave from the gatekeeper's lodge sprinted toward them.

"Life, health and prosperity to you, my masters," the slave called, bowing from the waist. The man wore a grim expression, and when Efrayim glanced toward the parchment scroll in the slave's hand, he realized why—the scroll had been sealed with the imprint of the royal house. "The message—" the slave bowed again "—is for Efrayim, son of Zaphenath-paneah."

Tarik studied the outside of the scroll, then gave it to Efrayim. His expression stilled and grew serious. "I hope no trouble is stirring."

With a casualness Efrayim did not feel, he took the scroll and weighed it in his hand, considering what message it might contain. His father had just returned from the palace at Malkata, and he had not sent word of any matter that would concern Efrayim. So why had a message come from the palace?

Despite his nonchalance, his hand trembled as he broke open the seal. He was well aware that both Tarik and Menashe watched as he read the carefully penned hieroglyphs.

"My father and I—" he snatched a quick breath of relief as he looked up at Tarik "—are invited to the palace at Thebes tonight for a banquet given by Queen Tiy and Sitamun."

The captain lifted a brow. "Just the two of you?"

"Just two," Efrayim answered, realizing the significance of Tarik's question. He shot a glance at Menashe, whose expression had hardened to stony indifference. It was odd that the queen should not have invited both of them, but perhaps this banquet had been Sitamun's idea. If so, she certainly would not choose to invite dour and disapproving Menashe.

But Menashe would not understand. "If you, brother, had not begun to grow that filthy beard," Efrayim joked in an attempt to ease his brother's embarrassment, "perhaps the queen would look with more favor on you. I don't know why you insist on being as hairy as a common sheep herder—"

"I look like what we are," Menashe interrupted, one corner of his mouth twisting. "We are descended from sheep herders, Efrayim, there is nothing shameful in it. Avraham, Yitzhak and Yaakov all kept sheep—"

"Enough, please." Efrayim tossed the dirty towel to a waiting slave, then snapped his fingers at a young girl who waited with a pitcher of water. "You may be a shepherd if you want to—" he stooped as the silent girl poured water over his bare shoulders "—but I am the son of a vizier, and tonight I shall dine with a queen and a princess." He paused as another slave handed him a clean towel. "And there shall not be a sheep in sight."

Tiy sat in practiced repose, her hands clasped at her waist and her ankles crossed, while her thoughts raced like the wind. Her intimate dinner, quietly arranged in her own private chambers at the Theban palace, appeared to be a success. At the banquet to welcome the Hebrews back from Canaan she had watched to see which foods Zaphenath-paneah particularly enjoyed, and those dishes were spread before him now: honey-basted quail, sweet pomegranates, ethereally light shat cakes, melt-in-the-mouth lotus bread. The vizier, devastatingly handsome as always, sat at Tiy's right hand; Efrayim and Sitamun sat at her left.

The dinner conversation had been light and inconsequential. If either the vizier or his son wondered at the reason for this banquet, neither of them had expressed his curiosity. They spoke of Pharaoh's construction at Opet, the recent trip to Canaan and the remarkable beauty of the Nile at sunset. Though Tiy attempted to guide the conversation into more personal channels, the vizier remained annoyingly aloof. He deflected her praise for his thoroughness, attributing his success to Pharaoh's insight; he murmured that his abilities were not his at all, but blessings from his god. And always, no matter how closely she leaned toward him or how intently she tried to breach the wall behind those dark eyes, an air of isolation clung to his tall, majestic figure.

Her daughter, Tiy observed, was enjoying far more success with her suitor. Efrayim's nature seemed as full of sunshine as his looks. Sitamun, who was too frequently given to pouts and temper tantrums, laughed freely in the young man's presence. She seemed a bit in awe of him, and was perhaps a little confused by his easy charm. But the girl had been ruthlessly spoiled and she needed someone who could inspire her to admiration. When Tiy noticed Efrayim's gaze focusing on Sitamun's lips, she leaned toward her daughter and suggested that Efrayim might enjoy a tour of the royal gardens.

Sitamun lifted a brow; the idea pleased her. Without hesitation, Efrayim stood and offered his hand. The gallant gesture touched Tiy. Amenhotep had once behaved in such a way…a long time ago.

Zaphenath-paneah swiveled his head to keep the young couple in view. "Are you certain, my queen, they should venture out alone?"

"No one is alone here in the palace." Tiy shifted in her chair to face him. "There are too many guards and slaves, priests and royal relatives. It is impossible to be truly alone here…yet it is quite possible to be lonely."

As the two young people moved away through the open doors, Tiy clapped her hands. Slaves materialized from several doorways, and with a languid gesture she indicated the bowls and dishes of steaming food remaining on trays scattered around the room. "Away, all of it," she commanded. The slaves sprang into action.

"You have been very gracious, my queen." Zaphenath-paneah

folded his hands and looked at her with polite and tactfully in-curious eyes. "The dinner invitation was most kind. Of course, I imagine Sitamun prompted you to issue it."

Tiy smiled, waiting until the last servant had exited the chamber. When the drapery had fallen behind the departing slave's form, she lifted her chin and allowed the heavy weight of her beaded wig to pull her head back. "Sitamun did no prompting at all." She studied his face unhurriedly, feature by feature. His eyes fell beneath the power of her gaze, and she smiled. "Have you wondered, our noble vizier, what compelled me to bring you here tonight?"

He looked away with a smile that seemed almost boyish in its shyness. Did she detect a grain of softness in his granite strength? Had he suspected her secret motivations?

"I did not want to be presumptuous." A look of tenderness crossed his exquisite face as he glanced back at her. "But I did wonder if you were attempting a bit of matchmaking."

She laughed. Perhaps he had begun to understand.

She shifted so the length of her leg showed within the split in her fitted skirt. "Would the idea displease you?"

Zaphenath-paneah's gaze did not leave her face. "I would be pleased if our houses were joined." His expression softened into one of fond reminiscence. "Since I tutored Amenhotep, I have often felt like his father. So of course I am honored to think that his daughter, whom I hold in great affection, might possibly consider my son for a husband."

Tiy looked away so he would not read the depth of her true feelings. He had grasped only the obvious; he was not as intui-tive as she had hoped. What had happened to the vizier's vaunted powers of intuition and observation? Could he not see that she wanted to offer him much more than a royal daughter-in-law?

Perhaps this conversation was premature. He had grasped the obvious, and she should be satisfied. She could use the growing relationship between Sitamun and Efrayim as a foundation for the future. With adroit handling, Zaphenath-paneah could be won over, and as the steward Senenmut had enabled the queen Hatshepsut to rule as Pharaoh, Zaphenath-paneah would aid her. She would promise him anything, even herself, but one day he would see that Amenhotep was unfit for kingship, that *she* was the real power behind the throne.

"You are wise, as always, Zaphenath-paneah." She looked down at the floor and sighed. "And I am grateful for your influence on my husband's past. Yet Pharaoh is not the man you knew as a boy—but of course I do not have to tell you what you already know." She paused and looked away, allowing her eyes to dwell on the family paintings that lined the walls of her chamber—idealistic images that portrayed her and Amenhotep offering sacrifices to the gods. "Pharaoh cares for little these days but his harem and his building projects. Once he considered me the flower and joy of his youth, but—"

"He still cares deeply for you, my queen," Zaphenath-paneah dared to interrupt. She lifted a brow and stared in disbelief, but he continued. "He places more trust in you than he does most of his counselors. In fact—" he chuckled "—I daresay he trusts you almost as much as he trusts me."

"It is true that he allows me to handle a few ceremonial affairs," she admitted. "That is why I live here at Thebes. I am honored that he encourages me to meet with the governors and counselors who come to bring him tribute."

"So you see how much Pharaoh needs you." The vizier spread his hands. "He depends on you. So do not doubt his devotion, my queen."

"It is not his devotion I doubt." She lowered her voice. "It is his wisdom."

If this slender, delicate thread between them were to strengthen, she must not move too hastily. Zaphenath-paneah was doggedly loyal; he would resist any outright proposition if he sensed the seeds of betrayal. But despite his closed, aloof expression, she felt his vulnerability. He had no wife; he had not known the comfort of a woman's arms for years, yet he was still an attractive, compelling presence. The pull of his personality grew stronger every time she saw him, but she was another man's wife. She would have to tread carefully, for only by conclusively demonstrating Amenhotep's incompetence could she hope to win Zaphenath-paneah's support.

"I suppose a queen should not expect to be more involved

in the government of the kingdom," she murmured. "After all, Amenhotep has you to guide his decisions. But wisdom is acquired by capacity, not by gender. And like Hatshepsut, who ruled for Tuthmosis III when he was a child, I have a great capacity for learning."

Zaphenath-paneah shook his head. "I don't know that Hatshepsut actually *governed*—"

"Then you don't know our kingdom's history," she retorted, annoyed with the vizier's impenetrable equanimity. "I am sure you have heard that Hatshepsut was only Tuthmosis's regent, but she had herself declared Pharaoh, she assumed the royal beard of kingship and wore the full royal headdress. The high priest of Amon-Re supported her, as did others of the royal court."

"Then where," Zaphenath-paneah interrupted, "is her royal tomb? If she was so beloved, where are the shrines to perpetuate her name and memory?"

Tiy stared at him across a sudden ringing silence. "Hidden, mutilated or destroyed." She clipped her words. "Though she was a powerful pharaoh, she was not without enemies."

"No one is." The vizier gave her a smile that seemed more an automatic civility than an expression of pleasure.

"Thank you for listening to my concerns." She cut him off with a smile of gratitude, which he acknowledged with just the smallest softening of his eyes. At that moment, the happy voices of Sitamun and Efrayim danced into the room, and Zaphenath-paneah's posture relaxed.

Tiy studied the vizier's handsome profile as he greeted the two young ones. One day she would make him realize that Amenhotep cared nothing for Egypt. She would make a better ruler; she and the vizier would be an invincible team. Like Hatshepsut and Senenmut, they could grasp and hold the reins of power.

Satisfied with the seeds she had planted, she rose and abruptly wished her guests a safe and happy farewell.

Yosef sat alone under the small ox-hide canopy of the bark as it slipped along the dark Nile toward his house. The evening with Queen Tiy and Princess Sitamun had left him feeling strangely out of sorts, and he could not understand why events had unfolded as they did. He had not been surprised by the invitation to dine with the queen, for the attraction between Sitamun and Efrayim was obvious to anyone who watched them. The dinner itself had passed without any remarkable developments and Efrayim had been at his charming best.

But after dinner, when Tiy dismissed the young ones to the garden, the gleaming light of hunger in her eye had unnerved him. Her breath had quickened as she leaned toward him and spoke of her unhappiness with Amenhotep; what was he to make of that? He had faced an aggressive woman in Potiphar's house, and that situation nearly cost him his life. But he was no longer a handsome youth, and Tiy was no affection-starved maiden. She could not want an evening of love from him; she often denounced Amenhotep for spending too much time in such sensual pleasures.

So what drove her toward him? What had inspired the glitter in her jet-black eyes?

His gaze fell on the river. The water running alongside the boat was the color of tarnished silver, smooth and glassy in the moonlight. Efrayim stood at the curved bow, his hands tucked into the waistband of his kilt in a relaxed, familiar pose. When he lifted his face to study the eastern moon, his profile was so similar to his mother's that Yosef caught his breath. Asenath had been in her tomb eighteen years, but when that particular wistful expression crossed Efrayim's face, Yosef almost expected the boy to turn and speak with his mother's soothing voice. Asenath's sweet love had lightened Yosef's heavy load and helped him endure those first turbulent and trying years as vizier.

An odd twinge of jealousy and pain stirred in his heart when Yosef recognized the expression in Efrayim's eyes. Love, youthful and idealistic, filled Efrayim's gaze just as it had Asenath's, and Yosef felt an instant's squeezing hurt at the memory of how love had evolved into grief during his wife's lifetime. For him, Pharaoh's welfare had always come first. Yosef had guarded his heart even during his marriage; not since his encounter with Tuya had he completely abandoned himself to love, the most fickle and passionate of human emotions.

Tuya. Even now, her name brought a smile to his lips. He

had not spoken to her in years, though he knew she still lived in the immense palace at Thebes. She was, after all, Pharaoh's mother and a national treasure. Years ago, Yosef had asked her to become his second wife, but she had wisely refused. After that, he had taken pains to avoid her, to keep old memories and powerful passions safely tucked away. For Asenath's sake he had never invited Tuya to his house; for his own sake he had never sought Tuya at the palace. And after Asenath died, he waited, half hoping Tuya would send a message, but she did not. Apparently she was happy, so Yosef left her alone.

After the dark days, he delved into his work for Pharaoh, avoiding his empty house where Asenath's laughter echoed in the halls and her scent lingered on the bed linens. Efrayim and Menashe, the fruits of her womb, were content to follow Ani and Tarik through the villa, and the maidservants were eager to spoil them. Yosef's days brimmed with Pharaoh's work: dispensing judgments in the great hall, receiving and recording reports from the far-flung nomes and outlying military posts. Among other duties, Yosef was responsible for managing the royal residences, supervising the public works, directing the military police and Pharaoh's elite Medjay troops, commissioning the royal artisans, overseeing the royal farms and granaries, monitoring the distribution of food to the king's laborers and officials, and the collection of taxes. Except for the priests, every individual in Egypt was directly or indirectly responsible to the king's vizier, and there were days when Yosef felt he had talked to or heard from practically every soul in the kingdom.

The work consumed him, but it had its rewards, and chief among them was the salvation of his father's people. When Yisrael and his children entered Canaan, Yosef understood the reason for his personal suffering, his pain and desolation. God Shaddai allowed it all to strengthen him, to defeat his pride, to bring him to a place where he could lead. He had learned how to guide men…and how to forgive.

Now Yisrael was dead and the past forgiven—what work remained? For the first time in his life, Yosef felt drained and hollow. The god who had guided through dreams and whispered in a still, small voice had not spoken in years. What if He did not speak again?

The bow dipped and rose again in a sudden gust of wind, sending a cool splash of spray into the air. Yosef felt droplets touch his face as he closed his eyes and wearily considered his existence.

Chapter Fourteen

If he were to win Sitamun, Efrayim realized, he might need more than the support of his father and Queen Tiy. The opinions of many counselors would have to be considered in view of a royal marriage, and Sitamun's would be no different. Efrayim would have to prove to all of Egypt that a son of Yisrael could move confidently in Egyptian society.

During the weeks following Tiy's banquet, Efrayim wrangled invitations to nearly every gathering and social occasion in Thebes. The citizens of that city, who were naturally fond of entertainment, music and gaiety, opened their doors to him in surprised gratitude, allowing him to grace their gatherings with the aura of his father's illustrious name. Diligently courting noblemen and their wives, he reciprocated their hospitality by hosting a few festive banquets in his own quarters at his father's villa.

As part of his grand scheme, Efrayim sent gifts to the governors of Egypt's nomes and to the king's most trusted counselors. Knowing that no marriage would be possible without the approval of the priests, he culled a dozen of his father's finest cattle from the herd and ordered them to be delivered to the temple of Amon-Re. These things he did without his father's consent, but in full certainty that Yosef would delight in the result to come.

Each morning Efrayim anointed himself and painted his

eyes, then donned his wig, a finely pleated kilt and a volumi-
nous cloak. In the finest homes of the highest nobles, he danced
and drank and discussed life, love and politics with sagacity and
wit. He wrote sweet missives to Sitamun and ordered slaves to
deliver them straightway to the palace. And while he attacked
his work with steadfast determination, he noticed that his
brother, Menashe, grew more melancholy with each passing day.

More than happy to let his queen attend to the meaningless
ceremonies of state, Pharaoh remained at Malkata with his harem
while Tiy placated his counselors and officials. Zaphenath-
paneah was forced to divide his time between Malkata and
Thebes, spending half his day listening to the plans of the impetuous pharaoh and the other half tending to vital matters of
taxation, productivity and foreign affairs.

Every third day he reported to Tiy at the Theban palace, more
out of courtesy, Tiy supposed, than out of any conviction that
she would be able to offer real help or insight. The vizier was
yet a long way from where he must be, and yet she never failed
to feel her heart flutter when his tall, beautifully proportioned
body moved into the throne room. She took great care not to
open her countenance before the prying eyes of those who
waited before her, but spoke with Zaphenath-paneah in tones
of dignity and resolve. On the pretext of asking for his help, she
dictated letters to kings of other lands and arranged for the
giving and receiving of tribute between Pharaoh and several
fledgling city-states bordering the Great Sea.

She felt her mouth curve into a smile when the vizier informed
her she was the first queen whose name had ever been inscribed
on official acts. So he had finally noticed her ability! The letter
in his hand, to which he had just penned her name, was an announcement of the king's marriage to yet another foreign princess.

"Send that papyrus to Malkata with the others," she told
Zaphenath-paneah. A group of six scribes sat cross-legged on the
floor at her feet, recording every word she uttered. "And thank
the Mitanni king for the offer of his daughter. Assure him that
Pharaoh would be pleased to receive her as a bride, and she will
be treated with every kindness, given every luxury and so forth."

She waved her hand and Zaphenath-paneah nodded in approval. With that matter out of the way, she rested her elbows on the arms of her gilded chair and laced her fingers, eager to be done with the business that had filled the hall with scribes and onlookers. "If there is nothing else, you may all go." She clapped twice. "Except the king's vizier. I need a private word with you, Zaphenath-paneah."

The eyes of more than one curious counselor flitted in her direction as her coterie rose and filed out of the room. She kept a tight rein on her expression until only the vizier remained. Then Tiy inhaled, deepened her smile and tried to contain the eagerness in her voice.

"I have wanted, honest vizier, to discuss a certain matter with you."

He bowed his head, lowering his gaze. "I am your servant, my queen."

"This matter concerns your title." She rested her head on her cheek, hoping he would lift his eyes. "The title of vizier has always been conferred by the king. But I have been thinking—with the situation developing between our children, might the vizier's title become an inherited one?"

He looked up, honest surprise in his eyes. "Inherited?" His mouth curved into an unconscious smile.

"Yes." She sighed, pleased that she had managed to discover the flinty edge of ambition within the man's soul. "Your son Efrayim is a worthy young man, is he not? I have been hearing good things about his generosity and insight. And I imagine that he has been trained by the best tutors Egypt can offer."

"He has, my queen." A flush colored the vizier's cheek as he bowed his head again. "But my elder son, Menashe, stands to inherit—" He lifted his gaze. "My father knew."

She lifted her brows. "Your father knew what?"

"He crossed his arms." A spark of some indefinable emotion lit the vizier's eyes. "He placed his right hand on Efrayim's head and said the younger son would be greater than the elder."

"That is interesting, but what your father did does not matter here. I wanted you to know what I am considering…and of course, to hear your opinion." She paused as her gaze froze on his long, lean form. "Is this something that would please you?"

"Yes." He answered a little too eagerly, and bowed as if aware that he had stumbled. "If it is for Pharaoh's good, of course. I want only to serve him."

She felt blood coursing through her veins like the Nile in flood and she made no effort to hide the longing in her eyes. "Which do you desire to serve most—Pharaoh or his kingdom?"

He stiffened, but did not look away. "I have never considered the difference. Pharaoh is Egypt, is he not?"

"Is he?" Her brows lifted the question. "You have today signed my name to Pharaoh's documents, you have allowed me to use Pharaoh's seal because Pharaoh has given me his authority. If I am then equal to Pharaoh, and Pharaoh is equal to Egypt, then it follows that I, too, must be equal to Egypt."

His eyes gleamed toward her like glassy volcanic rock. "Your logic is sound."

Tiy closed her eyes. "I am glad to hear you say it." The fullness of time had not yet come, but it was approaching. "Thank you for your counsel, Zaphenath-paneah. You may go."

Yosef shifted uneasily in the litter that carried him through the streets of Thebes. The gauzy curtains did little to block the gray dust that rose from the pattering feet of the litter bearers, and the oppressive heat of the day weighed heavily on his damp skin.

More burdensome than the heat, however, was the queen's offer. Every father yearned for his son to follow in the path he had forged, and today Tiy had practically promised that Efrayim would marry a princess and be the king's next vizier. But at what price? He had been watching Tiy long enough to recognize her negotiating skills, but she did not bestow benefits without expecting something in return. She did not even make offerings to her gods unless they had met her expectations.

Still, Yosef found it interesting that she had suggested Efrayim, not Menashe, to be the next vizier. Her offer harmonized with Yisrael's blessing, so perhaps God Shaddai had revealed the future as Yaakov lay so close to death. God could certainly raise Efrayim to power in Egypt; the Almighty had worked a far greater miracle when He transferred Yosef from a prison to a throne. Nothing was too difficult for God Shaddai.

But the hungry look in Tiy's eye still troubled Yosef.

Chapter Fifteen

The orange-red sun had not risen far above the cloud-studded horizon when Jokim, his father and grandfather disembarked at a dock outside Thebes. They had spent the night on the river, so Jokim walked unevenly for several minutes, unused to the feel of solid earth beneath his feet. The hard-packed paths of Thebes did not rock and yield like the deck of the felucca they had boarded for the journey, and as he thumped over the ground he knew he would never become accustomed to the Egyptians' sea-going ways.

His father paused by a merchant's stall. "Shall you visit Efrayim now?"

Jokim nodded, unable to tear his eyes from the brilliant wares lined up like treasures. "I will find you tomorrow at the docks. I hope you have a profitable day of trading."

He walked away with a quick step that implied more confidence than he felt, for he still spoke very little Egyptian and understood even less. The Hebrews spoke the Canaanite tongue, and despite the influx of Egyptian brickmakers who were helping his relatives erect permanent housing, Jokim had not had many opportunities to practice the foreign language.

An obese, kilted merchant directed Jokim to the vizier's villa, a sprawling, pink-washed estate south of the city. As Jokim followed a winding path along the river's edge, he noticed that the cultivated acres outside the tall walls were lush with grain and ready for harvest. The vizier's herds dotted other fields, a testimony to Yosef's wealth and power.

But the villa held Jokim's attention most. He had spent his life in tents of canvas and leather, so the marble beauty of the elegant home rising from within painted walls left him breathless with admiration. Nervous flutterings tickled his chest as he approached the gatekeeper's lodge and hoped that Efrayim would be willing to welcome a long-lost country cousin.

For not only did he seek hospitality, but Jokim had been entrusted with a solemn responsibility. He prayed Efrayim would prove willing to help him bear it.

After greeting Jokim with an affectionate embrace, Menashe explained that Efrayim was away. Jokim stuttered in embarrassment as Yosef's elder son ordered a slave to wash his guest's feet and bring him a clean tunic, then commanded that fruit and fresh bread be supplied.

When they had settled in the privacy of Menashe's comfortable chamber, Jokim breakfasted on lotus bread, dates and wild honey while his cousin asked about the family in Goshen—what were the uncles doing now that Yaakov no longer lived? After a few moments of trivial talk, Menashe flushed and asked if anyone had spoken of returning to Canaan.

Was he still set on that topic? Jokim changed the subject, but frustration filled Menashe's face when Jokim mentioned the brickmakers, masons and builders that had poured into Goshen since the clan's return from the burial journey. "The older people are tired of living in tents," Jokim said. "They want something stable. Something better. And while none of them will build a home as grand as this one—" he gestured to the elegant house surrounding them "—would you begrudge them the right to have a proper roof over their heads?"

Menashe leaned forward. "I don't begrudge them anything. I just hate to see them put roots into the soil of Goshen. It is not the land of promise. It is not where God wants us. But apparently no one wants to obey God Shaddai."

Jokim swallowed a stubborn lump of bread that had lodged in his throat. "So you have said." He did not want to tell his cousin that uncles frequently joked about Menashe's speech in the wilderness, mocking him as a youngster with hot blood, the one who would rush in and claim the promised land all by himself.

"Perhaps you should try to understand the others," Jokim said, reaching for a cup on a nearby tray. "You have lived here in splendor while they have lived in dust and dirt. Now they want the feel of stone under their feet. And many of them, my father included, insist that if God wants us to dwell in Canaan, nothing will prevent us from dwelling there."

Menashe's face darkened. "Do they expect God to pluck us up and drop us back into our homeland? God has told us what He wants. He gave the message to Avraham, Yitzhak, Yaakov and me! But our people do not want what God wants. They want an easy life in the Black Land where food is plentiful and comforts abound. They want brick houses and stone floors."

Jokim took another bite of the delicious bread and told himself to keep quiet. He had been warned that Menashe was like a young lion roaring after his prey. Though he yearned for the glory of the hunt, he would not be prepared for the effort of the kill.

He would say nothing else until he'd had a chance to talk to Efrayim. If Efrayim truly was the greater of the two brothers, he would be more suitable for the task ahead.

"Jokim!" Perfumed and staggering, Efrayim entered the room and held out his arms. "What a wonderful surprise!"

Menashe felt his stomach churn as the cousins embraced. Efrayim was drunk again, and the day not half spent. In the past few weeks he had changed. Though Menashe was not certain what motivated his brother's newly hedonistic lifestyle, he could guess at a reason or two.

Efrayim fell into a chair near Jokim, hooked one leg over the armrest and grinned at his guest. "We must celebrate your arrival. We will show you the city, take you to a few entertainments. Thebes is a magnificent place. The temples alone will make your eyeballs bulge from your head. And the women—beautiful!"

"I'd like to see a few things." Jokim smiled, then turned toward Menashe. "Will you come with us?"

Menashe shook his head. The last thing he wanted was to accompany Efrayim on a jaunt around the city.

A devilish look gleamed in Efrayim's eyes. "We'll have more fun if we leave my brother behind."

Obviously, Jokim did not want to venture forth with a drunken kinsman. "Please come, Menashe."

Menashe sighed and gripped the armrests of his chair. "I'll come, but we will not stay out long. And we will not go to any of your friends' parties."

Efrayim closed his eyes, then lifted a hand and shook it as if waving farewell to a host of people he would not be seeing. "We won't take the cousin to the parties. I promise."

Biting his lip, Menashe looked at Jokim, then jerked his head toward the doorway. "Let's go."

The pharaohs of the eighteenth dynasty had lavished considerable care and wealth on Thebes. The shrines, temples and buildings erected during this dynasty alone had earned the city a reputation for splendor and beauty that would last for centuries. Flanked on the west by a two-mile-long prominence of cliffs that formed a backdrop for the small valleys and plains sprinkled with the tombs of the dead, the living city lay to the east of the river and pulsed with life even in the heat of the afternoon.

Efrayim and Menashe led their disconcerted kinsman through a maze of winding paths in the heart of the capital, occasionally stopping to point out a spectacular statue, temple or a favorite merchant's stall. Efrayim, Menashe noticed, seemed to walk more steadily than he had at the villa, and Menashe hoped that the morning's beer had finally left his brother's system. The Egyptians drank only water, beer or wine, and Efrayim's free-wheeling friends favored the strong black beer that flowed like water at parties, regardless of the hour of the day.

They wandered through the city for more than three hours, Menashe dutifully following his brother and cousin while Jokim listened to Efrayim point out one architectural wonder after another. "There are hundreds of temples at Thebes," Efrayim boasted, gesturing around him. "Probably more than any place on earth. The temple of Amon-Re is the largest in the world."

"And yet there are no temples to El Shaddai," Jokim observed.

Menashe thought the remark would offend Efrayim's proud sensibilities, but his brother only grinned. "Why does an invisible god need a temple?" He lifted his shoulders in a shrug. "What are you going to put in it? Nothing! Why does nothing need a temple?"

"God Shaddai is not a nothing," Menashe muttered. Though he'd had his own doubts recently about God Shaddai's wisdom and purpose, Efrayim's flippancy galled him.

"I didn't say *He* was nothing." Efrayim pressed his hand to his chest and smiled as though out of pity for Menashe. "I said His temple would *hold* nothing."

The sun had begun to sink toward the west when Menashe gestured toward the river, hoping to lead his brother and cousin home. Jokim's tongue had loosened in the past hour, his previous awe and astonishment evolving into open admiration of the confident way his cousins moved about the city. Jokim was in the midst of explaining his father's reluctance to enter the foreign marketplace when a shadow fell across the path.

Menashe looked up, annoyed that someone else had entered the conspiracy to ruin his day. His frown faded, however, when he saw the hulking brute who had blocked the sun. The interloper wore the distinctive kilt and leopard-skin belt of one of Pharaoh's elite guards. He had probably come to Thebes from Malkata on a pass of some sort, but by the sour look on the man's face Menashe knew his holiday had not been pleasant.

"Ho! You river rats!" The man swayed drunkenly as he pulled a sword from its scabbard. His sour breath blew over them like a fetid breeze. "You'll not pass by me until you swear allegiance to my patron goddess. Nut's her name!"

With his free hand the barbarian pointed to a small stone statue by the tavern doorway. Menashe frowned; the statue depicted a woman wearing a sun disk and cow horns; it was the image of Hathor, not Nut. But this inebriated ruffian was in no condition to know the difference.

Jokim paled immediately and withdrew, cowering behind Efrayim's shoulder. The Hebrew was at a distinct disadvantage since he couldn't understand the slurred words of the drunk Egyptian.

Keeping his voice calm and steady, Menashe placed his hands on his hips. "Let us pass, friend. We will not give you trouble, but neither will we bow to an idol."

"You will." A vein in the warrior's forehead swelled like a thick, black snake. "Nut demands it."

"We will not," Menashe answered. He glanced around for a weapon, but saw nothing. He had no dagger in his belt, no club in his hand. Even Jokim's shepherd's staff would have been useful, but he had left it at the villa, not expecting this sort of harassment.

"Can I help?" Jokim asked in a low murmur. "I know trouble when I see it, and I have fought before. If he is determined to confront us—"

"He will let us pass." Menashe answered in Egyptian, raising his voice so the soldier could hear. "As Pharaoh lives, this man has no reason to detain us."

"A pox on the life of Pharaoh!" the warrior roared, waving his sword. Menashe cast a quick glance at Efrayim. The man was either out of his mind or senseless, for no one, especially a guard in Pharaoh's service, could curse the king and expect to live. If anyone else heard him—

"I can settle this." Efrayim advanced with a casual smile. "I would be happy to bow before Hathor—or Nut. Just clear me a space, will you?"

"Efrayim!" Menashe barked, disbelieving.

"Hush, brother, I'm going to bow." Efrayim kicked a pebble out of his way, then fell to his knees on the path. Mindless of his spotless white kilt, he sprawled in the road, extending his arms toward the stone statue and pressing his face to the dirt.

Menashe gaped in total incredulity, then realized that the warrior was staring as well. Menashe stepped forward, reached up and twined his hand in the savage's hair, then brought the man's head down to his own uplifted knee. The sudden, surprising blow knocked the last vestige of understanding from the savage's clouded brain. He staggered backward and collapsed unconscious in the pathway.

"Come!" Menashe grabbed Jokim's elbow and pulled his cousin toward home. Efrayim rose from his place in the dirt and ran to catch up with them, laughing as he sprinted toward home.

* * *

After dinner with the vizier and the chief servants of his household, Menashe said goodnight to his cousin, brother and father. He had scarcely lain in bed five minutes when a soft rap sounded on his door.

He sat up, alarmed. "Yes?"

"May I speak with you?" The words were Hebrew, the voice soft and conspiratorial. Menashe tossed off his linen sheet and padded to the door. Jokim stood there, his eyes glowing with a sheen of purpose. Menashe invited him in and directed him to a chair while he lit a lamp.

He took a chair opposite Jokim. "What is so important we could not discuss it this afternoon?"

A flush ran like a shadow over Jokim's tanned face. "This afternoon," he said, his dark, earnest eyes seeking Menashe's. "I saw something I never expected to see."

"A drunken fool?" Menashe laughed. "There is one on every street corner in Thebes. I am used to them."

Jokim used his finger to dash small sparkles of sweat from his forehead, then folded his hands and leaned forward. "Today I saw a son of Avraham bow down to a stone idol. *That* I never expected to see."

"Ah." Menashe slid down in his chair and rubbed the back of his neck. "Don't judge Efrayim too severely. His action was part of a ruse to help us escape. And his plan worked. We caught the drunken fool off guard and no one was seriously hurt. The afternoon could have ended quite differently."

"But you wouldn't have done what he did." Jokim's eyes were sharp and assessing. "I would not have done it. And neither would I have called God Shaddai 'nothing.'"

Menashe rested his head on his hand. "Maybe I wouldn't have bowed. But Efrayim doesn't worship idols. And he wasn't thinking clearly today, so his words were not what they should have been. I can assure you that he is not always so frivolous."

"He doesn't worship idols *now*. But we have heard things. Last week a trader told us that a dozen cattle branded with the vizier's mark had been offered to the priests of Amon-Re. My grandfather, Yehuda, said the man had to be mistaken, but the trader insisted he spoke the truth. My father was certain your father had been robbed—either that, or someone from the villa pulled the cattle from Yosef's herds."

"Impossible." Menashe shot Jokim a penetrating look, then rose from his chair and paced in the room. "That makes no sense. My father, Efrayim and I worship El Shaddai and Him alone. We have never sent offerings to any of the temples. But these things are easy to check. If cattle were taken to the temple, the steward will have a record of it."

Jokim nodded, but an almost imperceptible note of pleading remained on his face.

"There is something else?"

Jokim studied Menashe intently, then he continued. "I was not completely honest with you this morning when we spoke. I told you the old ones are content to remain in Goshen, and that much was true." A strange, faintly eager look flashed in his eyes. "But there are many of us, mostly young men, who are ready to return to Canaan."

Menashe let out a snort of disbelief. "No one listened to me in the wilderness. Why should you heed my words now?"

"You caught us by surprise, and we were silenced by the elders. But since we have returned to Egypt, we have seen our fathers cast off our way of life as easily as they disposed of their worn-out tents. They are old and tired, and they are resting on your father's promise to take care of them. They are depending on Yosef, the almighty vizier, instead of the Almighty God. And so we, their sons and grandsons, find that it is up to us to lead the return."

Menashe felt his knees weaken. Was this another cruel jest, or had God finally decided to equip him for the task ahead?

The memory of his own words passed through him like an unwelcome chill. *"If you had only moved one of them to support me,"* he had prayed. He had imagined himself alone and helpless, and all the while God had been working in hearts unknown to Menashe…

He sank into his chair and fixed Jokim in a steady gaze. "You are ready to go back? But now we have nothing. Before we had chariots, horses, warriors—"

"We can get those things." Jokim's eyes darkened. "We can get horses and camels, and already we have begun to talk to some of the border guards. For a price, they will join our company and fight with us."

"But we have nothing with which to pay them."

"We will have the spoils of Gerar, Gaza and Ashkelon. They will fight for the promise of riches."

The words rang in Menashe's head like a clanging brass gong. He would win spoils in the battle—riches he could use to buy another harpist, some man or woman he could present to Pharaoh in exchange for Jendayi. He wouldn't need to trade on his father's influence, nor would he have to bring her back to live in his father's house. He would take her to Canaan, where they could be married...

God Shaddai had not left him hopeless.

"We will have to train in a safe place," Menashe murmured, his thoughts racing along the track he had abandoned weeks before. "On the edge of the wilderness near Tura Quarry, my father has a house we can use as a base. It is isolated. He has not visited it in years."

"I had hoped we could count on you." A faint light twinkled in the depths of Jokim's black eyes. "The others thought Efrayim would be the one to lead us, but this afternoon I realized you are the one God has prepared. You know the Egyptians and the Hebrews, you can give us straight talk and simple answers. You, Menashe, are the one we need. Say you will come and help us, and we will follow you back to Canaan."

In that instant, Menashe's resolve to forget the past shattered. A sense of fulfillment flooded his soul as his doubts vanished. God Shaddai *had* called him. Here was another proof of the call.

Feeling alive for the first time in weeks, Menashe extended his hand to Jokim. "On his deathbed, Yisrael proclaimed that we would return to the land of our fathers. I will come to you soon, so prepare the others. And may God lead us home."

"He will." Jokim stood and clasped Menashe's arm. His voice rang with confidence. "Let the others do what they will, but we shall obey the will of God Shaddai."

Zaphenath-paneah

And Joshua said unto the children of Yisrael, How long
are ye slack to go to possess the land, which the LORD
God of your fathers hath given you?

Joshua 18:3

Chapter Sixteen

No element distinguished Pharaoh from the common man more than stone. Like other pharaohs before him, Amenhotep knew the magic of enduring stone would enable his name to live forever. To achieve that end, he secured the quarries that provided raw materials for statues, temples and pillars that would bear his name throughout generations to come.

Tura Quarry stood behind the green belt of the Nile like an aloof, august presence. Menashe paused on the trail that led to the quarry and gazed up at the chiseled cliffs from which ancient Egyptians had dug limestone for the casing of Cheops's pyramid. A score of slaves moved like ants over the cinnabar-colored walls, cutting stone for Pharaoh's latest project. A wagon loaded with meat, bread and drink tottered along the path leading into the quarry, and under a faded canopy near the gate a group of scribes sat cross-legged in a shady spot, each man's parchments resting on the taut spread of his kilt as he recorded his share of the daily business. The air vibrated with the incessant *tap tap tap* of the workers' hammers, keeping time with the heightened pounding of Menashe's heart.

A short distance away, south of the quarry but separated from the river by a rocky ridge, a whitewashed, pillared building stood out like a beacon in the midst of the crimson hills. Menashe pointed to it.

"You are right, cousin." Jokim's eyes narrowed as he followed his cousin's finger. "It is perfect. Isolated and quiet."

"My father used to stay there when he was required to supervise projects at the quarry." Menashe lowered his arm. "No one will think it strange that I am here...or that a few of my relatives have come to join me."

"But not your brother," Jokim murmured.

"No. Not Efrayim."

Before leaving his father's villa, he and Jokim had asked Ani about the vizier's cattle being accepted at Egyptian temples. To Menashe's horror, Ani confessed that Efrayim had ordered that two dozen of the finest beasts be sacrificed at the leading temples of Thebes and Heliopolis.

A tumble of confused feelings assailed Menashe at the thought of Efrayim's disloyalty. Had he no faith in El Shaddai? Was he so determined to remain in Egypt that he wished to placate a host of false priests?

Sickened by the struggle within him, Menashe turned his thoughts from his brother and gave his cousin a troubled smile. "It is good there are many who will join us. Efrayim must make his own decisions."

Behind him, Tarik broke into the conversation with a discreet servant's cough. "May I inquire," he asked when Menashe turned, "how long you intend to stay here? Your father will want to know."

Menashe studied the rocky hills and felt the power of the secluded spot. "You need not say anything to my father," he said, closing his eyes against the sun's brightness on the gleaming cliffs. "I doubt he will notice I am gone."

Even with his eyes closed, Menashe could sense Tarik's hesitation. The stalwart captain still tended to think of Menashe as an untried youth unable to spend a night unguarded and away from home...

"You will be quite alone in this place," Tarik said, confirming Menashe's suspicion. "If you are only planning to stay one night, why don't I remain with you? We can take the felucca back in the morning—"

"I would not keep you from your duties." Menashe opened

his eyes and turned, easing into a smile. "Besides, you taught me how to defend myself. Do not worry. No harm will befall us here."

Tarik inclined his head, but apprehension still flickered in his dark eyes. "Menashe—" he lowered his gaze "—can you not tell me what you intend to do out here? It has been my duty and privilege to protect you since the day you came into this world—"

"And it has been my privilege to have you as my guardian." Menashe lowered his hand to the man's shoulder and stooped to look into the shorter man's face. "But you, Tarik, are sworn first and foremost to serve my father, and I am not certain he will understand what Jokim and I intend to do. So if you do not know what we intend, your loyalties cannot be divided."

"Perhaps they already are." Tarik's jaw tensed, betraying his deep frustration, but he did not argue further. Instead he gestured toward a pair of servants who lingered on the trail. "Come," he called over his shoulder, not taking his eyes from Menashe's. "Take the supplies into the house. Then we must return to Thebes."

"Thank you, Tarik." Menashe shifted his hands to his hips as the servants drove the supply wagon toward the house. "I shall not forget your help."

"Grant me one request," the captain said, stopping in mid-stride. His brow furrowed as he hesitated, then a rush of words poured forth. "I don't know what you are planning—and I shall not ask—but if you should need help, there is a warrior at Malkata who might be willing to assist you. His name is Abnu, and he is a friend. He owes me a debt, and I give you permission to claim it."

Menashe grinned. "What is he? A guard of the royal harem?"

Tarik's mouth twisted in a wry smile. "He is a giant. A Medjay warrior. Sometimes he fights for Pharaoh's entertainment, yet I heard he was tiring of the sport, for he always wins. But he enjoys an adventure, so remember his name. He would enjoy this one, I think."

"A giant?" Menashe squinted. "When did you keep company with a giant?"

"My life did not begin with you, young master." The captain's brittle smile softened. "But the past is only important if it can be of use to your future. Call on Abnu if you need a strong arm. And may your father's god give you wisdom in the days ahead."

Tura lay a full day's river journey north of Thebes, but was only an hour's camel ride from the Hebrew camp at Goshen. After depositing their supplies in the deserted house, Menashe and Jokim bid Tarik farewell, then walked to the quarry to bargain with the overseer. The old man in charge of the stone-cutters fell to his knees as soon as he recognized Menashe, and Menashe felt his face color as the man groveled in the dust. Though he was accustomed to displays of respect from common folk, in Jokim's presence the man's obsequiousness embarrassed him.

"Rise, friend." Menashe extended a hand. "You should bow to the vizier, but I am only his son. If you are willing to be of service, however, my kinsman and I are in need of a camel—two, if you can spare them."

"For you, son of Zaphenath-paneah, we can spare anything," the man said, his grin toothless and stained in the midst of a ruddy face. He rose and squinted at Jokim, then his head bobbed like a cork on the Nile. "Two camels, yes, you may take my own. They should serve you quite well."

"We'll only need them a day or two." Menashe rested his hands on his hips. "I do not want to inconvenience you."

"Two days, two weeks, it is all the same to me." The old man bobbed again. "Where am I going? Nowhere. Take them, with any of my slaves you might require. I have a daughter, too, if you're interested—"

"No, thank you," Menashe interrupted. "We need the camels only."

Later, perched atop a gurgling, growling beast that moved with long strides across the silent sands, Menashe dropped the reins on his thoughts and let them wander freely. Solitude was a rare commodity in crowded Thebes, and especially precious to one who had come from the bustling vizier's household. Here in the wilderness he found it almost possible to forget who and what he was. In Egypt men bowed and scraped before him because they knew him to be the vizier's elder son. What a joke! Yisrael, the one whose opinion mattered most, had seen Menashe as inferior. And Yosef, who could have rebuilt the foundation of Menashe's self-confidence with a blessing of his own, seemed content to continue about Pharaoh's business. He spent the bulk of his time and energy on Amenhotep, apparently satisfied to ignore his sons and allow his brothers to remain in a land to which they could never belong.

A fierce, steady wind shrilled southward, blowing up clouds of sand that scraped Menashe's arms and legs. He lowered his head, delighted to let his cousin lead the way back to Goshen. Jokim, like the other Hebrews, was accustomed to the desert. Menashe knew he had much to learn, including how to dress. Like most other Egyptian nobles, he wore only a kilt, a cloak and a wide collar, and he found himself wishing he had donned a long tunic and head covering like the one Jokim wore. The scraggly beard he had begun to grow as a symbol of identification with his Hebrew brethren was not yet full enough to prevent the sand from scouring his neck.

If he was going to lead his people back to Canaan, he would have to dress, talk and think the way they did. They would follow a son of Yosef, but only if he behaved as a Hebrew.

After arriving in Goshen, Jokim led Menashe to his father's tent, then went in search of the men who had sent him to Thebes. Shela's tent stood empty when Menashe entered, so he sank onto a stool, then ran his hand over his face and tasted sand on his lips. Was there an inch of his body not covered with grit?

A flapping noise startled him, and he looked up to see a young girl standing in the tent's opening. She carried a pitcher of water in her arms.

"Jokim said you would want to wash your hands and face," she said, speaking Hebrew in a delicate whisper. She was a willowy creature, more child than woman, but the potential for loveliness was evident in her form and the elegant curve of her cheek. Her thick, dark hair hung in long, graceful curves over her shoulders, and the hands that held the pitcher were delicate and long-fingered.

She has Jendayi's hands, Menashe thought, his greeting sticking in his throat.

Seeing him hesitate, the girl lifted a brow. Menashe flushed and he cleared his throat. "Yes, I would like to wash."

"Hold out your hands." He obeyed, and with the glee of a small child she tipped the unwieldy pitcher, allowing a stream of water to splatter on his hot, dusty palms. The liquid felt wonderfully cool and cleansing. He looked up to smile his thanks.

She lowered the pitcher to the ground and wiped her hands on her tunic. Then, staring at him with curiosity, she leaned against a tent pole and thrust her hands behind her back. "Jokim says you are here to talk to his friends."

"That's right."

"He says I am not allowed to listen."

Menashe ran his hand over his mouth, hiding a smile. "Does the conversation of men interest you?"

She pulled her lips into a round rosette. "Not always. But it is not every day that *you* come to Goshen."

Was he the "vizier's son" even here? His good humor evaporated. "I am afraid you might be disappointed if you listened to us," he said. "We will not be discussing topics to entertain a child. And if you want to meet the vizier's son, go to Thebes. The better one is there."

"I'm not a little girl. I'm fifteen." Her dark eyes boldly met his. "You are as bad as Jokim, thinking of me as a girl. And what is the Egyptian vizier to me? Nothing. We are the children of Yisrael. Jokim says we are going back to Canaan, so I wanted to meet the man who will help us go."

She lunged toward the doorway, but Menashe caught her arm. "Wait." His mind bulged with questions. "You know about our plan? And you want to go back?"

"Jokim tells me everything." Anger edged her voice as she jerked from his grasp. "And I know enough to keep quiet. Father does not want to talk about leaving Goshen, and neither does Grandfather. They are surveying land right now, deciding where they should build their houses and pen their animals. My mother is with them, her head spinning with dreams of the jewels she will buy and the garments she will make. They want to stay here, but I do not. I am ready to go back to Canaan."

"But why? You are too young to have memories of the place." Menashe marveled that so small a frame could contain so fierce a spirit. "How do you know you will like Canaan?"

A flush rose on her cheekbones. "How does the eagle know how to fly?" She lifted her chin and stood on tiptoe, bringing her lips to within inches of his ear. "He hears the voice of God Shaddai."

Before Menashe could react, she whirled and raced through the tent opening. He started forward, intent on catching her, but Jokim blocked his path. He watched the girl go, and a wry grin split his face as he turned back to Menashe.

"I see you've met Atara." He sighed in mock heaviness. "It was all I could do to keep her at home when I left for Thebes. She wants very much to be a part of all this."

"She is your betrothed?" Menashe asked, staring after the girl's willowy form as she threaded her way through a huddle of women around a cooking fire.

"By heaven, no, and I pity the man who marries her. She is my sister—my curious, mischievous little sister." He clapped a hand on Menashe's shoulder, and when he spoke again his voice was lower and more intense. "The others are waiting outside the camp, in a wadi a short distance away. We cannot meet here, too many of those who disapprove would notice. We are trying to keep peace with our fathers, so we do not speak openly of our plans."

Shaking all thoughts of the girl from his mind, Menashe followed Jokim from the tent.

Nearly forty men had gathered in the dry streambed where Jokim led him. They sat on stones and various outcroppings of rock, and Menashe was pleased to see that most of them wore a look of determination. They were the new generation; most were his age or a few years older. These were the grandchildren and great-grandchildren of Yaakov, and they were eager to find their places in the land God had promised to His people.

Jokim led Menashe through the waiting Hebrews, then gave

a swift introduction. "Brothers and kinsmen, I am certain you remember Menashe, son of Yosef. When I went to Thebes I was certain God had sent me to bring Efrayim back to you, but God showed me *this* is the man to lead us. Listen to him, my brothers, as you once listened to his father and his father's father. For I am convinced God would have us journey back to Canaan. Menashe heard the voice of God Shaddai. He is the man to take us home."

Without further ceremony Jokim sank to a rock and looked to Menashe, his eyes alight. Menashe felt his mouth go dry as he looked at the crowd of bearded faces, remembering the last time he stood before his Hebrew relatives. On that morning he had proclaimed his dream and they had mocked him. But these few, at least, had carried his conviction with them.

He searched for words and found none, but God had promised to provide all he would need to obey. *What I need now, God Shaddai, is the gift of persuasion.*

"Kinsmen—" he spread his hands "—I stand before you dressed like an Egyptian because this is the land that gave me birth. But unless we leave this place, all men of Yisrael will look as I do within a few years. Our people will forget the promises of God, we will forget God himself. And the land that now binds us with goodness and generosity will bind us with chains and whips."

One man lifted his fist in protest. "No!"

"Never!" echoed another voice.

"It could happen," Menashe said, with a cautionary lift of his hand. "My father and my brother and I live according to the truth of God Shaddai. There are no idols in our house, but anything we serve more than God—whether it is a habit, an idol or a kingdom—will eventually enslave us. If our people begin to love and serve Egypt, they will be imprisoned. Hear me, for I speak God's truth."

"How could such a thing happen?" one young man shouted. He leaped to his feet and threw his hands up, fists balled. "The sons of Yisrael are not idol worshippers."

Jokim moved to the empty space between Menashe and the young man. "This is Hezron, son of Perez, son of Yehuda." Jokim turned to the audience and spread his arms in an expansive gesture. "We think we will never change, that we would never forget the god of our fathers," he called, his jaw tightening. "But though we love God Shaddai and our fathers have taught us truth, we cannot be sure our children will not be affected by the evil in Egypt. Just yesterday I watched Efrayim, who was elected to stand with Yaakov's own sons in the inheritance, bow before an idol. He committed the act in jest, but how do we know today's jests will not be tomorrow's practices?"

Menashe felt his cheeks burn for his brother's sake, but a hushed silence fell over the group. Hezron sat down.

Jokim hitched his thumbs in the woven belt at his waist. "Menashe is true to us and our god, and he knows the Egyptians. He has sympathetic friends in high places. With his help we can gather horses, chariots, weapons—all we will need to retake our land."

"But look at us," another voice called. A gangly youth with a blotchy face stood and lifted his thin arms. "There are scarcely forty of us, and there are thousands of Canaanites between Goshen and Hebron. Even if we had control of Pharaoh's army—"

"We might have the army, or at least part of it," Menashe interrupted. "The border police are mercenaries paid by Pharaoh to guard his borders. They will fight for any cause so long as they are compensated. They will join us if we guarantee them a part of the spoils."

"But we are not warriors." Another young man looked at Menashe with something fragile in his eyes. "I am Zimri, son of Zerah, son of Yehuda. I am a goat herder, but the goats stay close to the camp. I have never even fought a wild animal, so how am I to fight a Canaanite warrior?"

Menashe felt his heart swell. The youth had the mild eyes of a man who should grow old sitting quietly in his own house, but if God could use Yaakov, the trickster, He could use anyone willing.

"Zimri—" Menashe gentled his voice "—I will teach you all you need to know. My father's captain taught me swordplay and charioteering. I can hurl a spear with deadly accuracy, and I can teach you to do the same. Have no fear, cousin. If God is on our side, who can stand against us?"

Menashe folded his arms across his chest. "We may not have to kill. If we are bold, we will march first on the small settlement of Gerar. Those men will flee rather than fight. But we will take the city, and the inhabitants of Gaza will hear of it. When we move northward, the men of Gaza will flee to Ashkelon, and the word of our force will grow. We will tell any who listens that we come in peace and want nothing more than to return to our homeland."

Silence. They sat and stared at him, thinking.

"How many mercenaries might we enlist?" Hezron asked.

"One hundred, perhaps two hundred." Menashe unfolded his arms. "And they are skilled in combat."

Another moment of silence passed, then Menashe nodded and swept his audience with a piercing glance. "I have secured a place, a house outside the quarry at Tura. No one will notice us there, and we will have the entire desert in which to train. The overseer of the quarry will provide all we need, for he wants to remain in my father's good graces. As soon as we are settled, I will send word to the captain of the border guards. We should have his answer within a few days."

"One more thing!"

Menashe lifted his head. Hezron stood again, an implacable expression on his face. "How can we know—" he turned to face the others "—that God Shaddai is on our side? That we are following His will?"

Forty pairs of questioning eyes shifted to Menashe, arousing his old fears and uncertainties. "Did God not tell our father Avraham that Canaan was the promised land?" Menashe asked, his voice calm, his gaze steady. "Did God not tell Yaakov to fear not to descend into Egypt, for He would preserve us and make us a great nation here?"

"Yes," came the murmured reply from a dozen throats.

"Can you think of any reason why God would want us to stay here?"

The only answer was the moaning of the wind over the wadi.

"God has preserved us," Menashe said. "He has made us a great nation. And now it is not a question of whether or not God wills for us to reenter Canaan, but whether or not we are willing to obey Him. Are we willing to be obedient? Are we willing to march into the land He has promised?"

"Yes!"

"I am!"

"I am ready!"

"Hear him!" Jokim shot his fist into the air. "Now, kinsmen, go home to your families and take your leave. Bid your fathers and mothers goodbye, kiss your sisters farewell. But tell no man where we are going or what we are doing. The old ones disapprove, the women will weep and wail. But we will not be deterred."

As one, the group lifted their voices in a determined roar.

Menashe smiled as the hired warrior fell to the dirt, a trickle of blood streaking across his cheek. Hezron managed the battle-ax very well, especially when Menashe considered that the Hebrew had only been introduced to the weapon two weeks before.

"Very good." Menashe thrust his hands behind his back as he nodded. The burly shepherd extended his hand to help the warrior, one of the border mercenaries, to his feet. "You have caught the idea."

"You should not be surprised," Hezron answered, chuckling. "A battle-ax is nothing but a shepherd's staff with a blade attached. In the wilderness my brothers and I have battled far worse than this Nubian. Once a bear attacked me when I had nothing but a staff to defend myself. Another time Hamul used the sharpened point of his staff to kill a pair of Philistines who came on him in the night."

Menashe bit down hard on his lower lip, determined not to defend himself in front of these men. He had never intended to imply that they were less skilled than he, but animosity had flared toward him several times. Peace was not easily kept among men who purposely worked themselves into the frenzy of combat, and not all the Hebrews were ready to accept a leader who was so…Egyptian.

He turned and walked to the circle where Zimri and Shallum were involved in a wrestling match. Several of the others had gathered to watch, and Menashe found Jokim in the group. Someone had drawn a lopsided circle into the sand, and within it Zimri and Shallum hunched like prowling bears, each intent on the eyes of the other.

Menashe watched the circling men, then gave Jokim a nudge in the ribs. "I see new faces here." He frowned as he searched the gathering. "Who are these strangers?"

Distracted, Jokim tore his gaze from the wrestlers and looked around, then gave Menashe a one-sided smile. "They are quarry slaves. The overseer gave them permission to train with us."

Menashe's mind flooded with objections. "But what if Pharaoh learns of this? Or my father? We don't need these men."

"We need every pair of hands willing to join us." Jokim looked back at Menashe with a level gaze. "And if God chooses to help us by the hands of these Egyptians, who are we to say He should not?"

"We don't need the Egyptians!"

"We needed mercenaries."

"They are different. When the fight is done, they will return to their posts."

Jokim shrugged. "When the fight is done, these men will return to the quarry. They are slaves. They have no choice. But the overseer thinks he will please your father by having them help us, so he volunteered their labor. He has no great need of them. Pharaoh has not called for blocks of limestone in months. The overseer said these days Pharaoh favors black granite from a place called Ibhet."

Alarm rippled along Menashe's spine. Once again, a younger kinsman had stepped into his rightful place and usurped it without even thinking. Without considering the price that might have to be paid.

"What will happen when one of these slaves slips away?" Menashe asked, his voice tight. "When he takes a boat—or steals one—and goes up the Nile to tell everyone he meets about our work here? What will happen when my father finds out? I am still the vizier's son and my father still has the power to—"

"To do what?" Jokim asked, his eyes bemused and opaque. "To punish you? You are a grown man. Your father can offer you nothing but his blessing." He turned back to the wrestling match.

Menashe looked away, not trusting himself to answer. A

tumult raged as despair, anger, denial and aggression warred in his spirit. Jokim could speak so lightly of a father's blessing only because he was certain to receive one. He did not know the searing pain of being passed over, while Menashe felt a rock fall through his heart every time he thought of Yisrael and Efrayim...

"I am not unaware, Menashe, of what you are feeling," Jokim went on, watching the wrestlers. "But I am not the firstborn. I do not expect that blessing and will not be disappointed when I do not receive it."

"You cannot know," Menashe answered, the words tasting like gall, "what I am feeling."

"Perhaps not." Jokim turned to face him. "But I am not your adversary, nor am I trying to take your place. I must answer to my own conscience, and to what I know as truth. The truth is we need every man who will join us. I am grateful for any man, Egyptian or Hebrew, who will risk his life to help our cause."

"Still, if I am to lead, I should be consulted."

Jokim turned his gaze back to the contest. "I had planned to speak with you tonight, when we could talk in private."

Menashe crossed his arms. Jokim was right. The decision to accept the slaves was logical, sensible and smart. And if Menashe had not been so intent on believing only *he* could make decisions, he would have seen the merit in his cousin's reasoning.

He clapped Jokim's shoulder. "I'll be in the house if anyone needs me," he said, preparing to leave the circle of cheering men. "But perhaps it is good no one does."

Chapter Seventeen

"Captain Tarik!" A chubby little slave boy, clothed in a smudged and wrinkled kilt, lifted the tapestry over the doorway of the captain's small house. "The vizier calls for you!"

Tarik threw an apologetic glance at his wife, rose from his chair and tied his sword belt over his kilt.

"Is there trouble, do you think?" Halima asked, a frown settling across her pretty features. "Zaphenath-paneah does not often call for you so late."

"Nothing out of the ordinary, I'm sure." Tarik's mouth curved as he looked back at his wife. "Keep the roasted pigeon over the fire. I'll be back before you go to sleep."

He pulled his spear from the wall, then walked through pools of torchlight up the wide marble steps of the portico, through the vestibule, and into the vizier's grand reception chamber. Zaphenath-paneah sat in his gilded chair, still every inch an official, still intent on his work though the sun had set hours before.

Before him, in widely spaced seats, sat Efrayim and a heavily bearded man Tarik recognized as one of his master's elder brothers. He struggled to recall the man's name.

"Tarik, you remember my brother Yehuda."

Tarik bowed. "Life, prosperity and health to you, my friend!"

"Yehuda has come to Thebes to inquire about his grandson," Zaphenath-paneah went on, a watchful fixity in his face as his eyes searched Tarik's. "Jokim is his name, as I'm sure you'll remember. He came to visit Menashe and Efrayim several weeks ago."

Tarik nodded. Jokim had visited exactly fifteen days before, but Zaphenath-paneah was not always well-informed about the goings and comings in his household. Tarik thought it best not to correct him.

"We have passed a pleasant evening in conversation, but a few moments ago Yehuda asked to see Jokim." When the vizier paused, a quick and disturbing thought struck Tarik. By Seth's diseased toenail, did Yehuda think Jokim was *here?*

Zaphenath-paneah must have read the thought in Tarik's eyes. "Yes, captain, my brother has been led to believe that Jokim is visiting Menashe and Efrayim. And until this moment I believed Menashe was in Goshen."

Tarik lowered his gaze, dreading his master's next question. He had never lied to his master. He would die for Zaphenath-paneah or his sons, and that love had driven him to help Menashe—

"Where are they, captain?"

Tarik lifted his gaze. From the corner of his eye he saw Efrayim press his hand over his mouth, probably hiding a smile.

The day of reckoning could not be postponed forever. He lifted his head. "I believe, master, that Menashe and Jokim are at Tura."

Efrayim dropped his hand, his smirk wiped away by astonishment. "What are they doing at the quarry?"

Tarik took a deep breath; this would not be easy. He had promised to keep a secret for Menashe, but he had sworn loyalty to his master. "It is my belief," he began, choosing his words carefully, "that he is…training."

"For what?" This from the old man, Yehuda.

Tarik wished he had been away at the stables when the vizier's summons came. "For possible battle, sir. In Canaan."

He could say no more, but he'd said enough. Zaphenath-paneah and Yehuda looked at each other and Tarik knew they understood. Even he, an Egyptian, had felt the power of Menashe's burning conviction that the Hebrews should return to the land of their fathers. Menashe had insisted his summons came directly from God Shaddai, and though Tarik could not imagine life away from Zaphenath-paneah or Thebes, he would have gone to the Underworld and back if *his* master commanded it. Menashe could do no less.

"This is ridiculous." The old man's bony hand knocked against the arm of the chair in some sort of frantic palsy. "They are nothing but youths—"

"They are men, sir," Tarik interrupted, knowing he could be punished for the insolence of speaking without first being addressed. "Do not fault him for the crime of being a young man. My master's son is mature and responsible. Menashe possesses courage and grace in full measure. Time will only weaken his strength."

Yehuda scowled. "Time would improve his character," he snapped. "And his wisdom!"

Tarik looked away. In the other chair, Efrayim wore an expression of stunned surprise. "Jokim is my age, uncle," he whispered. "He *is* a man full grown."

"No man has the right to engage in war on a whim." Zaphenath-paneah's tense, clipped voice forbade any further discussion. "War is for kings and princes, not unrealistic young men. They must be brought home. Whoever is with them must return to their people."

Zaphenath-paneah brought his hands together in an explosive clap and two slaves appeared in the doorway as if they had materialized from out of the wall. "Fetch my scribe, and a runner," the vizier commanded. "I will write a letter that must be carried downriver tonight." His eyes flashed toward his captain of the guard. "Tarik, summon the boatman. The letter must be safely delivered to Menashe, and when the boat returns, Menashe must be on it. Take two of your best guards to make it so."

Cold dignity created a stony mask of Zaphenath-paneah's face; never had his eyes seemed so hard. "Captain, can I trust you to see that my orders are followed?"

"Yes, my lord." Tarik's voice, like his nerves, was in tatters.

Down at the docks, Tarik paused before dismissing the boatman. Yehuda had already spread out his cloak to sleep beneath the canopy, and the usual contingent of rowers and seamen lined the railing. There was no need for additional men, even though Zaphenath-paneah had expressly commanded that a pair of guards be dispatched to bring his son home.

Tarik's promise to obey weighed on him. Could the vizier truly know so little about his son? A pair of guards on the felucca's deck would arouse Menashe's suspicions. He would see their weapons and refuse to show himself; he would be hurt, angered and driven to disobey his father's summons.

"Is that all, Captain Tarik?" the boatman asked, wiping his face with the back of his hand. "We'll be off unless there's anyone else—"

"There is no one else." Tarik looked the man squarely in the eye. "Just your seamen, the messenger and the Hebrew."

The boatman ducked and moved out to the gangplank, his bare feet sliding over the weathered wood without a sound.

A wizened seaman pulled the gangplank into the boat, and Tarik caught his breath, the knowledge that he had disobeyed his master twisting and turning like a whirlwind inside him.

Menashe stepped out onto the villa's wide portico and lifted his arms to stretch. The rising sun swallowed up the wind that had howled around the villa all night. The house had begun to look like a barracks, for men slept everywhere they could find room to lie down. The slaves from the quarries deemed it an honor to sleep in the vizier's house, while the Hebrews dreamed of the green hills and lush groves of the Jordan River valley.

Menashe had dreamed of Jendayi. Despite her attraction to Efrayim, his heart still yearned for her. Perhaps, once he had proven himself a warrior, she might come to love him. But whether she did or not, he was determined to keep his promise and win her freedom. As soon as they had cleared the way back to Canaan, he would return to Egypt, make things right with his father and enter Pharaoh's palace. Before the gilded throne and the gleaming Wadjet eye on Pharaoh's headdress, he would offer sheep, oxen, everything he had gathered in the spoils of war. But he suspected Amenhotep would be more swayed by the proffering of praise than possessions.

Menashe wasn't sure when the truth had come to him, but

one afternoon as he sifted through his thoughts he had been struck by the realization that he and Pharaoh shared a father figure, Zaphenath-paneah. To both Menashe and Amenhotep Yosef was a daunting example, but did Pharaoh feel smothered to the same degree Menashe felt alienated? The common people joked that Pharaoh had built Malkata in an attempt to live with his harem apart from Queen Tiy, but perhaps he had built it to put distance between himself and his vizier. Though Zaphenath-paneah still spent a few hours each morning in ceremonial attendance on the king, he spent most of his day in Thebes.

Doing Pharaoh's work. Receiving Pharaoh's praise. And the people's. Everyone adored Zaphenath-paneah except the priests of Amon-Re—

No wonder Amenhotep had never converted to the worship of God Shaddai. In his theology, at least, Amenhotep could stand apart from the clouding shadow of Zaphenath-paneah's influence.

Alone with his thoughts, Menashe had come to understand the frightened god-king on the throne. Amenhotep was as easily intimidated as any man and he found it easier to withdraw to Malkata than to see his glory dimmed in the presence of one who shone brighter.

So when the battle for Canaan was done, Menashe would approach Pharaoh, massage the royal ego with sincere praise and offer whatever Pharaoh required in exchange for Jendayi's freedom.

As dawn draped misty veils over the little village where the quarry slaves and overseer lived, Menashe squinted toward the stocky brick structures. Already one of the slaves stirred along the small path winding among the huts—probably an ardent worshipper of Amon-Re, out to catch a glimpse of the god as he began his ride across the sky. Either that, Menashe thought with a wry grin, or the man was up early to answer nature's call.

Menashe yawned, stretched again, and was about to turn back into the house when another movement caught his eye. Far in the distance, near the western riverfront, the small triangular tip of a sail peeked from behind an outcropping of rock. Visitors, but from where? Who would risk the dangers of traveling on the river at night?

A wave of apprehension swept through him as he darted toward the rocky wall that bordered the path and partially hid the vizier's house. Reaching for foot- and handholds he had known since his childhood, he lifted himself up and over the edge of the sheer wall. Lying flat on the rock's broad back, he shimmied forward, pushing himself with his toes until his eyes peered over the rim of stone.

For an instant his heart expanded in relief. The felucca was his father's, for the vizier's crimson and white standard flapped from the single mast. So either Tarik had sent word of some emergency or his father knew—*everything*.

His stomach heaved. Without a doubt his father knew; Zaphenath-paneah realized everything eventually. Menashe should have known the confrontation could not be forestalled; a showdown was inevitable. But he would not be reprimanded in front of his men.

Sliding backward off the rock, he slid down the cliff as quickly as he dared, then hurried toward the river, determined to intercept his father's emissaries before they reached the house.

An hour later, Menashe sat alone on a mounded levee at the river's edge, a papyrus scroll in his hand. The messenger had been happy to leave the scroll with Menashe and depart for Goshen, but before the felucca moved on Menashe caught sight of Yehuda's set face, clamped mouth and flashing eyes beneath the canopy of the boat. Jokim would be glad he had not followed Menashe down the river path.

Now Menashe's eyes focused on the western horizon while his heart struggled with the knowledge that this time his father could not be obeyed and must not be trusted. God had spoken, and Yosef had not been willing to listen, nor had Yehuda. What was it about old men that deafened their ears to the voice of God?

"Who was it, Menashe?"

Jokim's voice startled him, but he did not turn around. Judging from the sound of their footfalls, more than one man stood behind him.

"The boat brought a message from my father." Menashe rested his elbows on top of his knees, wearily considering the river before him. "We have been discovered. And our fathers—mine and yours, Jokim—demand that we return to our homes. It is not the right time to indulge in battle, my father says, and only Pharaoh can declare an invasion. So when the felucca returns from Goshen, I am to board her and join my father in Thebes."

Jokim sank onto the levee beside Menashe while Zimri sat beside Jokim like a well-trained puppy. "Since the felucca is only going back to Thebes, apparently your father doesn't expect me to board her," Jokim said. "So I will stay, as will the others. Our fathers are not the vizier."

"You know what the elders will say." Menashe turned to Jokim with a critical squint. "They will say you are living in rebellion. And no good son rebels against his father."

"Unless a father rebels against God," Jokim answered. "In that case, we ought to obey God first. I will not disrespect my father. I will not argue with him, insult him or dishonor him. But I believe God has called us out, Menashe. I will not abandon the cause, no matter who summons me."

Menashe flinched at the subtle accusation in Jokim's voice.

"You do what you must do," Jokim finished, staring out at the river. "But now that your father knows our location and intent, it is too dangerous for us to remain here. We will move our camp into the wilderness, and we will relocate every night in order to escape detection. If you come back—"

"When I come back," Menashe interrupted. "I will go home, make peace with my father and do my part to keep things quiet. And then I will return. I would be a worthless warrior if I put my hand to the sword and proved unwilling to finish the battle."

Jokim smiled. "When you come back, stop at the quarry and ask the overseer where we have gone. We will leave word with him so you will be able to find us."

Menashe inclined his head, not looking at his kinsman, and after a moment Jokim and Zimri stood and walked away, their footsteps puffing over the sand as they climbed the trail to the marble mansion. Menashe closed his eyes to the sight of the shining river, hating it with every fiber of his being. Lying there, green and shining, it reminded him of a jungle python, sometimes thin and lazy, other times engorged and restless, but always moving, always pulling, always alive. You couldn't kill it or escape from it. It hypnotized; it drew people from the mountains and wilderness until they lived in a thin margin along its banks. And, like the others who had come from the forests and the deserts and the stony mountains, his father and Avraham's people had come from the holy promised land to live alongside the glowing water. The river had saved them according to God's plan, but now, still hypnotized by its beauty, they were loath to leave it.

He rose and crumpled the papyrus scroll in his hand. With all his might he flung it toward the controlling and treacherous Nile, then turned and stalked up the trail to fetch his cloak.

If he did not obey his father's order, Zaphenath-paneah would send others to search for him. So he would depart with the felucca; he owed that much to the men who had toiled with him under the blazing sun. He would meet the boat at the river, away from his warriors, so as not to reveal their faces or their number. He would reenter his father's house and pretend to be a properly obedient and chastised son.

But he would return to the fight as soon as possible.

The oarsmen rowed to the steady beat of the drum throughout the night. As the felucca raced over the crushed diamond water, Menashe leaned against the railing and crossed his arms, grateful that his father hadn't sent an armed guard to escort him home. That would have been the ultimate insult, a statement that the vizier's elder son could be trusted no more than a slave or condemned criminal. Menashe mentally thanked his father for the gesture of confidence even though he planned to abuse it.

The sun had begun to adorn the housetops with the first gray-pink tatters of dawn as the boat neared Thebes. Menashe gave a nod of thanks to the boatman who lowered the gangplank, then he stepped down the ramp and darted toward a huddle of fishermen who were gathering their nets.

Carefully, he scanned the crowd at the docks. Menashe thought his father would send a messenger to the river, a friend, perhaps, to escort Menashe home and sound out his feelings

about this ignominious return. He concealed himself among the
fishermen, stooping slightly to disguise his height, until he
spied a familiar face hurrying toward the waterfront.

Ani. Of course. His father had sent the villa's resident wise
man, the beloved tutor to whom Menashe had taken his questions about the earth, the sky, his body, his brain, even his heart.
Yosef had been wise to send Ani, for Menashe might have
shared his plans with him, but Ani's aging eyes would fail him
this morning. As the old steward peered across the crowds of
fishermen who prepared to set out on the river, Menashe slunk
away and moved northward through the crowd.

He would face Yosef, but not now. His eyes burned from
sleeplessness, and the malaise in him would choke off any
words he might want to say. He needed rest. He wanted the
company of a friend.

He spied an abandoned papyrus skiff near the reedy bank,
one of the ubiquitous rafts children often used to slide from one
shore to the other. Without a sound, Menashe stepped onto the
skiff and sent it winging westward across the river. With any
luck, the encroaching fishing ships would surround him within
a few moments, and in the river traffic he could move unnoticed
toward Malkata.

If he needed help, Tarik had promised, a giant called Abnu
might be willing to give it.

But another, more pressing reason lay behind his urge to visit
the king's palace. Jendayi waited there, and nearly two months
had passed since he had last seen her sweet face.

Amenhotep built his palace on a shore previously reserved
for the dead. Malkata lay just north of Thebes on the Nile's
western bank. Menashe knew it might be difficult to enter the
harbor without arousing suspicion, but in the past few days he
had been surprised at how many things were possible if one had
the temerity to attempt them.

When the towering granite pillars of Malkata rose from the
emerald ribbon of foliage bordering the riverfront, Menashe left
the bustling, noisy river and floated into the harbor, crouching
low on the skiff and paddling through the water with his hands.
High reeds edged the king's harbor, and he remained in the

rushes until he passed the royal docks without raising an alarm. Moving slowly so he wouldn't attract attention, he pawed through the reeds until he caught a glimpse of green water behind them—the secret canal. His father had mentioned it when they last visited Malkata, but Menashe had been too engrossed in his dreams of Jendayi to look for the hidden entrance.

Pointing the nose of the skiff into the reeds, he threaded the boat through the thick growth, using the willowy stems to pull his way through the camouflaged opening. Finally the tiny boat broke free and slid into the waterway beyond.

For a moment Menashe wondered if he had entered a different world. A pink granite wall rose at his left hand, tall and forbidding. The muddy banks had been cleared of reeds and plant growth so any approaching enemy would be exposed. The wall of reeds muffled the raucous sounds of the Nile's sailors and fishermen. Menashe heard only the steady slush and suck of the water beneath his small boat, and from somewhere behind the wall, a broom hissing over wet tiles. At his right, shimmering mirages made the western cliffs dance in the distance. The air vibrated with the wings of swifts that flew low to catch insects hovering between the shifting line of sun and shade.

He crouched, his hands dripping on the reed boat, as the muddy banks slid by. Finally he spied a gate in the granite wall. Two guards stood there, their backs to him, and Menashe ducked and lowered his hands into the water, turning the skiff into the bank. He beached the vessel out of the guards' sight, then paused to wet the edge of his cloak and wipe the previous day's accumulated grime from his hands and face. He moved cautiously, for danger lurked beneath the blinding dazzle of the sun's path on the quiet canal.

But crocodiles and vipers were the least of his worries now. Throughout the night he had considered ways he might slip into the palace, knowing that no one entered Malkata without an invitation. Unless he could convince the gate guards that someone inside the fortress had summoned him, he would pay dearly for this adventure. He had enough confidence in his physical training to think he might overpower these two warriors, but a noisy disturbance would force a general alarm. He considered sneaking in through the servants' quarters and skulking around like a drudge, but a lifetime on the fringes of the royal circle had taught him that a man could rise to success in Pharaoh's court only as long as he did not show his insecurity.

He would walk into the palace as if he were an invited guest. If apprehended, he could always throw himself on the mercy of Pharaoh, Queen Tiy or even his father the vizier.

Menashe tugged on the kilt he wore and ran his wet fingers through his close-cropped hair. If he had known he would find himself at Malkata, he would have brought his wig and a blade to shave his straggly beard. In this unconventional guise he would stand out more than most men, but he had no other choice. He had come too far to turn back.

Lifting his chin, he strode up the bank. The guards were Nubians, two of the famed Medjay warriors. He did not recognize them, but thought it safe to assume that at one time or another they had manned the guard post at the front gate. They certainly would know his father, and perhaps they had even seen Menashe enter with the renowned Zaphenath-paneah.

The warriors stood at the gate, laughing at some private joke, and Menashe positioned himself before them, spreading his legs in a bold stance and resting his hands on his hips.

He cleared his throat. The men looked up, and the taller blinked in consternation.

"Life and peace to you, my friends." Menashe thrust his hands behind his back. "By the life of Pharaoh, I pray you are well." He nodded at the larger man, who looked every inch an African warrior: tough, lean and sinewy. "Is that a new collar you are wearing, captain? I do not recall seeing it when my father the vizier and I dined here several weeks ago."

The guard's gaze traveled up and down Menashe, taking in the fine linen kilt, the soft sandals, the gold wristbands…and the beard. He transferred his inscrutable gaze to his companion.

"I know I look disheveled—" Menashe exchanged a smile with the second man "—but I have been training in the desert." He glanced pointedly at an angry-looking slash across his chest and shrugged. "This little scratch must seem like nothing to a pair of Medjay warriors. Tarik, the captain of my father's guard, has often told me of your bravery in battle. He says there are none in the world as skilled as the Medjays."

The big guard lifted his chin and stiffened his massive weight. "Life and peace to you, son of the noble vizier." He inclined his dark head in a deep bow. "We did not know you were expected."

Menashe held up a disarming hand. "I am not here to disturb Pharaoh, but to speak with a warrior. The captain of my father's guard recommended that I find the man known as Abnu."

At the mention of the giant's name, the smaller guard cast a quick, apprehensive glance toward his companion.

"I know Abnu." The taller guard lowered his voice. "I have sparred with him. Only the grace of Pharaoh saved my miserable hide. The giant would have run me through with a pike had the king not spoken." He said this proudly, as if there were substantial merit in living to tell about a bout with the giant.

"Pharaoh must think highly of you," Menashe murmured.

The guard shrugged. "You will find Abnu in the warriors' barracks, unless he is sparring in the courtyard. When you find him, tell him Nebu sends his greetings."

Menashe gave the man an apologetic smile. "Where are these barracks? I have only visited the gardens and the royal house."

The guard stooped to etch a drawing in the sand. "Here is Pharaoh's palace," he said, completing a rectangle with his index finger, "and here are the chambers of the queen, prince and princesses. Behind them is the royal harem. And behind the harem, in a building of whitewashed brick, are the quarters for Pharaoh's warriors."

Menashe studied the drawing, imprinting it on his mind. "Behind the harem?"

"Pharaoh wanted his guards kept between his treasures and his slaves." The second guard's dark face split into a broad grin. "The servants are housed behind the warriors."

Menashe felt his heart skip a beat. God be praised! Jendayi would surely be found in the servants' quarters. If all went well he would speak to both Jendayi and Abnu today.

"Many thanks, my friends." He stood and walked between their sharpened spears as if he were taking an afternoon stroll. "And I will not forget to give your regards to the giant."

Chapter Eighteen

A wide courtyard separated the main wall of the palace complex from the smaller residences within it, and Menashe hurried over the sand until he had passed the magnificent pavilions that housed the royal family. The shadows of the morning had shortened, fleeing from the spaces between the more humble buildings and the glorious villas, and Menashe realized the day was already half-spent.

The warrior had given him accurate directions. Three rectangular brick structures stood between the royal residences and the vast complex of Pharaoh's celebrated stables. The building closest to the palace was dedicated to Pharaoh's harem, the next to his warriors, and the final one to his slaves and servants. As much as his heart longed to explore the servants' chambers, Menashe knew he should find Abnu first. The men who waited for him in the desert would need reassurance when he returned, and a Medjay warrior would cheer their hearts. And if he spoke to the warrior soon, he might have the rest of the day to spend with Jendayi.

Two guards sat just inside the doorway to the middle building, a game of Hounds and Jackals spread on a tray between them. They looked up as Menashe entered the room, then returned their eyes to the board, each man intent on the game. Menashe sighed in relief when they paid him no attention.

"Prosperity and peace to you," he remarked to one of the

players as his eyes swept through the room. The interior of the hall was cut down the center by a single aisle; at least fifty low wooden beds were lined up against the walls in straight rows. Above the beds, a profusion of spears, shields, swords, bows and daggers hung from pegs. Sleeping men occupied several beds at the back of the room, probably the guards of the midnight watch, and at least a dozen warriors clustered in small conversational groups toward the front, their hands employed with awls and leather strips as they mended the tough leather of their shields.

Menashe crinkled his nose. The air smelled as if it had been breathed too many times, and someone had definitely neglected the chamber pots. The hall was drab and ordinary, not at all befitting Pharaoh's celebrated Medjay warriors.

"What do you want?" one of the gamers asked, not lifting his gaze from the board.

"I am looking for Abnu." Menashe searched among the Nubians for one who might be considered a giant. "Tarik, who serves Zaphenath-paneah, recommended that I find him."

The hall fell silent, as if every ear had decided to eavesdrop, then one of the groups near the doorway broke apart. A man who had been seated on the floor unfolded his tree-trunk legs and came toward Menashe, a stalking, purposeful intent in his walk. The shining skin atop his shaved head nearly brushed the nine-foot ceiling and his muscled, built-for-action body moved with an air of authority. His face bore the expression of a man who demanded instant obedience.

Menashe was almost sorry he'd come. He wanted a man to *serve* in his army, not command it.

"Who seeks Abnu?" The man's rumbling voice shattered the silence.

Menashe floundered before the brilliance of the man's gaze. With difficulty he coughed out an answer. "Menashe, elder son of Zaphenath-paneah."

The warrior frowned and placed his hands on his slim hips. "Why do you seek me? I have nothing to do with the king's vizier."

Menashe took a hasty half-step back. "I came to bring you greetings from Tarik, captain of the vizier's guard—"

"Tarik!" As swiftly as a chameleon changing colors, the man's face broke into a lazy smile. "That old son of Nut! How is he faring?"

"He is well," Menashe answered, blinking. "He and his wife are happy."

The giant scratched a faint growth of hair on his chin, then pinned Menashe with a long, silent scrutiny. "Tarik was your teacher?"

Menashe gave him an abashed smile and cleared his throat. "Years ago, he taught my brother and I how to fight. We learned to wrestle and to throw a spear…and to manage a bow and sword, of course."

The giant smiled again, but his expression held only a ghost of its former warmth. "Did Tarik teach you well?"

"Very well. He is an excellent teacher."

Without warning, the giant turned and yanked a copper sword from the wall. He hefted the sword in his broad palm as if weighing it, then he tossed it toward Menashe. Too late, Menashe thrust his hands into empty air. The blade clanged on the tile floor at his feet.

"I hope you are more skilled than you are alert." Abnu pulled a heavier sword of iron from a peg. He wound his thick fingers around the grip, then shot Menashe an impenitent grin. "We will see just how good a teacher my friend Tarik is. If he did not teach you well, I shall visit the vizier's house and scold him thoroughly. After, of course, I convey my condolences about your demise."

Menashe's heart leaped to his throat as he bent to pick up the copper blade. "Tarik taught me ably. But I am not a warrior by trade. My skills are certainly not as finely honed as yours." His stomach churned and tightened as he faced the man, the sword dangling at his side. "I have no wish to fight you."

"No wish to fight?" In three steps the giant moved close enough for Menashe to appreciate the muscles rippling beneath the skin of his abdomen. "Listen to me well, son of the vizier, for I shall not repeat myself. You have, I fear, already made the crucial mistake of believing that strong men are stupid. If I were not in a generous mood that mistake would have already cost you your life. But because I am not stupid, I know this—if Tarik sent you to see me, he wants me to help you, and that can only mean you are somehow involved in a fight. Whether you want me to battle one man or twenty remains to be seen, but if a man expects me to pick up a sword on his behalf, he had better be ready to pick up one on mine. If you have no heart to fight, you are doomed already."

Menashe swallowed hard and squared his shoulders. Though panic rioted within him, he could not help feeling exhilarated by the ferocity of the giant's passion. What a force he would be against the Canaanites! His size would intimidate any who came against them, and with God's power behind his weapon, the land would be quickly be restored to Yaakov's sons.

Menashe lifted his eyes to the giant's rigid face. "If I go a round with you—" he swiveled his blade until it pointed upward toward the warrior's jugular "—will you consider my request?"

Abnu's eyes flicked at the sword, then glared back at Menashe. "I will listen to you," he answered, a slight trace of cynical humor in his tone, "if you draw first blood. But if at any time you retreat or flinch, I will kill you, for a coward is a shame to his teacher."

"I am not a coward." Menashe kept his gaze locked with the giant's. "And I will prove it."

As if a signal had been given, the loitering warriors stood from their places, eager to watch what would surely be more entertaining than a game of Hounds and Jackals.

"You must fight outside," one of the men called. "And be quick about it! The captain does not tolerate disorder within our company."

"Don't worry," Abnu snarled, his rapier glance passing over Menashe again. "This will not take long."

Afraid to take his eyes off his adversary, Menashe turned and allowed the giant to pass by him. Outside, the sun had vanished behind a cloud bank that left the courtyard in shade. As he advanced, he wrapped his hand around the sword. The ill-fitting copper sword in his grip felt slippery and alien.

A dozen impatient hands shoved Menashe toward the empty space where Abnu shifted from foot to foot, his long arms hanging empty below his belt, the iron sword wavering in the sand a few feet in front of him. Menashe thrust his blade into the sand, too, then stepped back as the circle around them thickened.

Even over the uncontrolled sounds of the zealous crowd he could hear his heart battering against his ears. Never in his most far-fetched imaginings had he anticipated that he would have to fight in order to win an audience with this man. He was accustomed to people who obeyed his wishes, bowed before his name (or at least his father's title), and laughed at his humor, no matter how dry the joke. He had expected help, even affection, from an old friend of Tarik's.

But lately all his expectations had vanished like pebbles dropped into the Nile.

Through the roaring din, he breathed a prayer. "God Shaddai, help your servant now!"

Then, as the challenger seized his sword and lunged with an earsplitting cry, Menashe dove for his blade and rushed toward destruction.

Jendayi paused on her walk back from the palace kitchens. Warriors' cries echoed from the courtyard, battering her delicate senses with animal coarseness. She took a deep breath and plunged toward the safety of the wall that would lead her to her own quarters, far away from the rowdy warriors.

Pharaoh's men were at it again. She hated the soldiers' roughhousing; their grunts and cries and curses often echoed long into the night. But this fight seemed different, for a tremulous ring of clashing metals punctuated the crowd's cries in a recurring, steady beat. This was neither a wrestling match nor a drunken brawl. This sounded like a duel.

Her fingers found the wall that would lead her home, but she halted beside it, paralyzed by her aversion to violence. She heard a deep growl, a hoarse taunt and a gasp from the crowd. A deep thud vibrated beneath her feet, as though a heavy object had fallen.

Her blood rose in a jet when a familiar voice touched her ear. "Lie still, giant, and let me mark your cheek with my sword," a man demanded, his words punctuated by deep gasps. "You will grant me what you have promised."

Jendayi's mind swirled in a crazy mixture of hope and fear. That was Chenzira's voice. But why would he be fighting in Pharaoh's courtyard? Unless he had begun a brawl while his master met with the king—

Her breath caught in her throat. Was Efrayim visiting the palace?

She whirled toward the gathering and lifted her sightless eyes toward whatever confrontation had taken place. The crowd moaned in sympathy for the displaced champion, and several observers muttered soft curses as bracelets and armbands clinked and changed hands. Jendayi stepped forward, hoping to find someone who could tell her about Efrayim.

"All right, you slippery fish," a deep voice growled from the midst of the commotion. "I am yours to command…for a time."

"But you serve Pharaoh."

Jendayi felt a thrill of hope run through her as she confirmed Chenzira's voice. Her ears had not deceived her.

"I am a free man. I can serve whatever master I please," the defeated man answered, the depth of his voice lifting the hair at the back of Jendayi's neck. "And by trickery you have hired me. Where and when shall I report?"

"Meet me two days from today, at sunset, outside the vizier's villa. Do not approach the gate and do not announce your presence." A short silence was followed by the sound of two hands slapping in agreement. "And I will thank Tarik for teaching me that escape move. Only with his help could I have outrun your blade."

"Tarik is a better teacher than I knew." A smile echoed in the older man's voice. "Give him my regards, and tell him I will see him soon."

Jendayi put out a hand to make certain no one blocked her way, then edged closer to Chenzira. She was about to call a greeting, but he saw her first. "Jendayi!"

She couldn't stop a smile. "I recognized your voice and could not believe I heard correctly. What are you doing in the midst of a fight? And why are you here at all?"

"I—" He paused as his fingers grasped hers. "Let us go someplace where we can talk."

"I know a place." She kept a tight grip on his hand as she turned. "Stay close behind me."

"I would not lose you for the world."

She led him to a private garden, hidden from the rest of Pharaoh's palace by high walls. From the confident way her sandals moved over the path Menashe suspected she came here often. She did not hesitate, but moved with catlike grace, not in the least impeded by her blindness. His heart swelled with compassion as he followed. He closed his eyes, trying to imagine himself in her situation, but his feet immediately grew heavy and unsure of themselves.

"What has happened to you?" she asked, a mischievous note in her voice as she chided him for lagging behind. "Hurry, I want to show you a special place. But you must tell no one of it—except perhaps Efrayim."

"I will tell no one," he answered, opening his eyes. Golden sunbeams laced the branches of the flowering acacia trees; the foliage around them hummed with insect life. The pebbled path pointed a curving finger through beds of massed flowers, but Jendayi plunged off the trail and moved through the plants toward the garden wall.

"No, Jendayi." Menashe resisted the pull of her fingers. "You have left the path. This is not the right way."

"That all depends," Jendayi answered, tossing a smile over her shoulder, "on where you want to go." She stopped in a small clearing near the wall and released his hand. "Look around, will you? It is somewhere near."

She pressed forward, insinuating her way through the lush greenery growing against the wall, then she crouched and ducked behind a stand of flowering trees. He lost sight of her, then heard her urgent whisper. "Here! Come closer, Chenzira!"

Plunging through the plants, he reached the wall and found her kneeling before a door not more than three feet tall. "It is the door of escape," she said, her eyes squinting with amusement. "Akil showed it to me soon after we came here. If ever the palace comes under attack, we are to slip down to the canal through this little gate."

A brass ring had been set into the door; her fingers found it and tugged the door open. Without signaling her intent, she slipped through the rectangular opening and disappeared. Menashe crouched in front of the doorway, then crawled after her on his hands and knees. He scrambled through the thickness of the wall, then climbed out onto a rocky bank. The canal flowed twenty feet away, gleaming like copper as the bloodred sun streamed across the waters.

Jendayi was sitting on a stone, her face to the sun, her elbows tucked at her sides in a childlike posture of wonder. "Is it as lovely here as I imagine it to be? I know the sun is there—" she lifted her hand toward the blazing orb "—and the canal is before me. I come here nearly every night, for it is quiet and peaceful. And though odd wind-borne sounds sometimes reach my ear, I feel I am quite alone. Except now, of course."

"Why do you come here?" Menashe sank to the rock beside her. "It is a lonely place. The life of the palace is behind us."

"My life does not lie within those walls. It lies here." She pressed her fingers to her heart. "I live only in my imagination, Chenzira. There I can make music so fleet that my fingers cannot play it…and in my imagination I can visit Efrayim."

Menashe resisted the urge to groan as she fell silent. What had Efrayim ever done to deserve this beautiful creature's affection?

Her cool voice broke into his thoughts. "Are you going to tell me what brings you here? I was surprised to hear your voice, and amazed that you escaped the warrior you fought. Does your master know you have foolishly risked life and limb this afternoon?"

"No," he answered, managing no more than a hoarse whisper. He paused, desperate to confess the entire truth, but doubted she would be as willing to open her heart to a nobleman as a servant.

"I am here because the vizier is unhappy with me," he said truthfully. He bent one knee and rested his elbow on it, grateful for the opportunity to unburden his soul before a compassionate heart. "And I escaped the blade of Pharaoh's giant because God Shaddai brought an ancient wrestling move to my mind. Abnu was not expecting it, so I managed to trip him."

She hugged her knees to her chest. "Then you worship the same god Efrayim does." Resting her head on her knees, she was a picture of gentle innocence. "When I lived in the vizier's house, I heard much talk of the invisible god. Of course—" she shrugged "—all gods are invisible to me, for I can see none of them. But I can *feel* them. In the temples, the priests allow me to run my hands over the gods' carved faces. I can smell the sweet scent of their incense and hear the hymns of praise."

Menashe stared at an ibis that waded in the canal, prodding the shallows with his curved beak. "I can feel El Shaddai. Not with my hands, but with my heart. I can see His design in the way of an eagle in the sky, and His goodness in the bounty of a loaded fishing boat on the river." He turned and fastened his gaze to Jendayi's lovely face. "And I see His passion in the way a man looks at the woman he loves."

A shy smile played at the corners of her mouth. "I suppose you are right, my friend. I have yet to discover that feeling. But soon I will." Her tone hardened. "I must."

"Why Efrayim?" Menashe couldn't keep a note of impatience from his voice. "Why have you set your heart on *him?* He is cocky and arrogant. He gives too much attention to too many different women."

"You do not speak very respectfully of your master." Her tone had chilled.

Menashe swallowed an angry retort. "Efrayim is not my master, the vizier is. But I know Efrayim, and I must tell you, Jendayi, you are foolish to waste your feelings on him. He is not worthy of you."

Across her pale and beautiful face a dim flush raced like a fever. "Not worthy of me? No, I am not worthy of *him!* Do you think I hope to marry—that I want— Oh, how could you? I am not in a position to choose. I would never be so presumptuous. I am a slave. I hope only to enjoy the smile of a caring master again. Pharaoh is indifferent. I am one of thousands who answer to his command. But Efrayim cares for me, and if I can return to his house—"

Menashe pressed his hand to her arm. "How do you know he cares for you?"

"Because I have received a message from him." The fire left her voice as a gentle blush colored her cheek. "And years ago, in the garden of the vizier's house, Efrayim kissed me. Though he is a nobleman, and though I will never be more than a slave, he is the only person in the world to ever show that kind of affection for me."

"What sort of message?" Menashe choked on the words.

"I received it from my handmaid while we journeyed to Canaan. Efrayim promised to approach Pharaoh and ask that I be returned to the vizier's house." She lifted one delicate shoulder in a shrug. "He has not yet done so, but I am certain he is waiting for the right time. Perhaps he will take me with him when he establishes his own house."

Menashe sat back, numb with astonishment. The message she referred to was obviously his; somehow she had misunderstood. But Efrayim *had* kissed her. Jendayi had staked her hope and future on one brazen act of an impetuous, vain, spoiled boy.

Menashe clenched his fist as the bitter gall of jealousy burned the back of his throat. Efrayim had Jendayi's love, which he had not sought, and the right hand of blessing from Yaakov, which he had not deserved. Menashe had striven hard to please his father, his tutors and his god, all for nothing, while charming Efrayim had smiled at Yaakov and kissed Jendayi. And both of them had fallen in love with him.

So kiss her now. The thought came from out of nowhere, careening through his heart like an out-of-control chariot. If a kiss had given Efrayim the right to Jendayi's heart, might not another one, filled with tenderness and sincere affection, usurp that claim? Menashe could easily claim her lips now; he could crush her to him and make her hear the thudding, insistent drum of his heart. He could tear Efrayim's memory from her mind and overwhelm her childish devotion to an undeserving scamp…

But if a kiss alone could win her, she was not truly won. Menashe had not seen many examples of dedicated selflessness in his life, but he knew love involved more than physical attraction. His uncle Shim'on and Mandisa exhibited an almost wordless understanding of one another's moods; Tarik and Halima would have neglected the entire world rather than each other. Physical affection, it seemed to Menashe, was like the limestone casing on a pyramid—pleasant and attractive, it had little to do with the solid blocks that formed the building's foundation and structure.

He would not attempt to win her the way Efrayim apparently had. He would win her heart and mind and soul by proving his dedication. And he would wait for her to come willingly into his arms.

"Jendayi—" He paused, struggling to interpret the turbulent emotions buffeting his heart.

"I understand, Chenzira, you don't have to tell me. I can sense that you are troubled." She turned her face toward the flowing water. "I asked you to talk to Efrayim for me, and you weren't able to do it."

"No, I wasn't." He lifted his eyes toward the heavens. Sunset was beginning to stretch glowing fingers across the sky, but Jendayi could not experience the sense of exhilaration it elicited. She dreamed of slavery in a more pleasant house, yet he yearned to release her from bondage, to shower her with love and elevate her to a position of authority in his own household. How could he teach her to dream of higher things? How could he show one who had never seen love that it encompassed far more than a token kiss?

"Jendayi—" his words poured forth in a rush "—you should forget about Efrayim."

"Forget him?" She turned on him with the fury of a tigress. "How can I forget the only kindness I have ever known? He alone has shown mercy to me. I ought to serve him the rest of my life in gratitude for that alone! If you are my friend, Chenzira, you will talk to him for me. Remind him of his promise, tell him I am waiting."

He gritted his teeth, straining against the choice he had to make. The truth would wound her, but she would never open her heart to all he offered if she were bound to a counterfeit affection. "Jendayi…Efrayim does not love you."

She halted, shocked. Her mouth opened as she drew in an audible breath. "How would you know?"

Menashe closed his eyes, unwilling to see the hurt that would soon cross her face. "He plans to marry Princess Sitamun. Apparently the queen, Pharaoh and the vizier approve. I suspect the marriage will take place within the year."

She took a wincing little breath, then turned her face away. For a moment woven of eternity she said nothing, then he heard her voice, flat and final. "A political marriage does not matter. He could still take me into his house. As long as he cares a little, it is enough. I am a slave. I have never hoped to be more than that."

Menashe released a choked, desperate laugh. "By heaven above, do you love him so much? Would you be happy settling for crumbs from his table? If you will forget Efrayim, someone else might come into your life—"

"Love him?" She pressed her hand over her face. Her voice was muffled as she spoke through her fingers. "Ah, Chenzira, if you only knew."

Swallowing the sob that rose in his throat, Menashe studied the sand at his feet. If she cared for Efrayim so deeply, what right had he to persuade her not to love his brother? He wanted her to be free; he could not deny her the freedom to choose the man she would love.

"I should be going." He pushed himself up from the rock, his private anguish almost overcoming his control of his voice. "I shouldn't be here."

"You said the vizier was unhappy with you." As she lowered her hand Menashe could see the silvery tracks of tears on her cheeks. But she looked up and offered him a sweet smile of concern. "Why is your master unhappy? Are you in terrible trouble?"

"I suppose so," he answered. "I have been in the wilderness with a group of Hebrews who are preparing to launch an invasion into Canaan. God Shaddai promised that land to Yisrael's descendants. Now that Yaakov is dead, there is no need for the sons of Yisrael to remain in Egypt."

"An invasion?" She shivered. "But why must you go to war?"

"God called me," he answered, "and I must obey. But since the vizier does not understand or approve, I have left his house."

Her hand flew to her throat. "These Hebrews—is Efrayim with you? Is he in danger?"

"No," Menashe answered, his voice dry. "Efrayim is content to remain in the center of Thebes."

A shadow of satisfaction crossed her face, then her countenance settled back into delicate, composed lines. "All the same, troublesome slaves are whipped, my friend. I would not like to think of you being punished."

Her hand fell on his, burning his skin with her touch, and emotion clotted his throat so he could not speak. "I would be honored if you would think of me, Jendayi," he finally answered, extending both hands to help her up. Still holding her hands, he stepped back to regard her in the golden light of sunset. She would be a welcome addition to Efrayim's household if Pharaoh chose to make her a gift to his prospective son-in-law. But she would not be happy as Efrayim's slave, for he would give her no more attention than he gave the prowling housecats which rid the villa of vermin and occasionally demanded an affectionate stroke.

What should love do? Work toward what she wanted, or what was best for her? The question hammered at him.

"Jendayi, I must return to the vizier's house for a few days, but I will do what I can to help you," Menashe promised, his voice breaking. "While I am gone, accept my farewells and know this—the path toward Efrayim is not the best one for you."

One delicate brow lifted. "And have you knowledge of another secret garden door?"

"That all depends—" he dropped her hands "—on where you want to go." He turned and made his way down the bank of the canal. When he turned for a last look, she had vanished into the wall surrounding Pharaoh's palace.

Jendayi turned and slipped back through the wall, stunned by the void she felt when Chenzira left her alone. But she was only being foolish. Like a child who shivered when a cloud blocked the sun, she was growing used to the hope of Efrayim, and now she was alone again, with only a slave's promise of help.

She would have to accept her role in life, realize once again that she was nothing but a slave.

But one of Chenzira's questions kept slipping through her thoughts: *By heaven above, Jendayi, do you love Efrayim so much?*

"If you only knew, my friend," she whispered, feeling the cool breath of the garden on her face. "I must love or die forever. And Efrayim is the one who can best show me how."

Chapter Nineteen

Akil scarcely had time to hide himself behind a sycamore tree before Jendayi slipped back through the little door and brushed herself off. The chironomist stood very still, keenly aware of the girl's heightened sense of hearing, and only dared breathe again when she began to make her way back over the garden path.

Leaning on the gnarled tree trunk with one hand, he shook his head, amazed that she had managed to attract trouble even while safe behind the guardian walls of the king's palace. She had always given him more cause for concern than the others. Kissa, the lutist, was as lovely as the harpist, and the oboist, Sakmet, flirted constantly with the guards, but trouble focused on Jendayi with the unblinking eye of a god. When she was but a child, another slave trader had recognized her gift and tried to abduct her from Akil's tent, a hundred jealousy-spurred rumors had attempted to sully her name, and even in the vizier's house the younger son had taken her lovely face in his hands…

Thoughts of the vizier's sons lit a hot, clenched ball of anger at Akil's center. They were always appearing when he least expected them, upsetting his tidily ordered world. Today Sakmet had come running to report that Jendayi was leading a man into the private garden, so Akil hurried out to safeguard his treasure. His annoyance turned to speechless shock when he recognized Menashe, the vizier's elder son, and shock evolved into panic when the pair disappeared through the escape door. If Menashe was helping Jendayi escape, Akil knew his head would be in a basket before sunset. And so he had followed, sneaking like a viper up into the branches of a sycamore where he saw and overheard enough of the riverside conversation to know that Jendayi did not plan to escape. Menashe had come to say goodbye before departing to join a military corps intent on an invasion of Canaan.

The chironomist rubbed his expressive hands together and considered the information he had just gleaned. Pharaoh would not approve of this armed force; any action not sanctioned by the king would be construed as a direct slap against his authority. A mighty lion could not have two mouths or two heads, so the king possessed complete military power in Egypt.

The master musician smiled. Such information, dispensed at the right time and to the right person, could be invaluable. And Akil, who prided himself on his hardheaded pragmatism, knew this report would have to be presented with the utmost discretion. The mighty Amenhotep would never listen to a lowly musician, but other, more receptive ears had tilted toward Akil in the past...

Tiy would grant him an audience. The queen often asked for his impressions of the people who visited her throne room, for he was the perfect observer and routinely ignored by her guests. More than once after a pompous nobleman had passed out of the queen's chambers, Akil had ended that man's lofty ambitions by drizzling gray disapproval. Tiy, marvelous judge of character that she was, trusted him.

For news of impending treason, the queen would be most grateful. And if Akil handled this situation with Jendayi as quietly as he had others in her past, she would not be affected. She would never even know what had happened to her false friend.

"How do you know this is true, Akil?" Tiy asked, resting her chin on the dainty tip of her thumb. Her intelligent dark eyes shimmered with light from the torches in her chamber, and Akil found it difficult to find his tongue. No matter how humble her origins, she was a goddess, surely as divine as Pharaoh.

"I heard their conversation with my own ears," he said,

lowering his forehead to the marble floor where he had prostrated himself. "The vizier's son said he had to return to the
desert where the invasion force was training. So I took a boat
at once to bring you word—"

"A military force," the queen echoed, her voice dark with re-
strained power. "Pharaoh should be told of this."

"That's what I thought." Akil dared to lift his gaze to her
august person. "But who am I to tell him? My humble words
would be but a buzzing in his ear."

"I will tell him." Tiy's dark hair swung about her proud
shoulders as she stood. Akil bowed his head again, unable to
bear the sight of her curving, regal figure at so close a distance.

"Thank you, Akil," she said, her voice now coolly impersonal. "Speak of this to no one else, and I will send a message
to Pharaoh on the ship that carries you back to Malkata. But I
will urge him to do nothing until I have had an opportunity to
spy out the matter. If the situation is what it seems, something
must be done."

Speechless with admiration, Akil nodded.

"It is unfortunate, of course, for the young man." Tiy's dark
eyes, too hard for beauty, were now as flat and unreadable as
stone. "I liked Menashe, he seemed a great deal more sensible
than his brother." She tapped the fingertips of her hands
together. "But treason cannot be tolerated. We would commit
a great injustice if we executed our vizier's son without proof
of his sedition, so we will give him time, and a little rope…and
wait to see whether or not he will hang himself."

What a glorious gift of the gods she was! What a song he
would write to praise her cunning!

"Now go." Her words echoed in the chamber. "And
remember—tell no one."

Buoyed by the knowledge that he had been of service to the
queen of his heart, Akil backed away.

The inky sky faded to indigo and then to deep purple; the
silver stars gradually withdrew into the vault of heaven, leaving
Yosef alone with his thoughts. He had left his home before
sunrise for several reasons, chief among them his wish to avoid

a confrontation with Menashe. Last night Ani had come into Yosef's chambers and reported that the wayward son had finally returned to the villa. With an uplifted brow the old man had lifted the unspoken question—do you want to see him?—and Yosef had been forced to admit that he did not.

Why, Menashe? he questioned, walking through the nearly deserted streets. He locked his hands behind his back and kept his eyes intent on the smooth path beneath his feet. *Why did you embark on this foolish task without asking for my permission, even my advice? Could we not have discussed your ideas?*

As he approached the docks, his mind supplied the answers. Menashe wouldn't talk to him because he knew how Yosef would respond: *God is not calling the sons of Yisrael back to Canaan; I have already decreed that our people will remain in Goshen.* He was a decisive, busy man, he had no patience or time for theory or postulation or suppositions. In over twenty years, in fact, he had no time for his son. His time belonged to Amenhotep, to Egypt.

On his loneliest days, in snatched moments between the endless interviews and appointments, Yosef wondered if his burden was too much for one man to bear. But he had been fulfilling these responsibilities for over twenty-seven years, and he was still as strong and capable as any man in Pharaoh's service. He could serve another thirty years if God Shaddai so willed. Amenhotep trusted him, and such confidence was a rare gift.

The stars had completely faded behind a sky of dark blue velvet by the time his felucca reached the palace at Malkata. The guards at the gate bowed and allowed him to pass, and Yosef automatically turned through the halls that would lead him to Pharaoh's bedchamber.

Every morning after the divine pharaoh had been awakened by his hymn-singing priests, and then perfumed, painted and bedecked in a spotless kilt and the crowns of Upper and Lower Egypt, Yosef was the first official to greet him. Today, as the god-king ate his breakfast, Yosef sat at a respectful distance and outlined his work of the previous day.

Yesterday, he reported, he had interviewed three governors of Egypt's southern nomes, read an assortment of agricultural

and tax reports from all the nomarchs and inspected the king's
bodyguard. He had dispatched a detail to investigate a disturbance at one of the northeastern military posts, and asked for
information from navy officials who commanded forts on the
Nile. He had heard accountings from the leading priests of
Thebes's temples, received a full report from an assistant in
charge of overseeing the valuable timbered lands and asked for
a summary of the Nile's progress from the Nile readers at Ele-
phantine. After completing this work he had returned to his
villa, where a long line of complainants waited for him to hear
their cases and pronounce judgment.

He paused. Amenhotep, who usually ate his breakfast and
listened to Yosef's report with few comments, sat silently,
ignoring the priests' offerings, and gazed at his vizier like a bird
staring at a snake.

Supposing that the king had an upset stomach, Yosef continued to read. "Four hundred healthy cattle were gathered in
taxes from the city-states of Syria," he said, consulting the
scroll in his hand, "with two hundred bushels of grain, three
hundred barrels of wine, two hundred of oil, two hundred of
honey. And the princes of Mitanni have sent five hundred deben
weight of silver to secure your marriage to Astra, daughter of
one of their kings."

Ordinarily the mention of a woman would have elicited an
exclamation for good or ill, but Amenhotep still said nothing.
At the sound of Pharaoh's silence, Yosef lowered the papyrus
parchments to his lap.

"What is troubling you, my lord?" Yosef asked. "By the
love I hold for you and the trust you place in me, I beg you to
speak freely."

Amenhotep's square jaw tensed. "Last night," Pharaoh said
mockingly, "I learned that your son Menashe has been training
a secret military force in the wilderness east of Tura."

Yosef's body tightened, then he forced himself to take a deep
breath. Whatever had happened in the desert did not matter
now, for Menashe was home where he belonged. Though Yosef
had not yet spoken to his son, the young man was certainly no
longer involved with the scheme to retake Canaan. That

escapade—the misadventures of a few hot-blooded Hebrew youths—had been concluded.

Yosef shook his head. "There are no secret military forces in Egypt, my king. I am your vizier, and I would know if such a thing were true."

"Do you know every secret, then?" Amenhotep threw the words like stones. "Does your god tell you everything that goes on in this kingdom?"

"Not everything, Pharaoh." Yosef tipped his head back. "But He has given me guidance about all matters of importance."

The king's brows flickered and he settled back in his seat. "All matters of importance," he repeated, tracing his finger along the curved arm of his gilded chair. "Is your family not important, then? For I have it on good authority that your elder son has been recruiting my Medjay warriors for a foray into Canaan. He was seen *here,* yesterday, striking hands with my giant. If the rumor is true, he is planning to invade lands that have been under Egypt's authority and defense since the time of Tuthmosis III. How shall I explain to the Canaanite governors that *my* warriors are attacking territories under *my* protection?"

For an instant Yosef could not think. A wave of grayness passed over him, a dark premonition. For though the king's charge was preposterous, he knew with pulse-pounding certainty that Pharaoh spoke the truth. Menashe was stubborn and he might yet persist in this unreasonable and foolish notion. But would he go so far as to appear at Malkata to brazenly recruit Pharaoh's elite guards?

His temper rose. What would make a young man dishonor his father and even the king? Deliberately, consciously and in full knowledge that he would severely damage his father's reputation, Menashe had rebelliously plowed through a carefully cultivated character and position.

Anger and frustration surged in Yosef's soul, accompanied by a deep sense of shame. If his lack of parental control was obvious to Pharaoh, it would be apparent to the entire kingdom. Word of this misadventure would spread throughout the palace by nightfall and be repeated in the nobles' houses by the following sunrise. By week's end, every man and woman in

Thebes would know that Zaphenath-paneah had foolishly
allowed his son to anger Pharaoh—

By heaven above, what if Pharaoh cast Yosef off? He would
have every right to do so, for Yosef had permitted his son to
commit an abominable act…

Yosef slipped from his chair and lowered himself to the
floor, feeling for the first time in his life that he *groveled* before
his king. "Forgive me, my lord, for disappointing you and
failing as a father," he whispered, choking on the words. "And
forgive my son for his senseless actions. I will remedy the situation immediately. I will do whatever has to be done."

Pharaoh stretched the silence, his eyes icy and unresponsive,
then commanded his vizier to rise. When Yosef stood again before
him, the king smiled in a way that only emphasized that he hadn't
smiled before. "Find your son—" Amenhotep spoke in the tone
a father might use to reprimand a child "—and keep him at home.
The gods have blessed us since you and your people came here.
We have no wish to see you leave. And we will not hold the shame
of one son against the other. If your son Menashe forgoes these
foolish plans for battle, your son Efrayim shall marry my
daughter Sitamun. And our two houses shall be joined forever."

Intensely humiliated, Yosef could only nod.

"Now, back to your report." Pharaoh dipped his hand into a
bowl of succulent grapes. "Tell me more about this daughter of
the Mitannis."

"Did you not stop to think how this action would appear to
Pharaoh?" Yosef heard bitterness spill over into his voice, but
he did not care. Menashe stood before him, his hands hanging
at his side, his eyes closed, his head unbowed. A proud figure,
who might have swelled Yosef's heart with admiration if the
signs of pride had not reminded him so much of himself.

Yosef had chosen to address his wayward son from the authority of the dais in the grand reception hall. The regal height
of the chamber only seemed to emphasize his son's solitary
figure. Thirty men waited outside in the vestibule, anxious to
whine, complain or beg for justice, but at the moment Yosef had
no time for anyone but his own stubborn son.

Menashe said nothing, and Yosef clenched his fist, torn between confrontation and forgiveness. If Menashe would only confess and apologize, all would be forgotten. Amenhotep could be distracted from this mistake, the wedding plans for Sitamun and Efrayim would provide a pleasant diversion.

Yosef took a deep breath and forced himself to calm down. "Pharaoh has promised to forgive if you abandon this fool-hardy venture." He gripped the armrests of his chair. "He has promised that Efrayim will marry Sitamun, thus linking our houses for all time. In a few months, if you please the king, you may be offered one of the younger princesses—"

"I do not want to marry a princess." Menashe's voice grated in the spacious chamber. He lifted his gaze to meet Yosef's face. His eyes, cold and proud—oh, how well Yosef understood them!

"Well, then. If the royal women do not suit you, there are yet a hundred noble families in Thebes who would be happy for their daughters to be joined with Zaphenath-paneah's house."

"No." Menashe's well-formed mouth took on an unpleasant twist. "I love Jendayi, the harpist in Akil's orchestra. I will marry her or no one."

"A slave?" Surprise caught Yosef off guard, then laughter floated up from his throat. "You could no more marry one of Pharaoh's slaves than I could move the sun backward. Why would you hunger for a slave when a princess is within your reach? When you are ready—"

"Father, for a man of understanding, you are confused." Menashe's resolute, confident face mocked him. "God has called me to lead our people back to Canaan. I will not marry an Egyptian princess, nor any of the noble Egyptian women. I love Jendayi. If God can lead us to Canaan, He can arrange for her to be my bride."

Yosef had built his career on being patient and slow to speak, but now a raw and foreign fury rose in his throat and almost choked him. Never had anyone, king or commoner, slave or servant, guard or warrior, dared to speak to him with such determined resistance. And this was his son! The child he had brought into the world, provided for, prayed about, fretted over—

"You will not speak to me in that tone!"

Menashe's eyes glowed with intelligence and independence of spirit; when had they begun to look so adult? He thrust his hands behind his back. "What tone should I use, Father? I have tried speaking to you in a more humble voice, but you would not listen."

"I always listen to wisdom! But you speak foolishness!"

"I speak what God has told me."

"God has told you nothing! He speaks to *me!*"

"Can God not speak to me, too?" The young man opened his hands and held them before his chest. "Or must He always speak through Pharaoh's noble vizier?"

"Of course He can speak to others," Yosef said, irritated by his son's mocking tone. "But He would not contradict Himself. And He told me that the famine would come, and we would be preserved in Egypt—"

"Eighteen years ago." Menashe's eyes darkened with emotion. "God used you, Father, and now the Almighty has chosen to use me. He may choose to use others. Why can you not believe the truth?"

Yosef opened his mouth to speak, but the words died before they reached his tongue. He wanted to reply that *he* was the inheritor of Yaakov's blessing of the firstborn, and he was far from dead. His brothers were yet strong and powerful, and Efrayim had received a greater blessing than Menashe. God Shaddai might have chosen any of a host of deserving, righteous men before calling Menashe…but hadn't Yosef seen that God sometimes chose to work in inexplicable ways?

But God would not, He could not, call the Hebrews out of the Black Land without giving Yosef some sign. Menashe had to be mistaken. He was young, and the prospect of war had infected him like a fever.

"You are wrong," Yosef finally said, regretting that Menashe had chosen such a poor opportunity to unveil his talent for leadership. "God placed me in a position of authority over the family. If He wanted us to return to Canaan, He would have shown me."

A look of implacable determination remained on Menashe's face. "God set you apart as ruler in a foreign land," he countered, a hint of inexpressible sadness in his voice. "You are a

Hebrew, but you are not of the Hebrews, Father. You have sacrificed yourself in order to save your people, and God Shaddai
blessed you for your willingness to obey. But He calls the sons
of Yisrael out now, and He has called them through me, the least
of your sons, the least of the Hebrews. And I will obey, though
it costs me my life."

"It may." Yosef paused, hoping his words would sink into the
fog overpowering his son's reason. "Think, Menashe! Heed
the advice of your elders! No man is so old that he cannot live
another year, nor so young that he cannot die today. You may
think your uncles and I are used up while you are invincible,
but men of all ages die in war."

Menashe shrugged. "If I die, I die following the will of God."

Yosef flung his hands into the air, so furious he could hardly
speak. "It is Pharaoh's wish that you stop this nonsense. His
word is law. Will you obey it?"

"God's word is more powerful than Pharaoh's," Menashe
answered, his face full of strength. "I am not seeking to injure
Pharaoh, but I must obey God before any earthly king."

Yosef searched for another avenue of persuasion. "You say
you love this slave girl—then obey Pharaoh for her sake.
Remain here in Thebes and forget about Canaan, and I will see
what I can to do persuade Pharaoh to allow the marriage. It will
not be easy, but perhaps—"

An expression of pain crossed Menashe's face, but his eyes
still shone with a steadfast determination. "I love Jendayi with
my life, but even for her I could not remain here when God has
called me away. My men are depending on me."

"Then hear me." Yosef felt his flesh color as he rose from
his ornamented chair. "Give this up, Menashe. Give this up
because it is my wish, and I am the father who gave you life. If
you won't do it for Pharaoh or this girl you love, do it for me."

Menashe's mouth twisted, but his dark eyes flashed a
warning as he locked his hands behind his back. "Do not ask
this, Father."

"But I am asking. I am demanding—no, I am begging you."
Yosef held out his hands in entreaty. "Remain here at home with
your brother. The others will grow tired of the hardships of war,

and in time they will return to Goshen. Their families miss them. They do not approve of this venture, either."

"I can't give up even for you, Father. God told me to lead our people back, and I will."

The last vestige of Yosef's patience vanished. "You are as stubborn as a child! God did not speak to you!" He glared at Menashe with a thunderous expression that had quelled weaker men, but Menashe did not cringe or waver beneath his gaze. He stood in the hall, his posture militant, the shadow of his beard bestowing an aura Yosef had never noticed before. By heaven above, when had the man emerged from the boy? Yosef had enjoyed a passing acquaintance with the child, but this man he did not know at all.

"We will hear no more of this," Yosef finished, looking away. Best to leave this interview as if he had won, though he knew he had not. He stared at the colorful paintings on the walls of the chamber, occupying his eyes so they would not have to meet his son's gaze. "You will leave me now and say nothing more of a return to Canaan. And we will find a suitable Egyptian family who has a daughter, a girl who would be proud to be part of the household of Zaphenath-paneah."

"I am no longer proud to be part of the household of Zaphenath-paneah." A sudden chill hung on the edge of Menashe's words. "If I must leave it in order to obey God Shaddai, I will."

Yosef felt weak and vulnerable in the face of his son's anger. With stiff, brittle dignity he returned to his chair as Menashe moved confidently out of the reception hall.

The vizier of all Egypt turned and sank onto the woven rush seat. Clinging to the armrests of the gilded throne, he bit his tongue lest he call his son back and surrender.

Outside his father's reception hall, Menashe stood in the courtyard and considered the western sky. The horizon blazed with violent shades of bronze and sapphire; the last gleaming slivers of sunlight clung to the skyline as if reluctant to leave the realms of the living for Anubis's dark abode of night.

Just as he was reluctant to leave his father's house.

He had not been surprised by the passion in his father's plea.

Yosef had always been an ardent defender of Amenhotep's position and power. What had surprised him was his father's unwillingness to consider that God might speak to a lesser man than the noble vizier. How could such a wise man be blind to the truth? Why couldn't he open his mind to the possibility that God was preparing to do something new?

What could prevent a father from believing in his son?

Menashe thrust his hands into the fabric belt of his tunic and slumped against a wall, absorbing the familiar sounds and sights of his father's villa. The complex had always hummed with activity at all hours of the day and night. As a boy he had played amidst the wonder of it all, never dreaming that all households did not entertain visiting kings, beautiful women and sons of Pharaoh. His life had been so full of important people and events and festivals that he nearly reached maturity without realizing that while he had comfort and excitement, other children had *parents*.

His mother had died while he and Efrayim were young, and his father had always been out of reach. Ani, Tarik, Halima and a host of other servants had hovered near to teach, train and apply ointments to the cuts and bruises gathered by a pair of rambunctious boys. Going back, picking up the strings of time, Menashe could remember occasions when he and Efrayim had breakfasted with their mother and father, but even then Yosef had been quick to kiss his little sons and send them out to play.

He was always sending them away. And now Menashe was ready to go.

The shades of night had fallen. Soon the giant Abnu would be outside the gates, ready to fulfill his promise. Menashe lifted his chin and strode toward his chamber to gather his things.

Abnu was a Medjay, and therefore a man of his word, so Menashe was not surprised when he stepped through the gate and found the giant loitering against a palm tree outside the villa. Over his shoulders the warrior wore a crimson cloak; a finely pleated kilt displayed his lean, athletic form and sinewy limbs to intimidating advantage. Red leather sandals with long, upward-curving toes shod his feet, a footwear unique to exalted

Nubians. At Menashe's approach, the warrior whirled and gave a smart salute, his dark reddish-brown skin gleaming in the faint light of the moon.

"Peace and prosperity to you, friend." Menashe flashed the man a smile of thanks. "Are you ready to begin the journey?"

"A Medjay is always ready for adventure," Abnu answered, his deep voice rumbling through the night. His long fingers gripped the iron-tipped spear in his hand. "Lead on, trickster, until I tire of you."

Menashe extended a hand toward the river, and together they walked over the beaten paths. Bittersweet memories rose to haunt him; he and Efrayim had often played along these trails. Ani had taken them fishing on the river; Tarik had always served as an official escort when they were allowed to stand on shore and observe their father's comings and goings on his magnificent barge.

Nostalgia made Menashe's throat ache. He didn't want to leave home under a cloud of disapproval, but what other choice did he have? To remain meant denying the voice of God Shaddai.

The small skiff Menashe had reserved was waiting at the docks. He had deliberately chosen a boat small enough to slip through the reeds that hid the entrance to the canal behind Malkata, and he sighed in relief when Abnu did not complain when it became obvious that he and Menashe would be the only oarsmen.

As he settled into the boat, Menashe begged Abnu's indulgence and announced that he had to stop at Malkata before proceeding to join the others. "A lady waits, and I must say goodbye," he explained as the boat lanced its way out of the still waters of the lagoon and into the river.

"Surely you are not taking me back to the palace!" Abnu grumbled, his bent knees nearly scraping his chin in the small craft. "I have just come from there. And if Pharaoh has heard that I am gone, he may order my brothers to implore me to stay." He lifted his brows. "Do you hear what I am saying?"

"I hear you." Menashe tossed a grin over his shoulder. "And apparently Pharaoh has already heard rumors. But I do not plan to enter the palace walls. If you will be quiet, all will be well."

The moon, sailing on a sky of deepest sapphire, cast a narrow bar of silver across the river, leaving the banks in shadow. Menashe trusted his instincts, turning his boat into the harbor beside the gleaming palace, then allowed the craft to drift along the reeds until he spied the gleam of water beyond the curtain of reeds.

The royal docks stood silent; the king's boats bobbed in the gentle wavewash. While Abnu quietly cursed the sharp stalks that razed his arms, Menashe maneuvered the skiff into the camouflaged canal, then sent the vessel winging around the curve of the meandering waterway. The only sounds were the soft lap of oars pulling against calm water and the buzz of insects.

A thin rectangle of light poured from the gate where Menashe had confronted the two guards, but the warriors themselves were not visible. "Insolent curs!" Abnu muttered. "Lazy beasts! If they were of my squadron I would cuff their ears, I would cut off the ends of their noses for deserting their posts."

"Then it is good for them you are with me," Menashe replied, urging the tiny vessel swiftly past the opening. He had to be quick, for the guards might reappear at any moment. But though he heard the musical murmur of male voices, the warriors did not show their faces. The skiff moved past the opening toward the mounded bank outside the secret garden. He did not know if Jendayi would be there, but he had every hope she might appear.

"What are we doing here, trickster?" Abnu grumbled, looking around. "It is bad enough I am sworn to serve you, but if you are up to mischief—"

There. The little door was barely visible inside the wall. "If you are as soft of heart as you are strong of limb," Menashe interrupted, "this may be the most rewarding debt you have ever paid." With a final solid pull on the oars he seated the bow of the skiff into the thick mud at the edge of the canal, then scrambled onto the bank. The dry soil of the upper bank cried out for the refreshing moisture of the inundation. In a few months the river would run full again…and so, Menashe hoped, would his heart.

"What are we doing here?" Abnu's exasperated whisper drifted up the bank.

Menashe sank onto a rock. "Waiting."

"For what?"

"A woman. You have said your farewells, I must say mine."

"By the stinking wax in Seth's ear," Abnu grumbled, un-furling his long legs and arms. Stretched out on the skiff, the warrior was nearly longer than the boat. "I agree to fight, and find I must listen to the croonings of lovers."

"I can only hope." Menashe fastened his eyes to the tiny door in the wall. "Go to sleep. I will wake you later."

He crouched on the bank, determined to wait until just before sunrise if necessary. As long as darkness covered the earth his father would assume Menashe slept in his chamber. The morning would be half-spent before the servants discovered him missing. At that point, news of Menashe's departure would be published throughout the house. Tarik would hear of it, and so would Ani. Their hearts would be wounded, but their grief would be too late. Their mourning should have begun years before.

The land spoke to him from all around and the skiff rocked with gentle sloshing sounds as wavelets lapped against it. Moon-light sifted through the leaves of a tree overhanging the wall, forming strange silvery hieroglyphs on the ground at Menashe's feet. What did the shadows say, he wondered, studying the moving patterns. Did they promise him victory or foretell his defeat?

A dull wooden clop disturbed the quiet. The tiny door in the wall, wavering through shifting shadows, creaked. Menashe caught his breath, afraid that any sudden sound might frighten Jendayi away. As silently as a cat, he crept over the bank toward the wall.

Little by little, the young harpist's head and shoulders edged through the doorway, seeming to test the silence. Menashe froze in his place, his heart reveling in open admiration of her beauty and bravery.

"Trickster!" Abnu called from the boat. "Is the lady com-ing or not?"

Like a turtle zipping back into its shell, Jendayi's head dis-appeared behind the door. Menashe sprang forward to stop her. "Jendayi!" he called in a rough whisper, hoping she had not run back through the garden in a frightened retreat. "It is your friend! Please, there is nothing to fear!"

The door creaked open once again. Her head, wreathed by a lovely circlet of flowers, appeared and lifted toward him. "Chenzira?" she asked the darkness, her arms and shoulders tensed for flight.

"Yes, do not fear." He moved to her side. "You said you came here often, and I wanted to see you before I go."

"You are still going away?" She gave him her hands. He helped her out of the tunnel and she stood before him, her eyes dark and unfathomable.

Struggling with the sense of confusion her presence always elicited, Menashe had difficulty finding his tongue. "Yes," he said, aware of the pressure of her hands on his. "I am leaving the vizier's house, and I do not think I shall ever return. But I could not leave without telling you…everything. I want to be honest with you, Jendayi."

"Did you speak to Efrayim?" Her hands struggled to rise like a pair of tethered birds, but he held tight, strengthening his heart against the sting of Efrayim's name.

"I did not see much of Efrayim in these past two days," he told her. "He has been spending most of his time at Pharaoh's palace in Thebes. Princess Sitamun is there with her mother, and Efrayim has done his best to charm and entertain the princess."

Jendayi's face fell, but Menashe clung to her fingers. "Jendayi, do not let your heart be troubled."

"You are sweet to be concerned for me." She pulled away from him and took a few steps toward the black water, absently testing each footfall. "But you should not worry so much. What does it matter if Efrayim marries another? As long as he cares enough to ask for me, my future is assured."

Menashe felt the chasm between them open like a wound. "Why is Efrayim so important to you?" he stammered, not caring what Abnu might hear from the canal beyond. "What gives him the right to your heart—a kiss? A kiss is nothing but an intimation of love, sometimes there is no truth in it. People kiss one another all the time."

He moved toward her, fully expecting her to launch into an

impassioned defense of the man she loved, but was surprised when tears spilled from her eyes. "Not me," she whispered, her forlorn cry rending his heart. "No one kisses me. In my entire life, I cannot remember any other kiss. Only Efrayim's."

Menashe took a quick, sharp breath. "No one else? Not even your mother, a friend, a sister—"

"I have no mother, at least not one I can remember." Tears glistened on her delicate, heart-shaped face. "No friends, no sisters. Akil assigned me a handmaid, but Kesi serves me only because she would be beaten if she did not obey."

"Your master, then," Menashe suggested, though something in him recoiled at the thought of the old chironomist planting his pruned lips on Jendayi's face. "Surely he has shown some affection for you."

"Akil is a hard taskmaster." She palmed tears from her cheeks. "He cares for me only to please Pharaoh." She sniffed, then wiped her wet hands across the neckline of her gown in a helpless gesture. "But Efrayim kissed me once, so he must love me. And if my heart does not learn to love, I will die a thousand deaths. I will be eaten by the monster in the Underworld. I dream of it, and I know it will happen."

"Jendayi, hear me." Menashe moved to her side in one swift step. Though she tensed at his sudden approach, he gathered her into his arms and held her in a gentle embrace. "My dear girl," he said, one hand stroking her cheek while the other held her close, "you *are* loved. Forget Efrayim, he loves another. I love you, Jendayi. I would risk my life before Pharaoh himself in order to win your freedom."

She stiffened in his arms, and for an instant Menashe felt as if he held a statue of the most fragile glass. "You love me?" In spite of her sorrow a tinge of exasperation entered her voice. "Chenzira, I am not asking for pity."

"I don't pity you. I think you are the most beautiful, the most talented woman I have ever met."

"You feel sorry for me. I am heartbroken, and alone—and blind."

"I love you. I have loved you since the day I first saw you."

"Two months ago?" Firmly she placed her hands on his chest

and pushed him away. "Your kindness is touching, Chenzira. But you belong to the vizier, I belong to the king. Neither of us has the power to change our fates." Her polite smile faded. "Efrayim once sent word that he was willing to ask for me, but he obviously preferred to ask for the king's daughter."

"That wasn't Efrayim!" Menashe clenched his fist and took a deep breath. If ever God had sent an opportunity to tell her the truth, this was it. "This message from Efrayim came while you were in Canaan, after you played for the vizier's guests, right?"

Her brows lifted. "Why am I surprised you would know that. You serve in the vizier's house. You were probably in Canaan with us."

His lips trembled with the need to laugh. "Yes, I was there! But the message you received came from me."

"But Kesi said she spoke with the captain of the vizier's guard."

"She did." Menashe firmed his voice. "I sent the message. I did not carry it. Jendayi, I am not the vizier's servant, but his elder son. And you must believe me when I say I have loved you for years."

She backed away without speaking, one hand over her lips, the familiar mask of aloofness descending like a shadow on her face. She was retreating inside herself, a frightened slave scurrying away from a nobleman. If he did not catch her—

He rushed on. "I told you my name was Chenzira because I did not think you would confide in me if you knew the truth."

"You were right." She turned and faced the river, her head bowed. "It is not right for a slave to share her heart with a master. But you lied."

He edged forward until he could see her troubled face. "I am not your enemy, Jendayi. I would not hurt you for the world."

She lifted her chin, but kept her face toward the water as if she could see a world of mystery in the canal beyond. For a brief moment her face seemed to open, and Menashe saw a whirl of spinning emotions: bewilderment, a quick flicker of fear, pure and simple agony. Then the mask of detachment descended again.

"You are the vizier's son." She wrapped her arms around herself as though a chill wind had just blown over her. "Like Efrayim, you will marry a noblewoman whether you want to or not. This *love* of yours is not real. It is a childish fancy. I will not risk this life and the eternal one on the fickleness of a nobleman's heart. I should not even be speaking to you—"

"I am no longer the vizier's son," he said, moving toward her as though being closer would help her understand. "Tonight I left my father's house and everyone in it. My father will disown me, if he has not already. I have no family, no possessions, no support. I came here tonight to tell you the truth and to offer you my love. I must go to war, but when God Shaddai brings me back, I will stand before Pharaoh and give him a portion of the captured spoils as a bride-price. I will redeem you from Pharaoh, Jendayi. My god will arrange it. You will be free to choose your own path."

"You expect a lot of your god," she whispered.

"He loves to provide." Menashe moved to stand between her and the meandering canal. Carefully, he reached out and placed his hands on her arms, drawing her to him. She did not resist, but neither did she relax except to put out a hand to steady herself against his chest.

Her light touch unfurled streamers of sensation that left Menashe light-headed. "I will return for you." His pulse skittered as he felt the movement of her breathing against his skin. "As Pharaoh lives and God Shaddai provides, I will return."

Her face lifted to his then, and beneath the aloof loveliness he saw a suggestion of movement and flowing, as though a hidden spring were trying to break through. "Chenzira— Menashe, it is hopeless." Disbelief echoed in the tone of her voice. "I have seen my future. There is no love for me, not here, not anywhere."

"Yes, there is." Menashe locked her in his embrace. "Give me the opportunity to show you, Jendayi. One chance. That's all I ask of you."

"And if you do not return?" Her chin quivered and she lowered her head, her thick, dark lashes fringing her cheek. "If I trust you, believe in you, and you do not return for me, what shall I do then?"

Menashe cradled her head against his shoulder, not certain how to answer. "I will return," he said finally, releasing her head so he could study her sweet countenance one final time. "And if you will trust me, your heart will begin to live. Defeat your dream now, Jendayi. Have faith in me…and in my god Almighty."

Despite the sorrowful bend of her posture, the corner of her delicate mouth lifted in a half-smile. "You sound so confident. I could almost believe you," she whispered, just before leaving the circle of his arms.

And while the stars sprang out, one by one, from the cobalt dome of the heavens, Menashe watched her slip back into the palace garden and thought that nothing on earth had ever seemed more breathtaking than the simple grace of his beloved Jendayi.

Chapter Twenty

Akil frowned as the musicians finished their final song for Pharaoh's banquet. Fortunately the king had not noticed that the oboe and harp consistently clashed in the final cadences of Hathor's hymn of praise, but several of the guests had unconsciously cringed at the dissonant sounds.

A group of female acrobats took to the open floor now, leaping, twirling and undulating to the beat of their own drummer, and Akil nodded to his instrumentalists, granting them permission to retreat from the king's banquet chamber. He fixed his gaze on Jendayi as she slipped her arms around her harp and lifted it. A frown had occupied the space between her delicate brows for the past several nights, and he wondered again if she had received some message from the vizier's son. All of Thebes buzzed with rumors about Menashe's failure to appear at a recent palace ceremony with his father and brother Efrayim; Pharaoh had been much displeased. But Queen Tiy had caught Akil's eye and lifted a confident brow, and he knew she had matters under control.

But perhaps Jendayi was privy to information even the queen would not know. If Akil could bring that information to the queen's ear, her estimation of him would rise even higher. Perhaps she would award him with a golden chain, or a special suite of rooms within the palace...

The flutist and oboist pattered out of the chamber. As Jendayi followed with her maid, Akil followed them into the hallway, then caught Kesi's arm. Placing his fingers across his mouth to signal silence, he pulled her away from the harpist and drew her into a private alcove.

"What seems to be troubling your mistress?" he asked, painting on the warmest smile he could muster. "She is not herself these days. Tonight she played with less than her usual brilliance."

"I—I don't know," Kesi stammered. She paled before his questioning gaze. "I haven't done anything to displease her, I'm certain of it. Please, master, don't send me away."

"Hush, foolish girl." Again he forced a smile. "Something is troubling Jendayi. I know her too well to miss the signs of discontent. You must find out what is bothering her."

"Master, she does not often talk to me. She rarely confides in anyone."

"Make her trust you." His breath burned in his throat; were all slaves as stupid as this girl? But he must control his temper, or like a chattering bird she would fly and warn the harpist. He took a deep breath. "Speak to her tonight, draw her into your confidence about something. If you tell her a secret, she will want to confide in you. It is the way of women."

"I don't think it will work, master." The girl's eyes clouded with doubt. "She is most withdrawn lately. She does not talk about herself. I never know what she is thinking."

"Then find out." Not bothering to smile this time, he ripped the words. "Find out, or I will send you to the overseer, and he will beat you into obedience. Need I say more?"

"No, Master Akil." A familiar weakness settled about her eyes, the way all women looked just before they cried. "I will try to get her to talk."

"Don't try." Akil released his hold on her arm. "Do it."

Chapter Twenty-One

A shaft of sun angled down from a clerestory window in Pharaoh's chamber, trapping slow convections of dust. Feeling as distant as the stars from the priests who intoned the ritual blessings before Pharaoh, Yosef watched the dancing particles and considered the unsettling matters of his own household.

For two weeks Yosef had said nothing to his servants about Menashe's defiant departure. No one dared mention the young man's absence to him, correctly sensing that the subject was a delicate and difficult one. Ani, who made it his duty to know everything and everyone who passed through the vizier's villa, went about his work a little more quietly than usual, his face longer and his step slower than it had been in weeks past. And Tarik, that most inspiring of warriors, briefed his men every morning in a voice so dull and dry the words seemed to come from him after a lengthy journey through a desolate wilderness.

But his servants had been wearied by the extra demands of the settlement at Goshen, Yosef told himself. The sons of Yisrael were busy building proper houses, and Ani had been employed to help the Hebrews procure the necessary workers to form bricks and bring lumber from Lebanon. And Tarik had not only the safety of the vizier's household to worry about, but now also responsible for overseeing the caravans which traveled from Thebes to Goshen and back again.

Yosef went about his work as best he could, knowing the

situation with Menashe was a threatening cloud that would hang over his head until it burst. A week after Menashe left, Yosef had sent out patrols to report the movements and makeup of the Hebrew force. But though Tarik's men had scoured the area between Tura and Goshen, the patrols had not been able to find Menashe's recruits. Pharaoh had not yet asked how the situation with Menashe had been resolved, but if the phantom force still existed, the king would soon hear of it. Knowing his stubborn son, Yosef was certain the rogue army remained alive and well.

On his last visit Yehuda reported that one hundred fifty young men were missing from the Hebrew camp. Even a few of the younger women, Yehuda noted, had wondered aloud if a move back to Canaan might not be in the family's best interest.

"But we, your brothers," Yehuda hastened to add, "believe in your leadership, noble vizier. If you want us to remain here, we will stay. We wrested your dreams of honor and glory from you many years ago, but God Shaddai, all praise to His name, restored them. Who are we to doubt you? Besides, we are content and prosperous. You, noble Yosef, have bountifully provided for our needs. We do not worry about drought, crop failure or sickness. If disaster strikes, we know the vizier Zaphenath-paneah stands ready and willing to provide for us."

Now, as Yosef sat across the room from Pharaoh and listened to the priests praise the king, he wondered if he had not spoiled his brethren. He loved them, he wanted to make up for the many years they had been apart, and he knew God had brought him to Egypt in order to provide for them. Menashe was right about at least one thing—Yosef had been set apart. The hand of God had woven Egypt into the fabric of his life; he could no more wrest himself from the palace on the Nile than he could divide his soul from his spirit.

Yet a cloud of doubt hovered over his conscience. Years ago, while Yosef lived and worked in Potiphar's house, pride had been the seismic fault of his life. Had that most subtle and poisonous of evils returned to infect his soul when he least suspected it?

The priests finished their hymn of praise to the divine king, and Pharaoh extended his crook, bestowing blessings on his faithful servants. The worship concluded, Amenhotep stood in one regal motion and uncrossed the crook and flail from before his chest. The crook, a symbol of his duty to shepherd his people, seemed less prominent to Yosef today than the flail, a symbol of the *ladanisterion,* a type of whip used by agricultural workers to gather ladanum, the aromatic shrub that yielded resin when beaten. As Yosef stood and followed his king from the bedchamber, he wondered if Pharaoh had used a sort of *ladanisterion* on him. Ever since Amenhotep had confronted him with news of Menashe and the alleged uprising, Yosef had felt limp with weariness and defeat.

When they left the king's priests behind, Yosef lengthened his stride, falling into step beside the king. "A large crowd awaits your judgment today," he remarked, trying to discern the royal mood. "They are gathered outside in the courtyard."

The king's eyes seemed to study the tile floor where they walked. "And after a tiring morning. I don't know why they come to Malkata. Why do they not approach you? Why do they insist on bothering me?"

Yosef folded his hands and struggled for a tactful reply. If Pharaoh had been younger, Yosef would have reminded him that kingship offered both privilege and responsibility. But the time for character lessons had passed. Amenhotep's temperament and personality, for good or ill, had already been formed.

"The men who wait to see you are noblemen, and deserve an audience with their king. I have rendered judgment on hundreds of cases in Thebes within the past month. But these men serve you with their lives, they hold important posts throughout the kingdom—"

"They know I will agree with you," Pharaoh interrupted. His smile flashed, dazzling against his olive skin. "You are my teacher, my right hand. How could I not agree with you?"

Yosef smiled, glorying in the intimate moment. Surely there was no better time to bring up a disagreeable subject. Pharaoh was feeling nostalgic and anticipating the pleasures of his harem…

"My king—" Yosef dipped his head "—I have been considering something of great importance and would like to know your thoughts on the matter."

Amenhotep stopped in the passageway. A flash of humor

crossed his face as he turned. "It must be a troubling matter indeed, since you know everything except for the one subject in which I am expert."

Yosef lifted a wagging finger. "The matter has nothing to do with women."

Pharaoh released a throaty laugh as he crossed his arms. "Speak, then. What is it?"

"My people, the Hebrews." Yosef's gaze swept over the king's face. "You have said you do not approve of a military force to reestablish our home in Canaan, and in those words you have again revealed your wisdom. But if my brothers and their families could return to Canaan in peace, would you allow them to go?"

Amenhotep's eyes widened in concern. "Are they unhappy? Have I not made every allowance for them?"

"Yes, my king, you have been more than generous, and they are prosperous." Yosef smiled. "But this is not their land, it is yours. And some of the younger ones are hot-headed. They hear stories of the old days and yearn for glory. Their hearts desire to live in their own promised land."

"You must remind them that glory lies in Egypt." Pharaoh nodded. "No king has been greater than I, no king has fought fewer wars or seen greater contentment among his people. No one has starved during my reign, the land has bountifully brought forth food. The temples I have built shall last throughout eternity."

"Yes, my lord, but the younger ones—" Yosef halted, aware that his king was not listening. Pharaoh stood silent, gazing into private space, and his eyes were those of a bewildered, vulnerable child. Yosef felt his heart constrict in guilt. He had tried to prepare this fatherless boy for the throne, yet his work might never be finished.

"You taught me about life, Zaphenath-paneah." A momentary look of discomfort flitted across Amenhotep's face. "My mother and father both loved you. How could you think of leaving me?"

"I could not consider it," Yosef answered. He bowed to reinforce his sincerity. "As long as I live, I will not leave you. You have my solemn oath."

Though Pharaoh did not answer, the gratified expression on his face spoke for him. He moved ahead toward his throne room, humming the tuneless hymn the priests had sung earlier.

And as they continued through the passageway, Yosef knew he would not leave the Black Land alive. God Shaddai often spoke in miraculous ways; Yosef himself had heard God's voice in dreams and visions. So why could He not speak through the voice of a king?

The conversation with Amenhotep restored Yosef's confidence in his own reasoning, and with a lighter heart he approached the queen's apartments in the palace at Thebes. An urgent message had been waiting for him when he returned from Malkata, and the queen's messenger said Tiy would wait for the vizier's appearance, no matter how late the hour.

A guard led him to the queen's innermost private chamber; a pair of slaves took his dusty traveling cloak and removed his leather sandals. As he sat on a delicate chair and immersed his dusty feet into a basin of water, he closed his eyes and rested his head on a luxurious pillow. The day had been long and hot, his work a series of endless and vain repetitions. He hoped the queen's business was not urgent.

A slave dried his feet and urged him to recline on a cushioned chaise longue. Yosef moved to it, pressing the back of his hand over his tired eyes as he savored the sweetly mingled scents of lotus blossoms and incense. Notoriously tardy, the queen might keep him waiting an hour or more.

He had closed his eyes and drifted into a shallow doze when a hand fell on his skin. His eyes sprang open. Tiy sat beside him on a chaise built for one, her left hand lingered on his chest. He wondered if she could feel his discomfort, the sudden banging of his blood.

"My queen," he whispered, scarcely daring to move.

"My vizier," she answered, her voice no more than a soft purr in the silence of the room. The scent of her heavy perfume assaulted him; green malachite gleamed from her eyelids, reminding him that just this morning he had jokingly told Pharaoh that most women were not so young as they were painted...

Glancing left and right, he realized the servants had departed. No guards, no handmaids, no daughters lingered in the chamber. They were alone.

"Excuse me." He lifted his head in an attempt to sit up. "I was rude to fall asleep."

Her hand held him to the bench. "I understand, and I pardon both your weariness and your lack of manners. I know you have spent the greater part of the day at Malkata." She lifted her free hand and gazed at her henna-tinted nails. "And how is my husband's harem faring?"

"Everyone at Malkata is well." He lowered his head, tense and tired but not wanting to anger her.

"I know that, too." She turned the full power of her smile on him. "There is little about you I do not know, Zaphenath-paneah, known to the Hebrews as Yosef."

The mention of his familiar name sent a warning shiver through him, and his face burned as he remembered another woman, another house, another time. Sagira, Potiphar's wife, had caught him alone in a room decorated much like this one, and she, too, had held the power of his life in her hands. God had preserved Yosef then, though he had suffered mightily for his resistance. But Tiy was not a bundle of raw emotions like Sagira. Amenhotep's was an intelligent, pragmatic woman. Surely he could reason with her.

"My queen," he said, "forgive me if I overstep my authority. But I must beg you to reconsider what our surroundings lead me to believe you intend to suggest."

Her lower lips edged forward in a pout. "Ah, Zaphenath-paneah, you are no fun at all. My husband has a harem filled with women. Why shouldn't the queen be allowed to find love where she can?"

"Because the queen is wise," Yosef answered, daring to take the hand that clung to his chest. He lifted it, held it up as if in salute, then dropped it into her lap as he sat upright. "You do not want to do this. Later you would hate me. And such an act would betray the king's trust in both of us."

Though she did not move to touch him again, an invitation lingered in the smoldering depths of her eyes. "Think carefully, my vizier. You have no wife to smell the scent of another woman on your skin, and I am quite alone here. No one would know. We might take our fill of each other until the dawn."

"God Shaddai would know," Yosef interrupted, sliding away from her. "And so, I daresay, would those who know me well. A righteous man's eyes look openly on the world. If he should build a wall behind those eyes, the people who know him would wonder. My captain, my steward, they would know."

"I am surprised you did not mention your sons." Tiy quirked an eyebrow. "Particularly the elder, Menashe. Or do your sons not know you as well as your captain and your steward?"

Yosef flushed, helpless to halt his embarrassment. How much did she know about the situation with Menashe? She could have spies anywhere, even in his house.

"My people know me." He ignored her question about his sons as he swung his feet to the floor. "If there is no other business here, I should be getting back to my villa. I trust you see the wisdom in this course of action."

"I suppose—" she shifted on the chair to see him better "—you are right, as always, noble Zaphenath-paneah. I have offered you the chance to correct an injustice of history, and you have. Tonight you will leave the scorned woman clothed and with your full dignity, not at all like the other time when you ran naked into the stable."

Mercifully, the dim light of the chamber hid the extent of his humiliation. Her immodest comments, however true, were ill-suited to her position. Though he had not smelled beer on her breath, she was behaving like a drunken woman. Tomorrow she would remember…and feel shame.

"I give you good night," he said, inclining his head.

"Wait." Her hand, like a fist of iron, closed around his wrist. "I did not bring you here to seduce you, most noble vizier. I brought you here to discuss a matter of vast importance for the kingdom."

"And that is?"

She gave him a humorless smile. "Amenhotep. I love him, but though he believes otherwise, he is not the greatest pharaoh Egypt has ever known. I would be a better one."

Yosef looked up, startled beyond words.

"Yes." She stared at him in deadly concentration. "You know I speak the truth. Amenhotep spends all his time and energy on his women and his infernal monuments when he could be expanding Egypt's boundaries."

Yosef pressed his hand to his forehead, trying to force his confused thoughts into order.

"Just this week I have heard rumors of unrest in Hatti and Mitanni," she went on, her voice like velvet edged with steel. "With troops gathered from our nomarchs, we could send an invasion force and subdue those unruly kings. Pharaoh is always talking about Tuthmosis the great warrior, and yet he will do nothing to make his own reputation greater than that king's. Yet it could be done. Just as Hatshepsut placed a puppet pharaoh on the throne while she ruled with her steward's aid, you and I can rule more effectively than Amenhotep."

"Are you suggesting that we—" the word *murder* would not cross his lips "—get rid of the king?"

"Of course not." She frowned as if he'd suggested something distasteful. "I love my husband. I would not even go as far as Hatshepsut, who eventually took the throne, crown and royal insignia for herself. But I can rule in private and leave Amenhotep to his adoring public. Together we could do this. If you will sign your name with mine to letters to the governors of the nomarchs, we will state our intention to handle all domestic and foreign affairs from the palace at Thebes. In time, when Pharaoh finds out, he will be displeased, but then he will realize we have acted for his own benefit. He will be king in people's hearts, while we will extend the power of Egypt throughout Canaan, Hatti and Mitanni."

The heavy power in her eyes laid hold of something in Yosef's being, and for an instant he found himself caught up in her plans. Amenhotep *was* unsure of himself, he did spend too much time in pleasure and wasteful entertainments, and Tiy had always been the more resourceful and realistic of the two. Who could say that God had not called Yosef to Egypt's throne rooms for this time and purpose? If Egypt's warriors moved through Canaan and subdued the hostile kingdoms there, the sons of Yisrael could chose from the best lands in the world, while he, Zaphenath-paneah, made provision for their welfare…

When Yosef looked away, needing a moment to reorient himself, the voice of common sense attacked his grandiose dreams. The queen, he realized, was contemplating treason far worse than anything Menashe had ever suggested. The priests would consider her plan complete and unthinkable foolishness. She was not the divine pharaoh, Amenhotep was. She was not even the dynasty heiress; one of Amenhotep's sisters had married him to establish his place in the royal lineage. And Yosef had sworn to serve Amenhotep, Tuya's son, not Tiy.

"My queen—" he shot her a withering glance "—you cannot do this. I will never agree. Pharaoh is the king set apart by God, and you are his queen. Be his supporter, not his enemy."

For a moment her eyes met his with fierce determination, then she faltered and cast her gaze downward.

Confident that he had corralled a dangerous notion, Yosef straightened. "Have you spoken of this to anyone else?"

Tiy shook her head.

"Good." Yosef rested his hands on his knees, then stood. "I will say nothing of this to Pharaoh. I think it is best that we forget everything that happened here. Amenhotep is a fine king, content with his kingdom and his people. God has blessed his country. The people are prosperous and happy. Can any king ask for more?"

"No," she murmured, her expression pained.

"You are right, my queen." He moved toward the doorway and slipped into the darkness before she could say anything else.

Ever since her unpleasant encounter with Zaphenath-paneah, delightfully unpredictable thoughts had bounced in Tiy's head like loose bits of marble after a haphazard blow of the mallet.

The vizier had proved his unshakable steadfastness yet again, but she was nothing like Sagira, the empty-headed woman who had attempted to execute her vengeance in one mad accusation. Tiy was wiser, and she knew the vizier well enough to know that the threat of physical destruction would do little to disturb his cursed equanimity. In his lifetime he had survived slavery, imprisonment, poverty and a wife's death—how else could a man be broken?

Resting on her bed, she rolled onto her side and propped her head on her hand. She would accomplish nothing by engineering Zaphenath-paneah's imprisonment or execution. Pharaoh's proud vizier cared nothing for the wealth he had accumulated or his fine villa on the Nile. Unlike other unusually handsome men, he spent little time consulting with the royal costumers and jewelers. And though he loved his sons and his servants, his passion for Pharaoh overrode everything else.

Father to Pharaoh. In that title lay the key to the vizier's destruction.

She ran the gilded tip of her fingernail over a pattern in the rich linen bedcoverings and felt her lips curve into a smile. Poor Zaphenath-paneah, she could almost pity him. She had tried to appear chastised and humbled when he refused her, a difficult challenge when she yearned to spew hot defiance in his pious face. She might have overlooked his scorn for her loving attention, but she could not excuse his refusal to aid her quest for authority. For if his overwhelming devotion to Pharaoh should ever urge him to divulge the proposition she had made, she would be the one exiled from the source and center of all power.

Zaphenath-paneah, then, would have to go away.

She rolled over onto her stomach and propped her head on her hands. On the morrow she would take a barge to Malkata and speak to her husband. She would not be as foolish and obvious as the notorious wife of Potiphar, but she would destroy the vizier nonetheless.

"You see how it is, then," Tiy said, regarding Amenhotep with a speculative gaze. She had risen before sunrise and taken her gilded barge to Malkata. Now she sat with her husband in his bedchamber, face-to-face, with no intermediaries or meddling priests about.

"I do." Amenhotep studied her. "But I shall miss Zaphenath-paneah. He has been the vizier since my father's time and my mother adores him."

"Queen Tuya has nothing to do with your government of the kingdom." Tiy leaned forward and rested her hand on his arm. "And the vizier has everything to do with Egypt. Therein lies the problem—the vizier's duties are too much for one man, and Zaphenath-paneah has now lived more than twice as many years as your father. Since Egypt is two kingdoms, appoint a new, younger man to administrate each half. One man shall supervise Lower Egypt from the city of Memphis, another Upper Egypt, from Thebes. And rather than taking your time each morning, they shall report to me at each new moon."

And I will manipulate both.

Amenhotep stroked his chin. "There may be wisdom in what you say." He lowered his voice. "I would not admit it to anyone else, but often I have felt like a child who cannot shed his overprotective parent. But what shall we do with Zaphenath-paneah?"

"Have you not noticed the dark smudges of weariness beneath his eyes?" Tiy placed her hand over her husband's. "I think he is eager for a well-deserved rest. He has a prosperous villa, a reputation for honesty and two fine sons. Leave him alone, my husband, let him enjoy the leisure he has earned. Do not call him into your presence, do not ask his advice on any subject. Leave him in peace to enjoy his people, his home, his sons. That is all he would ask, I think, were he here with you now."

Amenhotep smiled with warm spontaneity. "It shall be done."

"Shall you tell him before the court at Malkata this morning?" She held her breath, hoping he would accept her suggestion. Nothing would make her happier than to see Zaphenath-paneah humbled before the pharaoh he had given his life to serve…

But Amenhotep was too much a coward. "I shall send a messenger to him." He clapped his hands. "Summon a scribe!" he bellowed to the chamberlain who appeared in the doorway. "And a runner! I have an urgent message to be carried at once to my vizier."

Pharaoh's uncertain eyes sought hers again. "Shall I at least consult him about choosing two new viziers? Zaphenath-paneah is a shrewd judge of character."

"He is not so shrewd as you think," she answered, giving him a careful smile. "He is old, so let him begin his rest today. The honorable and worthy Zaphenath-paneah has served his king well, but no longer shall he enter the palace at Malkata, no longer shall he be required to stand before Pharaoh and report the troubles of an entire kingdom."

Pharaoh nodded, considering. "In the name of my father Amon-Re, I think I shall commission a song to honor him." He sniffed and clapped his hands again. "Send me Akil!" he called to the flustered chamberlain who thrust his head through the curtained doorway. "And waste no time in fetching him!"

Tiy leaned back in her chair and steepled her hands before her chin, well-satisfied with the beginning of her revenge.

TIY

The LORD is slow to anger, and great in power, and
will not at all acquit the wicked: the LORD hath his
way in the whirlwind and in the storm, and the
clouds are the dust of his feet....
The LORD is good, a strong hold in the day of trouble;
and he knoweth them that trust in him.

Nahum 1:3, 7

Chapter Twenty-Two

Yosef lowered the papyrus scroll to his lap and stared dumbly at Pharaoh's imprint on the broken seal. *Dismissed,* the parchment said. Without a word of warning or a hint of displeasure.

Someone had made a grave mistake. He reread the message, searching for some combination of words his weary eyes could have transposed, some crucial phrase his staggered reason might have missed in his first reading. But Pharaoh's message was as clear as it was brutal:

> The Horus Living-of-Births, the Two Ladies Living-of-Births, the King of Upper and Lower Egypt, Amenhotep, Son of Amon-Re, Pharaoh, Living forever unto eternity!
> A decree of the king to the vizier Zaphenath-paneah:
> Life, health and prosperity to you, High Vizier of all Egypt, Zaphenath-paneah. Behold, your king and pharaoh, Amenhotep III, decrees that henceforth from this day, beginning with the rising sail of the sun-bark of Amon-Re, two viziers shall represent my divine throne throughout the double kingdom of Egypt. For today indeed you have begun to grow old, and will soon lose your virile powers. Be mindful of the day of burial, of passing to a revered state! A night will one day be assigned for you for oils and wrappings from the hands of Tayit, the goddess of weaving. You will be placed on a bier, with oxen drawing you and

singers going before you, and the mortuary dances will be performed at the door of your tomb.

Until that day, two younger men, sons of your teaching, shall be appointed in your place as vizier. This is done to give you a well-deserved rest and allow you to take your place of honor while life still pours through your heart. As for you, the king sends his thanks, faithful love and appreciation for your outspoken service to the two kingdoms. We shall rest well, knowing that your god will sustain and preserve your coming in and going out as He has from the beginning of your days on earth, and in the two kingdoms.

You have begun to grow old. Whatever did Pharaoh mean? Yosef had lost neither the quickness of his mind nor the sharpness of his wit. His hair, or what remained of it under his heavy wig, was streaked with silver, but the hoary head was a sign of wisdom and experience, not weakness. Feathery lines marked his eyes and mouth, but those webbed lines had been etched by his concern over Amenhotep, spun out of love and concern and guardianship.

Old? Young men needed elders, men who were unwilling to become pathetic imitations of younger rivals. What was Amenhotep thinking?

Yosef clenched his fist as ice spread through his stomach, then remembered he was not alone. The messenger from the king waited before him, as did Ani, who had been drawn away from his duties by this urgent message from Pharaoh. The steward waited, his bright, birdlike eyes alert to the signs of distress and urgency on his master's face.

"Pharaoh," Yosef began, dismayed to hear a strained tone in his voice, "will appoint a new vizier—two of them, in fact— very soon. Apparently I have finished my course of service to the king. He wishes me well. In time, perhaps—"

Despair rose in his throat, stifling the power of speech. *You have begun to grow old.* Of course he had! He had spent his life in service first to Amenhotep's father, then to the present pharaoh. He had set aside his own dreams, trusting his estate to Ani and his children to Tarik and a succession of handmaids.

Would he be rewarded for that sacrifice like *this?* By means of a simple parchment and a few formal phrases he had been thrown out like yesterday's vegetables.

Oh, the ingratitude and incivility of the young! Amenhotep's father would never have behaved so rudely; the king's mother, Queen Tuya, would rise up in fury if she had any idea her son had treated his vizier so cavalierly. Yosef had done nothing to deserve being tossed away like a worn and faded garment. Though he was older than most of the king's counselors, he possessed the health and longevity of Yaakov. With the blessing of God Shaddai, he would undoubtedly live to see Amenhotep himself entombed, and yet this stripling king had the gall, the unmitigated *audacity,* to cast aside the one who had been his protector and tutor, counselor and father…

In a silent fury that spoke louder than words Yosef crumpled the royal message, then a wave of remorse swept over him. He was still subject to the king, and he had just demonstrated a spirit of rebellion in front of Pharaoh's messenger. Amenhotep barely tolerated differences of opinion in his counselors, and with ordinary common citizens—which Yosef now was—he had no tolerance at all.

Ani, intuitive soul that he was, understood. As Yosef lowered his gaze he heard Ani commanding Pharaoh's slave to depart. The messenger bent to bow, then caught himself. His face and neck turned a vivid scarlet as he bobbed awkwardly before Zaphenath-paneah, noble *citizen,* and fled the room.

God of my fathers, help me. Yosef smoothed the crumpled papyrus against the linen of his vizier's robe as his blood ran thick with guilt. How could he justify his anger? God Shaddai had elevated him from prison to a throne overnight; he had been promoted and demoted before. But though Yosef's previous tribulations had been difficult, at least he had come to understand the reasons for them. By provoking his brothers to jealousy, he had opened the road for their betrayal. By tolerating the dangerous affections of a powerful woman, he had initiated his confinement in prison. In the past he had ignored dangerous thunderclouds on the horizon, but in the past few years the horizon of his life had been as clear as a sunny sky.

Or had it? Had he been too involved with Pharaoh's work to even look up?

He looked up now, but his eyes would not focus. Through a blur of tears he saw Ani standing silently, his hands folded at his waist, his head bent.

A heaviness centered in Yosef's chest as he met his steward's gaze. "I think I would like to be alone," he said, reaching for the solid arm of his gilded chair, the throne from which he had ruled the Black Land for nearly thirty years. That chair seemed the only solid reality in a shifting world, but it, too, was aging…

Yosef sat, wondering for the first time if he had more yesterdays than tomorrows. Had God finished with him? Was this parchment the Almighty's way of removing Yosef from the work that counted for eternity? Perhaps he had made mistakes; pride had always been his chief weakness. But he had tried to do his best for Amenhotep; he had placed Pharaoh and Pharaoh's house above even his own. Yosef had tutored the young prince while his own sons learned under Ani's patient teaching; he had spent hour after hour listening to the young king's problems while his own wife pined in lonely silence, feeding the insecurity that ultimately took her life.

Such joys he had sacrificed, all for Pharaoh! He had not withheld one precious thing from the altar of duty. And now his God-given work was done. Finished. Gone.

Ani gave him a bleak, tight-lipped smile, ruefully accepting the terrible truth.

Yosef lowered his head into his hands and kneaded his temple; his head pounded with memories. Ani did not speak for a long moment; he did not need to. The two men had been master and servant for so long they understood one another.

The older man held out his hands. "If you truly want to be alone," he said, his dark eyes brimming with compassion, "I will go."

Just then the double doors burst open. Tarik hurried into the room and flung himself onto the floor, unaware that he was no longer required to prostrate himself before his master. "Most noble vizier," he called without stopping to evaluate Yosef's mood, "my scouts have returned. Menashe and his men had been discovered in the wilderness. By sundown tomorrow I could have a squadron of men at their camp."

The captain broke off when his gaze met Yosef's, and the jubilant look of satisfaction left his eyes. He faltered, floundering in confusion as his gaze shifted to meet Ani's, then he finished with a question. "Shall I bring Menashe home?"

Yosef heard him through a vague sense of unreality. "Do what you will with the young men," he murmured, rising from his now-insignificant chair. "I do not care."

Rather than return to Thebes immediately, Tiy lingered in her chambers at Malkata, summoning her coterie and personal servants from Thebes to Pharaoh's pink granite palace. Surprised by her unexpected visit, Pharaoh's chamberlain stood in her chambers now, barking out commands as a host of slaves hastened to freshen the water basins, air the linens, light the tall cones of incense.

Wrapped in a cocoon of indifference, Tiy paced in the center of the hubbub and patiently counted the hours until she might command an audience with one who quite possibly knew more about Pharaoh's palace than Pharaoh himself—Akil. She knew Amenhotep had spent the morning with the musician, fruitlessly trying to appease the creative god who had laid the suggestion of a song on his pleasure-fogged brain, but the day was half-spent and Pharaoh would soon be calling for his dinner. Abruptly, she sent a slave to summon the musician, then she dismissed the chamberlain and settled back to wait.

Tiy's appreciation for Akil had grown since the chironomist approached her with news of the rendezvous between the vizier's son and the little harpist. A stiff, nearly bloodless individual whom she suspected of being even more clever than she, Akil was a valuable ally because Pharaoh tended to forget that his musicians had ears and wagging tongues. And Akil adored her; she had discerned that much when the chironomist traveled all the way to Thebes to tell *her,* not Amenhotep, of Menashe's treachery.

With Zaphenath-paneah out of the picture, Akil could serve as her eyes and ears. If he served her well, she would elevate him as Hatshepsut had exalted her steward Senenmut.

Feeling relaxed and invincible, Tiy smiled when the embroidered curtain to her chamber lifted. The musician entered and prostrated himself on the floor. "Rise, Akil." She pointed to a chair. "You and I are alone, so let us forget protocol. You will sit to talk with me, but you must swear that what I tell you shall never pass your lips."

"You may cut off my tongue if it does." The man rose and moved toward her with abrupt, purposeful strides, then took the seat she offered and clasped his hands on his knees. Out of long habit, he bowed his head, but kept his olive-black gaze affixed to hers. "How may I serve you, O Mother of Egypt?"

She gave him a mirthless smile. "I am sure you have realized that Pharaoh is about to appoint two new viziers."

One of his finely plucked eyebrows shot upward. "It is not for me to question the divine pharaoh, but I wondered why he was so intent on creating a hymn of praise to honor our noble Zaphenath-paneah."

Tiy made a soft sound of disgust. "Come, Akil, speak plainly. I know you have never liked the vizier. I have read your feelings in your eyes."

The chironomist lifted his shoulders and shrugged, though a suitably shamed look crossed his face. "Alas, the queen knows me too well. And I cannot hide what my heart tells me. The vizier is an opportunist. Can anyone deny that all he has done for Egypt has been accomplished to provide for the rabble living in Goshen?"

"You have guessed my concern." Tiy leaned forward. "Since you brought me news of this rebellious Hebrew army, my sleep has not been pleasant. I fear for our people, and particularly for my daughter. The sons of Zaphenath-paneah are like their father, attractive and charismatic, and yet we dare not trust them. But my daughter Sitamun has lost her heart to Efrayim, and several of Pharaoh's Medjay warriors have surrendered their loyalty to Menashe's flattery and cunning."

"The Hebrews are a formidable force," Akil agreed. "But they are not as formidable as Pharaoh's house."

"That remains to be seen." Tiy rested her chin on her hand.

"I am concerned. Pharaoh has hidden himself away with his harem, and my son—well, the crown prince's will is not as strong as it should be. He is too romantic, he spends altogether too much time with the priests of Aten." She released a nervous laugh. "If Pharaoh had other sons, I might allow him to become a priest. But aside from Neferkheprure' Wa'enre', my womb has brought forth only daughters."

"It is unfortunate—" Akil pressed his hands together "—but since your daughters are heiresses of the royal line of pharaohs, a marriage between Sitamun and the vizier's son might result in a Hebrew rising to the great throne of Egypt. But of course you have considered this—"

"Of course I have," she snapped, cutting him off. She frowned, disturbed that a mere servant had expressed her deepest fear. She was the Great Wife, the highest-ranking queen, and therefore Sitamun, as the eldest daughter, would carry the line of succession. If something happened to the crown prince, Sitamun's husband or child would inherit the throne of Egypt.

Zaphenath-paneah's grandchild as Pharaoh? The thought galled her.

She pressed her hand to her lips. She had advanced the idea of a royal marriage and even encouraged Menashe's idiotic flirtation with a slave in order to win influence with the vizier's sons, but they had failed to sway Zaphenath-paneah in her favor. Apparently the opinions of the sons mattered little to the father and, judging by Menashe's actions in the northern wilderness, the convictions of the father were of no consequence to at least one son.

Ignoring Akil's death-bright eyes, she sat and toyed with a strand of her wig. An idea had begun to form in her mind, an elusive notion which might prove unpopular in Sitamun's eyes but which would be acceptable both to the priests and to the people. And Sitamun, creature of comfort that she was, would be convinced of the plan's wisdom if the attendant benefits were adequately emphasized. Efrayim might rage, but who would care? If he behaved inappropriately, he would furnish yet another reason for Pharaoh to banish Zaphenath-paneah and his troublesome sons from court. The three influential Hebrew men had already proven themselves a danger to Egypt's welfare.

"Akil." She turned toward him. "Would you do anything for me?"

His eyes filled with fierce sparkling. "You have but to ask."

"I want you to be my spy within the house of Zaphenath-paneah." Her eyes locked on the musician's. "You and your orchestra shall return to the vizier's house. The annals shall record that you are a gift from Pharaoh to the former vizier, a tribute to his work and devotion."

She heard his quick intake of breath. "You would have me leave you?" He managed a tremulous smile. "But Pharaoh—"

"Pharaoh can employ any musician he wishes," Tiy answered, recognizing the sharp light of attraction within the man's deep eyes. As the chironomist's expression tightened, she placed her hand on his arm. "Do this for me, Akil, and all will be well with you. Go to the vizier's villa, make yourself one of the household, find a weakness I may exploit. Send word to me, and then I will bring you back to Pharaoh's palace and shower you with blessings. You will not regret leaving Malkata."

He smiled in relief. "As you wish, my queen. My only desire is to serve you."

With careful dignity he rose from his chair and slipped to the floor in a bow.

"Rise and go." Tiy tilted her head as she watched him obey. His eyes did not lift to hers before he turned to shuffle away, and she bit her thumbnail, hoping she had trusted the right man.

"Who is going where?" Jendayi lifted her head from her bed, not certain she'd heard Kesi correctly. She had been enjoying a nap, and Kesi had burst into the servants' quarters babbling about someone moving to a villa.

Kesi's voice brimmed with excitement amid the soft sounds of garments being pulled from their woven storage baskets and flung onto an empty bed. "We are to pack at once. The master says we will leave Malkata before dark. Can you imagine? We are going to live with the vizier!"

Jendayi dropped her head back onto the pillow of her arms,

convinced she was experiencing a lucid dream. But then Kissa and Sakmet rushed into the chamber, chattering like excited monkeys. Jendayi lifted her head again and strained to sift through their babble.

"Will someone please tell me exactly what is happening?" She pushed herself to a sitting position. She felt the bedclothes beneath her, the breath of the wind from the open door. This was no dream.

"According to Pharaoh's chamberlain, Zaphenath-paneah has earned a time of rest," Kesi explained. "Pharaoh will choose two new viziers tomorrow, one to govern Upper Egypt, the other to govern the nomes of Lower Egypt. And to show his gratitude for years of gracious service, the king is returning Akil and his orchestra to the vizier's house."

Jendayi caught her breath as the shock of discovery hit her full force. Could this news possibly be true? Zaphenath-paneah had been the one and only vizier since before she had been born; legends reported that he had bounced the toddling pharaoh on his knee. Paintings of the vizier graced at least a hundred buildings and granaries in Thebes and the people of the Black Land revered him as Giver of Plenty and the Bread of Life. Zaphenath-paneah was a living legend! He had been blessed by the gods; some people insisted that the spirit of a god rested on him…

So how could he no longer be vizier? The sun could not stop being the sun, nor could the river pull up its waters and refuse to refresh the land. And just two days ago the women had played at a banquet for the king and his vizier. The voices of both men had echoed with concern and mutual respect. It was neither natural nor logical that Pharaoh should suggest that the time had come for his vizier to go away.

But Pharaoh could be influenced by stronger voices.

Kesi's broad hand fell on Jendayi's shoulder. "Wake up, little sister!" she whispered, the sweet scent of beer on her breath. "Did you not hear me? We are going to the vizier's villa! You will sleep tonight under the same roof as your beloved Efrayim!"

Menashe will not be there. For some inexplicable reason that unsettling thought ricocheted through Jendayi's mind. Confused, she blinked up at her maid. "I suppose this is good news."

"Of course it is." Kesi sank to Jendayi's side and gripped the harpist's arm with her hot hand. "Do you remember how Efrayim kissed you in his father's garden? Perhaps the gods have answered your prayers. You will live in his house again, he will kiss you again. His affection for you, already in bud, will blossom in full. He no longer needs to ask Pharaoh to sell you! He must only ask his father's permission to make you a concubine, and surely the vizier would not withhold such a favor from his son. The gods have smiled on you, my lady."

"Efrayim is going to marry Princess Sitamun," Jendayi remarked, wondering why this unexpected miracle did not thrill her. For months she had hoped and prayed for such a turn of events, but now she could only think of the vizier's house as an incomplete, empty place.

Kesi placed a finger to Jendayi's cheek. "Those reports of Efrayim's marriage to the princess are only rumors." A teasing tone filled her voice. "Akil says the princess will be married soon, but not to the vizier's son. Our master has already begun to write a song in honor of the wedding."

Jendayi clutched the maid's arm. "Efrayim will not marry?"

"Akil says Efrayim will not marry any of Pharaoh's daughters." Kesi patted her mistress's hand with confident pressure. "And Akil is never wrong."

Jendayi turned her face away to consider this new development. Menashe had been wrong. He had tried his best to convince her to forget Efrayim. He had lied about his name, lied about Efrayim's marriage. Had he lied about *everything?*

Kesi hopped up to continue her packing, and Jendayi sat motionless while her head swirled with doubts. Why would Menashe tell her Efrayim did not love her? Did he hate her so much he was driven to break her heart? Surely not, she was a slave, she meant nothing to him. But if he did not hate her, then why would he attempt to—

She pressed her hand over her lips as her mind blew open. *Menashe hated Efrayim.* She had heard bitterness in his voice when he spoke of his brother—twice, the time he remarked that Efrayim would not join him in the desert, and another time when he'd said that Efrayim was cocky and arrogant, that he gave too much attention to too many different women. And there had been rumors on the caravan from Canaan, stories about a rivalry between the two brothers, something about a family inheritance which should have gone to the firstborn but which went instead to Efrayim.

Of course! Menashe was jealous of his brother, and bitter enough to sabotage the tender slip of love that had begun to grow in her heart. Menashe certainly cared nothing for a slave girl. His clumsy efforts to capture her heart had been part of a simple ploy to undermine Efrayim's attempt to redeem her from Pharaoh.

Like a weed among barren desert stones, hope sprouted in her breast. Somehow, through magic or divine influence, Efrayim had won. Menashe had been defeated, and Efrayim had managed to arrange for her transfer to his father's house. He, not Menashe, had sent her the message in Canaan, and now he waited at his father's house to reclaim the love his lips had sealed so many years before.

She stood and reached toward the wall where her harp rested. Let Akil write songs to praise the princess and her future husband. She would write a song herself, one unlike any she had ever written before. It would resonate with hope and love and the sweetness of a fulfilled dream. And when Efrayim heard it, he would know she had come home to him.

Night had spread her sable wings over Malkata by the time Tiy's spy arrived from the vizier's villa. She received him in her innermost chamber, anxious for any news from Zaphenath-paneah's house. To her surprise, however, the spy did not bring word of the vizier's reaction to Pharaoh's decree, but news of a different sort.

"We found the rebel camp to the west of Tura," the man reported, pausing to wipe a trickle of sweat from his brow. "They move every night, but have circled back to an area just east of Pharaoh's quarry. The captain of the vizier's guard expects Zaphenath-paneah to send us to apprehend them on the morrow—"

"I think not," Tiy interrupted. Resting her chin on her hand, she gave the Medjay warrior a bemused smile. "Remember that you do my bidding, and not the vizier's."

"Yes, my queen." If she had not known him to be as hard as

flint, she would have thought he flushed, for two dark spots appeared on his cheeks.

"Besides—" Tiy ignored his discomfort "—as of today, the vizier no longer has authority to arrest men in the king's name." She curved her long fingers around the armrest of her chair. "I doubt he is currently in a frame of mind to do anything."

The Nubian frowned, and Tiy snapped her fingers at the pair of slaves plying her with ostrich fans. They whirled and left the chamber, then Tiy propped her chin on her hand and considered the warrior standing before her. He was not the most handsome man she had ever seen, but there was a restless energy in his movements and strength in the shoulders and arms that gleamed in the soft lamplight. His legs were as brown and firm as cedars, and in his strong features she saw traces of a certain sensuality. His face was as hard as granite, like his eyes.

She raked his body with her gaze, then smiled as he peered at her with the wary gaze of an untamed animal. This one, she knew, would not be immune to her charms.

"So you are the notorious Hondo?" she asked, folding her hands at her waist.

Lethal calmness filled his eyes. "Yes, my queen."

"Even your name means war." She observed him through lowered lashes. He tilted his brow, studying her, and she knew he sensed the ripple of excitement flowing in her blood. Unlike Zaphenath-paneah, this man would do anything to please her.

She stared at him until he lifted his brows in a silent query, then she spoke again. "Hondo, I must take you into my confidence. Can you be trusted?"

The grooves beside his mouth deepened in a smug smile. "Implicitly, my queen."

"Good." She rose from her chair and moved toward him, compelled by her frustrated passion and the knowledge that Amenhotep frolicked with his harem only a few paces away. "I need a reliable warrior, a man who will be discreet. Most of all—" she moved so close that her breath warmed his face "—I need a man who is willing to die for me."

He stiffened, but began to melt when she lifted her finger to trace the shadow above his upper lip. "Of course you will not have to die," she said, noticing that the light of desire now illuminated his tumultuous dark eyes. "I ask only that you are willing to do so."

"I do not fear death, for a man may live forever in a queen's favor," he whispered, dropping his hand to her shoulder.

"You are a brave one." She lifted her hand and pressed it to the burnished mahogany of his cheek. "For the liberty you took in touching me just now I could demand your life."

"But you won't."

"No." She regarded him with a smile. "You, Hondo, will not die for touching me, nor for anything else your heart desires tonight. But if you do not do exactly as I tell you regarding Menashe, elder son of Zaphenath-paneah, you will most certainly die at Pharaoh's command." Her hand caught his and brought it to her lips. "A most painful and torturous death." Tilting her head, she gave him a sleepy-cat smile. "Do you understand?"

"I understand," he murmured in the instant before his mouth covered hers.

Chapter Twenty-Three

Efrayim moved through the villa with a loose-boned, easy gait, intent on finding his father. A full month had passed since Pharaoh had discharged his vizier, but Efrayim had seen no more of his father in the past month than he had when Yosef had been at Pharaoh's constant beck and call. His father used to fill his days and nights with work; Efrayim suspected that he now filled them with regret.

And to think he used to long for the day when his father would no longer be vizier.

Ani had said Zaphenath-paneah would doubtless be found in the garden, and Efrayim knew the vast walled sanctuary was one of the few places in the villa that brought his father any pleasure. The grand reception hall seemed to mock the vizier's former lofty position; and Yosef's own chambers, though spacious, must have seemed confining and claustrophobic when compared to the wide spaces of Pharaoh's palace. A master had no business in the servants' quarters, stable or kitchens, so Yosef had begun to haunt the garden. Among the mandrakes, acacia trees and lotus blossoms, Efrayim suspected Yosef was assuring himself that he and Pharaoh would stand as equals under the sun.

The time of mourning should soon come to an end, however, and Efrayim was determined to pull his father from the cloud of gloom that surrounded him. He did not know exactly what had transpired between Pharaoh and Yosef, but Efrayim knew the two younger men who had been appointed to fill the vizier's position were already showing signs of strain. Though they were bright and capable, the effort of carrying half the load of Yosef's job had left them haggard and drawn. Efrayim had heard from a dozen nobles that Amenhotep had already expressed reservations about the capabilities of his new viziers. But a great deal of responsibility had been placed in Queen Tiy's capable hands, and if she did not complain about her additional duties, the dual-vizier system would probably remain in place.

The rising sun painted a golden glow over everything in the garden, and Efrayim felt his spirits lift as he strolled along the paved path and nodded at the slaves who maneuvered the towering shadufs and watered the plants. Catching sight of his father's dark head beneath the pavilion at the far edge of the garden, Efrayim hurried toward him. He had an idea he thought his father would approve, a plan to unite the best Egyptian artists and Hebrew builders in order to create a trading center in Goshen, a signature city that would pave the way for others like it. If Yosef warmed to the idea, the work would fill his days, occupy his thoughts and please both Pharaoh and Yosef's Hebrew brothers.

Yosef sat motionless in his chair, his elbows planted on his knees, his eyes drawn into slits as if he concentrated on some vision nearly lost in the past or future. An aura of melancholy radiated from his handsome features, and for an instant Efrayim slowed his steps, caught up in the fearful reverence that had marked all his childhood meetings with his powerful father.

But he was a child no longer. The tide had turned, *he* was now the stronger one. Hadn't Yaakov foretold this? The old patriarch must have known that Yosef would be incapacitated and Menashe distracted by dreams of battlefield glory. The mantle of leadership had fallen squarely on Efrayim's shoulders.

"Father," he called, breaking the spell of silence. He rested one foot on the first step of the pavilion and leaned forward, held back by the old formality he and Menashe had been bound to obey since the beginning of their formal education.

His father's lids fell over his eyes as if guarding a secret, but after a moment he turned to measure his son with an appraising look. "Do you no longer bow before your father, Efrayim? Or have you joined the thousands who no longer respect me?"

Forever in control, he was still granting favors, making judgments, reading the will of both God and Pharaoh.

Refusing to prostrate himself on the tile, Efrayim inclined his head in a deep gesture, then looked up and gave his father a warm smile. "I will always respect you as my father." He took another half-step forward. "And I want to talk to you." Clearing his throat, he made an effort to lighten his voice. "You have avoided me these past weeks, but we ought to talk about Pharaoh's decision."

Yosef's gaze turned again to a faraway place. "It is not a subject I want to discuss."

"Why would you avoid it when everyone in Thebes knows what happened? It is not a story, Father, that can be hidden. But neither is the tale of Pharaoh's new viziers. Both of them have already encountered the royal wrath. The king cannot abide them, and the nomarchs are complaining that these men are not able to handle the details of taxation, the temple properties, the rituals of marking boundaries after the flood—"

"Pharaoh will find someone else, then."

"Perhaps." Efrayim lifted his brows, encouraged that his father was still listening. They had never been close, but in the past month Yosef's indifference had extended even to Ani and Tarik, the two most trusted servants in his household. Both men were more like lifetime companions than servants, but Yosef's grief had cut them off.

Efrayim decided to be blunt. "I have an idea to build a trading center in Goshen. We will need your knowledge and influence with the governor and merchants of that area. It will be a good work, and I am certain you will enjoy it. Pharaoh will be pleased, and when Sitamun and I are married, I will use my influence with Pharaoh to convince him to forgive whatever trouble arose between you."

"There was no trouble." The statement rang with reproach. "None whatsoever. If you have heard otherwise, you are listening to liars."

"So you say," Efrayim answered. The conversation had spun

out of his control, and his father's contemptuous tone sparked his own cynicism. "Of course Pharaoh had no problems with you. That's why he dismissed you without warning. That's why he gave your duties to incompetent men."

When Yosef did not answer, Efrayim's mood veered sharply to fury. Would his father never understand that his sons were capable of helping him? Yosef was so arrogantly self-sufficient, so infernally capable! Could he not admit that he had somehow failed Pharaoh? Counselors frequently disagreed with Amenhotep; if the confrontations were not too severe, they were brought back to court after an apology and a sacrificial offering of praise to the divine king. Why could his father not admit he was human?

"Almost—" Efrayim held tight to the bridled anger in his voice "—I am beginning to understand why Menashe left."

Yosef looked up. "Do you understand? Then explain it to me. I do not know why my elder son would rebel. He says he must obey God, and so he disobeys his father and breaks Pharaoh's law. And I, who have struggled always to obey, am the one who is punished." He looked away. His hand, trembling slightly, reached out to nudge a butterfly from the arm of an empty chair. "When I was young, I was told to grow up, to act like a man. Now that I have grown old, I am looked on as a child, even by my own son."

"Father, I only want what is best for you."

"Then leave me." When Yosef met Efrayim's gaze again, his wise, dark eyes had filled with a curious deep longing. "You are not as old as I am, Efrayim, but I was once as young as you are. You cannot know what is best for me. Only God knows...if He has not abandoned us."

Efrayim stepped back, shaken by his father's honesty. Whether he spoke as Yosef the Hebrew or Zaphenath-paneah the Egyptian, his father's proclamations had always been as certain as the sunrise, as sure as the force which pulled objects from the sky to the earth. But the uncertainty in his expression now shook Efrayim to the core.

Without another word, he slipped from the pavilion and retreated through the garden.

* * *

Jendayi took her seat on the stool against the chamber wall and strummed the harp strings to test the tuning she'd just given them. Almost perfect. One string was a little sharp, but she could adjust the pitch by pinching the string at the proper time. The men at this banquet probably wouldn't have noticed a slight dissonance of tone, but everything had to be perfect in Jendayi's ear, especially when Efrayim was present.

Dinner was Jendayi's favorite hour at the vizier's villa. With dependable regularity she and the others of the orchestra were summoned to the central hall where the aromas of rich foods mingled in a delightful symphony of smells. As her fingers fell into the independent motions forged through long hours of practice, her ears sought the smooth sound of Efrayim's baritone.

Today, like always, she found him. Over the past month she had managed to identify most of the major attendants at Zaphenath-paneah's midday banquet, and she was quietly astounded that so few visitors came to socialize with the esteemed nobleman who had been so illustrious a vizier. She remembered that as a child she had been overwhelmed by the vast crowds who came to consult with the vizier—every day the banquet hall had echoed with new voices, strange accents and lilting languages from all over the known world. But now she regularly heard the voices of only four men: Tarik, captain of the guard; Ani, the aged steward; the vizier himself; and Efrayim.

As long as Efrayim was present, she tended to ignore the other three. They did not speak much anyway; Efrayim held, controlled and enlivened the conversation. His sparkling wit, the rich timber of his laughter, the subtle crescendo of his voice as he strove to make a point when debating with the steward or the captain—all these things she noticed. And though she could not see him, she was certain that in moments of strained silence when only her harp spoke, he looked at her…and remembered.

The memory of Efrayim's kiss was now stronger than her recollection of Menashe on the riverbank. The elder son had vanished like a dream, no one at the vizier's house even spoke of him. She could not discover exactly why his name had been obliterated from all conversations, but though the four men spoke of many things, they never referred to Menashe's past, present or future.

She once asked Kesi if she found it odd that the members of the household behaved as if Menashe had never existed. "Grown men leave home and lead their own lives," she answered flippantly. "You imagine too much, Jendayi."

But Jendayi could see with other than physical eyes, and her spirit could not help but sense the thick cloud of disapproval that filled certain breaks in conversation, unexpected lulls in the laughter, conspicuous gaps in the questions of friends and relatives—all were empty spaces where Menashe's name should have been.

Perhaps he deserved to be ignored, she told herself. After all, he had lied to her, and he was obviously engaged in serious wrongdoing if the noble Zaphenath-paneah had disowned him.

Yet though she still felt anger for the lies he had told her, another part of Jendayi's heart squeezed in anguish as time passed and the obvious public omission of his name opened the door on memories she'd tried to lock away. How could the vizier pretend Menashe did not exist? How could any parent ignore a child? Had *her* mother, whomever she was, blotted out all memories of the daughter she birthed and then abandoned? Did she ever stop to sacrifice in the temple for Jendayi's health or prosperity or light a lamp on the anniversary of Jendayi's birth? Did *she* dream of standing in the Hall of the Two Truths and being eaten alive for her lack of love?

Jendayi heard the irritated snap of Akil's fingers; she was rushing the beat. She inhaled deeply, forcing herself to slow down, and commanded her fingers to divorce themselves from her feelings. Just as she had ordered her heart not to think about Efrayim.

Efrayim had promised to arrange her release from Pharaoh's house, and he had. But a month had passed and he had not spoken to her or sought out her company. She often took her harp into the garden alone, hoping he would seek her there, but he did not. Though Jendayi followed his voice every day in her blind darkness, she was no closer to being loved than she had been in Pharaoh's palace. Yet here she had to endure the sting of jealousy, for the other female servants talked constantly of Efrayim, praising his charm, his wit, his attractive face and form. They twittered when he walked by while Jendayi sat in silence, awaiting some word of confirmation that he had acted on her behalf.

But in the uncomfortable silences and dirgelike conversations of the household she discovered one possible reason for Efrayim's reluctance to approach her: Zaphenath-paneah's household mourned. No one had to tell her that the former vizier had not accepted his fall from grace, for often the atmosphere within the villa was as heavy and desolate as a tomb. And while the father agonized, she assured herself, the son could not speak of love.

So she would have to wait, even though waiting demanded every ounce of patience Jendayi possessed. Since her return to the vizier's house her nightmares had intensified; nearly every night she dreamed of standing before the scales of truth and watching her granite heart sink like a stone opposite the feather of Ma'at.

Just last night the ebony eyes of the jackal-god had blazed fire on her. "You are a waste of flesh and blood!" Anubis's voice ripped through the Hall of the Two Truths like a screaming cyclone. "Why did we give you life? You are nothing, you have loved nothing, you have done nothing but waste the gods' gift."

"What did you want me to do?" she cried. "How do you expect me to find love as a slave? You may as well tell me to count the waves of the Nile!"

Anubis did not defend himself, for he was a god, and Thoth did not offer a word in reply. As Jendayi nervously tested the hold of the treacherous floor on her bare feet, Ammit crept forward, his crocodile head gleaming, his lion's paws thick and heavy on the shining floor. Iron-willed and hard as steel, he bore down on her. She thrust her hands before her eyes, coveting her mortal blindness, while a high, shrill, piercing ring deafened her ears—

Her own scream. Kesi had awakened her, prying her from the terrible dream.

Now, in the scented banquet hall where blessedly mortal voices wrapped around her, Jendayi caressed the familiar strings of her harp and urged them to speak the secret language of her soul, soft sounds that would draw Efrayim to her side. And more than once, as she played with unusual brilliance, she felt a flush steal over her cheek…and knew he was watching.

While the other female musicians spent the hot afternoons in sleep or gentle conversation, Jendayi preferred the solitude of the walled garden. The spot was a favorite of Zaphenath-paneah's, but he avoided it during the heat of the day so she did not worry about disturbing him. After dinner every afternoon, as the engorged guests retreated to their work or their chambers, she picked up her harp and slipped away from Kesi to find her way to the garden.

One of the servants had described the garden's design, so she knew the reflecting pool lay beyond the portico, and behind the pool stood the master's pavilion. Around the pool, the servant told her, date-palms and dom-palms had been arranged with clumps of papyrus, while figs and sycamore mingled between those plantings. A host of flowers grew in planters near the water's edge, red poppies and blue cornflowers, purple irises, white lilies and yellow chrysanthemums.

Jendayi could smell the biting scent of the chrysanthemums as her sandals clapped against the tile of the garden pathway. The servant had not told her that blue lotus blossoms floated in abundance on the surface of the pool; those beauties announced their own sweet presence. The lotus, long a symbol of rebirth and beauty in Egypt, was the Queen Mother's favorite flower. Whenever the orchestra had been summoned to play for the regal Queen Tuya, the sweet scent of the flowers seemed to linger with Jendayi for days.

Her questing feet found the pavilion; she carefully managed the stairs and fumbled for the armrest of a chair. After seating herself, she paused a moment to listen. Water splashed near the pool, but those sounds came from the slaves watering the thirsty flowers. Except for the servants, she was alone.

Sweet silence. Nodding to herself, Jendayi pulled her harp to her chest and began to play a tune that had surfaced in her imagination during dinner. Two fanciful melodies had played themselves again and again in her head, and Jendayi knew they were meant to be played together, one voice complementing the other, one rhythm serving as a dynamic contrast to its mate. *Like you and Efrayim,* a little voice spoke in her head. *He will teach you to love and you will teach him to…what?*

Her hand slipped and she frowned, curling her mutinous fingers into a tight ball. Her body wouldn't cooperate, one hand refused to play its melody independently. As a child she had easily managed the old trick of simultaneously patting her head and rubbing her stomach, but commanding one hand to play smoothly while the other plucked out a sharp, bright countermelody seemed as impossible as scratching her ear with her elbow.

"Why the frown, my dear?"

Jendayi flinched, startled. She must have been deep in concentration not to hear the old steward's approach. But though he had surprised her, she was not afraid. His voice, as always, brimmed with concern.

"I'm sorry, master." She ducked her head. She tried to rise and bow, but the harp stood in front of her.

"Do not bother with formalities here." The old man sank into the empty chair beside her. His voice sounded tired. "What I heard of your song was lovely. So why do you frown?"

"It wasn't all I meant it to be." She slapped her hand against the strings, risking a small display of temper. "I hear the tune in my head and know how it ought to come out of my fingers, but they will not obey. If I can create it in my head, I ought to be able to play it."

"The gods create us, but they cannot always bend us to their wills," Ani answered, a surprising degree of warmth in his voice. "But they have given you a great gift. Except for the enchanting melodies you put there, no music would dare enter my weary head."

The steward fell silent, and Jendayi felt her polite smile fade. He had not sought her out to talk about music. So why had he come to her?

Her whole being concentrated on sounds that might give her a clue, but she heard nothing but whispers of foot traffic drifting over the high walls of the garden and the soft lap of irrigation buckets scooping up the pool's calm water.

Ani's hoarse whisper finally broke the silence between them. "I thought you might like to talk about my master's son."

"Efrayim?" Anxiety spurted through her. Had Ani's legendary insight uncovered her hopes? Had she, in an unguarded moment, allowed her face to reveal too much of her heart? She might have looked adoringly at Efrayim; the others might have seen and cast knowing looks toward one another. Perhaps the entire household was laughing at her! One of the worst things about blindness was missing the myriad ways people communicated through glances, gestures, expressions…

"Why would I speak to you of Efrayim?" The old steward spoke in a neutral tone, without inflection, but a warning voice whispered in Jendayi's head. Was this a test?

"He is the only son here in the villa," she answered, her adrenaline level beginning to rise. "And what I have heard here leads me to believe he is the only living son."

"Bah! You and I both know the vizier's elder son lives." She heard the steward sigh. "Misery weighs on my heart like an iron weight, for Menashe has been like my own son for many years. He has often shared his heart with me, even more than with his father. The vizier, you understand, has always been busy with Pharaoh's affairs."

"I don't understand," she said, wincing at the tortured sound of his voice, "what this has to do with me."

"Don't you?" His short bark of humor lacked laughter. "Menashe told me of your…*friendship* with him." The cold edge of irony crept into his voice. "He also told me you fancy yourself in love with Efrayim—on account of a kiss given years ago."

Her cheeks burned. "I told him those things in confidence. He should not have told you."

"I am his friend," the old man continued as casually as if he discussed the grain harvest and not the critical state of Jendayi's heart. "I know him better than anyone in this household. And because he considers you his friend, I thought perhaps I could help you."

Fueled by hopeless anger, a ripple of mirth bubbled into her voice. "You are an old man," she answered, trying to be respectful. "And though you love Menashe, he is gone, and you cannot bring him back. Apparently you could not even change his mind about leaving. So how can you help me?"

"I had thought to prevent your heart from being more blind than your eyes." A thread of warning laced his voice. "If you truly love Efrayim, I cannot hope to command the passions of your heart. I love him myself. But because I have been like a father to both Zaphenath-paneah's sons, I know their natures. And Efrayim will not make you happy, little harpist, no matter what your heart may tell you."

"He will!" she blurted out. "He loves me, he can teach me to love."

"Ah, my child." The aged man's hand came to rest on the top of her head, and Jendayi fought the impulse to jerk away. "Perhaps you live in an imaginary world. Certainly you hear things I cannot. But you are alone there. If you want to find love, you must seek it as resolutely as Isis sought the coffin of her beloved Osiris."

How? She wanted to scream, but her pride kept her from crying out. She resisted, not speaking, and after a moment the pressure of his hand lifted and his sandals shuffled away over the marble tiles on the garden path.

How could she seek love? She was as helpless as a plant without water. She owned nothing, not even her freedom. She shuddered as the floodgates opened and her torment found its way out through her tears. She was a waste of flesh and blood. Nightly the gods railed at her, foretelling her destruction, and Jendayi could do nothing but agree that they had judged correctly.

Ani strolled slowly, watching his sandals fall on the smooth tiles of the garden path, his thoughts far away. Menashe had been foolish to lose his heart to such a faithless young girl, but love was often as unexpected as a midnight assassin.

In spite of Ani's long-standing resolve not to dwell on the past, his mind returned to his youth. Long before he came to Zaphenath-paneah's villa, he had fallen in love with a young slave called Salihah. A slim, graceful beauty, she had stolen his heart in just one look. They worked together for weeks, each one shyly loving the other through tender words and teasing glances, until the master took Salihah to his chamber. She resisted his advances and in his anger he cut her face, marring her loveliness forever. As a helpless, primitive grief overwhelmed Ani, the steward of the estate took Salihah away and sold her as damaged goods at a slave auction.

Ani never saw or heard from Salihah again. Yet even now, when he had time for introspection, his vision colored with memories of the woman with whom he had shared only a few words, a score of stolen smiles and one brief caress as their hands touched. Through the shadow of memory, one terrible, gnawing thought haunted him: had he unwittingly been the instrument of her destruction? Did she resist the master for Ani's sake?

A slave, he decided after many restless nights, should not risk loving anyone. And because he adored both Efrayim and Menashe, he did not want either of them to hurt the little harpist and suffer the guilt he had borne for a lifetime.

At the sharp smell of burning wood, Ani lifted his head. The odor of burning wood usually meant that a clumsy kitchen slave had allowed a grease fire to get out of hand. He sniffed the air and frowned. The scent was not coming from the area of the kitchens, but from the front of the villa.

In a zigzag crouch Ani raced to the courtyard. Tarik's guards would certainly have the situation under control, but Ani wanted to vent his displeasure. The household could not afford to squander valuable materials now…

He rounded the corner and stared wordlessly across the open space of the courtyard, his heart pounding. The fire was not accidental. Ani had never seen anything like the sight which greeted his bleary eyes.

Zaphenath-paneah stood in the center of the courtyard before a towering formation of lumber piled waist-high. Thirsty flames licked the base of the dry wood, tonguing high into the shimmering air. Behind the master, a host of wide-eyed guards stood at attention. A line of slaves stood to one side, their linen kilts stained with blood, their biceps bulging under the weight of loaded bowls and trays.

Ani was barely able to control his gasp of surprise when he

realized that the servants carried the butchered remains of a bull. The last bowl, he noted with distaste, brimmed with blood.

Surprise siphoned words from his tongue. Had the master lost his sanity? Though the Egyptian cult of Apis venerated the bull, the priests accomplished all things decently and in accordance with the prescribed order of rituals, not in the center of a courtyard and certainly not in the most extreme heat of the day. The sacred bulls—those with a white crescent on one side of their bodies or a black lump under their tongues—were considered the offspring of Ptah, born of virgin cows and destined for a life of service in the temple. The priests of Ptah cared for the bulls for twenty-five years, then quietly drowned and embalmed them.

A rise of panic threatened to choke Ani as he stared at the bloody scene. Never would a priest of Ptah consider such a violent act. And Zaphenath-paneah, who devoutly worshipped the invisible and almighty god of the Hebrews, had never spoken of Ptah. In all the winding length of Ani's memory, Zaphenath-paneah had never, ever offered a sacrifice—particularly one as gruesome as this.

"What should we do?"

Startled by Tarik's voice, Ani glanced up. Intense astonishment was also inscribed on the captain's tanned face.

"He gave you no warning?" Ani whispered, sneaking another glance at his master. "There was no hint of what he had in mind?"

Tarik jerked his chin toward the vizier. "This morning he asked for a bull, free from blemish," he answered, locking his hands behind his back. "Then he instructed the kitchen slaves to butcher the entire animal, reserving no part of it for themselves or for dinner. Even the blood has been caught."

"I noticed," Ani remarked, his voice flat.

Tarik lifted an eyebrow. "Have you ever seen anything like this? You are a wise and learned man, you should know what he is doing."

"It may be a Hebrew custom, but I know nothing of it." Ani's voice faded to a hushed stillness as the master stepped back and lifted his hands.

A tense silence enveloped the courtyard; even the nesting birds on the rim of the villa's walls ceased their warbling. Zaphenath-paneah closed his eyes and lifted his face toward the blue vault of heaven. "El Shaddai, god of Avraham, Yitzhak and Yaakov," he prayed, his voice breaking. "Forgive, I beg you, the sins of this household, of my sons. For You have taken Your blessing from us, and we are lost without You."

Ani searched for the meaning behind the words. Zaphenath-paneah was the wisest man in the kingdom, the spirit of a god rested on him always, everyone said so. So how could he believe his god had deserted him?

Lowering his hands, the vizier opened his eyes, then took two sizable hunks of raw, wounded meat from the first servant's bowl and tossed them into the flames. "Without the shedding of blood there is no pardon for sin." His eyes remained on the flames as his hands moved again from the bowl to the fire, offering other portions of meat to the sizzling inferno. "And just as I have ordered that the entire bull shall be offered unto You, with nothing held back, know that my entire household shall be dedicated to You, O God Shaddai."

The line of servants continued forward, each man bearing his burden in silence as Zaphenath-paneah emptied each tray or bowl onto the altar. The pungent aromas of roasting meat and sizzling fat permeated the air. Finally, as the last servant offered the bowl of blood, Zaphenath-paneah took it and held it high above his head, then moved around the fire, spattering the lower logs with the crimson liquid.

When the last drop of blood had been spilt, the master clasped his bloodstained hands in front of his once-spotless robe and bowed his head. "The sacrifice has been offered as Noah and Avraham and Yaakov offered it," he said. "May God forgive those of my household who have sinned." After a moment of silence, he lifted his head. His powerful dark gaze raked the gathering until he found Ani and Tarik.

"See that no one disturbs the offering," he commanded, moving toward them. "Absolutely nothing is to be eaten, all is to be consumed by the fire."

Tarik lifted his arm in salute. "Yes, my lord."

The master nodded and moved through the crowd, but the nagging fears in the back of Ani's mind refused to be stilled as Zaphenath-paneah stalked away.

Three days passed with snail-like slowness while Yosef waited for word of Menashe's repentance and return. He had offered his sacrifice with every expectation that God would honor a public confession and humiliation, and yet there had been no sign that his erring elder son had experienced a change of heart.

Breakfasting in the garden, Yosef waved away the slaves who lingered with fresh wine and steaming loaves of sweet lotus bread. He had not touched the dainties on the tray before him; his appetite had disappeared days before. He wanted nothing more than to be left alone with his thoughts.

The king's disdainful dismissal had left him reeling, but Yosef was now certain the situation was God's call for him to set his house in order. Efrayim had pointed out something Yosef had been too upset to see—trouble *did* exist between Yosef and Amenhotep, and that trouble was Menashe. This ignoble discharge had to be a direct result of Menashe's rebellious actions, and once Menashe had seen the error of his ways, things would certainly be set right. And so Yosef had humbled himself and offered a sacrifice like those of his forefathers, doubtless shocking his household and the nobles of Thebes, but worth every rumor and uplifted eyebrow if God worked and sent Menashe home to repent…

Tarik's frantic voice nudged Yosef out of his musing.

"Hail to the Mother of Egypt," the captain of the guard called, his voice hoarse with surprise and urgency. "She who is the Most Favored Lady, the Graciousness of the Nile, the Beginning-of-the-Divine-King desires an audience with you, Zaphenath-paneah."

Yosef took a quick breath and turned toward the portico where Tarik had fallen prostrate on the tile. Two of the palace guards stood there facing each other with the tall, graceful figure of Amenhotep's mother, Queen Tuya, between them.

For a moment the sight did not register on Yosef's dazzled senses. The Queen Mother had gone into seclusion after her son's marriage, forfeiting her own enormous popularity in order to allow her son and his wife to hold first place in the people's devotion. She rarely left her apartments in the palace, and never went about in the streets of Thebes. But here she was, her luminous eyes fastened to Yosef's face, regarding him with a look that drove his breath from his body.

Tearing his gaze from hers, Yosef rose from his chair and slipped to the floor, a wave of despair crashing over him as he felt the warmth of the sun-warmed tiles on his hands. By heaven above, what had she heard? She must have thought him near death if urgency had compelled her to come to him.

"Rise, Zaphenath-paneah." Her voice rang with an infinitely compassionate tone, and Yosef's soul shrank from the sound of it. Pity? He had never accepted pity from any man, and would not welcome it from a woman, even one he had loved.

He rose and stared at her. She wore a short, full wig, a surprisingly youthful style for a woman of over fifty years, and her graceful figure had ripened to a womanly fullness. Uncommon delicacy and strength mingled in her lovely face; color lingered in her sweetly curved lips. On her pale face she wore the fine lines of age with a serene elegance; time had not diminished her beauty.

"Leave us, please," she said. Instantly the pair of warriors moved from the shade of the portico into the house and, after an instant's hesitation, Tarik followed them. The lingering slaves who carried the remains of Yosef's breakfast took their cue from the departing men and scurried away like rodents.

Yosef searched for words and found none. Reading the surprise on his face, Tuya smiled and strolled from the portico to the garden pathway. "I am afraid I have put you at a disadvantage." She folded her hands as she glided over the walkway. "Perhaps I should have sent word that I would come."

Yosef inclined his head. "My villa is always open to you."

"I appreciate the welcome," she answered. "Though I am not sure you are happy to see me."

She had reached the pavilion, and Yosef extended a hand to the empty chair at his side. "I am thrilled you have come."

"Liar," she whispered, sliding into the carved chair. She

leaned back, allowing the heavy fullness of her wig to tip her chin toward him. "You never could lie, Yosef, that's why Tuth-mosis valued you so." One corner of her mouth dipped. "I'm only sorry Amenhotep doesn't value you in the same way. He is a good king, but he is not the man his father was."

Yosef lowered himself to the edge of his chair. "Is that why you are here? To tell me what we both know about Pharaoh?"

"No." She crossed her legs and leaned forward, one elbow resting on the arm of her chair. "You were at my side when Tuth-mosis passed into the Other World, but I was unable to stand by you when your wife died. You were a very public figure then, and I couldn't risk the rumors."

"No need to explain." Yosef cut her off with an uplifted hand. "I know the dangers of palace gossip."

She nodded almost imperceptibly. "But I believed you did not need me. You had your sons to comfort you, and you had God Shaddai. But now, Yosef, you grieve and I wonder if you have either your sons or your god."

Yosef's jaw clenched as he rejected the softly spoken statement. "What do you mean? One son has left my house, just one, and God Shaddai would never leave me."

Tuya's face emptied and Yosef felt a sudden icy silence surround her. He had hurt her, but he didn't care. Like a scolding mother, she had stepped out of her pristine palace to rebuke and comfort him when he did not need comforting or rebuking.

"God has not left you," she went on in a strangled voice, turning her gaze toward the lotus blossoms in the pool, "but is it possible you have left Him? This is not like you, Yosef. I have never seen that look on your face, that anger in your eyes. I have heard about Menashe, I heard about your sacrifice. I thought perhaps you might feel as alone as I often do."

A weight of sadness lay on her elegant face, and Yosef shud-dered at the thought that he had put it there. "I am sorry, Tuya, to have caused you pain. Menashe has done much to hurt all of us, but I believe God will bring him home. And when Menashe returns, all things will be restored to the order of God's will."

"God's will…or yours?" Tuya's dark eyes brimmed with unquenchable warmth. "Think, Yosef, before you believe your own words. And know that I will not cease to pray for you."

She straightened her shoulders, then stood and moved with regal elegance toward the house, leaving Yosef alone with his thoughts.

Chapter Twenty-Four

The desert sun stood proud in the white-blue sky, baking both man and beast in its heat haze. Efrayim shifted on his camel and slipped the reins from his sweaty left hand to his right. He and a bodyguard had taken one of his father's boats from Thebes to Tura, then led two cantankerous camels from the ship and set off for Menashe's rebel camp. Tarik's last report placed it somewhere in the wilderness beyond the jagged mountains; Efrayim suspected he would find his rebellious brother and kinsmen at an oasis five miles south of his father's house at Tura quarry.

Menashe was the root cause of their lives' upheaval, and Efrayim was determined to confront him and end the havoc of the past few weeks. Because Menashe had defied the king and returned to war, Yosef had been dismissed from royal service. And lately it had become clear that because Zaphenath-paneah was vizier no longer, Efrayim would never be allowed to take Sitamun as his wife. Though there had been no formal announcement that Efrayim would not be accepted as a suitor, he knew such a match was inconceivable as long as Menashe remained outside Pharaoh's will. But if the rebel would come back to Thebes and apologize to Pharaoh, everything could be made right.

The camel's jolting gait had reduced Efrayim's muscles to jelly, but he shifted in the saddle again and continued sorting through his thoughts. Menashe *had* to come to his senses; the fate of Egypt and the sons of Yisrael rested on his decision. The future had begun to unfold the way Efrayim thought it would—his father had withdrawn from leadership, leaving Efrayim in charge, just as Yaakov had foretold. Of course Efrayim hadn't realized how quickly his father would falter, or how *publicly* he would lose his grip. Only four days before Yosef had demonstrated his deteriorating reason to the entire household; in broad daylight he had ordered the butchering of a perfectly healthy bull, then had offered a sacrifice that blackened the skies over Thebes and attracted every stray dog and cat within ten miles of the villa.

Efrayim had been at a party during the unprecedented event, but Ani, Tarik and a host of other servants had been quick to tell him of their concerns when he returned. Before the day ended he knew the slaves had spread the story at the wells, in the markets, on the streets. All of Thebes, probably all of Egypt, would soon know that the mighty Zaphenath-paneah's wit had broken, and before long people would be praising the divine pharaoh for having wisdom enough to anticipate the tragedy.

And everything was Menashe's fault.

Urging his camel into a trot, Efrayim forbade himself to lose his temper. He had not set out to quarrel with his brother, but to reason with him, to help him see the far-reaching folly of his actions. Perhaps news of the little harpist's arrival at the villa could persuade Menashe to return to Thebes. If that enticement would not work, then a report of their father's gory sacrifice might spur him homeward. Menashe imagined himself the deliverer of the Hebrews, after all, but he was doing little to help their cause and reputation by driving Yosef to outmoded sacrificial rites.

Menashe had to be turned away from his intention of making war. Rumors were rampant, Pharaoh was unhappy, the family was falling apart.

"There, master!" The guard behind him shouted and pointed toward the horizon. Just above the slope of sterile golden dunes, Efrayim caught sight of movement. The tents had been cleverly camouflaged to blend in with the sand, but in this heat the dancing image of huddled men proved impossible to ignore.

Efrayim kicked his heels against his mount's side. "Onward, then."

"You are fortunate my men didn't kill you." With his hands on his hips, Menashe paced back and forth, blocking the opening of his tent. "If you insist on coming, you must send word."

Efrayim clenched his jaw to kill the retort in this throat. Locking his arms across his chest, he stared at his brother. "It is easier to come than to send a messenger, and my purpose cannot wait."

"Your purpose?" Menashe stopped pacing, and amusement lurked in his eyes. "What new purpose could send you flying across the desert after me? Nothing has changed. You want me to ignore God's call, and I will not."

"You are flaunting Pharaoh's wishes and breaking our father's heart. He is not himself—"

"So I have heard." Menashe spoke more quietly, and a muscle quivered at his jaw.

"Then come home." Efrayim moved toward his brother, extending his hands in a desperate plea. "The way to peace and prosperity is through Egypt, can't you understand? We are at peace here, and the Egyptians leave us alone. We can learn from each other, and in time we shall be like them—"

"That is the problem!" Sudden anger lit Menashe's eyes. "You are blind to the truth, Efrayim, and so is our father. God Shaddai brought us here during the famine so we might be preserved, yes! But not only did He protect us from famine, He brought us to Egypt in order to keep us as the unique people of El Shaddai! We were torn from the idol-worshipping Canaanites—"

"A senseless argument, for the Egyptians worship idols," Efrayim interrupted, clenching his fists.

"Not in Goshen," Menashe countered. "Our people are isolated there, or at least we were until we began to plan cities and build brick houses. If we persist in remaining, it is only a matter of time before we adopt Egyptian gods. Today our uncles are building brick houses, tomorrow they will build brick temples and shrines. We must leave before we bow before idols, before we forget God Shaddai altogether."

Efrayim shook his head. "Well-spoken, Menashe, but you forget *you* are a son of Egypt, not Goshen, whether you like it or not. You have not forgotten our father's god. And why would God Shaddai call you to lead the sons of Yisrael? He set our father aside to bring them to safety, and as long as our father lives, they shall be part of Egypt."

"For an Egyptian, you sound very much like the Hebrews in Goshen." Menashe raised his voice in a mimicking cry. "As long as Yosef lives, we shall remain here where the grass is rich and the river blesses our fields." He paused, running his hands through his hair in a detached motion. "If they are comfortable, they will never leave. When Father dies, they will cling to someone else—you, perhaps. And after you, they will find someone else. And soon they will forget why they are remaining here, and they will hold fast to prosperity and comfort—"

"They will become *powerful* if peace is made," Efrayim interrupted. "And if you will forget this nonsense and return to Thebes, I will be allowed to marry Sitamun—"

"You will never marry Sitamun." Taking a deep, unsteady breath, Menashe lifted a warning finger. "You never will, not even if I surrender and crawl on my knees to declare myself Pharaoh's slave. Can you not see how Queen Tiy fears us? She trembles in Father's presence. She knows a mightier god than Amon-Re has blessed us. She would never allow a Hebrew to marry into the royal family, for the people adore Zaphenath-paneah. If the Egyptians grow disenchanted with Amenhotep's dynasty, they might yearn for Father's descendants to be their leaders. Tiy knows this."

Efrayim snorted. "You are dreaming again."

Menashe crossed his arms. "The Egyptians don't care who rules over them as long as they are fed and not overtaxed. When the eastern Hyksos overran this land during the fifteenth dynasty, the Egyptians welcomed them with open arms. As long as the river flooded and the crops grew, they accepted the foreign kings as the gods' will."

Not knowing how to answer, Efrayim fell silent. As always, Menashe had prepared his arguments. But one truth, at least, he could not dispute. "Father wants you to come home. And because a good son honors his father, you must obey him."

Menashe gave him a quick, denying glance. "I am doing my best to honor my father." Turning to face the open door of his tent, he placed his hands on his hips. "I am honoring him by following his god. God Shaddai began a work in Yosef, and He calls me to continue it."

Menashe's words froze in Efrayim's brain; from them a thought grew and flowered. "Then all this—" Efrayim gestured at the spears, shields and battle-axes piled around him in the tent "—is to prove yourself a worthy son. You are not here to win Canaan. You care nothing for those miserable Hebrews out there in the heat."

"God called me," Menashe answered.

Efrayim stepped closer as conviction took root within him. "You have always tried to prove yourself. You were always the show-off, the one who had to demonstrate your lessons, to prove you could throw a spear farther than me—"

"You are mistaken."

Efrayim fingered the stubble on his chin. "It is all clear to me now. Yaakov gave me the blessing of his right hand, and now you feel you must prove yourself. Why else would you claim to have heard the voice of God? Your dream was not inspired by the Almighty. Your holy call was nothing but an invention of jealousy."

"You…are…wrong!" Menashe spoke in a thick and unsteady voice, and Efrayim knew his words had struck his brother's heart. Nothing could be gained now by pressing the issue; he would only drive Menashe to a fury that might prove dangerous for them both.

"War demands a high price of a man," Efrayim whispered, moving close enough to place his hand on his brother's back. Menashe flinched beneath his touch, but he did not pull away. "Think twice before you risk your life. You may think you are gaining Father's respect, but what will you accomplish if you lose your life? The little harpist will have genuine cause for weeping if you do not return to Thebes. And more's the pity, because she now waits for you in our father's villa."

He caught an expression of mingled wonder and fear on Menashe's face, then Efrayim left the tent and mounted his camel for the long ride back to the river.

Alone in his tent, Menashe slapped his hand to his forehead and railed against Efrayim's timing. Surely his visit was a trick of the Evil One, for on the morrow their band was to make its first foray into enemy lands. They were now a force of four hundred—two hundred Egyptian mercenaries and an equal number of Hebrews. Each man had his own reason for joining the force, but most had come for gold, glory or God.

As Menashe left his tent and walked among them, every eye gleamed with eagerness, every warrior's belt held a winking sword that had been polished and honed to the sharpest possible edge. Imposing an iron control on his countenance and his emotions, he returned their salutes with a resolute nod. He could not afford to allow Efrayim or his father to upset him. When next the gold-veiled sunrise crept over the desert, he and his men would no longer be sons and brothers, but warriors on a divine mission, urged forward for God's people and His purpose.

"Sons of Yisrael and our Egyptian comrades in arms!" Menashe shouted, climbing atop a smooth rock in the midst of the camp. "Tomorrow is the day! At sunrise we reenter the land of Canaan, we fight at Gerar, we begin to retake our homeland!"

"Listen to him!" Jokim yelled, hurrying to Menashe's side as others spilled out of their tents. The men who had been sitting around the cookfires stood and folded their arms as Jokim continued. "The sons of Yisrael know their true place! The Hebrew homeland is Canaan, the land promised to Avraham, Yitzhak and Yaakov!"

The Hebrews cheered; the Egyptians and Nubian warriors looked nonplussed. Menashe caught sight of their confused expressions and smiled. "Never fear, my warrior friends," he said, catching Abnu's eye. That giant had been invaluable to their cause, for a mere glimpse of his assuring strength had silenced the quailing of many an anxious heart. "For when we attack on the morrow, the men of Gerar will flee as if before a bear out of the woods! They will run to Gaza with news of our strength, and the men of Gaza will run to Ashkelon and Ashdod, till all of Canaan knows we are coming back to live in the land God promised to Avraham and his descendants. And for you—" he extended his hand toward a knot of mercenaries standing nearby "—because your valiant hearts have not feared to join us in this endeavor, you shall be granted first choice among the spoils and captives. The bounty and plunder of Gaza, Ashkelon and Ashdod shall be yours. Then you shall return home to bedeck your wives and your concubines, and all who see you shall marvel at the riches won by your bravery."

The Egyptians slapped each other on the back, enjoying their imagined success. Even the reserved faces of Abnu and his Medjay cohorts spread in wide grins, thoroughly enjoying the danger-excitement of the moment. Menashe had been surprised and a bit alarmed that so many Nubians left Thebes to join them, for Pharaoh's captains must have noticed an obvious thinning of the royal troops. But if the king could not hold his warriors, he did not deserve them. As long as Amenhotep remained in his pleasure palace at Malkata, the valiant Medjays were as restless as penned bulls. They lived for battle, and probably considered this venture a mere exercise to sharpen their skills.

Menashe paused, waiting for the riotous merrymaking to cease. "When the battle is won, all of us shall know we heard and obeyed the voice of God Shaddai. It is His will that we be holy, and we have kept ourselves pure as we trained here. No women, no idols and no thievery have been allowed in this camp."

Shouts of agreement rang from the hills; even the heathen Nubians nodded in earnest accord.

"It is the will of God that we be submissive." Menashe continued, "to all the authorities except when they conflict with the voice of God Himself. And we have harmed no peaceful citizens of the desert, we have not stolen from the Bedouin in his tent or the temple priests who gather the offerings at the river shrines."

The hurrahs returned with a deafening surge of sound.

"But though Pharaoh and his vizier have asked us to abandon this holy cause," Menashe went on, "sometimes God wills that we suffer." Silence met this statement, followed by a murmur of dissent. Menashe softened his expression as he looked out on his men. "Yes, my brothers," he said, his gaze meeting that of Zimri, the gentle youth who had learned how to throw a spear and wield an ax under Jokim's tutelage. "When we obey God rather than men, we shall have to pay the price. On the morrow some of us will be injured. Some of us will give our lives in the fields of Gerar or, in days to come, in the streets of Ashkelon or Ashdod. But God is faithful. He will reward our suffering by bringing our wives and children into a green land flowing with milk and honey. That is the unchangeable, unshakable will of God. And all men, be they Hebrew or Nubian or Egyptian, will be blessed if they honor God Shaddai, the Holy One of Yisrael."

The cheering began among the Hebrews first, then lifted from the throats of every man present, rising in great waves until the dunes rang with the sound. Menashe lifted his hands toward heaven in anticipation of victory, then led his men in a dance of praise. He twirled slowly at first, then increased his tempo, hoping to exhaust himself. He knew he would not sleep through the night to come.

With wary eyes, Hondo watched his dancing companions. Let them cheer and rant and rave. Let them expend their precious energy; they would not live long enough to restore it.

He and the twenty men he had recruited had been living with the rebel force for over a month. Though Hondo had kept to himself, quietly hiding his face from Abnu and the Hebrew leaders, no one had questioned his motives, timing or skill. He was a Medjay, so they supposed him faithful to Abnu; the foolish Hebrews had not stopped to think that he might actually be loyal to Pharaoh…and his queen.

His brow wrinkled with contemptuous thoughts as Zaphenath-paneah's son trotted by, out of breath and delirious with adrenaline-fueled energy. That young imbecile should have known Hondo's face and name, for he was one of the most skilled assassins in the entire Egyptian army. Zaphenath-paneah certainly knew of Hondo's reputation, but apparently the vizier had never discussed the king's special weapon with his son.

He smiled to himself as he studied Menashe. A shame, really, to cut down such a handsome and passionate youth. A pity the young man had chosen to follow this ridiculous quest instead of remaining at home like his displaced father.

The young man's dance had spread like a fever; the men around Hondo jostled him, clapping him on the shoulder and moving him into the frantic circle which turned to the inaudible beat of war. Hondo smothered his smile and slapped his arms about his comrade's shoulders, then joined in the frenzy of the dance.

Long after sunset, sleep finally came nudging in among Menashe's thoughts.

He dreamed he was a child again, standing in the chamber where his mother and father often breakfasted. "Come here, my boys," Yosef called, his voice sounding ghostly and faraway, but Menashe and Efrayim ran to him, crawled up in his lap and covered his cheeks with kisses.

Asenath, their mother, remonstrated: "You must always bow before approaching Pharaoh's vizier."

Menashe looked at his father, hoping for a word of rebuttal, but Yosef only patted him on the head, his eyes distant, his expression aloof. "Go with Ani now, my sons, and study your lessons. Make me proud of you." Menashe accepted the challenge but left with a heavy heart, knowing he would not see his father again until the morrow.

"Father," he murmured through the embracing folds of sleep. His hands reached out and closed on empty air, then his arm brushed the handle of his battle sword. The cold kiss of metal brought him back to wakefulness.

He was not a child, but a man preparing for battle.

A decidedly non-dreamlike cry shattered the night. Menashe fought through the cobwebs of weariness and fumbled for his sword, then squinted into the night, struggling to focus in the heavy darkness. For an instant he panicked, not seeing the other tents or campfires, then he remembered that Jokim had insisted they separate from the others in order to clear their thoughts in preparation for battle. But now, sequestered behind a sand dune, Menashe felt dangerously isolated.

"Menashe!" Jokim crouched beside him in the dim moon-light, his sword in hand and a cold, hard-pinched expression on his face. "They are upon us!"

Menashe hefted his sword and squatted beside Jokim. His breath seemed to have solidified in his throat. "Who moves out there in the dark?"

Jokim flattened himself against the dune that separated them from the camp. "I can't tell."

Menashe joined Jokim on the dune; together they crawled upward on their elbows until they peered over the lip of sand. Without speaking they parsed the sounds that came through the night beyond: cries, screams, shrieks of agony. Prickles of cold dread crawled over Menashe's back.

"Someone is attacking," Jokim mumbled, stating the obvious. "But who?"

"It matters not." Menashe stooped to pick up his shield. He thrust his arm through the leather loops that held it to his arm, then turned to look at his cousin. "Our first battle begins tonight. Are you ready?"

Jokim blinked with bafflement, then thrust his jaw forward. "Yes." He bent for his own shield. Like Menashe, he girded it to his arm, then nodded.

"We should go into the fray together," Menashe said. "Side by side, the two of us will make a more considerable foe."

"Or a bigger target." Jokim gave Menashe a humorless smile as he moved out from behind the dune.

The damage had been done by the time they arrived, but there was no sign of the marauding foe that had passed through the camp. With fearful curiosity Menashe wondered if an enemy could rise from beneath the sand itself. If not for the viscous pools of blood surrounding the bodies scattered around the campfires, Menashe would have thought his men asleep. Man after man appeared to doze, their hands folded across their chests or tucked beneath bearded cheeks. The enemy, whomever they were, had moved confidently, swiftly killing with silent strokes of a blade across the jugular. But others of Menashe's force lay facedown on their bellies, their hands extended for swords that had been kicked away, their bare backs opened by an ax.

The darkness, laced now with the smells of blood and death, enfolded Menashe like a suffocating blanket. What enemy had done this? And how could they appear without warning and strike in the dead of night? Whomever they were, they had fled, either to hide or to pursue the survivors who sought escape in the darkness.

"Jokim—" Menashe turned to his cousin "—why did you insist that we not sleep in my tent tonight?"

Jokim gaped in horror. "By the name of God Shaddai, I swear to you that I knew nothing."

"Do not swear by His name." Menashe turned. The silhouette of his tent stood black and awkward at the edge of the clearing, backlit by the moon rising beyond the silvered sands. "At least my tent was empty. An enemy would search it first, hoping to kill me."

Jokim's hand tightened around his sword. "Zimri! I asked him to sleep there and guard the weapons."

Menashe darted forward, zigzagging between the bodies on the ground, until he reached the tent. The canvas flap that served as a door had been sliced from top to bottom, and an inky puddle marked the rug where Zimri lay.

"My fault!" Jokim cried, pushing past Menashe. He dropped to his knees beside the boy's body. "He is not a warrior. I should never have let him come. What shall I say to his father? How can I face his mother?"

Keening in sorrow, Jokim scooped up a handful of sand and poured it over his head while Menashe stepped back to study the scene. Zimri had not been struck while sleeping, for he lay sprawled at an unnatural angle, one leg tucked under him. Blood spangled the sword that lay a few inches from his hand.

"Look there." Menashe pointed to a mounded shape among the shadows of the tent. Distracted, Jokim stopped wailing and turned.

Menashe moved to light an oil lamp, then held it aloft and brought it near the stacks of shields and weapons. Another warrior lay on the ground, his eyes glazed, his mouth frozen in a spasm.

"I know him." Jokim's voice filled with fresh sorrow. "He

was one of the newer arrivals. A Medjay. Alas, even our friends are dying for our people."

Menashe left Jokim in the tent and returned to the field, searching for survivors. But in the lurid red glow of smoldering campfires he found only death. In the space of an hour the army of four hundred had been transformed to a corps of two hundred corpses. The others had fled in the night.

Engulfed in tides of weariness and despair, Menashe crouched beside an ashen campfire. There was now more darkness in the darkness, more threat in the world. If God had called him to win Canaan for the Hebrews, why had He allowed this atrocity to befall them just as they prepared to obey?

"Was it men from Gerar?" Jokim's voice startled him. "Spies? Somehow they must have been forewarned of our intention."

"The enemy was not from Gerar," Menashe answered. He looked across the dead fire to the body of a boy scarcely fifteen years old, one of Yehuda's grandsons. "The killers made no noise, they carried no torches, they left no tracks in the sand around us. These murderers rose up and killed their sleeping neighbors."

Jokim shivered and knelt beside Menashe. "Were half our company traitors?" He lowered his voice as if ashamed to speak of such things. "Was it the Nubians?"

Menashe fought to control his swirling emotions and jerked his thumb over his shoulder. "Behind me lies one of Abnu's men. He was one of the first to die, I think. He still wears the smile of contented sleep."

Jokim remained in an attitude of frozen stillness for a long moment. "The Egyptians, then."

Menashe shook his head. "There are as many Egyptian dead as Hebrew."

"But surely there was no conspiracy among the men." Jokim settled back on his haunches. "You saw them tonight. They were in one accord and ready for battle. They were all willing to fight, to die if necessary."

"Some of them were willing to die, but not for us." Menashe stood, brushed sand from his knees and picked up his sword. "Did you look closely at the scene in my tent? Zimri is dead, but he killed the Medjay who lies in the tent with him."

Jokim frowned. "But Abnu's men—"

"Not all Medjay are Abnu's men," Menashe answered. "I believe the men who rose up against us tonight were sent from Pharaoh and charged to destroy us before we could venture into Canaan."

"If they were sent to execute traitors," Jokim asked, the line of his mouth tightening, "then why are we still alive?"

"Because we slept apart," Menashe answered, moving away from the fire. "They have not finished with us. But neither has God Shaddai."

Knowing that their enemy had slipped away under cover of darkness, Menashe and Jokim crept away from the camp, cowering in shadows, avoiding the open patches of moonlight where a man might easily become a target for a silent spear. From time to time they heard movement in the dunes beyond; once or twice a sharp cry twisted through the silence of the night. Menashe had no doubts that Pharaoh's guards were tracking survivors in the hills beyond.

After seemingly endless night, a gentle radiance low on the eastern horizon indicated where the sun would rise. Menashe and Jokim kept that horizon at their backs and crept toward the river. Once they reached the Nile, they could either find a boat or beg a ride from a passing barge. If they did not encounter the enemy in the desert, they would reach the river within a day; within two days they could be back in civilized Thebes, where assassins did not work so openly.

At last the horizon's glow spread and brightened until the gleaming sun rose swollen and red above the dunes. Menashe felt his fear abate in direct proportion to the sun's advent, and by the time the horizon glimmered blue he felt he could again stand tall and face any approaching adversary.

He and Jokim talked little on their long walk across the sand. The sun spread its rays over the dunes, baking their skin and parched lips, but neither man dared to speak of his thirst, hunger or weariness. Any admission of weakness was tantamount to surrender, and Menashe had given up all he intended to during the previous night of horror. The enemy would have to be content with divesting him of his dreams—for a short time. Once he had regrouped the survivors, he would undertake another incursion into Canaan, even if he had to launch it from Edom or Moab.

If there were any survivors. Guilt, heavy and sharp, avalanched over Menashe as Zimri's earnest face rose in his memory. If not for Menashe that young man would not have been in the desert. If not for his dream, none of the Hebrews would have left their homes and families. His relatives would look askance at him now; mothers would weep at the mention of his name, fathers would curse the day Menashe had been born. Even the Egyptians would consider him a pariah, a young fool who had flagrantly rebelled against his father and led four hundred men to ignominious deaths in the desert.

A man could die honorably on the field of battle.

No man died honorably sleeping by the fire.

The dead Egyptian warriors, denied the glory of battle, would have no funerals or tombs. Some of the wealthier families would send search parties to bring home the mortal remains of their sons, but the poor families would have no way of gathering their loved ones until the desert sun had dried and desiccated the corpses, leaving them to a sorrowful, sandy afterlife with no provision for eternity…

Menashe swallowed hard, wanting to forget every moment of the past twenty-four hours. What a cruel joke the divine will had played on him! He had done all he could to please God Shaddai, and yet he had been defeated. How could God allow such a thing to happen? Was He not a god of justice and fairness?

His mind skittered away from the unsolvable dilemma. He could not think about God in his present state; his thoughts scampered around in confusion and made no sense.

"At last," Jokim said, sighing. He paused a step ahead of Menashe and gestured beyond the rocky hill they were climbing. "I can smell the river."

Menashe's heart thumped with relief as he lengthened his stride, passing Jokim. But at the top of the rim he thrust out his arm to hold his cousin back.

The river lay as bright as a spill of silver across the barren sands, but Menashe's joy was tempered by the sight of a ship anchored in the small cove south of Tura quarry. A standard featuring Pharaoh's royal insignia flew from the barge's mast. At least a dozen seamen and warriors wandered over its deck, and another dozen lingered on the shore, their blades glinting in the sun. Judging from the depth of their firepits, Menashe guessed they had been situated at this location for several days.

"Our traitors," Menashe whispered, dropping to the earth like a stone. Jokim fell beside him and they lay flat on their bellies, peering over the rim of rock. Laughter and the taunts of the warriors echoed among the hills; the scents of roasting meat wafted up from their cookfire.

Menashe's stomach clenched in sudden hunger, and he realized he had not eaten or drunk anything all day. Jokim had to be starving, too, and yet food and water lay within reach.

"What do we do?" Jokim whispered, watching the men below with an observant eye. "If we advance northward we can move around them."

Menashe cut him off. "We take them just as they took us. Their work is done, so why haven't they left? They are waiting for others to rejoin them. So we will lie in wait here, in these hills. I know these rocks, I know the path that leads down to the cove. We will guard it, and any traitor who passes by us is a dead man. And then tonight, if they still remain here, we shall slip among them like shadows. They are guilty of ruthless murder, and so we shall avenge—"

"You shall avenge nothing."

Menashe lifted his head and felt the sharp bite of a blade against his neck. His gaze darted toward Jokim; he, too, had been pinned to the ground by the sharp point of a spear.

The pressure at Menashe's neck eased slightly. "Stand up," came the terse order, and he did, rising slowly from the sand. Behind him stood a half-dozen men wearing the distinctive kilts and leopard belts of Medjay warriors. Their eyes glittered with battle-lust.

The group was dominated by the dark figure of a powerful and familiar man. The set of his chin suggested a stubborn streak, and he folded his powerful arms and smiled. "A very great honor to meet you face-to-face, Menashe, son of Zaphenath-paneah. It was not even an hour ago that I asked of your whereabouts and was dismayed no one could recall having killed you."

Menashe stiffened at the challenge in the man's voice. "God Shaddai spared me. As He will spare me again." He squinted toward his captor, remembering the man's voice and face and form. They had met before, on a winding pathway through the marketplaces of Thebes—but today the barbarian was not drunk.

"You are Hondo." Jokim spat the words in anger. "I remember you. You joined us at Kadesh Barnea."

The warrior smirked. "On the direct orders of Queen Tiy my men and I joined your pitiful band. And I fully intend—" his gaze darted back to Menashe "—to bring my lovely queen the gift of your head, Menashe. Though I personally think beheading is rather too merciful a punishment for traitors."

"You are the traitor." Menashe jerked away as two men stepped forward to bind his arms. "You trained, slept and ate with us and then rose in the night to murder your own comrades in combat."

"You are not my comrade, *Hebrew.*" Icy contempt flashed in Hondo's eyes. Visibly trembling with suppressed fury, he jerked his thumb toward a narrow path. "Take them down to the river. We shall have some fun with them while we wait for the others."

Chapter Twenty-Five

In later life, Menashe would have trouble clearly recalling the next several hours. The traitorous Medjays drove him and Jokim down the narrow path that wound through the rocky cliffs, urging them forward with the points of their spears and an occasional jab of a sword. Breathless and bleeding, they finally arrived at the makeshift camp on the shore where a host of men stared at them with the wide eyes of cowardly conquerors. Hondo barked out an order; eager servants dragged the Hebrews into the shallows of the drought-wasted river and tied their hands to mooring posts.

Standing in knee-deep water with his hands bound together, Menashe wondered if Hondo truly intended to take his head back to Thebes or if he would simply leave them in the river as crocodile bait. Nothing, he realized, would be too horrific for Hondo to consider. His actions had already demonstrated that he had no morals, no conscience and no royal mandate other than to stop the Hebrews.

Menashe lifted his eyes and blinked up at the sky. Now that Zaphenath-paneah no longer served as Pharaoh's vizier, Hondo did not even fear retribution from the second-highest throne in the land.

Jokim, overflowing with bravado, poured a steady stream of vituperation on his captors. Ignoring Jokim's insults, Hondo and his men retreated to the cookfire, and now their bloodstained hands lifted hunks of meat in mock salute to their starving captives.

"Sons of dogs and jackals!" Jokim yelled, struggling against the ropes that held him tight. "If Pharaoh has ordered this, he is the son of a water buffalo! A curse on all your idolatrous gods! May your wives and mothers bear illegitimate curs! May your daughters marry vile— Arraugh!"

One of the warriors, tiring of Jokim's curses, had picked up his bow and sent an arrow winging through the air. It struck Jokim squarely in the thigh, pinning him to the mooring post. Jokim screamed, then clenched his teeth and grimaced at Menashe as he twisted in a vain effort to move his hands toward the painful spot.

"I am a dead man, cousin," he whispered, sweat beading on his forehead.

"Don't speak of defeat."

He closed his eyes and screwed up his face against the agony. "We are in the water, and the blood—see, it gushes already."

"Jokim, listen to me," Menashe commanded. "We are not going to die, not at the hands of these men."

"The others died." Jokim's voice was now a husky whisper. "Why shouldn't we?"

"I don't know," Menashe admitted. "I don't understand any of this." A cold lump grew in his stomach as he looked at Jokim, and he turned away, frustrated by the niggling guilt of his own inadequacy. When had he ever claimed to have all the answers?

"You said—" Jokim's voice scraped terribly "—God sometimes calls us to suffer."

Menashe said nothing. And so, while Hondo and his men ate and drank and occasionally splashed through the shallows to buffet or spit on their prisoners, the afternoon passed into history.

When the sky began to glow red in the west, forecasting the sunset, Hondo moved to the center of the camp and lifted his massive arms. "We are still missing five men," he called, peering through the crowd as if the absent warriors might be hiding among the others. "We can only assume they have met with misfortune. So load the barge, for we will depart at sunset."

Hanging by the rope that secured him to the mooring post, Menashe opened his swollen eyes. One warrior had punched his face at least a dozen times, and Menashe was certain another had broken several of his ribs. At one point during the afternoon a pair of men had used Jokim and Menashe as targets in an archery competition. Though arrows fell in a whistling cloud around the pair for the space of an hour, the wobbly Medjays had been drinking and could not hold their bows steady. One arrow grazed Menashe's bare arm, leaving a nasty red streak, and Jokim took another arrow in the leg already lacerated by the spear. But they were still alive.

Menashe glanced over at Jokim. Blood from a wound in his forehead had transformed his face into a gruesome mask. He hung limply from the ropes that held him, weak from the slow seepage of blood from his wounds. Menashe frowned as he looked at the crimson-tinted water. The noise from the men on the beach had kept crocodiles at bay throughout the day, but the creatures were irresistibly drawn to blood, and they would grow more brazen once darkness fell. Menashe began to hope that Hondo would choose to take his captives' heads back to Thebes. A quick beheading would be more endurable than being torn apart by battling crocodiles in a feeding frenzy.

Hondo's warriors, seamen and slaves busied themselves with carrying provisions and weapons back aboard the ship. Their heavy footsteps thudded up and down the narrow gangplank, reverberating like the dull roar of thunder in Menashe's weary consciousness.

His arms, pinched by the constant pressure of the rope around his wrists, had no feeling. He had the fuzzy impression he possessed only a head and chest; he was nothing but a trunk tied to a pole, and soon he would be only a head, stuffed inside a gift basket for Queen Tiy. Would she invite his father to the ceremony during which Hondo would present her with trophies taken from the traitors? Yes, a voice inside Menashe murmured, she would. She was a capable and charming queen, but something poisonous lay just beneath the pleasing, polished surface of her personality, something dangerous…

"Men of Egypt, gather around me," Hondo called. Menashe

lifted one battered eyelid. The light was fading fast, color bleeding out of the atmosphere. The sun hovered over the western horizon, a gigantic ball of fire, the last sunset he would ever see. He closed his eyes again and waited for the inevitable.

The gangplank thundered with footsteps, every soul emptied the ship, anxious to observe Hondo's bloody entertainment. When at last the gangplank stood silent, Menashe heard the barbarian's bold voice again. "Today you shall witness the justifiable end of traitors." His words were punctuated by the soft swish of a weapon cutting through the darkening air. Against his will, Menashe's eyelids lifted. Hondo stood at the edge of the river, surrounded by his men, a battle-ax in this hand.

Despite his emptiness, Menashe felt the rise of panic. He had nothing with which to resist, no weapons, no strength, no will. The horror of the previous night and the constant abuse of the day, combined with his anger and thirst, had completely depleted him. And as weak as he was, he knew Jokim was even weaker.

He had no strength in himself. None at all. And no hope. He had been called of God and he had tried to rally his people, but they had not been willing to join him. They had journeyed to the promised land and felt its wonderful goodness beneath their feet, but then had turned back for the luxury and empty comforts of Egypt.

But God knew he had been faithful. Menashe closed his eyes and found strength in knowing that.

A noisy splash told him Hondo had entered the water, ax in hand.

"Are the baskets ready?" the assassin called. Now Menashe heard the rhythmic slap of the weapon's wooden handle against Hondo's open palm.

"They are asleep! Wake them up!" one of the men jeered, and Hondo laughed. He drew near, so close that Menashe could smell the rancid sweat of his body. Water splashed in Menashe's face.

He thrust out his tongue, hoping to ease his thirst by catching a drop or two, but still he kept his eyes closed. He was not certain his eyes could mask the emotions reeling in his heart, and he would not give Hondo the satisfaction of seeing his fear.

Another splash rained on his face, then his tormentor's voice dropped in volume. "Open your eyes and give them what they want," Hondo insisted, his hand splashing into the water a third time. "Or I shall cut off your companion's arms, then his legs, and finally his head. You may keep your eyes closed, but you will still hear his screams!"

Open your eyes, and you will see my deliverance.

Menashe's eyes flew open, not at Hondo's threat, but at the urgency in the numinous voice that seemed to vibrate from the mountains, through the air, up from the water. The voice had been so strong, so clear, he was amazed no one else heard it.

Perhaps someone had. "Jokim?" he called, his eyes focusing on Hondo's malignant face. The warrior pulled the ax back over his shoulder for the swing.

"I heard, Menashe!" A trace of laughter lined Jokim's weary voice. The sound must have alarmed Hondo, for his eyes widened in midswing. One of his legs shot forward in the water, and he teetered off balance, then screamed and fell into the shallows.

The men on shore laughed, imagining that the fierce warrior had lost his balance, but Menashe knew better. The hair lifted on his arms and his heart thumped against his rib cage as the water at his feet churned and boiled. Hondo reappeared, his clenched hands empty, his face frozen in an expression of atavistic horror. "Sobek!" he cried, then another scream clawed in his throat as an unseen force yanked him beneath the surface again.

Menashe blinked in numb terror. Sobek was the Egyptian god represented as a crocodile. Did Hondo think he had seen the god, or had a croc snagged him?

The men on shore stood in stunned huddles, then one of them shouted and pointed to the water. "Crocodiles!" he yelled, his bony face twitching in a paroxysm of fear. Menashe swiveled his eyes to follow the man's finger. Beyond the boat, from all directions, the unruffled surface of the quiet cove dimpled with the horny ridges of crocodile flesh. The river teemed with them; a man could have walked from one shore to the other on their backs without wetting his feet, and they moved steadily toward the men on the sand.

As the water around them blushed with Hondo's blood, Jokim let out a scream that chilled Menashe to the marrow.

Anyone who lived long in the Black Land knew the impossibility of escaping crocodiles caught up in the ecstasy of feeding. Energized by the sight of death in another guise, Menashe strained at his bonds while the men on shore ran for the narrow gangplank of the barge.

A sense of foreboding descended over Menashe with a shiver. He caught his breath as a particularly large beast emerged in the water a few feet away. He smelled the sour stench of wetness and rotted flesh caught between the creature's ragged teeth. Warning spasms of alarm erupted within him and he turned his head away, unwilling to look death in the eye—

But the animal glided past him with a strong side-to-side movement. Menashe felt the displacement of water as the creature swam by; the mighty tail brushed the benumbed flesh of his leg and yet the creature seemed unaware of him. Menashe shivered through fleeting nausea, then turned to look at Jokim. Though coated with blood and as pale as death, he, too, had been spared. A pair of creatures hovered atop the water to Jokim's right and a gigantic bull croc had thrust his pointed eyes up through the water at his left, but none of the animals had harmed him.

But this peculiarity had not been noticed by the panicked men on shore. Screaming and yelling, they hurtled toward the barge, overloading the gangplank until it teetered and tipped over, spilling at least twenty men into waist-deep water. A chilly dew formed on Menashe's skin as the carnage began in earnest, but a merciful shadow thrown by the setting sun blocked his view of the terror in the water.

The barge shifted, agitated by the death struggles in the river, and the handful of men who had managed to get aboard quickly loosened the mooring ropes and applied themselves to the oars. Thus abandoned, the men remaining on shore ran for the hills as the vicious creatures lumbered out of the water after them. But the towering figure of Abnu appeared from behind a rocky crest, and behind him stood at least a dozen of his loyal warriors. Hondo's frenzied comrades, bereft now of both weapons and sense, either ran pell-mell into the Nubians' spears or threw themselves on the ground to beg for mercy.

We are saved. The thought struck Menashe in an instant of understanding, then everything went silent within him as he pitched forward in a faint.

"They must have anchored directly above a crocodile nesting area," Abnu explained after freeing Menashe and Jokim. He and Menashe sat now by the fire, while Jokim shivered under a blanket someone had pulled from the sand. The giant clamped his jaw tight and stared at the now silent waters. "It *is* nesting season."

"It was a miracle of God," Menashe answered, holding his raw hands and wrists up to the warmth of the fire.

Abnu looked down at the ground and shook his head. "A natural mistake. They should have scouted the area."

"They did. They'd been here for days. We did not see a single crocodile until the first one grabbed Hondo." Menashe brought his knees to his chest, then folded his arms atop them and smiled at the giant. "If what happened here was not a miracle, then why weren't Jokim and I eaten alive? We were bleeding, and we could not escape."

Abnu pushed at a pile of dirt with his enormous foot. "Sometimes strange things happen. I have seen many things that do not make sense."

Menashe fell silent. He was convinced God Shaddai had worked a miracle to preserve him and Jokim from the Egyptians, but why hadn't God spared the others? And why had He allowed the massacre at the camp? Menashe understood why Abnu might have difficulty accepting the wisdom of God Shaddai. Menashe didn't always understand it himself.

"I do not understand everything God allows." He looked fully into the Nubian's somber eyes. "But it is enough to know He has a purpose for me. I know it is His will that the children of Avraham return to Canaan. And I know He called me to lead them. But only a few would take the step with me. Most chose not to believe." His eyes gravitated to the roaring fire. "Perhaps they never will align themselves to the will of God. But when they do, He will give them all He has promised."

"Are you giving up?" Abnu frowned, and his expression

sharpened. "That is not the way of a warrior. Tarik should have taught you better."

"I'm not giving up," Menashe answered, realizing that he could not. "But right now there are urgent things to consider. Jokim's wounds are serious. He will need a physician, and he cannot travel to Thebes on foot."

"What do you want me to do?"

Menashe paused. The danger had not passed. Tiy still wanted him dead and he was still a fugitive in Pharaoh's eyes. Who could he trust? Not his father, and certainly not Efrayim. But perhaps there was one…

"You must go to my father's house," he told Abnu, "and ask at the gate for a slave called Jendayi. She is my father's harpist, and she can be trusted. Tell her I will take Jokim to my father's house at Tura, and she must send a trustworthy physician to me."

"I myself will bring the physician back," Abnu volunteered, his heavy brows rising.

"I hoped you would." Menashe's smile widened. He reached out and clapped the other man on the shoulder. "You are a gift from God, friend."

The giant grinned back with no trace of his former animosity. "We shall see," he said, unfolding his long legs.

"And why," Tiy snapped, her patience evaporating, "would the river crocodiles attack you and not touch the Hebrews? Perhaps you did not see how your prisoners suffered. Perhaps their legs were eaten away."

"No, my queen. They stood in the midst of the beasts as if they were invisible." The protesting warrior pressed his hands to the floor of her chamber as if he'd been glued there. The trembling fool had been ushered to her quarters as soon as the royal barge had arrived back in Thebes, and she had already interviewed four other infiltrators who survived the skirmish with Menashe's rebel army. All of them gave the same incredible account, and every man shook before her like a dry palm in a high wind.

She looked away from the senseless man and considered her options. If Menashe and his comrade still lived, as all five survivors seemed to believe, they would be hiding in some safe refuge. And the younger man had been injured, so he would not be fit for travel. Menashe would need help, food and supplies from someone he trusted…someone from Goshen or his father's house. But if many Hebrews had died in the desert, Menashe would be about as welcome in Goshen as a plague of locusts.

"Get up, you fool," she told the quaking man before her. "Go immediately to the villa of Zaphenath-paneah, and ask for Akil, the chironomist. Tell him I have sent you, and that I command him to be alert for one who will come to fetch help for the troublesome son."

"If no one comes—"

"Someone will," she hissed. "And when he does, tell Akil to follow him. You bring word to me, so I can send my warriors to aid him." She waved him away. "Go at once. Your duty is not yet fulfilled."

Gulping in obvious relief that she had not ordered his execution, the man nodded and slunk from the room like a shadow.

Tiy rested her chin on her manicured fingertips. She would never cease to be amazed at the incredible talents of Zaphenath-paneah and his sons. In bygone days the vizier had been able to charm the birds from the trees, and his sons obviously followed in their father's footsteps. Zaphenath-paneah had always claimed his unique abilities came from his invisible and almighty god, but Tiy believed them to be the fruit of his intelligence, compassion and devastating handsomeness. Apparently his sons had inherited the same qualities, for Sitamun had been sincerely smitten by Efrayim, and Menashe obviously possessed his father's aptitude for leading and motivating men.

A terrifying thought rose in her consciousness. What if Zaphenath-paneah's special favor *did* come from his god? The Egyptians fondly credited their deities for all sorts of happy daily happenstances, but the survivors of the massacre on the river seemed convinced that they had witnessed a miracle in the midst of the crocodile attack. Could this invisible god wield that kind of force? And if He could and would, had He set His face against her?

Suddenly she yearned for Amenhotep's company. He would not be able to offer advice or wisdom more valuable than her own, but it would be comforting to rest in his arms and feel the burdens of the throne lifted from her shoulders. But the sun would soon set on what had been another royal wedding day. Amenhotep would sleep tonight with his latest bride, a match Tiy herself had arranged. And though her heart contracted a little to think of that royal couple, petty heartaches had to be borne in silence.

Tiy was the Great Wife, the reigning queen and the power behind the throne. And more than any of her blue-blooded predecessors she understood what the title required.

Chapter Twenty-Six

Though Jendayi could not see the exact moment when the sun slipped behind the western Theban mountains, she knew darkness had fallen by the way life in the vizier's house subtly gentled. Voices lowered in the night, laughter softened. The stern-voiced guards seemed to relax, for she heard smothered laughter and the clink of weapons as they put their swords, shields and spears away. Only a quartet of guards remained on duty during the night, and these four manned posts outside the villa's walls, away from the quiet hum of life within.

Once the vizier had been seen to his chamber and provided for, the sweet scents of lily oil streamed through the darkness as the women of the slave house anointed their arms and necks and went forth to entrance the men. Zaphenath-paneah was a more liberal and easygoing master than most—he allowed his slaves to marry, frequently granting them manumission as a wedding present. But no one, slave or free servant, could find a better master than Zaphenath-paneah, and only a few had ever left his service.

Of all locations in the house, Jendayi liked the garden best, but even it seemed different in the night. The ceaseless drone of insects became more melodic in the darkness, and the white lotus blossoms, which hid from the immodest brightness of daylight, generously opened their petals and perfumed the air. Occasionally Jendayi would hear a soft splash and imagine that some cricket or toad had leaped into the reflecting pool. The night sounds never unnerved her, for they belonged to the darkness, and darkness was as familiar as the strings of her harp. Daylight and dreams, she had discovered, brought things far more frightening than the night.

She had just settled down by the edge of the reflecting pool when Kesi came hurrying over the tiled pathway. "Come quickly, Jendayi," the handmaid whispered, a tinge of anxiety in her voice. "Someone at the gate of the vizier's house asks for you."

Every nerve in Jendayi's body jangled as she straightened. Who would ask for her? She knew no one outside the circle of this house and Pharaoh's, and she doubted that anyone from Malkata would venture here to ask for her. Efrayim was away at some party, as always, so who would seek her out?

"Is it—" her hand went to her throat "—a man or a woman outside the gate?"

"I don't know," Kesi answered, moving away. "The gate-keeper just sent me to fetch you. But you'd better hurry, because he doesn't like visitors after dark."

Jendayi rose and hurried forward as quickly as she dared, one hand extended to feel her way through the familiar passage-ways. Within a few moments she felt the courtyard sand under her feet, then she turned in the direction of voices and moved toward the gate.

"I am Jendayi." She spoke to the air.

"You?" The deep voice echoed as if it came from the bottom of a well. Jendayi shivered when she realized she had heard it before—at Malkata, at the center of a duel.

She folded her hands and tried to keep her voice steady. "Have you a message for me?"

The man's voice grew closer as it dropped in volume. "Menashe and Jokim have been wounded. Menashe bids me tell you that you must send a physician to his father's house at Tura quarry. Without aid, a man may die."

A strange surge of alarm ripped through her heart, fright-ening her. Menashe might be a liar and Efrayim's rival, but he had taken her into his arms when she needed a friend. "Is Menashe wounded?"

"Menashe will mend, but Jokim is in great distress. Do you know a physician?"

Jendayi pressed her fingers to her lips. The priests knew the healing arts, but Zaphenath-paneah employed no priests in his house. He called for his steward whenever one of the servants was ill—

"Ani," she gasped, a little surprised by her leap of logic. "He will know how to help." She whirled toward the house, then turned as an afterthought struck her. "You will wait, won't you?"

"I'll wait, little one," the voice growled from a great height. "But hurry. A boat is waiting, but we must be away before daylight."

Ani asked no questions when Jendayi told him Menashe needed help, and if the old man was surprised at her news he did not remark on it. He told her to wait a moment, then returned to the doorway of his chamber with his feet properly shod in papyrus sandals that made a delicate shooshing sound across the floor. She heard the soft creak of reeds and smelled the bitter tang of herbs; he carried a basket of medicinal plants. "I am ready," he said, nudging her with his elbow.

She took his arm, for her heart was pounding like a drum and she feared she would move too quickly in her haste and trip over some unexpected object. Within a few moments they had reached the gate, and she heard approval in the giant's words as he greeted the steward. "You are prepared. Good."

"If Menashe needs me, we should not delay," Ani answered. The heavy gate creaked, a guard snapped to attention, then Efrayim's oath echoed through the silence of the night.

"By the life of Pharaoh!" Alarm rang in his tone. "What brings a Medjay to my father's house after dark?"

Ani hissed in response, but the warrior said nothing. Jendayi felt her cheeks burning. What must Efrayim think, coming on her like this, with these men? He would imagine her a trouble-maker, a spy or worse.

"Ani?" All traces of humor vanished from Efrayim's voice. "Tell me why you are dressed for travel and carry your herb basket. And who is this giant?"

"This matter does not concern you, Master Efrayim," Ani said, his tone lightly respectful. "Now let the two of us pass. We have work to do."

"By all the gods, it's Menashe, isn't it?" Efrayim sounded distracted. "What happened? He is my brother, Ani, you must tell me!"

"He might not welcome your company just now."

"Listen, Ani," Efrayim said, his voice raw and harsh. "We may have our disagreements, but Menashe and I will be brothers until the day we die. Now if he needs help, you must tell me where he is."

The silence grew tight with tension, then Ani broke the quiet with a long sigh. "I suppose if you are with us you cannot run to Pharaoh." His words were playful but his meaning was not. "Come. Your brother is with Jokim, and they are hurt."

"Where are they?"

"That," the giant said, "you will discover when we have reached the place. If you are coming, wipe that arrogant expression from your face and join us."

Still clutching Ani's arm, Jendayi stepped forward as the steward moved through the gateway.

"No, Jendayi." Ani pulled her hand from his arm. "You must remain here."

Momentarily lost in her own reverie, she hesitated. A startling notion kept repeating in her mind like a haunting melody, and the harder she tried to ignore the it, the more it persisted.

"He told me the truth, didn't he?" Though she spoke to Ani, she turned her face toward Efrayim. "He told this warrior to ask for me…because he had faith in me." She could not stop herself from pondering the significance of Menashe's message. "If he had lied, if he had only used me to spite Efrayim, he would not have dared to ask for my help."

"I don't know what you're talking about, but Ani is right. This is not the journey for a little harpist."

Did he even know her name? "If Menashe is in trouble, I want to go." She lifted her chin. "He won't mind my coming."

"I'm sure he wouldn't." She heard sympathy in Ani's voice. "But this is a dangerous journey."

"The old one is right," the giant affirmed. "A barge escaped us, and the spies have undoubtedly reached Thebes by now. Menashe's enemies are powerful, little one."

"Powerful people have nothing to do with me," she insisted, reaching out. Ani had moved his arm away, but she caught the fabric of his cloak and clung to it. "You must let me go."

"No."

"We are wasting time."

Jendayi's heart thrilled to hear Efrayim rise to her defense. Though he would never be what she had dreamed he could be, if he wanted her on the journey he believed she could help.

"Efrayim is right, we haven't time to argue," the warrior broke in. "Already the stars have shifted. We must reach them soon."

"All right," Ani muttered. Jendayi felt his shoulders contract in submission, then she slipped her hand into the crook of his arm and let him lead her through the gateway.

"Not a word of this to my father," Efrayim told the guard and gatekeeper as they moved away. "He will know soon enough. You will only upset him by telling him of our departure. Say nothing."

By the profound silence which followed, Jendayi knew they would obey.

While Abnu had gone to the vizier's house to relay Menashe's message, one of his companions had slunk along the river, looking for a boat which might be easily unloosed from its moorings. At length he found a narrow felucca with its sail still unfurled. He tied a bit of red scarf atop the high mast, then crouched in the shadows of the railing to wait for Abnu's approach.

Beneath a shining net of stars the quartet found the marked ship and slipped into the boat without a word. Abnu, his Nubian comrade and Efrayim paddled in earnest, while Jendayi sat behind Ani. The warm night breeze caressed her face as she turned to inhale the pungent scents and sounds of the river. The noises of the creaking ship, straining cordage and flapping sail-cloth sent a jet of happiness through her heart. She was on her way, not to entertain faceless nobles and kings, but to help a friend.

She gripped Ani's bony arm and sighed, her soul expanding with the first real sense of purpose she had known in eighteen years.

As the ship pulled away from the darkened shore, Akil lowered the disguising edge of the tattered cloak and released an anxious cough to signal the warrior a few feet away. The Medjay spy turned and sped away toward the palace, and Akil paused on the bank and glanced toward the crowded city and a row of meager hovels where he might be lost for a week or two. Eventually the queen's guards would find him, of course, but at least he would not have to participate in his beloved queen's action against the vizier's son.

Any plan formed against the vizier would not prosper. Akil now understood that truth. The quaking warrior had just told Akil about the episode at Tura quarry.

Fear of the unknown knotted in his stomach, fear of the unknown god who could send crocodiles after every man except two Hebrews who stood bloody and broken in the water.

But Tiy's men would hunt him down if he left his post. The Medjay captains had been reasonable under Zaphenath-paneah's command; a runaway servant might have been sentenced to a year or two in prison. But now Tiy commanded the troops at Thebes, and the mistress of malice might order a runaway chopped up into little bits and fed to the crocodiles.

Shuddering, Akil turned his back on the hovels and searched for a small boat he could use to follow the men Tiy sought. His soul rebelled against the order—he was a musician; what did he know of spying?

An unexpected splash from the black river sent his heart into sudden shock. A dark premonition held him still for a long moment, then he turned and walked toward the brightly lit taverns of Thebes.

Let Tiy look for him when he was reported missing. With any luck, when she found him he'd be too drunk to care.

The wavelets that had flecked the surface of the river flattened out as the felucca slipped into the sunlit harbor built for

hauling stone from Tura quarry. Efrayim leaped from the boat
and splashed his way to shore. He should have known that
Menashe would retreat here, for in their youth they had spent
an endless parade of summers at the quarry house. The whitewashed villa offered privacy, comfort and a warning system, for
the quarry overseer might be enlisted to sound the alarm should
an enemy approach from the river.

"There's a narrow path leading back to the house," Efrayim
called, catching the rope Abnu tossed him. He helped drag the
felucca near the muddy bank. "I want to run ahead, so I'll meet
you there."

Ani gathered his things; the two Nubians jumped from the
boat into the water and stretched their cramped muscles. But
before he departed, Efrayim caught a glimpse of Jendayi's
sleepy expression and thought the little harpist had never looked
more beautiful.

"Guard your heart, brother," he murmured as he sprinted up
the stony path. "I hope it is strong enough to withstand the shock
of surprise."

"Menashe!" Efrayim's voice echoed among the outcroppings of the rocks, but no one answered from inside the house.
The villa had not been maintained in several months, and the
wide doors at the front entrance hung at an angle as if sprained.
But Menashe would not have hidden in the main reception hall.
He'd tuck himself in some out-of-the-way corner, perhaps in the
servants' quarters or the stables.

Efrayim darted around the house and jogged down a trail that
led to the brick servants' house. "Menashe!" he cried, a worried
note of impatience in his voice. "If you're here, speak up! Ani
is with me, and Abnu. Even the little harpist has come. I know
that will please you."

A hot wind blew past him with soft moans, punctuated by the
pebbly noises of his companions' approaching footsteps on the
gravel path. But the servants' quarters remained as silent as a
tomb.

"If this is a trick, I will wipe the ground with your face."

The voice came from behind him, and Efrayim whirled

around to see Menashe standing behind an elaborately carved pillar, a useless bit of ornamentation that should have been installed in the garden. Menashe came forward, moving gingerly, while Efrayim gaped at his brother.

Surely a man could not change so much in such a short time! Menashe looked ten years older, and his face bore evidence of a severe battering. One eyelid had swollen shut, and the area around it was green and purple with bruises. The mouth that had been so quick to smile in more carefree days hung unbalanced and puffed in an unnatural thickness above the dark beard, and a rumbling noise punctuated every breath Menashe drew. An angry red gash ran across his upper arm, and the skin of his wrists had been marred by burgundy marks.

One corner of the swollen mouth lifted in a smile. "If you think I look bad—" Menashe moved closer "—you should see the ones who didn't get away."

"I heard," Efrayim said, his mind still reeling in shock. "Abnu told us everything on the boat."

Menashe nodded. "God preserved us, brother. I don't know why, but He did. And now I can only hope you have come to help."

"Ani is with me." Efrayim jerked his thumb back toward the trail. "And Jendayi. She could not be persuaded to remain behind."

A hopeful glint lit Menashe's eyes, then the cries of the others distracted him. Ani hurried toward his wounded ward, tears welling in his eyes as he lifted his hands to exclaim over Menashe's battered face. Abnu, Jendayi and the other Nubian stood at a respectful distance while Ani wept over the vizier's wayward son.

"Menashe, my boy! How I feared I would never see you again!" Ani cried, tears streaming down his wrinkled cheeks.

Menashe bore the embrace, then pulled away. "Jokim is inside, and at this moment he needs you more than I do," he said, leading Ani toward a back entrance to the house. "But I know you will make him well."

"If the god who preserved you will strengthen me, I can try," Ani answered, following Menashe into the house. "Tell me yourself about the miracle of the crocodiles. These old ears want to hear the truth from your lips."

* * *

"I believe you *thought* you heard the voice of God," Efrayim said, explaining himself again to his brother. They were sitting together on the floor in the large bedchamber of the villa, a few feet away from the bed where Ani and Jendayi were tending Jokim. In a corner near the doorway, Abnu and his companion sat with their backs to the wall, their eyes closed in fitful sleep. The other loyal Medjays had dispersed into the desert to look for survivors of the Hebrew camp.

"But I cannot believe you were following God's will when you went into the desert with an army." Efrayim searched his brother's face for signs of surrender. "Look at the damage you've caused. How many dead, over two hundred? And what of the ones who ran away? Do you think they all found their way back home? No, many of your Hebrew kinsmen will be cast out for rebelling against their fathers. Others may have died in the desert. You do not know, Menashe, what destruction you have wrought."

Menashe clenched his fists. "Can you deny that Canaan is our land? God Shaddai promised it to us. Why, then, should we not go there at once?"

"God willed that Avraham would father Yitzhak, too, and he and Sarah waited years for the promise to be fulfilled," Efrayim answered. "Yet Avraham became impatient, and fathered Ishmael with the Egyptian handmaid. By rushing ahead and trying to implement God's plan himself, Avraham brought dissension into his own family."

Efrayim grinned as an expression of surprise crossed Menashe's face. "Yes, I've learned our history. Now that Father has nothing but time, I have enjoyed many dinners with him. And he has taught me many things."

Menashe's expression grew hard and resentful. "For you he has time. But he has not tried to find me, his firstborn."

"You were not willing to be found," Efrayim said, shrugging. He glanced over at Jokim. Their cousin's face was as pale as papyrus parchment, but he had stopped moaning in that pitiful nonstop way. Efrayim wasn't certain whether his cousin's silence boded good or ill.

He was about to remark that Menashe should have taken the time to find their father, but when he turned again he saw that Menashe's gaze had shifted to Jendayi's face. Though swollen and bruised, his eyes betrayed his silent ardor.

Efrayim snapped his fingers to get his brother's attention.

Menashe jerked his head around. "What?"

"Go to her," Efrayim whispered, aware of the girl's keen hearing. "She is here, you are here. Why are you waiting?"

Menashe looked at the floor and ran his hand over the dusty tile. "She does not love me, brother. I've opened my heart, and she has been honest with me. She loves someone else."

"Whoever he is, he can't be half the man you are."

Menashe stared at him, then burst out in a laugh so loud Ani screeched in alarm.

The older man tossed a warning look over his shoulder as he hunched over Jokim. "You boys will wake the dead with your noise!"

Efrayim grinned at his brother, a little mystified by his response but grateful for the gleam of humor in Menashe's eyes. This moment felt like old times...before Yaakov's blessing had torn them apart.

"I think you're right." Menashe ran his hand over his swollen jaw. "I am twice the man. But she knows how I feel. If she changes her mind, she knows I will be waiting."

"Love." Efrayim spat the word like a curse.

"Sitamun?"

"Yes." Efrayim looked away. "I love her. And I never realized how much until the queen stopped allowing me to see her. But after Father's dismissal, my invitations to the palace dried up like a wadi in drought."

"I'm sorry."

"I can't blame you, though I tried to." He managed a choking laugh. "If you hadn't ridden off into the desert, the queen would have found something else wrong with me—or Father, or Re'uven, or one of the other uncles."

"I know."

"But it is wrong to hurt Sitamun! I will admit that at first I sought her while thinking of the palace and power, but then I came to know her. She is so bright and beautiful! I would wed Sitamun even if we had to live in a fisherman's hovel."

"You could keep Sitamun in a mud hut about as long as you could squat beneath a bull with a milk bucket!" Menashe's swollen smile deepened into laughter. "And it would take a brave man to attempt either feat!"

Efrayim couldn't keep from chuckling. "I'm afraid you're right."

They sat in companionable quiet, but the brittle sounds of tramping footsteps shattered the silence. The Nubians woke and reached for their swords; Jendayi paled and seemed to fade into the whitewashed wall. Menashe pulled a stubby sword from his kilt and held it in his bruised fist as he stared at the doorway.

"Hear me, sons of Zaphenath-paneah!" a voice called from outside the house. "We are the warriors of Pharaoh's guard, and we have surrounded this place. There is no avenue of escape, no hope of recourse unless you return with us to Thebes and face your queen."

Menashe shot Efrayim an inquiring look, his mouth tight and grim under his beard. "This is not your fight," he said. "Let me go out to them. I will surrender, and you can help the others escape after I have gone."

"He said the 'sons of Zaphenath-paneah.'" Efrayim moved to his brother's side. "They know we are together. They know we will defend each other."

"Will we?" Menashe asked, one eyebrow lifting.

"We will." Efrayim pulled his own dagger from his kilt. It was an ornamental blade, not very practical in a duel and even less useful in a situation of war. But if his instincts proved true, Menashe would not allow this confrontation to end with blows. He would not put the harpist in harm's way.

Menashe squinted, then turned to look at Jokim and Jendayi. The wounded man lay as still as if he already slumbered in death's embrace, and the young woman trembled. Only the Nubians and Ani, distracted by his ministrations, seemed unaffected by the situation outside.

"We cannot risk a fight." Menashe lowered his sword. "They would kill the others, and I cannot have the blood of Ani and

Jendayi on my hands. I would give my life for either of them.
I cannot ask them to die on account of my stubbornness."

"That is the wisest thing you have said all day." Efrayim
sheathed his own blade, then walked to the doorway and lifted
his hands. A dozen warriors waited outside, their swords drawn
and their eyes narrowed.

"Hail, you of the royal guards," Efrayim called, stepping out
into a bright rectangle of sunlight. He frowned, finding it hard
to believe that a few weeks ago any one of these men would
have given their lives for *him*. "My brother and I surrender to
you. Take us to your queen, only let the others in this house
depart in peace."

The commander jerked his head toward Efrayim. As half a
dozen men came forward with ropes, Efrayim heard labored
breathing behind him. Menashe had joined him on the portico.

Efrayim flinched as a pair of warriors tied his bonds too
tightly in enthusiastic zeal. "Are you doing this for her?"

"For her, for Ani and for you." Sweat beaded on Menashe's
upper lip as the same energy was applied to his wounded flesh.

As soon as the brothers were bound, the commander climbed
the steps of the portico and looked into the chamber. "Bring the
others, too," he told his men.

"Not the girl!" Menashe thrashed in the grips of two burly
guards. "My brother and I surrendered. You must let the others go!"

The commander shot a bright grin of amusement over his
shoulder. "I made no such promise."

A barge transported the prisoners to Malkata instead of the
royal house at Thebes, and Efrayim felt the nauseating sinking
of despair as the boat turned into the royal harbor on the western
bank of the Nile. He had not spoken to Sitamun in several
weeks. All his messages had been ignored or returned, and he
doubted she would be allowed to leave her royal apartments at
Thebes if the queen was truly intent on keeping them apart.

But a constant hope burned in his heart, for surely love could
find a way to unite them. With a single private word in
Sitamun's ear he could assure her of his devotion and steadfast
heart. Did she still think of him? With a woman as bright and

flirtatious as Sitamun, one could never be too sure of oneself, but perhaps even at Malkata he could bribe a guard or servant to carry a message to his love.

He bit his lip as he surveyed the royal harbor. As he had suspected, the queen's barge was tied to the dock; her royal standard fluttered and snapped from the highest mast. Farther down the dock, like an ostracized relative, stood the gilded barge which had once hoisted the regal standard of the vizier. His father's boat.

Turning his back to the docks, Efrayim crossed his arms as a new anguish seared his heart. The realization that Yosef would have to observe his sons' trial and disgrace wounded Efrayim as deeply as the thought that he might have to surrender his hope of marrying the love of his life.

Chapter Twenty-Seven

Their father waited at the palace gate. Menashe's steps slowed when he recognized Yosef's somber profile and proud bearing, and even Efrayim seemed to stutter on the path. Memories opened before Menashe's eyes as if a curtain had been ripped aside, and for a moment he and Efrayim were small again, compelled by Ani or Tarik to face their father and suffer the consequences for some mischief they had committed. Menashe's knobby knees knocked with fear; Efrayim's chubby face twisted in a spasm as he bent forward and declared that he would have to relieve himself before he could go one step farther...

The memory vanished in a sepia haze. If only they could go back.

Menashe lifted his eyes to his father's face. The past weeks had carved a new series of lines about Yosef's eyes and forehead, diminishing the impression of strength. A muscle clenched along that chiseled jaw as Yosef's gaze met Menashe's. He did not speak, but hurt and longing lay naked in his eyes.

"Zaphenath-paneah." One of the guards stepped forward and bowed his head in a perfunctory salute. "Your sons are commanded to appear before Pharaoh."

"I know."

Menashe winced. His father's voice, which had once rung

with the power to command ten thousand men, now seemed empty and deflated.

Yosef moistened his dry lips. "My sons will appear, but the old man and the girl are of no interest to Pharaoh. The two slaves are mine. Release them so they may return to my house."

Menashe looked at the ground, knowing what the guard's answer would be. "I can't," the guard snapped, leaning on the security of his spear. "The slaves are runaways. They must be tried with the two malefactors."

"No," Menashe groaned through stiff lips.

His protest was useless. The palace gates opened, and without a further word or gesture, Yosef folded his hands and turned, walking forward with a steady and even tread, clothed in his spotless vizier's robe and the rags of his dignity.

The guards who had escorted Menashe and Efrayim untied their prisoners' hands and fell back, knowing the captives could not run. Efrayim followed Yosef while Menashe limped beside him. Behind the brothers, a pair of guards pulled Jendayi and Ani forward. As Menashe moved toward the throne room he bitterly reflected that his stubbornness might yet result in the destruction of everyone he loved.

Throngs of nobles, suppliants and visiting kings waited outside in the vestibule, but the sea of sycophants parted as Zaphenath-paneah approached the gilded double doors. A pair of trumpets blared, a chamberlain announced the former vizier's presence, and the doors swung open. As one, the waiting suppliants fell to their knees and bowed, lest some ray of the divine pharaoh's presence fall on them. Tense with anticipation, Menashe stumbled forward, walking in the wake of bewildered and curious looks directed at his father.

The long, narrow throne room, pillared by columns painted to resemble lotus blossoms on luxurious stems, was lit by high clerestory windows that allowed bright light, not heat, to enter the stone sanctuary. Pharaoh's artists had painted his throne room with scenes of Amenhotep and Queen Tiy in scenes of familial bliss: conversing with the gods, entertaining their many children, cavorting in the garden. As he progressed toward the dais at the end of the room, Menashe let his eyes roam over the paintings, wondering if he would see some representation of Jendayi among the dancers, musicians and slaves depicted in service to the royal family. He sighed in relief when he did not find a harpist pictured on the wall. Perhaps Pharaoh had forgotten—and would forget—all about the girl.

Surely the enormous throne room had never been more crowded. As Zaphenath-paneah and his sons passed by, men and women stood silent and as still as portraits, their black eyes glittering like polished obsidian. Armed soldiers, nobles, priests and scribes stared, watching the Hebrews like a snake watches a rabbit. The muscles in Menashe's arms tightened involuntarily when he thought of those stares fixing on Jendayi, who followed behind him. Silently he thanked God that she could not see their darkly accusing eyes.

Finally they reached the platform where Pharaoh perched on the edge of a chair covered with gold, his expression petulant and bored. At Pharaoh's right hand sat Neferkheprure' Wa'enre', the crown prince; Queen Tiy sat in the gilded chair at his left. Members of the king's bodyguard stood at attention behind the thrones, their spears at the ready. Behind the queen's guards sat a bevy of her daughters and handmaids; a similar group of counselors and priests lingered behind the divine king.

Menashe had stood in the throne room a dozen times before, but today the position of the royal family members had changed. Sitamun, whose former place had been behind the queen with the other royal daughters, now stood immediately behind the king's chair, her hand resting on his bronzed shoulder. Haunted by the suspicion that Tiy wanted to foment trouble, Menashe squinted toward the queen. What could this mean? Had Sitamun been brought forward in order to provoke Efrayim?

Menashe cast a quick look at his brother. The significance of Sitamun's new position was not lost on Efrayim, for his brows drew together in an agonized expression, then a congested expression settled on his face. He must have felt Menashe's gaze, for he turned and tried to smile, but his features only flinched.

"She has done it," he whispered in a voice so low only Menashe could hear. "The queen was too afraid of us, frightened of the people we might become."

"What has she done?" Menashe asked, frowning.

Efrayim stared at the queen, amused resentment evident in the slight curl of his upper lip. "You have been away, you have not heard. Pharaoh took another royal bride a few days ago. The marriage was arranged on Pharaoh's behalf by the Mother of Egypt herself."

Menashe shook his head, his thoughts confused. "Who is the bride?" he asked, searching for an unfamiliar face among the royal women.

"Don't you see? Tiy is afraid Amenhotep or the crown prince will lose the throne if one of her daughters marries an outsider. She's afraid of *us.* Sitamun is Pharaoh's new bride."

Menashe blanched. Though it had long been reported that Egyptian royalty approved incestuous marriages in order to avoid diluting the divine royal bloodline, he knew of no such marriages within his lifetime. Until now.

His heart twisted as he looked at Sitamun. He might not live through the day, but at least he had been able to tell Jendayi of his love. But Sitamun, now a royal consort, would never taste anything of the world beyond the royal harem and the palace walls.

The crowd caught its breath in an audible gasp as Pharaoh lowered the ceremonial crook and flail. At this signal, Yosef stepped forward and prostrated himself before Pharaoh.

"Rise, Zaphenath-paneah." There was a note of regret that went beyond nostalgia in Pharaoh's voice.

Yosef stood and met the king's gaze, his hands clasped in front of him, his eyes silent pools of appeal. The Gold of Praise, the ornate chain symbolizing Pharaoh's favor, hung about his neck, a visible reminder that he had once been a valuable counselor.

As the king lifted the crook and flail, silence fell on the stirring crowd like a dampening cloak. "I have no quarrel with you, Zaphenath-paneah." Pharaoh frowned. "It is your elder son who must answer to my will."

As if on cue, the high priest of Amon-Re stepped forward. "Menashe! Your king the divine pharaoh summons you!"

Menashe lowered himself to the floor as quickly as his bruised body would allow.

"You, Menashe, son of Zaphenath-paneah, stand accused of

treason," the priest recited as Menashe lifted his head and shoulders. From lowered lids, Amenhotep shot a commanding look at him, and Menashe found it hard to believe he knelt before the same man he and his family had dined with so many times. There was nothing of the genial father and host about Amenhotep now. In this room he was king, Pharaoh of Egypt, and nothing else.

"You have conspired to commit acts of war," the priest went on, reading from a parchment scroll. "You have defied the authority of your father, Zaphenath-paneah, Egypt's noble vizier. You lured the king's warriors from their places of service. You have waged war and brought death on loyal Egyptian warriors." The king's glare burned through Menashe as the priest looked up with one final question. "Have you anything to say in your defense?"

Menashe licked his swollen lips and looked up through his half-closed eyelids. He wanted to rise but feared he would fall, so he remained on his knees.

"Life, prosperity and health to you, mighty Pharaoh!" He felt himself wavering, and put a hand out to Efrayim's shoulder for support. "If it please the king, know that I did conspire to return my people to their homeland, but I acted in accordance with a command from God Shaddai, the Almighty God of Yisrael, whom I must obey before any man on earth. I did ask one Medjay warrior to assist me, and others followed him in hope of spoils. But we did not wage war on Egyptians. Another enemy rose up in the night and slaughtered half my company. My god and my comrades know that as of this hour I have not turned my sword against any man, not even in self-defense."

The king's painted eyes remained as expressionless as a hawk's while the queen regarded Menashe with impassive coldness. Menashe inclined his head, knowing they had not finished with him.

Tiy lifted an imperious finger toward the priest. "Read the other charge."

The bald man shuffled for another scroll and cleared his throat. "Efrayim, younger son of Zaphenath-paneah," the priest droned. "You stand accused of rushing to aid your brother as he did rise up in treason against this throne. You have also taken liberties with a princess of the royal family—"

Sitamun flinched.

"—and conspired with ruthless ambition to take the throne of Egypt for yourself and your posterity."

Efrayim's eyes glowed with a savage inner fire. "Not true!"

"Did you not tell my daughter that Egypt could grow great under the influence of Avraham's offspring?" Tiy hissed, leaning forward.

"But I never did conspire to take the throne! And I journeyed to meet my brother in an attempt to stop him, not join him!"

"Silence!" Pharaoh held up his jeweled hand. Behind him, the two young viziers watched, their faces clouded with anxiety.

A murmur of voices, a palpable unease, crept through the room as the king considered his judgment. Menashe understood Pharaoh's predicament. If the king condemned him for obeying the voice of God Shaddai, Amenhotep would face severe criticism from the priests who claimed that the gods could and did speak to men. Furthermore, Menashe had not actually injured any Egyptians, nor had his men participated in a battle. Finally, Pharaoh could not forget that Menashe was the elder son of Zaphenath-paneah, the Bread of Life, who still enjoyed enormous popularity with the people.

The accusations against Efrayim were as worthless as chaff, but his fate would rest on Menashe's. By marrying his daughter, Pharaoh had eliminated the danger posed by Efrayim's wooing of Sitamun. And if Pharaoh decided that Menashe had not committed treason, the charge of conspiracy would be a moot point.

But Menashe's heart sank with swift disappointment as he considered an undeniable and dreadful question. How could a divine king acknowledge that a mightier god had the right to command men to disobey the Voice of Egypt, the physical incarnation of Horus and Amon-Re? Pharaoh could not. Admitting that a mightier god than himself existed would be tantamount to admitting Amenhotep was no god at all, only a puffed-up godling with dreams of divinity...

Queen Tiy's voice, velvet-edged but strong, broke the silence. "If I may speak, my king—" she inclined her head toward him in a stiff gesture "—your decision seems to rest on motive. Did the sons of Zaphenath-paneah act out of a sincere desire to follow their god, or did they choose to indulge in war for the sake of rebellion?"

Amenhotep glared at Menashe from beneath his paint-lined eyelids. "You are right."

"I know you have already discerned the truth, for you are god." The queen continued in a voice as cool as water. "But if this god of the Hebrews has the power to command men to disobey Pharaoh, why not let Him reveal His will in a physical manifestation? Amon-Re rides across the sky every morning, Hapi pours her floodwaters forth to bless our land. Surely this God Shaddai can do something to reveal Himself to your people."

Menashe stared at the queen while the chamber buzzed with whispers. What sort of insanity was this? Even Pharaoh's face was as blank as a slab of marble.

Realizing that the king did not understand, Tiy continued. "Your game of Hounds and Jackals," she said, her eyes bathing him in admiration. "The tiles out in the garden. Let the brothers play against each other. Menashe says he had to obey the powerful God Shaddai, Efrayim says he was trying to stop Menashe. How could this god send one brother to make war and the other to stop it? One of them lies, so let them play the game. At the conclusion, all who are assembled here will know the winner spoke the truth."

Pharaoh's face brightened. The idea of sparing one of Zaphenath-paneah's sons obviously appealed to him.

"What shall the winner win?" Sitamun's high, silvery voice rang through the anxious whispers in the room, and Menashe glanced toward her in surprise. Her wide eyes, filled with longing regret, had fixed on Efrayim as if she had just realized she might lose her flattering suitor forever.

"The winner shall save his life," Pharaoh answered, voice rumbling through the chamber. "And as an added prize—" He glanced about the room, his bright eyes bobbing for some treasure within his power to bestow, then he pointed past Menashe. "The winner shall have her!"

Menashe felt his heart constrict, knowing that the king pointed to Jendayi. No one had dared to suggest that she and Ani were anything more than slaves obeying their masters' will, but she was still property, and she had belonged to Pharaoh...

Amenhotep turned to Yosef, his finger still stretching toward Jendayi. "Have you any objection, Zaphenath-paneah?" The beginnings of a smile tipped the corners of his mouth. "After all, I did return the girl to you."

Menashe pressed his lips together as his father shook his head. How could he object? Pharaoh had already stripped Yosef of his life, his calling and his sons. What did it matter if he repossessed one blind harpist?

"Then that is how it shall be." Pharaoh lowered his hand and folded his hands in satisfaction. "The winner wins his life and the harpist. The loser forfeits his life. And this god of the Hebrews will decide the course of the game...which we shall play on the morrow."

He smiled, anticipating the event to come, and Tiy rose and extended her hand. Taking the hint, Pharaoh stood as well, and the two of them departed the throne room, trailed by a sea of daughters, priests, wives and counselors.

Motivated either by compassion or spite, the captain of Pharaoh's guard put Efrayim and Menashe into different cells separated by a far expanse of sandy courtyard. Menashe thought the arrangement a good idea, for depression had engulfed him after Pharaoh announced the bizarre contest. Efrayim had always enjoyed more luck at games and sporting events than had Menashe, and he found he had little to say to the brother who would undoubtedly win the game. The comforting words he would have called out across the courtyard would not move past the knot of jealousy in his throat.

So this is the meaning of grandfather Yaakov's blessing, Menashe thought, stretching out on a thread-worn strip of blanket some other prisoner had left behind. *Efrayim shall be the greater nation because Efrayim will live long enough to beget sons and daughters! Whereas I shall die on the morrow, and the last thing my eyes will see is Pharaoh placing Jendayi's hand in Efrayim's.*

His misery was so acute that his heart ached worse than his physical pains, which were considerable. He turned onto his bruised side and moaned, regretting but not surprised that life had boiled down to a choice between him and his brother.

He lowered his head to his arms and sighed. His father would not be sleeping either. Despite his own unhappiness, Menashe felt a stab of compassion for the man who had risen from slavery to the dizzying heights of power. But the tide had turned. Now Zaphenath-paneah had no wife, no power and little respect. Would God also take his sons? He had already lost one. Though Yosef kept his features deceptively composed during the audience with Pharaoh, Menashe knew the day had been especially agonizing for him when Amenhotep, Yosef's surrogate son, visibly and publicly demonstrated that he cared so little for Zaphenath-paneah's judgment that he would consult a game board before asking advice from the former Father to Pharaoh.

Menashe closed his eyes and lifted a prayer. "God Shaddai, forgive him for not believing. You have spoken through him for so long, he has found it difficult to accept that You would speak through someone like me." He gulped as a hot tear slipped down his swollen cheek. "I still find it hard to believe myself. You led me into the wilderness where we met with failure, You have led me to Pharaoh's court where I will probably die on the morrow. But I am willing to do whatever You require. I beg You to make me ready."

Deep within the palace at Malkata, Pharaoh tossed and turned, refusing to be borne to the world of dreams. Beside him, stretched across the spacious bed fit only for a king, Sitamun lay asleep, her gentle snores punctuating the darkness.

Looking at her, Pharaoh frowned. He would never have agreed to marry his daughter if not for the queen's insistence. He knew Tiy's insecurity could be traced to her own humble roots, but sleeping with his daughter was about as thrilling as counting bricks in a pyramid. Once Sitamun produced an heir, he would send her to the harem and let her live out her days in peace.

Tiy's other suggestion, the game of Hounds and Jackals, had at first struck Amenhotep as delightfully fitting, but now it bothered him. Should a man's destiny be determined by a roll of the knucklebones? Zaphenath-paneah would never agree to adjudicate a case this way, and the former vizier's injured, sorrowful expression had revealed to the entire court just how deeply the queen's idea offended him. Amenhotep knew he should not have wounded Zaphenath-paneah, for the people still revered him and his unseen god. Though very few even knew how to worship this God Shaddai, Amenhotep could not refute the consensus of opinion that an invisible god had blessed the Black Land for the sake of its vizier.

That opinion had grown stronger in the days since Zaphenath-paneah's departure from court. A host of intolerable situations had recently developed—an incurable fungus had blighted the harvest at Opet, a rich vein of black granite had disappeared at the Ibhet quarry, even the normally easy-to-please harem women had developed a habit of ceaseless squabbling. Someday soon, he realized, he might have to bring Zaphenath-paneah back to court…

Amenhotep could never openly espouse belief in God Shaddai, but having Zaphenath-paneah next to him as a shield had deflected trouble before. He would be wise to restore his old friend to the vizierate, but nothing could be done until this matter of Efrayim and Menashe had been settled.

But—the contest! It was too late to pardon the young men; he had already publicly declared that he and God Shaddai knew the game's outcome.

Sitamun moaned softly in a dream, and Amenhotep rolled his eyes and chewed on the edge of his thumbnail. The game would have to be played. One son would live, one would begin the long journey to his tomb. And, after burying one of his sons, Zaphenath-paneah would hear the king's offer to return to the vizierate, spit in Amenhotep's face and be promptly executed for his effrontery.

Pharaoh covered his face with his hands, tasting defeat for the first time in his life.

* * *

"Hush, my girl, don't weep," Ani whispered, his thickened voice rising above the wails of other slaves in Pharaoh's prison. He and Jendayi had been thrust together into the same rank pit, two pieces of property not worthy of any special considerations for modesty or propriety.

Jendayi lifted her face from the matted straw and tried to swallow the sobs that kept rising from her throat. "I can't help it. I don't know what to do. It is too terrible, Ani, too unjust. Menashe has hurt no one, and Efrayim sought only to help his brother."

"You speak both their names with affection." A slight trace of cynicism lined Ani's voice. "How convenient, since it appears you will leave Malkata tomorrow belonging to one or the other."

"But I don't want anyone to die!" Her anguish peaked to shatter the last shreds of her control. "I only want to be loved."

"My dear girl, don't weep." The straw rustled as Ani slid to her side. She felt aged hands on her head, and he pulled her to his shoulder, cradling her in his arms. "If you want to be loved, do not fear. I believe you already are."

"I know," she murmured in a despairing whisper. "I see that now. I thought Efrayim loved me, but all the time it was Menashe, quietly caring, trying not to hurt me—"

"Hush, child."

Bitter laughter bubbled to her lips. "I never knew how blind I was until last night. Menashe's love was there all along for me to see, to *test,* and Efrayim never gave me any indication that he cared. Oh, I do not fault him, for I imagined and invented every sign of affection I thought I saw…"

She closed her eyes and flung out her hands in simple despair. "I didn't *see* anything! Menashe asked me to have faith in him, but I couldn't! I could only hear Efrayim's voice. I dwelt on memories of Efrayim's kiss. I put Menashe out of my mind—"

"No, child, you didn't." Ani spoke with cool authority. "You didn't forget him. And when he called for you, you risked everything to answer. Whether you know it or not, you have already made the choice…to love."

Jendayi listened in silence, then gave the old man a grateful kiss on the cheek. Perhaps he was right. Curling up in the straw, she carried the hope in his words back to the bitterly cold caves of her lonely soul.

Could she choose to love? Was the answer to her nightmare really so simple?

Only the gods could tell.

Chapter Twenty-Eight

Though adults and children alike enjoyed the game of Hounds and Jackals, there was no sign of childish merrymaking when a squadron of Pharaoh's warriors escorted Menashe and Efrayim into the royal garden the next morning. Pharaoh and Queen Tiy had already been seated in tall chairs before the reflecting pool, and a host of curious nobles lounged behind a specially cordoned observation area. A team of archers, Menashe noticed with a grimace, stood stiffly at the far end of the garden, ready for the execution order.

Abnu was not among them. Menashe had heard from one of the guards that the giant and his loyal comrade had been transferred to the palace at Thebes just after the sick man in their care mysteriously escaped. Pharaoh was not pleased with the mercenary Medjays, but he valued them too highly to discipline them harshly.

"Look." Efrayim nodded toward the archers. "Our pharaoh is not willing to risk criticism in his handling of this matter. The sentence will be carried out before anyone can protest."

"Who could protest?" Menashe rubbed his stiff arms. "He has already announced that God Shaddai will rule this contest. And so one of us will be dispatched to the Other World according to the will of Almighty God."

"I am not worried," Efrayim answered, swinging his arms across his chest as if he prepared for a wrestling match. "You think I have no faith in God Shaddai, but I do. And I know Pharaoh is right in at least one thing—the god of Avraham, Yitzhak and Yaakov *will* prevail here today."

"If you have such faith, why didn't you go with me into the desert?" Menashe lifted a brow. "If you believe in God, you should have believed Canaan is our home, for it is what He promised—"

"I didn't go with you into the desert because I didn't want to go," Efrayim interrupted. He shook out his arms, then slapped his hands on his hips and gave Menashe an abashed smile. "I hate the desert. I hate sand, and heat, and lousy food. And I hate pain, the kind you felt when someone plastered those bruises on your face. But today, brother, I have no choice but to follow you. And if I have to endure pain, I hope God will be merciful and dispatch me quickly."

Baffled, Menashe stared at the brother he loved more than he cared to admit. Charming Efrayim could tell you his worst faults with a smile and still you'd want to take him home and keep him forever.

Menashe's gaze moved over the crowd until he spied Jendayi, Ani, Yosef and Tarik. The four of them stood apart from the others in a little knot, united by fear and despair. His father's eyes, large and fierce with pain, were fixed on nothing, while Tarik looked straight at Menashe. *Concentrate,* the captain's piercing eyes seemed to say, *take care. Remember all I have taught you.* Jendayi's unseeing eyes were wide, but a look of intense, clear light seemed to pour through them as she nestled against Ani's birdlike chest.

Which brother did she want to win? In either case, she would belong to a man who would take care of her. So why did she cling to Ani as if she were afraid?

Menashe stepped forward as the king's guard gestured to him. One of the king's new viziers, a portly fellow who only a month before had been a scribe tending to requisitions for the king's tomb, mounted a stand and held up his hands. When the crowd fell silent, his gaze focused on Efrayim and Menashe. "You must each choose a representative to roll the knucklebones for you." His brown eyes flickered. "Whom shall you choose?"

With the cocky grin of earlier days, Efrayim lifted his head and searched the crowd. Menashe shook his head when his brazen brother flashed a smile at Sitamun. "I would enjoy the honor of having Queen Sitamun cast the bones for me," he said, fixing her in a dark-eyed vise.

Murmurs swept through the crowd, but the new queen rose from her chair and moved with fluid strides toward the tray containing the bones.

"And you?" the vizier barked at Menashe.

Menashe looked over the crowd again. He could not ask his father to participate in an activity that might condemn Efrayim, and poor Ani would be just as torn between them. But Tarik—he caught the bantam guard's gaze and saw the captain nod. Tarik was a warrior with a heart of steel. His courage would see them through this day.

Menashe shifted his gaze back to the undeserving vizier. "I choose Tarik, captain of Zaphenath-paneah's guard."

The stout man nodded and rubbed his hands together. "Good. You, Menashe, will be the hound. You will run this course." He pointed toward a looping pathway which wound through the eastern half of the garden. "And you, Efrayim, will be the jackal, and will run the opposite course."

Efrayim gave the vizier a grudging nod, then positioned himself before the first tile. Menashe looked at Efrayim, they shared a smile, then Menashe moved to his starting position and turned toward the small dais where Sitamun stood next to a polished stand.

As Tarik shouldered his way through the crowd, Sitamun gathered the bones from their tray, cast a winning smile at Efrayim and tossed the knucklebones with a triumphant flourish.

The vizier bent over the pan and read the bones. "Six!" The sixth tile, to which Efrayim proceeded in a burst of energy, was linked to the lower half of the jackal's course. Efrayim paused on the tile, and in an instant the bark-carriers appeared with the fanciful carved boat of Amon-Re. They lowered it, Efrayim climbed inside, and then, amid a smattering of applause from the observers, the slaves lifted the long poles to their shoulders and carried Efrayim forward to a point only eight tiles away from the end of the course.

Menashe watched, astounded both by the casual attitude of the staring nobles and his brother's nonchalance. He was surprised Efrayim did not wave as the boat passed by.

Tarik stepped to the dais where the vizier held the metal pan containing the knucklebones. Tarik picked them up, jostled them in his palm and dropped them clattering into the open container.

"One!" the vizier called out. Menashe closed his eyes in relief and took a step forward. Though his roll had not been nearly as favorable as Efrayim's, at least he had been able to begin the game. Many times as a child he had sat in morose silence waiting to throw a one or a six while Efrayim gallivanted around the game board.

Bowing from the waist, the vizier presented the metal tray to Sitamun, who cast a longing look at Efrayim as she scooped up the knucklebones and pressed them to her lips for good fortune. Menashe cast a quick look at Pharaoh to see if he noticed the unspoken language between his wife and the accused criminal, but Pharaoh's eyes were fixed on the crowd, not the course.

The crowd stilled as Sitamun shook the bones, then released them into the tray.

"One!" the vizier called, his face pinking with eagerness. Sensing that Efrayim was the royal favorite, a few observers applauded as he took the next tile.

Tarik stepped forward again, his chin lifting in iron determination as if he would not allow Menashe to fail. With vigorous intensity he picked up the bones and clattered them together in his hand, then released them with a vigorous gesture.

"Six!" the vizier called. A chorus of ahhs rose from the crowd as Menashe paced out the allotted number of tiles. He had missed linking with the shortcut by one tile, but as he reached the sixth he bellowed in delight.

"This tile is marked with the ankh!" he called, rejoicing in the small but satisfying victory. Efrayim's insanely inappropriate gaiety was contagious. "Roll again, Tarik!"

The vizier's mouth spread into a thin-lipped smile as he handed the bones to Tarik again. Tarik picked up the stones, held them in his hands and then did something Menashe had never seen him do before. In the manner of the Hebrews, Tarik the great Egyptian captain held his hands aloft, lifted his face to heaven and moved his lips in a silent prayer.

The vizier's eyebrows rose. "By the power of Hathor's sun disk, what are you doing?" he asked, his voice heavy with sarcasm.

Pharaoh leaned forward in his chair and stared, but did not speak until Tarik lowered his head. "Captain," Pharaoh said, his impersonal tone breaking the uncomfortable silence, "if this is some form of protest—"

"It is not, my king." Tarik dipped his head in a formal bow. "But since you said God Shaddai's will should command this event, I thought one of us should ask His blessing on it."

Pharaoh sank back in his chair and clapped his hand to his cheek. Tiy leaned forward, her face marked with loathing. What might she do? Menashe tensed when Tarik shook the bones again.

"Three!" the vizier called when the bones had come to rest in the pan. Menashe took three giant steps forward, only to grimace when he realized that the third tile connected to a shortcut that would force him backward. The toothless old priest tipped his basket and a pair of cobras slithered forth to chase Menashe back to the beginning of the shortcut. He retreated, but noticed that the tile where he finally stood was one ahead of where he had begun at the beginning of his turn. He tossed Tarik a smile of encouragement.

While a pair of shaven priests chased the harmless cobras through the skittish crowd, Sitamun stepped forward to roll the bones again for Efrayim. There was a clatter, a clang, then the vizier yelled, "One!" and Efrayim moved forward again.

Jendayi grew more uncomfortable with every moment the game progressed. She had scarcely rested the previous night; she had not even slept long enough to visit the netherworld of her nightmare. But still the old fears haunted her. She awakened in a panic, her mind congested with doubts and regrets that did not vanish in the activity of the morning.

Ani had taken her arm and escorted her from the prison to the palace, but exhaustion blurred the scents and sounds in the garden around her, blending her nightmares with reality. Now she stood on tiles that radiated heat just like the glowing tiles of her dream. And even though she clutched the comforting fabric of Ani's cloak, eerily familiar sounds seeped through her darkness to haunt her. Those in the crowd who rooted for Efrayim were now howling like jackals, giving voice to Anubis and his gleaming ebony eyes. Somewhere in the gathering a papyrus reed scratched across parchment, recording every action just like Thoth the Scribe. And was that sound the clatter of bones or her teeth chattering in fear? The object clanging in the pan was her own hard heart, the useless and atrophied vessel which would compel her toward the vicious jaws of the One who Eats the Dead...

You have not loved! She had developed an uncanny sense of hearing; now she heard Anubis's accusation as if it came to her on an inner pulse that had nothing to do with the anxious crowd around her.

"I tried to!" she whispered, wringing her hands. "And I will! If given the chance, I will love him who first loved me!"

Stupid girl! The darkness enveloping her congealed and shifted; Anubis's shadowy face took on shape and thickness. The jackal looked at her with narrow, glinting eyes. *You are too late! Menashe will die here today, and you will be lost. And so we must surrender you to Ammit.*

"No," she whimpered over her choking, beating heart. "Menashe will not die. You have no power over him. And he loves me."

He lies.

"No! He does. I don't know why, but he does."

He will die here, Jendayi. Already he is losing the game. The archers stand ready, they will shoot at Pharaoh's command, and you will be given to the one who does not love you.

"No!"

The jackal's curling fangs seemed to lift in a smile. *Perhaps there is a way you and Menashe can be together. Run, Jendayi, toward the queen's chair. Pharaoh wears a dagger in his belt, take it and strike the queen. You cannot hope to harm her, for the guards will strike you down as soon as they guess your intention. But you will die in the same hour as your love, and together you shall enter into the Other World. If you love, prove yourself. And thus you may save yourself from Ammit.*

Hideously alluring, the jackal's suggestion fluttered through her thoughts. She knew where the royal couple sat; she could hear Tiy's shrill nasal tones through the voices of the gathering. Anubis was right—the guards would be on her as soon as she neared the dais, and she would be helpless to fend off any blow…

And Menashe was losing. She could tell by the low murmurs of the crowd that followed Tarik's toss of the knucklebones. He would die today, so she could precede him into the Hall of the Two Truths.

Quietly, she let her hand fall from Ani's cloak. He didn't seem to notice.

She turned to face the royal pavilion. Her questing fingers felt the cordoning rope, but it was merely decorative; she could slip under it in a heartbeat. If she ran, she could be on the steps of the pavilion before Tarik had to take another turn.

A tight knot within her begged for release; was this not the answer she sought?

Her thoughts turned toward Menashe, whose name echoed in the stillness of her mind. She recalled the rhapsody of being held in his strong arms, the comfort his words had brought her troubled heart. "If you will trust me, your heart will begin to live," he had promised. "Defeat your dream now, Jendayi. Have faith in me…and in my God Almighty."

Menashe would not want her to die. Menashe had urged her to defeat her nightmare, to believe in his love, to trust that he would return for her. And he had promised that he would, with the help of his Almighty God.

If she loved him, she would believe him.

"I will not do this," she whispered, turning back to the dark image of Anubis. "Menashe worships another god. At the end of my mortal life, I choose to stand before Him."

You are forever a fool, you are truly blind.

Snatches of cheers and the raucous sounds of laughter filled the air, noises from the progressing game, but Jendayi could not tear her inner eyes from the jackal's face.

Menashe's love is as invisible as the god he serves. Has he ever kissed you like Efrayim?

"No," she admitted in a broken whisper.

Didn't he leave you in Pharaoh's house? He went away, not caring what happened to you!

"He went away...to obey. He would have come back for me. He did come back."

As a traitor. Surrender your life to his god, and you are lost to us forever. You shall not again enter the Hall of the Two Truths, you will never pass through these portals into the Other World.

Suddenly all the formulas, incantations and rituals seemed a senseless and heavy burden. Why not surrender their uncertainty and falseness in exchange for faith in one who loved her?

"Go from me, I will never seek to please you again!"

An indescribable softening took place within her as she uttered the words. She smiled as a warm light permeated the dark recesses of her soul. "I will never again place my heart within the pan of your scales, Anubis. Another god shall judge my heart...and another man shall claim it."

The darkness before her eyes swirled in a fierce churning of textures, then the figure of Anubis retreated into inky blackness. Shaken, Jendayi reached out, half expecting to find that the physical world had dissolved away, too, but her groping fingers found Ani's thin arm at her side.

Just then the assembly erupted in a collective groan.

"What has happened?" she asked, afraid to hear the answer.

Ani paused. "Menashe has been catching up. They are both three tiles away from the Shemu square." Awkwardly, he cleared his throat. "Neither player has moved in several turns. Whichever man first rolls a three will win."

Jendayi tightened her grasp on the old man's arm, fully understanding what he had *not* said. Whichever player did not roll a three would die.

Chapter Twenty-Nine

It was Sitamun's turn to roll, Efrayim's turn to move. Smirking in confidence, Pharaoh's newest queen picked up the bones and blew on them for luck. Bored with the lull in the action and aware that every eye had focused on her, she transferred the bones to one hand, then mimicked the vizier's captain and lifted her head and hands as if pausing in prayer.

She heard Pharaoh chuckle behind her and several of her ladies-in-waiting twittered. Sitamun kept up the pretense, doggedly moving her lips in a nonsense incantation, the bones sharp against her palm.

The crowd began to snicker. Sitamun lifted one eyelid to peek at her father's former vizier. Beside his steward and the little harpist, Zaphenath-paneah stood as motionless as an idol, his head bowed, his eyes closed. His lips did not move, but Sitamun knew he was praying to his god in earnest.

She tired of the game. Efrayim had been a irresistible diversion, a pleasant way to aggravate her parents and the stuffy Hebrew vizier. But now she was a queen, and no longer a child.

She would never be a child again.

"For Amon-Re!" she cried, lowering her head. She opened her hand; the bones clanged into the pan.

"Two!" called the vizier.

Bored now with Efrayim, the game and her life, Sitamun crossed her arms and frowned in bitter fury.

* * *

Menashe noticed Sitamun's restlessness; so, undoubtedly, had Efrayim. The game was nearly over, and the thin layer of his brother's bravado had worn away. Efrayim might be willing to accept God's will in principle, but Menashe was certain his brother did not want to die. And Efrayim would be good to Jendayi; perhaps he would even grant her freedom.

Menashe lifted his eyes to Tarik and held the captain in his gaze. One of Tarik's brows shot up in a mute question, and Menashe blinked, signaling his wishes. Tarik frowned in wordless protest, but Menashe nodded again and tilted his head toward the area where his father stood with Ani and Jendayi.

He would do this for them. And for Efrayim, the favored son who carried Yaakov's best and brightest blessing.

Tarik lifted the bones and rattled them in his palm, but Menashe knew they would not fall into the pan this time. Tarik would do as Menashe wished and drop them onto the ground, effectively surrendering the game to his opponent.

Perhaps God had spared him in the desert so he could rescue Efrayim now.

Tarik's granite chin quivered. He extended his hand over the pan, then shifted his weight and moved his hand away. Opening his palm, he dropped the bones into the sand at his feet.

Efrayim's features twisted into a horrified expression of disapproval. "No!"

"Menashe forfeits, Efrayim wins!" the vizier cried, signaling the archers.

Tiy stiffened in shock as the captain threw the bones to the ground. If she'd had a moment's warning she might have forbidden the man to end the game this way, but she had never expected the captain to sacrifice Zaphenath-paneah's elder son.

She leaned forward as the archers advanced, then lifted her hand to shade her eyes. The sun had shifted, casting a pallid light over the gathering. The crowd stirred, then an odd coldness settled over the area, a darkly textured sensation like a gust of wind from the Other World. As voices shrieked in rising confusion, a whirlwind materialized from the paling sky and towered over the garden in a sullen yellow spout, bellowing over their heads like a river crocodile in mating season.

The claws of the wind snatched wigs and ornaments from the heads of men and women alike, including Pharaoh, forcing a frantic priest to dive for a covering with which to cover the sacred royal head. Across the garden, the sharp and brittle snap of wood cracked through the roaring noise. Tiy trembled in hypnotized horror as the funnel attacked the archers' bows and arrows, then moved on to snap Pharaoh's beloved acacia trees as easily as toothpicks.

Windblown sand scoured her cheek and blew between her teeth; she opened her lips to scream, but a mouthful of dirt and hot air rushed in to prevent her. Whimpering like a lost child, Tiy threw her arms over her head and sank to the ground, cowering before the fierce presence of the pirouetting whirlwind. The great current of roaring air drove everyone around her to their knees, then swirled overhead like an angry, warring creature waiting to breathe death on anyone who dared stand and defy it.

But two were standing. Whether through shock-induced stamina or sheer courage, Tiy saw Efrayim and Menashe on their feet, each brother as steady on his golden tile as if he had been rooted there.

A new kind of fear shook Tiy's body from toe to hair when the whirlwind moved toward the brothers, slowly, purposefully, like a probing finger. The pair stood less than ten feet apart, separated only by the reflecting pool and the Shemu symbol. The tip of the whirlwind nosed forward until it hovered over the Shemu, mocking Pharaoh's cartouche. Then, in a vast explosion of noise and color, the undulating column widened. The queen let out a tiny whine of mounting dread as the edges of its hot breath expanded to envelop the two brothers.

A thunderbolt jagged through her as the funnel lifted. Efrayim and Menashe no longer stood on the tiles, nor were they broken and sprawled on the ground. The monster wind had swept them up like a gigantic hand.

The cyclone retreated into the heavens, shifting and lifting until it metamorphosed into a boiling gray cloud a few feet above the surface of the pool. The cloud hung there as if it waited for something. From a few feet away, Tiy saw Amenhotep lift his head and gaze upward; the new vizier stared, slack-mouthed, a tenuous stream of drool dripping from his lips.

Pharaoh rose to his hands and knees. When he spoke, his voice was high-pitched and reedy. "What—what would you have me do?" he asked the swirling cloudbank.

The dark mass appeared to thicken and congeal as it wheeled around its invisible axis. A wild wind hooted and two human forms fell from the black shadow, landing with loud splashes in the reflecting pool. After depositing its human cargo, the cloud whirled again, and a thousand sparks of diamond light brightened its canopy. Still on the ground, Tiy tilted her head and strained to hear the chorus of mellifluous sounds that emanated from it, voices that could only come from supernatural throats. The strangely melodic song rose and fell, then the cloud spun one final time and lifted, vanishing into a sky of perfect blue.

Wave after wave of shock slapped at her. Tiy lowered her gaze to the pool where Efrayim and Menashe were laughing and wringing water from their garments. Efrayim looked about the garden with a devastating grin on his face while Menashe wore a slow, steady smile of happiness. Though they were dripping wet, Efrayim's wig had not been blown from his head, nor did either brother appear to be injured from the fall. In fact, Tiy noticed, peering at them, the bruises that had marked Menashe's face only a few moments before had faded.

Pressing an unsteady hand to her head, she realized that her own wig had been ripped off, leaving her shorn head exposed. Grasping the sheared top of a plant, the only material within reach, she held the mangled greenery to her head and cringed like a scolded dog, keeping one wary eye on the sky.

Amenhotep faltered and ducked as if he would prostrate himself before the sons of his disgraced vizier. But after a hasty glance upward to make certain the funnel cloud had disappeared, he remembered his own divinity and forced himself to rise.

Pinching his lower lip with his teeth, he turned to the younger, more easygoing son. "What does this mean?"

Efrayim thrust his hands on his hips. "Ask my father. He will know."

Amenhotep lifted his chin and turned to Zaphenath-paneah. He and his party had taken cover on the ground, too, but like Efrayim and Menashe, their clothing and wigs had been no more than ruffled by the claws of the wind.

"I ask you, Zaphenath-paneah," Amenhotep called, uncomfortably aware that his temples had begun to throb. "What has happened here? What does this mean?"

"It means," the former vizier answered, a faint look of amusement on his face as he paused to brush debris from his robe, "that the players reached the oasis at the same time. God Shaddai declares that they have both won and both must be exonerated."

"But the whirlwind—"Amenhotep gestured toward the sky, then pressed his hand to his throbbing head and surveyed the damage to his precious garden. "Such power!"

"It is a fearsome thing to trifle with the Almighty God." Zaphenath-paneah folded his hands and dipped his head in a sign of proper respect. "You wanted Him to adjudicate your game, honored Pharaoh, and so He has."

Amenhotep cleared his throat. "Well," he said, crossing his arms. He frowned at the sight of so many nobles and warriors still cowering on the ground. This was not good. If he did not handle this situation properly, the story would spread like the plague. Rumors would soon have the mighty king of Egypt cowering before a simple desert whirlwind...

He gave his vizier a forgiving smile, determined to be done with the matter. "Your god has decreed that both men are innocent, as I knew He would. But what would He have me do with the prize? The winner was to take possession of the little harpist, and she cannot serve two masters."

"No, my king, she cannot." Zaphenath-paneah turned to the slave girl, who stood behind him, her arm linked through the old steward's. "Jendayi," Zaphenath-paneah asked, his voice gentle, "you may choose your master today. Who will you serve most willingly? Menashe or Efrayim?"

* * *

Menashe heard his father's words as if through a thick fog. The events of the past hour had trampled him like a runaway horse, and he needed time to absorb them. But a few feet away the love of his life was being offered the opportunity to choose her future, and he had not had a chance to share his heart with her since that long-ago afternoon at Malkata. She would certainly choose Efrayim, but before she did, he wanted to tell her he would always love her.

He staggered forward, his eyes intent on Jendayi's bright face. But she would not give him time, for she dropped Ani's arm and stepped forward. "Thank you, master." Unusual determination rang in her voice. "I am ready to make my choice." Her face lit with affection and delight—the expression she always wore when speaking of Efrayim.

Menashe braced himself for disappointment. It was enough that God had spared his life and Efrayim's. He would be asking too much if he expected God to also fulfill his fanciful dreams.

"If God Shaddai wills," Jendayi said, the warmth of her voice sending shivers down his spine, "I choose to serve Menashe."

Menashe tensed, surprised and more uncertain than ever. She had chosen *him?* Why?

He did not have time to ponder the question, for Efrayim slapped him on the back while Yosef gestured for him to come forward and claim his prize.

"I wish you every happiness, brother," Efrayim said, sunshine breaking across his face. "Every happiness in the world."

And then Menashe was standing before Jendayi, and her small hands were on his arm, her smile beaming for him alone.

Efrayim turned away, unable to bear the sight of his brother's joy while his own heart still ached. He looked toward Pharaoh's dais and caught Sitamun's gaze. Had she gone willingly to the wedding canopy with her father? Had she been given a choice? He would never know the answers, for now a great gulf stood between them. The girl he had hoped to wed would never be his.

Time to face the future.

"Great Pharaoh." His voice echoed above the sounds of the bewildered crowd. "I beg a favor of you."

"Ask your favor," Pharaoh answered, his arms folded across his bare chest. Queen Tiy, uncharacteristically silent, rocked behind him on the ground, a handful of greenery pressed over her face.

"If you will," Efrayim said, looking back at Menashe, "allow me and my brother to dwell with our brethren in the territory of Goshen. Though we have grown up as your loyal servants in Thebes, perhaps it would be best if we raised our families with our kinsmen."

Pharaoh's eyes narrowed, and Efrayim knew the shrewd king would understand many of the reasons behind his request. If Efrayim left Thebes, he would not have to see Sitamun, he would not dwell in her thoughts. And if Menashe wanted to train another military force, at least he would be doing it in a far-off region.

Amenhotep nodded. "You and your brother may live in Goshen, and I wish you well. But your father, my own Zaphenath-paneah, shall not leave Thebes. I will want him by my side for as long as I live."

This announcement brought an immediate hush to the gathering. Tiy's face appeared through the shrubbery, her brows pulled into an affronted frown. The countenances of the two new viziers fell.

"Zaphenath-paneah." Pharaoh stepped down from his dais and walked toward Yosef. "Will you remain in Thebes to serve as my chief counselor? I covet your wisdom above that of all my servants, above my two viziers, above my priests, above my counselors. I value your judgment—" he thrust out his chin "—even above that of the Great Wife, Queen Tiy, who shall from this day be banished to chambers in my harem while a new queen is installed in her place. Remain with me, Zaphenath-paneah, for you and your god have prevailed again."

Efrayim stared after the king, astounded, as his father bowed before Amenhotep. "As always, Pharaoh, I am your servant." Yosef looked up at Pharaoh with true affection in his eyes. "God Shaddai has called me to serve you. You may count on my loyalty until I draw my last breath."

Pharaoh extended his hand—a truly intimate gesture. Efrayim smiled at the sight, yet had to blink back unexpected tears as his father pressed his lips to the royal palm.

* * *

On his barge, where Pharaoh's standard again fluttered from the center mast, Yosef traveled the distance from Malkata to Thebes in full, satisfying silence. He disembarked at the royal dock and proceeded straightway to the palace, driven by an unaccountable need to see Tuya. "Old wood is the best to burn," he whispered as he climbed the slope to the palace gates. "And old friends are the best to trust."

The palace at Thebes seemed strangely deserted with both the queen and Pharaoh at Malkata, but the handful of guards on duty at the gates bowed before Yosef and opened the double doors to the central hall without question.

News travels on the wind, he thought as he moved past them. *How could they have already heard that Zaphenath-paneah is again in Pharaoh's favor? A servant, perhaps, or one of the seamen from the barge.*

He had not traversed the narrow passageways that led to the House of the Women in years; he was not even certain he would be able to find his way to Tuya's chambers. Turning a corner, he surprised a pair of slave girls in the hall. One of them squeaked, the other immediately fell down and pressed her palms and forehead to the floor.

He folded his hands. "Pray tell me which apartment belongs to the Queen Mother."

The squeaking slave, still too startled to bow, pointed down another torchlit hall. Nodding his thanks, Yosef moved away.

Only one door lay at the end of the hallway where a single torch hung from an iron bracket and sputtered in the gloom. Timidly lifting his hand, Yosef knocked.

"Enter."

Tuya herself had uttered the command, and as he proceeded she smiled at him from the security of a delicately carved chaise longue. Long-stemmed and lovely, she looked up. Her exotic eyes tilted catlike toward him and seemed to probe his soul.

She had been waiting.

She had known he would come.

She had always understood him...better than he understood himself.

"Tuya," he began, lifting his eyes to the shadows that played flickering games around the high ceiling.

"There is no need to explain, Yosef." She held out her arms and in one forward motion he had entered her embrace, his head pillowed by her softness, his arms clinging to her as if she were a steady raft and he a drowning man.

"What have I done?" he murmured as she stroked his head, the touch of her hand almost unbearable in its tenderness. "I nearly lost my sons. God Shaddai preserved their lives, but for years I should have seen that I was losing their hearts."

"Fret not, my friend." The sound of her voice warmed his ear. "God is always at work, how could you forget? Your brothers sold you into slavery, and yet God raised you up. For better or worse, you placed my son above your own, and yet God will bless Efrayim and Menashe. God works even through human frailty—that is why He is Almighty, and we are as dust."

Her words were a soothing balm to his heart, and for a long interval he said nothing, then his eyes melted into hers. "In my youth I remembered my god…how could I think He would forget me in my age?"

"I don't know, Yosef." Her hand stroked his hair. "He will not, if you seek Him. You offered a sacrifice for your sons, now it is time to again offer yourself."

In silent agreement, he closed his eyes and lowered his head to her lap, lifting his thoughts to God Shaddai and finding comfort in Tuya's presence.

Chapter Thirty

The next morning, Menashe rose from his old bed in his father's villa for what he assumed would be the last time. The astonishing events of the previous day had cleaved his future from his past; from this day forward he and Efrayim would belong to the Hebrews. But more important, from today on he would belong to Jendayi.

He swung his feet out of bed, splashed his face with water from the washbasin and patted his face and beard with a linen square. A new robe, a long striped garment designed in the fashion of the Hebrews, draped a stand in his chamber, and Menashe slipped it over his head, relishing the feel of the fine linen against his skin. The robe had to be a gift from Halima, Tarik's wife. This would be his wedding garment, and he suspected Halima knew as much.

He paused in the garden to pluck a lotus blossom from the reflecting pool, then hurried toward the courtyard. The open space flurried with activity as he entered it. A half-dozen camels had been loaded with provisions for their new start in Goshen, and Efrayim seemed almost happy about making the journey. His bright smile shone on everyone from Ani, who wept openly, to the lowest slave, and he was directing the preparations for their trip with an unusually efficient air.

Watching his younger brother, Menashe felt his heart contract in pity. Though Efrayim would not admit it, yesterday in

Pharaoh's garden he had abandoned a lifetime of dreams. Neither the glory of Egypt nor its spoiled princess would ever be his. But he still had Yaakov's blessing, and now Menashe actually felt grateful that Yaakov had stretched his right hand toward his brother's head. Efrayim had surrendered more than Menashe; it was only right that God Shaddai honor him with blessings.

Jendayi stood with Kesi by the side of a groaning camel, a traveling cloak billowing about her slim figure. She had chosen to leave her Egyptian wig behind, and her own hair, dark and cropped close to her head, ruffled out in waves as the wind blew through it. She was laughing at some secret the girls shared, but as Menashe approached, Kesi dipped in a bow and retreated.

He expected Jendayi to stiffen in alarm, and was pleasantly surprised when she looked up, her gray eyes shining toward him like brilliant stars. "Master Menashe?" she asked, contentment in her voice.

The sound of her happiness struck a chord within him. "Yes," he answered, forcing the word over his tongue. He stepped closer and passed the flower under her nose. "For you."

Smiling her thanks, she reached out to take the lotus blossom, then wrapped the long stem about her bare arm. With a quiet confidence that caught him by surprise, she caught his hand, then fell to one knee. "Master, I am so pleased to belong to you. And I am ready for the journey. Kesi has packed my things and, with your permission, I have asked the servants to place my harp in a basket on my camel—excuse me, *your* camel."

"Of course, do whatever you like, but rise," Menashe answered, grateful that the noise of the courtyard drowned out the pounding of his heart. He lifted her. "Your harp shall go wherever you go. I look forward to hearing you play it every night."

"Yes, my lord. As your slave, you may command me at any time."

"You will not play as my slave." Menashe dropped her hand and drew her into his arms. "You will play as my wife, but only if it is your desire."

"Can it be true?" she murmured, lifting her face. "I don't deserve such freedom. A week ago I was a slave, troubled by nightmares and facing a dim future. Now I sleep as peacefully as a baby, and my heart brims with joy. Never in a thousand days could I have imagined I would be free from bondage, and never in ten thousand years would I have dreamed that I could be your wife." A blush of pleasure colored her lovely face. "You are too good to me, Menashe."

"Jendayi." She smiled as he said her name, and a quiver surged through his veins at the sight of her happiness. "I told you I have always loved you. For years I have been waiting—first for you to grow up, then for the opportunity to tell you how much I cared."

A blush ran over her exquisite face and tears trembled on her lashes. "I don't know why you were so patient. I knew I needed to love and be loved, it was all I wanted in the world! But I had been misled by my own ignorance. I didn't know what love was, and I never dreamed I could be someone's *wife*—"

"God planted my love for you long ago," Menashe answered, pulling her head into the hollow between his shoulder and neck. "And as God is eternal, so shall my love be. I would give my life for you, Jendayi. I want to serve you as I serve God."

He might have remained locked in her arms for the rest of the day, but from the corner of his eye Menashe saw his father approaching from the portico. He released Jendayi, then gestured to Kesi and told her to place her mistress safely within a camel basket. After promising to speak to Jendayi again before they left the villa, he stepped out to exchange farewells with his father.

Yosef waited in the center of the courtyard, his beautiful, long-fingered hands folded, his coal-black eyes wistful. He nodded. "So you are ready to go, then."

Menashe felt an odd twinge of disappointment. This was not the parting he had imagined.

"We are ready." He lifted his chin. "And I think you should know that I intend to marry Jendayi as soon as we reach Goshen. I want to take her as my bride among our own people."

Yosef nodded, the light of understanding flickering in his eyes. "I am glad you will not be alone," he said. "Loneliness was the first thing God pronounced not good at creation. I am certain you will make each other very happy."

Menashe glanced around, then nudged a small mound of

sand with his sandal. How tragic that he could think of nothing to say! His father had just denounced loneliness, and yet today both his sons would leave him. Perhaps he would not even notice their absence, for Pharaoh had thrust himself back into Yosef's life. But though Menashe had been far closer to Ani and Tarik than he had ever been to his father, still…

He floundered in a maelstrom of emotion, torn between eagerness to go and the feeling he ought to stay.

The corner of Yosef's mouth quirked. "Menashe, I know what you are thinking, and you should not deny your own happiness on my account. I will not be lonely. As soon as Pharaoh gives his permission, Tuya will be coming to live with me. I will take her as my wife."

"The Queen Mother?" Menashe burst out. "But you scarcely know her."

"I know you may not believe me, but I lived a varied and interesting life before you were born," his father answered, one dark eyebrow lifting as he smiled. "Tuya is a part of my past. We have decided it would be wise to combine our strengths in order to face the future."

Menashe grinned. "I suppose congratulations are in order. Let me wish *you* every happiness!"

"Thank you." His father rocked back and forth. "Will you try again?" he asked. "Will you lead them to Canaan?"

Menashe sighed and looked away. "I don't know. It would be harder now than before. I don't know if the people have the heart for it. They may not even receive me into the camp."

"They'll receive you." Yosef nodded with conviction. "You are family. You are my son."

Menashe was about to respond, but Yosef held up a quieting hand. He seemed preoccupied, as if a memory had surfaced and overshadowed his awareness of their conversation, and when he spoke again his voice was grim. "You asked me once why I did not tell you the stories of Yisrael," he said, brushing Menashe's arm. His gaze moved into his son's. "Perhaps I was afraid to speak of things gone by. Before my brothers came to Egypt, I wanted to forget the past, to bury every story I had ever heard. After my family arrived, I was so busy with my responsibilities to Pharaoh and to my brothers…"

His words trailed away, and Menashe lowered his gaze, shrinking from the self-accusation in his father's eyes.

"I think I wanted you to understand Egypt first, since this is where God placed you," Yosef went on, his voice stronger. "But now, Menashe, it is right that you live as a son of Yisrael. You have come to understand both worlds, and you have chosen between them." His eyes grew large and liquid. "You have chosen wisely."

Menashe fumbled for words. "I think… Thank you, Father."

Yosef turned his face toward the horizon. "When I was younger, I had many dreams. Some of them got me into trouble, just as your dreams brought you face-to-face with adversity. But God spoke to me through dreams, and though He has been silent for many years, He spoke to me again last night."

Menashe's heart stirred with interest. "What was His message?"

"In my dream I saw a king." Yosef's brow furrowed as he revisited the scene in his memory. "Not an Egyptian king, but one of our own people. He was deathly ill, and God Shaddai sent word that he should prepare to die. But the king begged for his life, and God revealed that He would grant the king another fifteen years."

Yosef's eyes clung to Menashe's, waiting for a reaction, but Menashe shook his head, not understanding. "So—did the king die?"

"Fifteen summers later," Yosef continued, looking at the ground. "But during that fifteen years, the king fathered a son who built altars to idols in the holy place dedicated to God Shaddai. He worshipped the stars and spirits. He seduced the children of Yisrael to commit more evil than the heathen nations around them, then he killed the true prophets of God until the streets ran red with their blood." Fear, stark and vivid, glittered in Yosef's eyes when he looked up. "The son's name was Menashe."

"This is not me, Father!" Menashe protested, stepping back.

"I know." Yosef forced a smile. "But the will of God is a mysterious thing. We know his promises will come to pass, but we don't always know when. Sometimes we are not to do the will of God, but we are to rest in it. We are to love God, seek Him and trust Him."

He paused a moment and thrust his hands behind his back, holding a powerful emotion in check. "We are called to obey, and sometimes we are called to suffer. It is through suffering that we realize the limits of our strength…and the greatness of our god."

Yosef placed his hand on his son's shoulder. His eyes shone with a tenderness Menashe had never seen in them before. "You were not a failure, son. God called you to lead, and you obeyed. In doing so, you have become a wiser man." His hand tightened on Menashe's neck. "The children of Yisrael will return to Canaan, for God Shaddai's will is always accomplished. And when they go, let it be known that my bones are to journey with them. God called me to live my life here among the children of the Nile, but one day I shall sleep with my fathers in the promised land."

"Father—" A deep, unaccustomed pain in Menashe's breast cut off his words, so he could only nod in assent. Yosef smiled, satisfied, and drew his son into the cradle of his arms.

After a long moment, Yosef released him. "Fetch your brother," he said, the glow of his smile warming Menashe's heart. "And I will bless you both for the journey."

With a heart too full to speak, Menashe obeyed.

Epilogue

Yosef, or Zaphenath-paneah, outlived Amenhotep III by thirty years. Shortly after ascending to the throne, the crown prince Neferkheprure' Wa'enre', who had never approved of either his father's lifestyle or his halfhearted approach to religion, abandoned Malkata, Thebes and even his royal name. Calling himself "Akhenaten," meaning "He Who is of Service to Aten," the sun god, the new pharaoh and his wife, Queen Nefertiti, built a great city in middle Egypt and called it Akhetaten. This pharaoh, oddly enough, worshipped one invisible and almighty god, Aten.

Akhenaten repudiated everything his father had idolized, attacking the cults of other deities in Egypt and destroying their idols. He confiscated the great estates belonging to the temples of local deities. He reigned only eighteen years, but his impetuous acts destroyed the foundation of Egypt's stability. His major contribution to the welfare of the Hebrews in Goshen was his determination to leave them alone.

Yosef lived long enough to hold his great-grandchildren from Efrayim, who married Jokim's sister, Atara. He cradled his great-grandsons from Menashe, too, but remained so close to his elder son's family that Genesis tells us the babies born to Makhir, Menashe's son, were "born on Yosef's knees," that is, considered to be his own. On many of his visits to Goshen, a crowd of little ones waited at the harbor for his barge to arrive. Plump young hands tugged at his flowing robe as he made his way down the gangplank; round, rosy faces eagerly sought kisses from the Bread of Egypt, the Father to Pharaohs, the Servant of God Shaddai.

As he counted the last of his mortal days, Yosef sent for his brothers. "I am dying," he told them, "but God will take account of you. He will bring you up from this land to the land about which he swore to Avraham, to Yitzhak and to Yaakov."

And Yosef had the sons of Yisrael swear that they would carry his bones up from Egypt. So Yosef died at the age of one hundred ten years, and was embalmed and placed in a temporary coffin in Egypt.

A rapid succession of pharaohs followed Amenhotep III: Akhenaten, Smenkhkare', Tut'ankhamun, Aya and Horemhab. And after Horemhab, who died without an heir, a new dynasty arose, kings whom the Bible describes as those "who knew not Yosef."

* * * * *

QUESTIONS FOR DISCUSSION

1. Had you thought much about why the Hebrews remained so long in Egypt before reading this novel? Why do you think they stayed?

2. How would you have felt if your parent or grandparent gave the blessing you expected to a younger sibling? How did this action affect Menashe?

3. Why do you think Yaakov, or Jacob, asked that his body be carried back to Canaan and buried while Yosef was content to wait until the children of Yisrael left Egypt permanently? What do their wishes suggest about their self-identity?

4. Since God had clearly said that the children of Yisrael would return to Canaan, was Menashe wrong to try to convince the others to return after Yaakov's death? Did he somehow misunderstand the will of God?

5. Someone once said that to find the will of God we need to "lie passive in His hand and know no will but His." Do you agree? How is this possible?

6. Psalm 37 says, "The steps of a good man are ordered by the LORD: and he delighteth in his way. Though he fall, he shall not be utterly cast down: for the LORD upholdeth him with his hand" (vs. 23,24). Do you believe the Lord was directing Menashe's steps? Efrayim's? Yosef's?

7. Why did Jendayi's recurring dream have real power to frighten her? How is she like other people who have based their lives on false beliefs or false powers?

8. Jendayi was physically blind, but other characters were emotionally and/or spiritually blind. Who, and in what ways?

9. What sort of lessons can you take from the story of Yosef's children? How do their trials apply to your life?

10. Who in this story did you most relate to—the "parent" characters (Yosef, Tiy) or the "child" characters (Menashe, Jendayi, Efrayim)? Why do you think this is so? Are you trying to make your way in the world, or are you more accepting of your place and willing to remain there until God moves you?

11. If you've read all three novels in this series about Yosef—*Dreamers, Brothers* and *Journey*—which story was most meaningful to you? Most surprising? What did you learn that you did not know before?

12. When God called Abraham/Avraham, He foretold that the patriarch's descendants would wander in Canaan and Egypt for 400 years and suffer in captivity. In Galatians 3:16–17, Paul repeats that 430 years stood between Avraham and Moses: "And this I say, that the covenant, that was confirmed before of God in Christ, the law, which was four hundred and thirty years after, cannot disannul, that it should make the promise of none effect." But in speaking to Avraham, God explained why the children of Yisrael would not return to Canaan immediately: "But in the fourth generation," He said, "they shall come hither again: for the iniquity of the Amorites is not yet full" (Gen. 15:16).

Despite Yosef's reasons for not immediately claiming the land of Canaan, God had another purpose: the Amorites were a sinful people, but they had not yet reached the limits of God's patience.

But God does not break his promises. Exodus 12:40 tells us that "Now the sojourning of the children of Israel, who dwelt in Egypt [and Canaan], was four hundred and thirty years. And it came to pass at the end of the four hundred and thirty years, even the selfsame day it came to pass, that all the hosts of the LORD went out from the land of Egypt."

Sometimes we grow impatient when God does not immediately answer our prayers...and we forget that He is dealing with other people, too. Have you found this to be true in your life?

RESOURCES

Bianchi, Dr. Robert S. *Splendors of Ancient Egypt.* London: Booth-Clibborn Editions, 1996.

Brier, Bob, Ph.D. *The Murder of Tutankhamen.* New York: G.P. Putnam's Sons, 1998.

Budge, E. A. Wallis. *The Mummy: A History of the Extraordinary Practices of Ancient Egypt.* New York: Wings Books, 1989.

Budge, Sir Wallis. *Egyptian Religion.* New York: Barnes & Noble Books, 1994.

Bunson, Margaret. *The Encyclopedia of Ancient Egypt.* New York: Facts on File, 1991.

Cahill, Thomas. *The Gifts of the Jews.* New York: Doubleday, 1998.

Coleman, William. *Today's Handbook of Bible Times and Customs.* Minneapolis, MN: Bethany House Publishers, 1984.

Comay, Joan. *Who's Who in the Old Testament.* Nashville, TN: Abingdon Press, 1971.

Coogan, Michael D., ed. *The Oxford History of the Biblical World.* New York: Oxford University Press, 1998.

David, Rosalie, and Rick Archbold. *Conversations with Mummies.* New York: William Morrow, 2000.

Davis, J. D. *Illustrated Davis Dictionary of the Bible.* Nashville, TN: Royal Publishers, Inc., 1973.

Editors of Time-Life Books. *The Age of God-Kings.* Alexandria, VA: Time-Life Books, 1987.

—. *Egypt: Land of the Pharaohs.* Alexandria, VA: Time-Life Books, 1992.

—. *What Life Was Like on the Banks of the Nile.* Alexandria, VA: Time-Life Books, 1997.

Fox, Everett. *The Five Books of Moses.* New York: Schocken Books, 1995.

Grower, Ralph. *The New Manners and Customs of Bible Times.* Chicago: Moody Press, 1987.

Halley, Henry. *Halley's Bible Handbook.* Grand Rapids, MI: Zondervan Publishing House, 1927.

Hart, George. *Ancient Egypt.* New York: Alfred A. Knopf, 1990.

James, T. G. H. *Ancient Egypt: The Land and Its Legacy.* Austin, TX: University of Texas Press, 1988.

Jenkins, Simon. *Nelson's 3-D Bible Mapbook.* Nashville, TN: Thomas Nelson Publishers, 1995.

Kaiser, Walter C., Peter H. Davids, F. F. Bruce, and Manfred T. Brauch. *Hard Sayings of the Bible.* Downers Grove, IL: InterVarsity Press, 1996.

Kaster, Joseph. *The Wisdom of Ancient Egypt.* New York: Barnes & Noble, 1993.

Manniche, Lise. *An Ancient Egyptian Herbal.* Austin, TX: University of Texas Press, 1989.

—. *Music and Musicians in Ancient Egypt.* London: British Museum Press, 1991.

Metzger, Bruce M., and Michael D. Coogan, eds. *The Oxford Companion to the Bible.* New York: Oxford University Press, 1993.

Montet, Pierre. *Everyday Life in Egypt in the Days of Ramesses the Great.* Philadelphia: University of Pennsylvania Press, 1981.

Murray, Margaret. *The Splendour That Was Egypt.* London: Sidgwick and Jackson, 1949.

Osman, Ahmed. *Stranger in the Valley of the Kings.* San Francisco: Harper & Row, 1987.

Potok, Chaim. *Wanderings: Chaim Potok's History of the Jews.* New York: Fawcett Crest, 1978.

Pritchard, James, ed. *HarperCollins Atlas of the Bible.* London: HarperCollins Publishers, 1997.

Romer, John. *Valley of the Kings.* New York: Henry Holt and Company, 1981.

Schaff, Philip. *Through Bible Lands.* New York: Arno Press, 1977.

Schulz, Regine, and Matthias Seidel, eds. *Egypt: The World of the Pharaohs.* Cologne, Germany: Konemann, 1998.

Spencer, A. J. *Death in Ancient Egypt.* New York: Penguin Books, 1991.

Steindorff, George, and Keith C. Seele. *When Egypt Ruled the East.* Chicago: University of Chicago Press, 1957.

Stern, David H. *Complete Jewish Bible*. Clarksville, MD: Jewish New Testament Publications, Inc., 1998.

Unstead, F. J., ed. *See Inside an Egyptian Town*. London: Barnes and Noble, 1986.

Vercoutter, Jean. *The Search for Ancient Egypt*. New York: Harry N. Abrams, 1992.

Wilkinson, Richard H. *Reading Egyptian Art*. London: Thames and Hudson, 1992.

Willmington, Harold L. *Willmington's Bible Handbook*. Wheaton, IL: Tyndale House Publishers, 1999.

Love Inspired®

HEARTWARMING INSPIRATIONAL ROMANCE

Experience stories
centered on love and faith
with a variety of romances
just for you,
with 10 books every month!

***Love Inspired*®:**
Enjoy four contemporary,
heartwarming romances every month.

***Love Inspired*® Historical:**
Travel to a different time with two powerful
and engaging stories of romance, adventure
and faith every month.

***Love Inspired*® Suspense:**
Enjoy four contemporary tales of intrigue
and romance every month.

Steeple Hill®

*Available every month wherever books are
sold, including most bookstores, supermarkets,
drugstores and discount stores.*

LIINCREASE

REQUEST YOUR FREE BOOKS!

2 FREE INSPIRATIONAL NOVELS
PLUS 2
FREE
MYSTERY GIFTS

Love Inspired
HISTORICAL
INSPIRATIONAL HISTORICAL ROMANCE

YES! Please send me 2 FREE Love Inspired® Historical novels and my 2 FREE mystery gifts (gifts are worth about $10). After receiving them, if I don't wish to receive any more books, I can return the shipping statement marked "cancel". If I don't cancel, I will receive 4 brand-new novels every other month and be billed just $4.24 per book in the U.S. or $4.74 per book in Canada, plus 25¢ shipping and handling per book and applicable taxes, if any*. That's a savings of over 20% off the cover price! I understand that accepting the 2 free books and gifts places me under no obligation to buy anything. I can always return a shipment and cancel at any time. Even if I never buy another book, the two free books and gifts are mine to keep forever. 102 IDN ERYA 302 IDN ERYM

Name	(PLEASE PRINT)

Address	Apt. #

City	State/Prov.	Zip/Postal Code

Signature (if under 18, a parent or guardian must sign)

Mail to Steeple Hill Reader Service:
IN U.S.A.: P.O. Box 1867, Buffalo, NY 14240-1867
IN CANADA: P.O. Box 609, Fort Erie, Ontario L2A 5X3

Not valid to current subscribers of *Love Inspired Historical* books.

Want to try two free books from another series?
Call 1-800-873-8635 or visit www.morefreebooks.com

* Terms and prices subject to change without notice. N.Y. residents add applicable sales tax. Canadian residents will be charged applicable provincial taxes and GST. Offer not valid in Quebec. This offer is limited to one order per household. All orders subject to approval. Credit or debit balances in a customer's account(s) may be offset by any other outstanding balance owed by or to the customer. Please allow 4 to 6 weeks for delivery. Offer available while quantities last.

Your Privacy: Steeple Hill Books is committed to protecting your privacy. Our Privacy Policy is available online at www.SteepleHill.com or upon request from the Reader Service. From time to time we make our lists of customers available to reputable third parties who may have a product or service of interest to you. If you would prefer we not share your name and address, please check here. ☐

LIH08R